GRACIE'S SURRENDER
SHENANDOAH BRIDES ~ BOOK 4

BLOSSOM TURNER

Copyright © 2022 Blossom Turner

All rights reserved. No portion of this book may be reproduced or transmitted in any form or by any means - photocopied, shared electronically, scanned, stored in a retrieval system, or other - without the express permission of the publisher. Exceptions will be made for brief quotations used in critical reviews or articles promoting this work.

The characters and events in this fictional work are the product of the author's imagination. Any resemblance to actual people, living or dead, is coincidental.

Unless otherwise indicated, all Scripture quotations are taken from the Holy Bible, Kings James Version.

Scripture quotations marked (NKJV) are taken from the New King James Version®. Copyright © 1982 by Thomas Nelson. Used by permission. All rights reserved.

ISBN-13: 978-1-942265-53-5

I dedicate this book to the celebration of close writing friends God has brought into my life who have encouraged, elevated, and endorsed my writing. These women are all writers themselves who have given of their time and talents to lift me up and make me a better writer.

To Kay Strom, a teacher and mentor, who was one of the first to encourage and endorse my writing.

To Jan Hooper and Jennifer Sienes, whom I first met at Mount Hermon and who have grown rich in friendship and love and who have tirelessly encouraged my writing.

To my Lady Inklings group: Holly Varni, Tisha Martin, Karen Moderow, Kathryn Hughes, and Ginny Yttrup. You are so loved and appreciated.

To my local Word Guild Chapter with too many names to mention. A special thank you to those who have reached in and personally touched my life: Heidi McLaughlin, Marilyn Kriete, Karen Barnstable, and Susan Debeeson.

And to my critique partner, Laura Thomas, who reads chapter after chapter, book after book, with amazing insight and encouragement.

To all you lovely ladies, I thank you from my heart. I am humbled and filled with gratitude for the gift you are in my life. My writing career is lifted on the wings of your friendship, inspired and empowered by the Jesus we share.

But Jesus said, "Let the little children come to Me, and do not forbid them; for of such is the kingdom of heaven."

Matthew 19:14 (NKJV)

CHAPTER 1

March 1879
Shenandoah Valley

"You're turning down *another* marriage proposal?" Ma put her hands to her temples and rubbed. "But, Gracie, he's such a fine young man."

The walls of the parlor room closed in on Gracie. Why did men continually misread the situation when she gave them no encouragement at all? It was so frustrating.

"You're eighteen now and quite old enough to become a wife. And George is an upstanding—"

"I never meant to encourage George. And I certainly didn't think he was about to propose. We barely know each other."

"What do you mean?" Pa said. "Our families go way back."

"But I've never looked at George that way." It was time to tell them a truth they may never understand. Especially Ma. Gracie lifted her head high, knotting her trembling hands together. "I have no intention of marrying. Ever." She added a firmness to her voice she did not feel.

"Why not?" Pa's bushy brows knit together. "Thought most every girl looked forward to that day."

That familiar memory came flooding in. Would Rosina's outstretched bony fingers forever haunt her? "Not this one. I like George, but I don't love him. I want to devote my life to Jesus and—"

"For heaven's sakes." Ma's hands flew into the air. "There's that Jesus talk again." She turned to Pa and wagged her finger in his face. "This is your fault. One by one, every one of our daughters have followed in your footsteps, but this is taking it too far. Set her right." She pointed at Gracie.

Rather than prolong the agony, Gracie took a deep breath. She might as well get it all out. If they weren't happy with her now, they sure wouldn't be after she told them the rest of her plans.

Pa moved across the room to stand in front of her and gently placed his hands on her upper arms. "Tell us what you're thinking, girl. Neither Ma nor I understand. A woman can love Jesus and be married too."

"I feel God is calling me to move to Richmond and work in the orphanage."

"Richmond?" Ma's voice rose a few octaves. "It's not bad enough you don't want to marry George, but you want to move to Richmond as well?"

"Please give me a moment to explain." Gracie pointed to the parlor chairs. *Dear God, please help Ma understand. I don't want to hurt her.* "Can we sit?"

Pa put his arm around Ma and guided her to a chair. "She is an adult, Doris. We should at least bend an ear." Ma slumped into the chair and turned her head to look out the window.

Pa chose the chair beside her and gave Gracie his full attention.

"Ma, remember when we visited Grandmother and Grandfather when I was twelve and I met that street urchin named Rosina?"

Ma nodded. "I'll forever regret letting you and Bryon go back and try to find that child the next day. You've never been the same."

"You're right. That experience, and then revisiting the orphanage with Amelia and Bryon again last year, has deeply impacted my life. The need is so great, with not enough hands to—"

"See." Ma's head snapped toward Pa. "Every time I let one of my children go to Richmond for a visit, they come back with the fandangled idea of moving there." Her eyes blazed as she returned her gaze to Gracie. "And what about a family of your own? How are you going to do that without a husband?"

Pa took Ma's hand, but she pulled it free and turned her head back toward the window.

He nodded at Gracie to continue.

"I don't want to be distracted by men when there are so many children in need."

Ma let out a loud harrumph.

"Besides," Gracie continued, "weren't you just talking about how Grandmother is grieving Grandfather so terribly? I could cheer up her lonely days."

Pa glanced at Ma. "Doris, you did say you were worried about your mother. Amelia confirmed she hasn't been doing very well since your father passed. We could let Gracie give the orphanage a trial run and give your mother some much-needed company at the same time."

"Well, I never!" Ma shot up from her chair and pointed at Pa. "You're siding with her. Was all this cooked up ahead of time— you two and that God of yours?"

"No." They answered in unison as she marched from the room. The stomp of her feet could be heard on every step up to her bedroom before her door slammed shut.

Gracie's hands scrunched her dress tightly. She relaxed and smoothed out the wrinkles. "Pa, you understand, don't you?" She stared at the floor planks. Would he be disappointed in her as well?

"I'm not sure I do."

Gracie looked over into his kind brown eyes.

"But far be it from me to get in the way of what God is telling you to do. Your ma on the other hand…" He rubbed his work worn hands back and forth on his brow. "She's going to need some time. When were you hoping to go?"

"As soon as possible. Thought it would be easier for George if I'm not around. And I've already secured an invitation from Grandmother to stay as long as I like."

"Must you cut the tie so abruptly? Your ma's heart is going to take a beating to let her baby girl go."

"She still has Jeanette, and weren't you both just willing to marry me off to George?"

"George is a ten-minute buggy ride away. Richmond is another story."

"I'll promise to come home for visits."

"Well, I'll be holding you to that, girlie. And don't worry about your ma, I'll talk to her." He stood. "She may not be tickled pink, but she'll come around. Just be sure this is something you really feel you need to do."

"Thanks, Pa." Gracie flew across the room into his arms and planted a big kiss on the top of his brow. She was finally going to fulfill the calling God had whispered into her heart all those years ago.

~

The sky was as blue as forget-me-nots, the morning sunshine teasing the buds on the trees to respond to its glory. A beautiful spring day to travel. Gracie settled in her seat, eager for the train to leave. A thrill pulsed through.

A lurch and a chug, and they were off, her new adventure unfolding. Each mile the train rumbled down the track away from the Shenandoah Valley, Gracie's excitement grew. Why did she feel as if her life was finally about to begin?

"May I sit here?"

Gracie turned from the window to see a strapping young man with a wheedling smile. Instinct told her to keep her distance, but politeness forced a response. "I haven't paid for two seats." She laughed to hide her nervousness. The last thing she needed was attention from any man.

A distinguished gentleman from across the aisle looked their way and raised his eyebrows. What had she done that was inappropriate? Should she have told the stranger to sit elsewhere? Having been raised on the farm, she had little knowledge of worldly etiquette.

"John Deleware." The stranger tipped his cowboy hat in her direction and slid into the seat. His smile widened, and he moved a tad too close.

Gracie turned toward the window and gazed out. She didn't want to be rude, but neither did she want to encourage him.

"May I have the pleasure of your name?"

Gracie sighed heavily. She hated to be discourteous. "Gracie…I mean Grace Williams."

"I like Gracie a far cry better than the formal Grace. I would wager a bet that your personality most likely suits Gracie?" He pulled out a small can of chewing tobacco and popped some in his mouth.

"I suppose it does." She answered, not comfortable with the stranger's overt interest. Why did her looks always have to be a magnet? She had prayed she would make it to Richmond without undue attention.

"Where are you coming from, and where are you headed?"

he asked between chews. He turned toward the aisle and spat. A rivulet of spittle hit the back of the seat in front of him. He did nothing to remove it. Gracie took the opportunity to look back out the window, hoping to ignore him.

"Well?" he said, not taking the hint.

She turned his way. "Mr. Deleware, please don't take this personally, but I have a lot on my mind, and I would prefer to be left alone."

"Oh, too hoity-toity for the likes of the working cowboy, hey? I know a brush off when I hear one."

"It's not that. I've chosen to give my life in service to God and—"

"To God?" A loud mocking laugh filled the air. His voice doubled in volume. "What, a nun?"

Gracie's cheeks bloomed hot. "No, not a nun—"

"What a waste of God-given beauty. You're meant to make some man very happy, not be closeted away in some monastery somewhere."

"I do believe the lady was politely asking you to leave her alone." The man from across the aisle was glaring at Mr. Deleware.

Gracie glanced his direction, trying to communicate gratitude in the look.

Mr. Delaware swiveled in his seat. "What's it to you?"

The man slid across the two seats to the aisle and stood. He removed his top hat and still stood a head above Mr. Delaware, who had also popped up.

"What? Are you her guardian?"

"As a matter of fact, I'm her brother. Now, move along, cowboy." His deep voice resonated authority.

Mr. Delaware looked back and forth between the two. "A nun is not worth my time anyway." He spat out a large gob of chewing tobacco and sauntered away.

"Thank you, brother." Gracie smiled up at him.

He leaned close, his sweet breath fanning her face. "I overheard you saying you were giving your life in service to God. I'm a Christian too, so that makes you my sister in Christ." He straightened and looked down at her. "Best not to give that smile so freely to strangers. Offers the wrong impression."

Gracie could feel the happiness melt from her face, and her ire rose like steam from the train engine. A girl couldn't even be friendly in this world without men taking it the wrong way.

The man slid back into his seat without a sideways glance in her direction. Much to her vexation, his strong jawline and formidable countenance drew Gracie's interest the rest of the way to Richmond. She found herself peeking his way one too many times. A man without a wedding ring who was not bent on making her acquaintance was a rare find indeed. They could be friends. Too bad their paths would never cross again.

~

Matthew kept his eyes riveted to the landscape out the train window. He could see nothing but a blur. Who would let their young and beautiful daughter travel unchaperoned? Was she really so naïve that she thought she could smile that alluring smile and not draw the men in like the bell chime of a Sunday morning steeple?

Women who looked like her were not the kind who gave their lives in service to God. They were the kind who got snatched up and married off in record time. If she wasn't going to be a nun, who was she and what was her plan? And why didn't she have a guardian with her?

It bothered him that he wanted to turn and stare at her like most of the men had done when she entered the train—married and unmarried alike. She had smiled at everyone and stopped long enough to chat with a little girl sitting beside her mama. That was when her big doe-like eyes came alive and sparkled with joy. Though he had wanted to be immune to the attraction he felt, he was not. Her dark wavy hair was plaited in a braid that swung around to the front and hung long down her torso. Her hairstyle and clothing were not the latest fashion, but all was eclipsed by the petite vision of loveliness she made. Slim, delicate bones, with curves in all the right places.

He shook his head against the pull and closed his eyes. When was the last time a woman had consumed his thoughts? He was prepared to wait for the one God had for him, not get sidetracked by mere physical attraction. He knew better than that. He usually wasn't so shallow. He ventured a sideways glance, hoping to dispel the odd sensation causing the erratic beat of his heart. Her profile was turned toward the window, so he took a moment to do what almost every man on the train had already done…enjoy God's creation of perfection. Round, bright cheeks that looked petal soft, delicate earlobes, and a button mouth that was curved upward at something outside. Did she smile all the time?

Before he could avert his eyes, she glanced his direction. He quickly turned away. Richmond could not come fast enough.

He did not look again. When the train jostled and screeched to a stop, he wasted no time in gathering his few belongings and standing to leave. She did the same. The gentleman in him bid he allow her to go first. "After you."

"Thank you, brother," she said, with definite sass on her lips.

He felt an uncontrollable urge to kiss that smile right off her generous mouth. Instead, he followed her off the train and watched a coachman hail her. The two of them disappeared into the crowd. Good thing. What was happening to him, this sudden attraction to a perfect stranger?

She was perfect, and it irritated him to the core. Any longer in her presence, and he would've done something completely out of character—like ask her to dinner.

CHAPTER 2

"These past two weeks have so lifted my drowning spirits."

Gracie set her tea on the table at Grandmother's words.

"Having you here...well, it's pulled me out of the sadness and given me a reason to get up in the morning."

Gracie offered a slow smile of agreement. "For me, too, Grandmother. You've been so kind and generous. And your home is so welcoming." She looked beyond the veranda into the perfectly manicured garden, where spring tulips, daffodils, and violets provided a riotous show of color.

"Paush." Grandmother's hand batted the air. "Having you here is much more to my advantage than yours."

"I love it here." Everything about Richmond felt right. Her promise to God to return to this very city and that orphanage was of utmost importance to her. She was eager to get started. Surely, her services would be needed somewhere. It would've been wise to have written in advance and worked out the details herself instead of relying on Amelia. Why hadn't she done that? She lifted her baby finger to her mouth and nibbled at a hang nail.

"Amelia's family will arrive soon for the midday meal. After that, Bryon will take you to the orphanage and introduce you to the superintendent."

She and Grandmother had discussed this already. "I'm so looking forward to it." Gracie lifted the pendant from around her neck and looked at the time. "Like right now."

"Heavens. Is it noon already? Time spent with you just flies on by. We best head into the dining room." Grandmother tried to pull herself up from the veranda chair and failed. "Give an old lady a hand." She waved Gracie over. "Goodness, there is no preparing one for how difficult aging is."

Gracie placed her hand under her grandmother's elbow to help lift and then held her arm into the dining room. She didn't let go until Grandmother was safely in her place at the head of the table.

Gracie took a seat next to her, and Grandmother patted her hand. "And if you find meaningful employment at the orphanage, you'll be here to stay. That will make this old woman very happy indeed."

"Oh no, I'm not looking for employment, Grandmother. I'm quite prepared to volunteer my time. Both Amelia and Katherine have offered to help pay my expenses. They want to support my life of ministry."

Grandmother's eyebrows arched. "A life can be a very long time." Her eyes clouded, and she looked heavenward. "I should be thankful I had your grandfather for as long as I did, but honestly, I feel so lost without him." She dabbed at the corner of one eye.

Gracie folded her fingers over the wrinkled translucent skin of her grandmother's hand and gave a slight squeeze. "That's another reason I feel God brought me here...for you."

Grandmother turned in Gracie's direction. Her full head of white hair pulled up in a chignon gave her a regal look, but her eyes spoke of the pain in her heart. "Do you really think God cares about individual lives, and mine in particular? I haven't given Him much mind over the years."

"I believe with all of my heart that He cares about you."

"Well then, girl, you'll have to rub some of that faith off on me, and I shall be delighted to be counted in that number of those who want to support you and your good cause."

Voices and laughter echoed down the hall. Amelia, Bryon, six-year-old Jenny, and four-year-old Pearl spilled into the room.

"Just in time." Grandmother waved them in. "The meal is hot and ready."

"I still can't believe I have a sister living so close." Amelia hugged Gracie and slid into the chair beside her. "I sure hope you love Richmond and your work at the orphanage because I want you to stay."

"I just said the same," Grandmother admitted.

The smell of fried chicken, vegetables, and mashed potatoes and gravy wafted up from the table, but Gracie was too excited to eat. "About the orphanage. What's the superintendent's name? And what is he like? Do you think he'll allow me to work with the girls if I have a reference from you?"

"Whoa, whoa. So many questions." Amelia laughed. "How about we say grace and then Bryon and I will fill you in. Girls, come get seated."

"I want to sit beside Aunt Gracie." Jenny slipped onto the chair next to her.

"No, I want to sit beside her." Pearl pulled at her sister's clothing.

"Stop, girls," Amelia said. "You can both sit beside her. Pearl, come over here." Amelia rounded the table to sit beside Bryon. And Pearl climbed up beside Gracie, swallowed by a chair far too big for her frame. But her eyes shone with happiness.

"They shouldn't get their own way when they're misbehaving like that." Bryon raised his eyebrows at the girls, his tone firm.

"We'll excuse the excitement this time," Grandmother said. "Gracie is a bit of a novelty right now. Bryon, why don't you say the blessing?"

Gracie did not hear the prayer. Her head was swimming with a hundred questions as Bryon offered a quick thanks for the meal.

The prayer was barely finished when Gracie blurted out, "Tell me everything you know about the orphanage."

"Where to begin?" Bryon plopped a large spoonful of mashed potatoes on his plate. "I better start from the ground up. I'm part of the board that oversees the three most important things about keeping the orphanage doors open—running it like a business, keeping it like a house, and involving the community like neighbors."

"Sounds like there's a lot more than looking after the children," Gracie said.

"Absolutely. If you can't keep the money flowing in, the children will have no home. Hence the board."

"What do they do?"

"There are twelve volunteers who take on this task, both men and women. You'll get to know all of us, as we all have different roles, so the sooner you learn the names the better. Mr. Lewis is the board president. He is a financial whiz. I work closely with him and Edwin Fuller regarding the finances. We invest in real estate, stocks and bonds, particularly the railroad at the moment. It's booming—"

"Goodness. Don't bore her with too many details about the finances." Amelia patted his arm. She looked across at Gracie. "He does tend to rattle on about what he loves."

They all laughed.

"Are you finished mocking me, my dear?" But the look he gave his wife was filled with affection.

"Remember. Short and sweet so poor Gracie has a hope of remembering the pertinent information."

"All right, I'll get to the point." He smiled across at Gracie. "My mother, Melinda Preston, has been a longtime member and sits as first vice president. She works with Dorothy Greenbrier and Eliza Whittle on community involvement and fundraising. Whatever you do, stay on the right side of Eliza. She is one problem you do not need."

Amelia nodded. "'Tis true."

"Reverend Peterkin is secretary and collaborates with local churches drumming up volunteers, who help with the donation of their time and money. Then, the three sisters—"

Grandmother tittered. "Oh, do let me tell." Her eyebrows danced with delight. "I've had the pleasure of having Myrtle, Matilda, and Margot Hampshire as friends for many years. They are a delightful trio, indeed."

Bryon smirked. Amelia grinned, and Grandmother looked like she had just swallowed the truth.

"What are you not telling me?" Gracie asked.

Grandmother leaned nearer as if sharing a secret. "Let's just say these three spinsters have a lot of time on their hands. They are as helpful as it comes, but goodness can they talk. Unless you have an hour to waste, run in the opposite direction." Grandmother shook her head. "I think they are spinsters because any man who came near that household could not take the three of them on. They stick together like peas in a pod. Always have, even as children."

Bryon chuckled. "They do the monthly inspections at the orphanage, so you'll get to know them well…very well."

"Though overwhelming at times, they're the epitome of kindness and helpfulness," Amelia added. "You name it…housekeeping, staff issues, shopping for goods, even helping out with the children, they'll pitch in."

Bryon nodded. "And then there's Doctor Parker, who aids Amelia with all things medical, and that's the board."

"Who runs the orphanage on a daily basis?" Gracie took a bite, trying to stuff the food past her nervousness.

"That's Matthew. He's the superintendent entrusted with the management of the home. Well, two homes to be accurate. We're doing an experiment never done before to see if we can cut costs. We purchased a new property with two separate homes—a house for the girls and another for the boys. With the homes on the same property, we save on staff. One common kitchen and eating area, one menu for all, one gardener, one superintendent salary, and so on."

"How ingenious." Gracie was getting more excited by the moment. To be part of something so well run and progressive would be amazing. Her dream to make a difference in the lives of orphan children in Richmond was about to unfold.

"Wish I'd thought of that myself, but it was Matthew's idea," Bryon admitted. "He's quite brilliant and presented the idea as a way of saving money, but also with the children in mind. Never seen anyone so insistent that, for normal social development, a mixture of male and females just like one would find in a family was needed. Having two homes on the same property allows for some interaction between the boys and girls. When we crunched the numbers, it made good sense on many levels."

"What is Matthew like?" Gracie's stomach rolled, and she pushed at the food on her plate. What if he didn't like her?

"Matthew is a no-nonsense fellow, but fair. He's young to be in such a place of authority, but he's very intelligent and a gifted leader. My mother insisted upon him, and since he took over a year ago, that orphanage has improved a hundredfold. I look after their bank account, and somehow Matthew miraculously does more with less."

"You can sing his praise all you want, my dear," Amelia said, "but does he have to be so…I don't know. What's a kind way of saying he acts far too old and strict for his age?"

Bryon faced his wife. "One has to have those qualities to handle all those ruffians, and he's had a tough life. That makes anyone grow up fast."

"Tough life?" Grandmother asked.

"I can say no more on the matter. It's his story to tell." He popped a bite of bread in his mouth as if to accentuate the point.

"Fair enough." Amelia patted her husband's arm and looked across the table at Gracie. "You may find Matthew a tad brittle, but now Marianna, the dear old soul who oversees the girls, is an absolute sweetheart, and the children…oh my, the children will break your heart but bring so much joy."

Gracie's insides twisted and knotted at the thought of this Matthew man. What if he thought she was too young and didn't want her at the orphanage? Or like Ma and Pa, thought a woman's destiny was no more than marriage and children of her own? He had the power to squelch her dream right then and there. She had no backup plan, and she certainly didn't want to go home and face Ma with the possibility that she had not heard from God. That would damage the name of Christ and reinforce Ma's belief that God didn't speak nor answer prayers.

She stuffed her worries and tried to concentrate on the chatter of the children.

"Auntie Gracie, do you think I can come play with the orphan kids when you're there?" Jenny asked.

"Let's just allow your aunt Gracie to get settled in before we pile on visitors."

"But I'm not a visitor. I'm her special girl. She already told me that."

"Me too," yelled Pearl in a shrill squeal. "Me too."

They all laughed. "Now look what you've started," Amelia

said. "Two weeks in and my girls are already spoiled by their Auntie Gracie."

"Oh, and about that...I'd prefer to be called Grace. Gracie sounds so immature, and if this Matthew guy is a little starchy, I think Grace will sound more professional. Don't want to give him the wrong impression right from the get-go. Or have you already told him my name?"

"I haven't spoken to Matthew about you coming, but Bryon..." Amelia turned toward him.

"No." Bryon shook his head. "I haven't said a word to him."

Amelia's eyes widened. "But I told you she was coming to help at the orphanage."

Bryon's eyes narrowed. "You didn't clear it with Matthew?"

Gracie's eye's flickered from one to the other. Was she hearing right? Her body broke out into a cold sweat. "Neither of you talked to him?" Gracie's voice wavered.

Grandmother lifted her dinner napkin and waved it in the air. "Surely there's nothing to fret about. Who would turn down free help? Especially from a woman who is as dedicated and lovely as our Grace."

Gracie did not miss the raised eyebrows that Bryon gave Amelia and her odd look back at him. A needle of concern stitched its way up her spine. She'd promised Pa that, if she should fail in her plan to help the orphans, she'd return to the valley for the sake of Ma. And then, the next time some man proposed, there would be little doubt she'd be forced into a shallow marriage. If only she could believe that George's proposal—the fourth she'd received—would be the last. But it seemed most every man from her school days had asked to court her or had worked at getting close to her family to make an inroad. She was so tired of the constant pressure to marry. *Please, dear God, make a way for me to fulfill my destiny helping the orphaned children. Give me favor with this Matthew man. Answer my plea, and let it be a testimony to Ma of your divine love and plan for each life.*

~

"Thanks for letting the girls stay with you, Grandmother, while we take Gracie—I mean Grace—to the orphanage." Amelia's brows lifted. She slipped on her cloak. "That's going to be a hard one, changing that up."

"That is my name," Gracie said as they waved goodbye to the children and slipped out the door. They each took an arm that Bryon extended and walked toward the awaiting carriage. The scent of a nearby lilac bush, which spilled in prolific blooms over the picket fence, filled the air. Gracie paused a moment and took a deep breath in before she entered the carriage. "Hmm, I love that fragrance."

"So do I," Amelia said.

Once settled, Gracie took the opportunity to voice her concerns. "You don't think that Matthew will have a problem with my helping, do you?"

"Oh heaven's, no. Why would he?" Amelia asked.

But Bryon's eyes widened, and he clamped his mouth shut.

"What is it?" Gracie focused on her brother-in-law. "I can see you're hesitant."

"It's most likely nothing, but I remember not long ago when he didn't want Sophia there."

"Sophia? That's what's bothering you?" Amelia jabbed him in the side. "She was not at all interested in helping with the children. She had one agenda only, and that was Matthew and a wedding band on her finger. He is rather handsome, you know."

Bryon laughed. "If you say so."

"Well, he most certainly doesn't have to worry about me wanting a ring. I've made my decision about men and marriage, and my life is taking another path." Gracie pressed her lips together and looked out the carriage window.

Amelia leaned across and patted her leg. "Don't you worry, Gracie…Grace. We've timed our visit perfectly. The children will be having their afternoon quiet time. You just let me do the talking."

Gracie nodded, but bit down on her lower lip. She prayed Matthew would give her the chance to prove she was very serious about her calling. Good looking or not, this Matthew man would not be a temptation to her. A smile broke through her worries. God had this. He had called her out of the gray and into the light the day she met Rosina. It had to be Richmond, and it had to be that orphanage, or she had not heard from God at all.

~

Matthew moved across the dining hall between the sturdy wooden tables toward his good friend Bryon, dodging the benches. He smiled at Amelia, then promptly lost his welcome with one look at the petite dark-haired beauty his friends had in tow. What was she doing here? Shock flooded his veins. It had been two weeks since he'd first laid eyes on her on the train, and she was still in his head.

"It's you."

"It's you." Both their voices blended at the same time.

Matthew forced a deep breath and a pleasant expression. "Gracie, correct?" He tried to keep his voice even and disinterested.

"I don't believe we introduced ourselves," she said, "so how do you know my name?"

Even her voice sounded inviting, like the music of the wind. "I overheard you telling the cowboy."

"You two know each other?" Amelia's eyes were laughing. "How lovely." She clapped her hands together.

"We do not know each other." Matthew's tone was cold and aloof. "We merely met on the train."

"He's my brother." All heads turned toward Gracie. She laughingly smiled up at him. "Brother-in-Christ, of course. He helped me out of a sticky situation, for which I never properly thanked him." Gracie held out her petite gloved hand.

He took it for a brief second. A jolt of awareness shot up his arm and rushed at his heart, and he dropped it quickly.

This was one complication he did not need. Turning abruptly from the smile that lifted her all-too-pretty mouth, he focused on Bryon. "What brings you and Amelia our way on a Sunday? That's your family day is it not?" He ignored Gracie's expressive brown eyes, which he could feel pinned on him.

"Family day?"

Amelia jumped in. "Gracie is family. She's my sister, and we have some great news. You know how you're always so short staffed?" She did not wait for an answer. "Well Gracie has it in her head—"

"In my spirit, dear sister," Gracie said. "Big difference." They smiled at each other.

What were these two up to? And why did Bryon look like he wanted to be anywhere but present?

"I stand corrected. My sister believes the Lord wants her to devote her life in service to helping children. What better place than this orphanage? And you won't have to worry about any extra costs incurred, as she has the support of two wealthy benefactors who champion her cause."

Matthew swallowed back a lump in his throat. They couldn't be suggesting this distracting beauty work at the orphanage, could they? Bits and pieces of the conversation he overheard on the train filtered back. Something about her desire to serve God. He had better think of a good rebuttal and fast. Despite desperately needing the help, Gracie was one complication he could not afford. Visceral attraction was not how he imagined God would introduce his future wife. They would be friends first, share common goals, grow into a love relationship. He didn't want this woman and his immediate attraction to lead him astray.

He worked hard not to frown and to keep his voice steady as he answered. "No. I do not think that would be a wise idea."

"Why ever not?" It was Gracie who stepped forward, a fiery glint in her eyes.

Amelia placed a hand on Gracie's arm. "Matthew, I don't understand. Just last week you were telling me that Marianna is run off her feet, and she's certainly not getting any younger."

"Sorry to say, but I've tried young women before, and they're flighty and uncommitted." He chanced a glance at Gracie but made himself focus on Amelia. "The children fall in love with them, and then they're off and married at the drop of a hat. It's most unsettling for all concerned."

Gracie stepped forward. "I assure you"—a glint of amusement played on her lips—"unsettling is the opposite of what I intend."

"Oh, how delightful…Bryon, Amelia…" Marianna waved from across the dining hall floating toward them as if she were a lady of leisure rather than the house mother of over thirty girls. It never ceased to amaze him how, even in her sensible dull dress and flat shoes, her upbringing of culture and breeding seeped through. What terrible timing. He had hoped to have the beautiful Gracie on her way before Marianna happened upon them. Maybe he could slip away.

Amelia and Bryon gave Marianna a warm hug and introduced Gracie. Matthew waited politely for an opening. "There is precious little quiet time to get things done before the kids are busy once again, so I will bid you farewell." He turned to go.

"Matthew," Marianna said, "do take a moment with your

friends. I just put on a spot of tea and was coming to see if you wanted to join me. Why don't we all sit for a blessed moment?" Marianna waved her hand. "After all, it's the Sabbath, and the good Lord instructs a little rest. You work far too hard."

Matthew rocked on his feet. He wanted to clear out, not sip tea with a group that would be sure to return to the one discussion he did not want to continue.

Settled around the table in the warmth of the kitchen, his large fingers dwarfing the teacup, he worked hard at keeping the conversation flowing in every direction other than where that dark-eyed beauty wanted. She said little, but her lips were moving ever so slightly as if she was praying in their midst. Just when he began to breathe easily, his tea almost done, she began talking.

"Marianna, how did you decide upon this life?"

Marianna turned to her. "This life?"

"Working with the children, I mean. From what you've been sharing, you could've chosen a very different path."

"Ah yes, but no path would've been as rewarding. I do not regret one moment. I just wish there was more of me to go around. These children are starved for love and affection, and quite frankly I'm getting old and tired. I've been praying God will send someone."

Matthew jumped up from his chair. "I hate to be rude, but I really must go."

"Please wait." Gracie was on her feet. "All I want is a couple of weeks to prove my worth. If you don't think I'm a fit, I'll respect your decision."

"Whatever is she talking about?" Marianna's focus was on Matthew.

He expected Gracie to plead her case and was astounded she stood in silence. He admired that. "She thinks she wants to help with the children, but you know how that goes. The kids get attached, and she'll lose her enthusiasm and be gone in a matter of weeks, leaving little broken hearts all over the place."

"Oh heavens, not everyone has stars in her eyes like that Sophia," Marianna said. "Besides, each kind word, each warm hug is an extra one those children would otherwise not have. I only have two arms Matthew, and I'm not about to say no to two more."

Marianna set her teacup delicately on her saucer and stood. "I always honor your leadership, Matthew, but I've been praying for some help. I believe this beautiful young woman is God's answer."

Every eye was upon him. He gritted his teeth and clenched his jaw. That was the problem—Gracie was too beautiful, but how could he say that? Common sense said they needed her, but everything within him recoiled at the distraction. Marianna would have help, but he'd find it tough to concentrate on the upcoming yearly budget he needed to get done for the board with Gracie floating in and out of his day. The sound of his pounding heart drowned out his "fine then."

Amelia clapped her hands, and Bryon smiled.

Marianna hugged Gracie. "Welcome, my dear."

Matthew looked on. How in the world was he going to guard his heart?

His so-called *sister* moved with grace to stand in front of him. Her petite head tilted. Joy dawned gradually in her innocent eyes. "Thank you for this opportunity. I promise, you'll not be disappointed."

Disappointment was not what he was afraid of.

CHAPTER 3

The past two weeks had been a living hell. Matthew had never been more distracted in his life. There he was again, focused on the melodic lilt of Gracie's laughter echoing off the walls and the children responding to whatever game she was playing with them. He needed to be tending his work. The joyful sound filtered down the hall and through the door he now kept open just so he could hear it.

He had to get this budget report done. He rose from his desk and made his way to the door, but instead of closing it, he found himself walking down the hall to peek in on the playful banter. The caress of Gracie's gentle voice tugged at his heart. He stopped outside the entrance and looked into the main hall, watching from a distance.

Gracie sat on the floor, her skirt billowing around her, surrounded by the children intently awaiting her instruction.

"Come over here, Emma. It's your turn to spin the top, and we'll all count to see if you get the longest time."

Shy little Emma took her thumb out of her mouth and made her way over to Gracie. She plopped on her lap.

"We'll give Emma one practice try, since she's new and has never done this. Agreed?"

The children nodded.

"All right Emma, just as I showed you. It's all in the flick of your wrist."

Emma somehow got the top spinning her first try, and all the children clapped and started counting out loud. Ah, she was smart. Gracie had them practicing their counting, and they didn't even know it. And the way she was able to get shy Emma involved touched his soul. He didn't want to feel the admiration rising up within him, but there she was, winning him over, consuming his thoughts both day and night. It embarrassed him how he lay on his bed at night imagining…

Gracie dropped a featherlight kiss on Emma's head, and he closed his eyes and pulled back out of view. What would it feel like to have those lips upon his? Heat rushed up his spine.

This was insane. How could a snippet of girl he barely knew create such turmoil within? This was not going as planned. There was no rationale to this burning attraction other than the fact that she was turning out to be a kind and loving help to the children.

He turned back toward his office and made sure he closed the door behind him.

~

*G*racie loved her work at the orphanage. The past few weeks had been all she'd dreamed of and more. God had given her the desire of her heart, and the work could not feel more right. Rosina would be proud of her. She was living her promise.

Working with Marianna was fluid and easy. The older woman was more like a sister than a matriarch. They shared many of the same aspirations for the children. Marianna was more than willing to pass the torch, having confided how tired she was of late. There was a definite need for her help. Now, if only she could convince the austere Mr. Weston. She had the routine down and was careful to follow each and every protocol. She had no desire to give him any excuse to send her packing.

A hum slipped from her lips as she collected the tin bowls from the lunchtime soup and piled them on the tray. One glance at Jonathan, and her heart sank. There had to be some way to get the quiet boy talking.

"What do you think, Jonathan, can I stack yet another bowl and make it to the kitchen?"

Jonathan's sad eyes shot wide open. He was new to the orphanage and painfully shy.

Beside him, Nellie's mischievous grin spilled across her round face. "Yes, yes." She clapped her hands. "Add at least three more."

Games were the way to any child's heart, but Gracie was not prepared to allow the stack to tumble. "Ah, ah, ah, Nellie. It's Jonathan's call. This is a way to get to know me, and you'll all get a chance at the guessing game. Today's question is, how strong am I? Keep in mind that, if the bowls topple, you must help me clean up and clear the rest of the dishes, but if they do not, then a candy stick is yours."

Jonathan eyed the stack with careful contemplation and turned to the rest of the room where all eyes were upon him. "Hmm…" He put a finger to his mouth. "She was carrying around that real fat baby all morning." They all giggled. "I think her arms are stronger than they look."

Many heads bobbed in agreement.

"How very astute of you, Jonathan. So, what say you?"

His slumped shoulders straightened a little. "How about a stack of ten like Nellie suggested. That would be three more than you have now."

Nellie beamed at him, and the room erupted in cheers.

Gracie placed three more bowls on top of the seven. It wobbled precariously as she lifted the tray. The bowls were heavier than she'd anticipated. Maybe this was not such a good idea after all.

Jonathan snapped up from his seat to walk beside her. "Come on, you can do it."

"What's going on in here?" Mr. Weston's clipped tone split through the laughter, and Gracie's body jumped at the sound of his voice. Her heartrate accelerated. The stack wobbled to one side and then another. Gracie managed to steady the tray and kept walking with her head held straight. Drat. Not a great idea at all. She slid the tray on the kitchen counter and turned around with a smile.

"Why the unnecessary load? What if they had toppled?"

"I'm...I'm—"

"She's helping us get to know her, sir."

Matthew turned toward Jonathan, who stood in the doorway. "Get to know her?"

"Yes, we were guessing how strong she is, and I guessed right. She's much stronger than she looks."

Gracie pulled a candy stick from the jar and moved across the room quickly. "Right you are, Jonathan." She tucked the candy into his small hand. "Run along now."

"What if those dishes had fallen and hit a child, not to mention the mess?"

A lump clogged Gracie's throat. She swallowed hard. Her game may have not been the wisest choice, but neither did it warrant this overreaction. She didn't want to give him reason to send her away. She'd better think fast.

Numerous sets of curious eyes peeked into the room from the doorway.

At one flick of Matthew's hand in their direction, the children scattered. "Meet me in my office, where we have some privacy."

"Marianna is running some errands, and I'm to get the children settled for their afternoon quiet time."

"Then come the minute she returns." His voice held a sternness that sent a shiver down her spine.

"Yes, sir," she said as sweetly as she could.

He turned and walked away. The hardwood reverberated under the stomp of his heels.

Dear Jesus, help me. Soften his heart. I love this work and these children more than I ever imagined I could. You must've fashioned this into my being while I was still in the womb. Oh Lord, make a way where there seems to be no way.

~

Matthew tapped the end of his ruler on his desk. His ledgers sat before him beside expense receipts piled high, waiting to be recorded. Not to mention the yearly budget he had not touched for days, which was due at month's end. The past few weeks, his concentration had taken a nosedive, and he was getting little done.

That woman had to go. Gracie had no idea how many times he'd left his stuffy office in search of her dark-eyed beauty. He told himself it was to surmise her work ethics, but he knew the truth. She drew him like the Shenandoah river's undertow.

He flung the ruler. It hit the wall and clanged to the floor. In one swift movement, he stood and paced the room. This obsession of his had to stop. He finally found a good reason to terminate the distraction she had become, and he would do it.

"Sir." She rapped on his open door.

There she stood with her deep-set brown eyes, a sea of chocolate he longed to swim in. He shook his head. He had never been given to irrational thinking. What on earth was happening to him?

"Come in." He pointed to a chair and promptly put the desk between them. She sat on the edge with her back ramrod straight.

He raked a hand through his hair and let out a deep breath before speaking. "It's best you do not return to the orphanage tomorrow."

"Why?"

Why indeed? He would have to make his words sound intimidating and convincing. "Today's display of—"

"I'm so sorry." Her eyes widened and glistened with unshed tears. "I was trying to get little Jonathan to engage. My little game got out of hand. I admit the stack of dishes was less than ideal. I promise it won't happen again."

Her words tumbled out one after the other. He could not get a word in.

"Please, sir. I've found that games bring even the shyest soul out to play. And Jonathan—"

Matthew held his hand up, and she pursed her lips shut.

"Gracie, you'll make a fine wife and mother someday. But overseeing many children takes a certain gift and maturity you currently lack."

"Please, Matthew."

His first name slipped from her lips, and his heart twisted into a knot.

A single tear slipped down her left cheek. She brushed it free. "I can learn most anything."

He had to finish the unpleasant deed with precise sharpness. "Yes, I do believe you can. But maturity takes time, time I do not have the luxury of giving you. These children are already getting way too attached. I cannot afford to have them devasted when you leave. It's best you do so immediately." He slid into his chair refusing to meet her gaze.

She stood, all five feet of her, and moved close to the desk, towering over him. "Have you discussed this with Marianna?"

The tone of her voice made his head snap up. Fire spit from her dark eyes. He stood, unable to take the heat of her passion searing a hole through his flimsy excuse for dismissal. "I'm in no way obliged to discuss this with anyone. I manage this orphanage, and my decision is final."

He expected her to turn away in defeat, but instead she came around to his side of the desk and stood very close. "You're a Christian, right?"

He could smell the sweetness of peppermint on her breath. "Yes."

"Have you prayed about this?" Her head tilted up in such a way that made him want to shake her and draw her into his arms all at the same time.

Where were those thoughts coming from? Everything about his attraction to her rankled. It felt too early, too superficial, too based on her beauty. How was he any different from the cowboy on the train?

Pray about this? Of course he hadn't. He'd been too busy thinking of all the ways she distracted him. He straightened to his full height and tried to match those flashing eyes with his full Matthew Weston intimidation.

She was unfazed. "Well, I have prayed. And I know with all my heart I'm not only to give my life in service to children, but I'm to give it to *these* children." With that, she turned and stalked away, slamming the door behind her.

A few minutes later, Marianna barged in. "Matthew, I love you like a son, but you've gone too far. A little fun with the kids and you demand Gracie go home and not return? What is with you?" Both her hands were planted firmly on her wide hips.

"She's too impulsive and too immature."

"And possibly too pretty?"

Was he that obvious? How embarrassing. He'd best sound convincing. "Her comely looks have nothing to do with this."

"Not so fast." Marianna's brows knit together. "Don't think I haven't noticed your sudden interest in our daily activities with eyes for one pretty lady in particular."

Was he that blasted obvious, or did Marianna just know him too well? "I'm doing my job in running this place, and my word on the matter is final."

"Ahh, you protest too vehemently. I think you finally met a woman you cannot ignore, and it scares you."

"That's not it at—"

"Are you sure? You have that analytical brain that wants to control everything with sensible reasoning. But falling in love never follows a well-laid plan."

Love? What was she talking about? He pulled at the cravat around his neck and leaned back in his chair.

"You may think I know little about that," she said, "but you'd be surprised to hear I fell in love when I least expected it. But then..." Her eyes held a faraway look. "He left for war and never returned."

"I'm sorry to hear—"

"I do know how love can catch one by surprise."

He raised one brow. He did not trust himself to speak.

"I need the help, Matthew. I'm not getting any younger." She inhaled a deep breath and blew it out. "I was going to wait until Gracie was more experienced to tell you this, but the doctor is no longer suggesting I slow down, he's demanding it."

Matthew stood and came around the desk. "Are you all right?"

Marianna placed a cold, wrinkled hand on the side of his face. "I'm old and worn out. You know how much I love the children, but I can no longer remain in charge of the girls. And frankly, I've never seen a more gifted person with children than Gracie."

Matthew took a deep breath. "What will we do without you?"

Marianna pulled his stiff body into one of her world-class hugs and held on tight. "God has this all under control. But if you're asking my advice?" She leaned back so she could look into his eyes. "Gracie is a gift from heaven, and you'd better skedaddle over to her home at once and beg her forgiveness. We need her back."

~

Gracie opened her grandmother's front door, slipped in, and closed it as quietly as possible. She had walked for over an hour in the warm May sunshine but still had no desire for conversation. The privacy of her room and a good cry were what she needed. She tiptoed through the entryway and past the parlor.

"Gracie, my dear. Whatever are you doing home so early?" Grandmother's high-pitched voice pierced the air.

Gracie froze. There was no point in postponing the inevitable. Her heart sank at the thought of leaving her grandmother to return home to the Shenandoah Valley in failure. How had she been so wrong in hearing from God? Had her promise to Rosina, and then consequently to God, been birthed out of emotion, not of the Spirit? That thought made her tremble. If she had not heard from God and was not supposed to be in Richmond at that orphanage, then the very fiber of her faith felt ripped asunder. How would she reconcile that?

And what was she to do with her life?

She turned into the parlor with emotions brimming at the surface. Would she make it through this conversation without blubbering like a fool? Her voice warbled. "I…I've been told I'm not a good fit for the work at the orphanage."

"What?" Her grandmother's voice rose a few octaves. "That

will never do." She tried to rise from her favorite chair and failed two times before standing and tottering across the room. Her balance relied heavily upon the support of her trusty cane. She drew Gracie into a warm hug. "Now, now child. Sit. We'll get this sorted." She called down the hall, and Lydia came running. "Tea, please." She waved her cane in the direction of the kitchen, and Lydia was off.

"Now, what's all this nonsense about you not being needed at the orphanage? Last time I checked, free help was hard to come by, and that place needs all the hands it can get." She lowered her body slowly back into her chair.

"I am needed, Grandmother, just not wanted." Gracie tried to swallow the pain, which only made things worse. Tears clouded her view.

"How dare they insult my granddaughter in such a way. I will forgo all donations in the future."

"No. That would only hurt the children."

"Ahh, you're a kind soul, aren't you? Just like your sister Amelia. How many times she has taken me to task for wanting to take things into my own hands." Grandmother shook her gray head.

"Sorry to interrupt you." Sixteen-year-old Sarah stood in the doorway. Ripples of shiny black hair bound with a colorful checkered turban complimented her pretty round face.

"Can it wait?" Grandmother turned to Lydia's daughter.

"Ma sent me to get the door, and there's a man named Mr. Weston." She focused on Gracie. "He insists he must see you, Miss Gracie." Sarah pulled at the sides of her apron, her dark eyes darting between the parlor and the hall.

"Mr. Weston?" Grandmother placed one hand to her temple and creased her brow. "I don't recall that name—"

"That's Matthew Weston." Gracie popped up. "The head of the orphanage. The man who…"

Grandmother waved her hand at Gracie to sit. "Do send him in, Sarah. He shall endure a tongue lashing from me."

"Now, Grandmother—"

"Don't you *now grandmother* me. No one is going to mess with my granddaughter's dreams and not have to deal with me."

Before she could protest, Matthew Weston stood in the doorway, and Gracie's tongue suddenly felt glued to the bottom of her mouth. She wanted to tell him to leave, but nothing came out.

Grandmother waved him in. "I'm glad you came by, because I have a bone to pick with you."

Mr. Weston held up his hand and moved across the room. "Please, allow me one moment to speak. I owe your granddaughter an apology. Then you can pick away."

The only smiles Gracie had seen from him in the past few weeks had been directed at the children, but there he was, winning her grandmother over with a wide grin and a kiss on the back of her hand like a perfect gentleman. Then he turned that smile on her, and everything she wanted to say was silenced.

"Please forgive me, Gracie. I over-reacted. Our orphanage desperately needs your help and your natural gifting with children. Would you please accept my sincerest apology and consider returning?"

He sounded sincere. His generous smile was indeed welcoming, not something she had witnessed before. Crescent dimples emerged like the thin slice of a new moon on both sides of his mouth. And those blue eyes, which earlier had been colder than glacier ice, were soft and pleading. Even his tall stature, with its natural air of authority, was tempered by this new relaxed approach. She would love working with Matthew Weston if this side of him surfaced more often.

She wanted to jump up and hug him and shout yes, but she

would not make it too easy. "Have I suddenly grown in maturity, Mr. Weston?"

A frown puckered his brow, and his smile flattened. "I deserve that. A rash judgment warrants a refutation of the matter." He took a few steps closer where he could look down directly into her eyes. "Your maturity is not in question. Mine is."

Gracie stared up at him. Who was this man?

"Wonderful. That's settled." Grandmother clapped her hands, cutting through the awkward silence. "Who could reject such a contrite apology? Certainly not my good Christian granddaughter. Come now, Mr. Weston, have tea with us."

"I'd be honored." Matthew Weston slid into a nearby chair.

"Gracie. Be a dear and pour the man a cup of tea."

Gracie took a moment to catch her breath before she stood. Had she just been bamboozled by the both of them?

CHAPTER 4

Matthew stifled a whistle as he walked into his office and plopped into his chair. What was happening to him? He was walking around the place with his head in the clouds and a certain dark-haired girl in his thoughts. When was the last time he had let his emotions rule and thoughts of whimsical impossibilities ferment? He had always had it in his head that there would be no shock to the realization of true love. Life would unfold in orderly fashion, and love would come slowly and logically. What were these erratic feelings? And why did he have to work so hard to temper them?

His eyes flitted around the room. A wall of bookshelves—the books ordered alphabetically for easy access. The one lone plant flourished under his tender care with just the right amount of water, sunlight, and soil maintenance. His mahogany desk was spit-polished clean with neat stacks of work in order of priority. He loved his latest purchase, a bureau that neatly held his ledgers and files on each orphan registered. Everything in his life exuded order—except the crazy thoughts of *her*.

Spring had turned into summer, and the last three months had held a lightness in his countenance that could not be accounted for. Every moment in Gracie's presence somehow felt crisper and more vibrant than the one before. Thankfully, he had finished his budget, albeit a month late, and was learning to concentrate despite the disruption of her floating in and out of his day.

She was attractive, very much so. All the more reason to be wary of the weakness of the flesh. Max, his assistant with the boys, was a perfect example of the lure she created. He had been back two months now from his trip to New York and was already smitten.

But with her comely appearance and standing in the community as the granddaughter of Mrs. Frances Brunson, not to mention that she was the sister of Amelia and Bryon Preston, it would not be long before every man in a ten-mile radius would be calling. Competing. Contending. With his past, it was better he remained fully cognizant of her social standing. The worst thing ever would be to let his emotions have free rein and then have to watch as a much more suitable life partner for her came along. What did he have to offer over the clearly better choices out there?

You have love.

He started and sat up straight. Where had that thought come from? Was God speaking, or was it just longing and a need to abate the loneliness that crawled into his soul every night?

He was not without options. Many women found him attractive, but how many would still be interested if they knew?

Sophia came to mind. She was beautiful and had all the social standing he could possibly hope for, but she only tolerated children at best, and children were his life. She had hinted at him working for her father, but he would never leave the orphanage. Plus, he'd felt nothing for her, therefore never felt compelled to share the truth. That would have been sure to send her running and would have adversely affected the orphanage. But this was different, no one had come close to drawing the regard he instinctively felt for Gracie. No one had come close to drawing his regard, which he instinctively felt for Gracie.

She's the one I have chosen for you.

He sat back in his chair. Every follicle on this thick head of hair stood at attention.

Why, in the middle of the day, with a hundred things pressing, would God choose that moment to speak?

But He was indeed speaking.

"I'm listening, Lord," Matthew whispered. The canted rays of afternoon sun spilled through the window as if on cue. The day had been a mixture of black cloud and rain. Somehow the sunlight now winked free, slicing through the dreary.

She's the one.

His heart slammed against his chest and kicked up speed as he heard the words spoken into his spirit. A smile split loose.

"You wanted to see me?" Gracie stood in the doorway of his office.

He righted his relaxed body into a more professional position. "Ahh...no." He could not think straight. His head felt like it was swimming in joy, yet he had so much to think through.

"Marianna said you needed to go over a few changes with me."

"Oh yes. Sit." He motioned to the chair. *Relax, boy. Take a deep breath. Inhale. Exhale. That's better.* The softness of her mahogany eyes pulled him in. How was he to concentrate?

"I...I do have something to discuss with you." Was he now going to stutter in front of her? He had never stuttered in his life.

"Yes?" She moved her chair closer. "Should I get my notebook and pen?"

"No. No. Not today. But we'll be brainstorming together in the future, where pen and paper would be an asset." He sounded like such a dolt when all he could concentrate on was the soft fragrance of wild roses wafting in his direction. "I sincerely hope the following news concerning your future will meet with your approval."

Her shoulders dropped, and she relaxed into the chair, but she kept folding and unfolding her hands.

Did he make her nervous? There was little doubt. If that message he heard from God had been a directive to pursue this lovely creature, he would have to mitigate that problem immediately. A mental note to be friendlier would be a good start.

"It's been three months since you came to us, and I would normally never suggest such a huge advancement so quickly, but circumstances dictate the necessity."

Her beautiful eyes widened, and his train of thought vanished. He turned his head away and stared out the window. If he was to get through this conversation, he best look elsewhere.

"Yes." The softness of her voice pulled to him, and he turned toward her but did not make eye contact.

"Marianna's doctor has ordered her to not only cut back on her hours, as she has been since you so graciously have taken some of the pressure off, but to stop working entirely. On behalf of the board, Marianna's recommendations, and mine, I'd like to offer you her position, with remuneration of course—a fulltime position overseeing the girls. I know this is a huge responsibility, but I believe you can handle it."

"What? You want me to take over Marianna's role?" Her brows rose, and her back straightened.

"Yes. Now keep in mind, Marianna will still be available for any questions or training you feel you need, and we'll see to hiring an assistant for you. I'm sure you'll at least want weekends with your grandmother. But from what I've seen thus far, I have full confidence in you."

"You have confidence in me?" A half giggle slipped from her mouth. "Really, Mr. Weston?"

"Why are you so surprised?"

"You haven't said one word of encouragement to me in three months. Yet I've heard you encourage almost every other volunteer and worker. Honestly, I thought you were less than impressed with me."

He could not tell her the truth that he dared not begin with the compliments or he would not be able to stop. Distance and aloofness had been his guard, but if he'd heard God correctly, he no longer needed to fight what he was feeling. Relief flooded through his being. He could just be himself.

"When you first came, I doubted you, but you have proved me wrong again and again. I believe you're serious about the wellbeing of our children, and this work at the orphanage is not just a pastime but a calling. Am I correct?"

"Absolutely. It is, and will continue to be, my life commitment."

"May I ask you a rather personal question?"

She nodded.

"What about marriage and a family of your own? This has been my key hesitation."

"I have zero interest in marriage."

"Zero?" His heart tightened like a vice clamping down.

"I fear a husband would be a distraction. And as far as children go, one look at this orphanage should tell you there's more than enough need to fill any motherly instinct I have."

He gulped back the warring reaction unfolding inside his head. How could he hear God tell him in one moment that she was the one, and in the next, hear that she had zero interest in marriage?

"I do mean what I say, Mr. Weston. And I would be honored to learn from Marianna and sign any paperwork needed to confirm my long-term commitment to this orphanage."

Matthew's heart sank and soared in waves. On one hand, he had her commitment to the orphanage. On the other, her aversion to marriage.

"Am I to understand you will not be courting the suitors who will surely be calling as you integrate into the social scene?"

"Absolutely not. Ask Grandmother, if you so desire. After I made the mistake of attending one event for her sake, I have said no to every man who has come calling. I will not be attending any further social engagements, including the upcoming fall gala, which Grandmother insists is the rage of the season."

"Sounds like you're serious."

"Nothing will come before my love for Jesus and this work He has called me to do. You can count on that."

Who was this wisp of a girl, so filled with fire and gumption? And how would he begin to win her love when she had such an aversion to marriage? "You are indeed an unusual young woman." He planted both hands on the desk. "I shall not need a signed agreement. I trust you have given this much thought and prayer."

"I have indeed. And as for a wage, please use that to hire more help. I have generous benefactors who are supplying my daily needs."

He smiled the most winsome smile he could muster and rose, leaning forward. "I know this is unorthodox, but shall we shake on our agreement?" He extended his hand across the desk.

"I would like that, Mr. Weston."

Her smile tunneled into him, melting the hard edges. The moment her small hand joined his, a shot of awareness exploded up his arm. He wanted to hang on forever. Reluctantly, he let go, and she pulled away and headed for the door.

"And Gracie?"

She spun.

"You're more than welcome to call me Matthew now that we'll both be part of the management team."

"That would be lovely," she said. "Quite frankly, you've scared me with your stern demeanor. If I didn't love the children so much and wasn't certain God wanted me to stay, I would've been long gone."

She laughed and his gut twisted. What an idiot he had been. "You'll see. There is another side to the serious Matthew."

She pressed a finger to her smiling lips. "Hmm. How about I test that theory?"

"Test away."

"When I walked in, you had the most amazing smile on your face. What were you thinking?"

He gulped. She was not ready for that answer. He stalled by walking around the desk toward her and pointing to the window. "The sun had just come out, and I don't know… I got this overwhelming sense of the Lord's presence." That part was not a lie.

She tilted her head up to him and nodded. "I know the feeling. Isn't He wonderful?" Her lips turned up in the kind of smile that spilled joy into the eyes.

"Wonderful, indeed." She would have no idea that he was referring to her and the God they served.

⁓

Gracie knocked on Matthew's office door at the end of the day with trepidation. She would put that declaration of him promising to be less serious to the test.

"Come in."

She stepped into his office, and rather than the stern demeanor that she had become accustomed to, dimples appeared on both sides of his mouth, accenting a row of perfectly white teeth. The sudden smile pulled at her heart strings, and she felt a strange sensation curl in the pit of her stomach.

"Can I help you with something?" he asked.

"I have an idea I need to run by you. First to get your permission, and if you agree, your help."

"That sounds interesting."

"Oh, but it is." She purposely threw him a grin as she slid into the empty chair across from his desk. "You know how we play hide-and-seek most days with the children, girls against boys?"

"I'm aware."

"Unfortunately, the girls always lose because the boys are more aggressive in the hunt. I want to secure a win but need your assistance."

He leaned back in his chair, his smile only broadening.

That was encouraging. "I thought of the perfect hiding place, but I'll understand if you have reservations." Her hands turned clammy, and suddenly her idea did not seem that safe at all. "I totally understand if—"

"Gracie, spit it out. The worst I can do is say no." He was still smiling. The transformation was startling.

"I...I thought that maybe...you could possibly help me, but only if you want to—"

"Oh, my goodness. Am I really that much of a sourpuss?"

She didn't want to admit that she was scared to death of his disapproval. And, if he thought it a dumb idea, she'd feel embarrassed and juvenile. Best to just get it out. "I was thinking of hiding the girls under the veranda at the far end, but I'd need your help to create a gate with the end slats for easy access. I'd of course clean it up under there, make sure it was free of spiders and put some old blankets down on the ground."

Matthew laughed and slapped his hand on his knee. "That's a brilliant plan. Give me a few days to work on that gate in clandestine fashion, and your win will be secured."

"You...you don't mind?"

"Ha, but of course. Those boys need a tuning up. They're getting far too big for their britches."

Gracie relaxed back in the chair. "Why thank you, kind sir. The girls will be tickled pink."

"Did you think I was going to say no?"

"I didn't know what to think, but I was hoping—"

"That I wouldn't be too much of a spoilsport."

"Yes." She giggled. "The new improved Matthew is much more to my liking."

He raised his eyebrows.

"What I meant to say—"

"Is exactly what you said, and that's what I like about you. You're honest."

It was her turn to give him a smile from her heart.

~

Windblown leaves rustled through the nearby oak. A few sifted to the ground, adding touches of yellow and orange. The air held that hint of crispness, signifying the impending change of season September always brought. Gracie took a deep breath in as the children poured out of the building. How much fun was this, getting to play with them in the great outdoors?

She clapped her hands, signaling the children to gather around. She winked at the girls. Full smiles broke free. Turning to the boys, she asked, "Ready for the girls to whip you in hide-and-seek?"

"Ha, that would be a first," Max said. All the boys snickered in agreement.

"We hide first, but you must count to thirty." She took off running with the girls squealing behind her. Over the veranda their feet pounded. The only rule was that they had to remain outside in their daily game of hide-and-seek. The opposing team had to find each person in fewer than ten minutes. The stage was set. The boys always won, but today, the victory would be theirs.

"Shh. Shh." She herded the girls around the side of the rambling main building and opened the board skirting at the far end that had been fashioned into a perfect gate. "Quick now, under you go."

She was amazed at the difference in Matthew. To her utter surprise, he had not only created the perfect gate but had snuck the girls out during their quiet time the day before to practice. They had cleaned out the area, placed old blankets down on the dirt, and had pillows to stifle their laughter.

"Ready or not, you're going to get caught." Max's loud voice boomed out.

Gracie placed her index finger to her mouth, and the giggling girls hushed. "Remember," she whispered, "if you have the urge to laugh, laugh into a pillow."

Enough light filtered through the slats in the boards to see the dancing eyes of the girls. Sheer joy filled Gracie's heart. What a wonderful life she had. The pitter patter of running feet rounded the corner of the veranda, and they could hear the boys scatter as they searched in all the usual places between the two houses. One by one, the girls lifted a pillow to their mouths and stifled the laughter. Especially when Max was right above and the boys were whining about the girls cheating.

"They must have gone inside," one said.

"Yeah, we can't even find one of them." Another one stomped his foot right above them.

"No. Gracie wouldn't let them go indoors," Max said. "They're somehow moving around, and you're not seeing them."

"Then they went out of bounds, off the property. Can we go down the street and look for them?"

"Absolutely not. Gracie would never allow anything that

unsafe. But we only have a minute left to find them. Let's split up. Half of you on this side and half on the other."

The girls heads bobbed up and down with their tiny cheeks stuffed into the pillows.

The ten-minute whistle blew, and the boys groaned in defeat.

"Wait." Gracie whispered. "Maybe if they all reconvene at the front of the house we can slip out and reuse this hiding place tomorrow."

Smiles split free. Gracie slowly opened the makeshift door and nodded. The girls spilled out as fast as they could. Their secret was safe for another day. They took the opposite way around the building between the houses back to the meeting place at the main house.

"Where were you?" the boys shouted.

"We didn't break any rules," Gracie assured them. "But our lips are sealed. Right girls?"

Even Emma, aged five, nodded. Her chubby thumb went in her mouth as Gracie picked her up. "I no tell," she said. The little girl with no smile beamed, and Gracie's heart lurched. That smile made the spikes of loneliness in the late evening worthwhile.

She had expected once she devoted her life and was living her promise, all loneliness would cease. To her disappointment that had not happened. What was she missing?

∼

"Aren't you going to tell me?" Max's charming, crooked smile lit up his face as he cozied up to Gracie. "Where were you?"

Matthew was not impressed with how familiar Max had become with Gracie. He was leaning in too close for propriety, touching her arm, bunting her with his elbow as he cajoled. And she was laughing it off, her eyes sparkling with mischievous merriment. The only saving grace was the knowing smile she tossed Matthew across the table every now and again throughout the meal.

He finally put a stop to the banter when the supper tables erupted in mayhem as the boys tried to fandangle the truth out of the girls and Jason took to twisting Nellie's arm. Her blood-curdling scream had the adults on their feet.

"Enough." Matthew's voice silenced the room. "A game is a game. And, boys, you have been outsmarted. It's your turn to take the loss as well as the girls have done in the past. Jason, apologize to Nellie at once. And Nellie, don't think I missed you sticking your tongue out at Jason. This was supposed to be fun. Remember?"

The boys nodded their heads. Even Max joined in.

"Any more nonsense, and there'll be no game time tomorrow, and the boys and girls will remain separated all day." He knew how much the children loved to be together. To take away their interaction at meals and game time was always an effective punishment.

It would be cruel to keep the kids apart, but at least that would also separate Max and Gracie. What could he do about the man's flirting? That had to stop as well. He slid back onto the bench. He didn't always join for the evening meal, but whenever he could manage the time, he liked to be part of the children's lives. But if he were truly honest with himself, lately his joining the children had less to do with them and more to do with Gracie.

She stood. "They're short-handed in the kitchen tonight, so I'm going to help with the dishes while the kids have dessert."

"I'll help too." Max jumped up.

"But what about the children?" Gracie asked. "Someone has to watch them."

"Matthew is more than capable. Didn't you see how

everyone cowered when he spoke? Wish I had that kind of power."

Max didn't have a malicious bone in his body, but Matthew didn't appreciate having been made out to be the ogre. He watched the two of them disappear through the open doorway into the adjoining kitchen.

Curiosity got the better of him, and he started gathering plates for an excuse to hear their conversation. He entered the kitchen with a stack in hand.

"How old are you, Max?" Gracie asked.

"How old do you think I am?" Max puffed out his chest and straightened to full height, all five foot six inches of him.

Matthew wanted to laugh. Max's infatuation with Gracie was obvious. Matthew wasn't far behind, but was he that transparent? He sincerely hoped not.

"I'd say twenty."

"You're right." His chest deflated a little. "How did you do that?"

"I'm good at that kind of thing."

"Well then, how old is Matthew?"

"Hmm, considerably older, I'm guessing."

Matthew set the dishes on the counter with a clunk to make his presence known.

They both jumped.

Max smiled at Matthew and back at Gracie. "Right you are, but how much older?"

Matthew wanted to deck him. How dare he be made out to be the old one in the bunch, even if he was.

Gracie turned to Matthew. "Hmm, I'm guessing thirty something?"

"Did you say *thirty* something?" Matthew spat out the question.

Max laughed. Could he not see how angry Matthew was?

"That wasn't meant to be an insult," Gracie quickly added.

"With all it takes in running this place, I can't see anyone younger being trusted with so great a responsibility."

"I'll have you know I'm twenty-six, and I've been running this place for two years already. Not to mention the fact I apprenticed for five years prior to that. I guess in your eyes, that makes me old."

"I didn't mean—"

"Max." He turned away from her. "Get out there and keep an eye on the children. I have some work to do in my office."

Matthew hated himself for stomping away and sounding gruff. He slid into his office chair with a groan. Why hadn't he laughed it off?

He placed his head in his hands and leaned forward to rest his elbows on the desk. Thirty something was exactly the persona he loved to give off.

Unless the girl he was falling in love with was fun-loving and only eighteen.

He was still beating himself up, head in his hands, fifteen minutes later when there was a slight rap at the door. He straightened. "Come in."

The hem of a dress and the poke of a head were all he could see.

"I have to tuck the children in, but I just wanted to say I'm sorry. I didn't mean anything by—"

"I guess I do act rather old for my age."

She slipped all the way in, her hand still on the doorknob.

"No excuses, but life has been tough. It has a way of making one grow up fast, and possibly I've become too serious."

She moved halfway across the room. "I just wanted to tell you how much I respect all you've accomplished and…and that I don't see you as old."

Matthew was tongue-tied. He wanted to tell her to go and yet to wrap his arms around her, all in the same moment. "Thank you," was all he could muster.

"These past few weeks have been wonderful, and I value our growing friendship. I hope my ill-spoken words have not jeopardized that."

He gazed into her searching eyes. "And I hope my lack of a sense of humor can be forgiven."

She smiled and nodded. "Already done." She turned to go. "Good night, Matthew."

The whisper of her voice and the way she said his name followed by the click of his office door had him aching to run after her. Of course, he would do no such thing. He drew his hands through his hair in frustration. He was feeling way too much for a woman who valued a *growing friendship.*

CHAPTER 5

*G*racie loved fall. The oppressive heat of summer was over. The crunch of leaves beneath her feet brought joy. A breeze swept through the row of oak trees that lined her grandmother's street, and she lifted her cheeks to let it kiss her face. Leaves gently sifted to the ground in colors of gold, red, and yellow making the walk to and from the orphanage one of her favorite times of the day. Soon Marianna would be moving in with her sister for good, and Gracie would take up residence in her room near the children, coming home to Grandmother's only on the weekends.

Life was grand. Except for the knotty situation of Max showing her far too much attention. Why did men always fall for her? She was so thankful for Matthew, the one man who had truly befriended her without designs for more. He would know what to do.

She lifted her head into the blue and whispered her morning prayers. "Lord, please help Jonathan's shyness. And Becky has grown out of another pair of shoes, but the finances are so tight with all the new kids. Lord, the place is filled to capacity, and the kids keep coming. The need is great, the workers few. Please help us know what to do. On a smaller note, Nellie is far too mischievous, and I'm losing patience, not to mention Emma's stealing my heart, but she's not adjusting. Lord, there are so many needs, and now this Max problem. Please send the right girl his way... Oh and Lord, bless Matthew and all his work. Help him to relax a little and not be so driven. He doesn't need to have the best run orphanage in the country as he insists upon. All he needs is to do his best and leave the rest with You. Give wisdom—"

"Who in the world are you talking to?"

"Goodness, Max, must you insist on sneaking up on me like that? I've told you numerous times I pray on my way to the orphanage, and every time you insist on joining me, you steal time from God."

"Ha. If you were a good Christian like me, you'd be on your knees at five, not still sleeping in that warm bed of yours." His eyes were full of laughter as he fell into step beside her.

"Like you're up at five, on your knees." She slapped him on the arm with the gloves she had removed.

He placed a hand on his heart. "I'm wounded. You don't believe I'm a spiritual giant? Look at me, the word giant is what everyone sees at first glance." He laughed and tapped his short head.

She loved that about him. He was short and stocky in stature but lacked no such boundaries in personality. He laughed at himself readily and invited others to join in. So different from the all-too-serious Matthew. For two people who could not be more opposite they actually complemented each other and worked well together. Now, if she could resolve Max's growing infatuation with her, all would be perfect.

They walked up the stairs of the main orphanage building, and he touched her arm before she could enter. "Honestly, Gracie. The best part of my day is waiting for you to come down the street and joining you for a few uninterrupted minutes." His eyes oozed tenderness and longing. The laughter was gone.

Gracie gulped back a sharp response. She was so tired of this same conversation over and over. She had hoped that, once she dedicated her life to God's work, He would make sure the men left her alone. But once again, it was the same words, different face. "Please, Max, let's not complicate our wonderful friendship. My first love is Jesus, my second the children, and with that, my life is full to overflowing." She stuffed down the fact she still felt pangs of loneliness. The truth was that, even if she were looking for a husband, Max was not the one. Her voice softened. "Do you understand what I'm saying?"

He looked down at the planks on the veranda. "I understand, but I don't agree. We both love Jesus. We're both devoted to the children. We share a passion and interest that most don't have. What better partner in life could you find than me?"

She stalled as she placed her hand on the doorknob. "You assume I'm looking for a partner. I'm sorry, but I'm not. I believe a husband would be a distraction and a complication I don't need."

"But could we—"

"No." She shook her head, hating to be unkind. But she had learned from past experience to be honest up front. "Please, Max, let it go. It's important to me that I don't lose your friendship."

He looked away and said nothing else.

She entered the hall, and five children came running for their morning hugs. As she crouched down, allowing small arms to encircle her neck, her heart filled to capacity.

She caught Max's eye. He looked as dejected as the trees stripped of their leaves. She'd have to pray that spring came for him soon in the form of a beautiful girl.

The sound of his voice lost all life. "Have a good day, Gracie. Lord knows, I won't." He stalked away.

~

Matthew fought to stay on task. Thoughts of Gracie were ever crowding in. Surely, he was more mature than this. He had noticed in the past couple weeks that Max had overcome his infatuation. And God was not moving any mountains regarding a softness in Gracie toward him. So, he'd best follow suit. Bookkeeping of utmost importance needed to be done, and half the day had ebbed away with little to show for his efforts.

He stood from his desk and made his way to the window. Maybe a little fresh air would motivate him. He slipped the bottom sash open as he heard a rap on his office door. Drat. He had no time for interruptions. "What is it?" His voice came out sharper than he'd intended.

Gracie's head poked in. "Should I come back later? The kids are down for their afternoon quiet time, and I have a few free moments. I've been meaning to ask your opinion on something, but if you're too busy, I can schedule for this evening before I head home."

One sight of her, and his heartrate responded. Oh, how he hated that he couldn't control that uptick. "Come in. I was taking a breather anyway. Getting some much-needed fresh air." He pointed to the open window.

"Would you walk with me?" she asked. "I find a little time in the sunshine midday revives me for the afternoon work."

"No." His voice sounded severe and unyielding. But the thought of walking beside her without at least the desk between them was most unsettling. "It wouldn't be wise for us both to leave the premise, just in case there's an emergency."

A cloud covered her expressive eyes. "But of course." She nodded.

He slid back into his chair behind the desk, but she didn't

take her usual spot across from him. She instead resumed his position at the window, looking out.

"I'm sorry to have to discuss this with you. I was hoping the situation would work itself out, but I'm no longer hopeful that will happen."

Was she on to him? Could she read the truth in his eyes? He had worked so hard to create a safe boundary of decorum until such a time that God opened the door. Truth be told, he was second-guessing that he had ever heard from God on the matter. The imagination was a powerful thing when someone as beautiful as Gracie floated in and out of a person's day. And yet that moment had been so clear, so unexpected. *Dear God, give wisdom like only you can.* He wanted nothing to hinder the comfort level of his most gifted and hardest working volunteer, not even his growing desire to make their relationship a whole lot more.

"It's been over two weeks since Max has spoken a word to me. He refuses to even answer a question when directed his way. I'm afraid I'm the reason for his behavior."

She turned from the window to gaze at Matthew. Her eyes darkened from brown to a drowning swirl of black. Haloed in the light of the afternoon sun, the thick braid she always wore toward one side and down the front gleamed a glossy ebony. He wondered what it would feel like to undo that braid and bury his head in the softness.

"Matthew. I clearly interrupted your work. You're miles away. I'll come back later." She moved toward the door.

"No. No. Sorry Gracie, I heard every word."

She spun back around.

"And I've noted a difference in Max. Quite frankly, I was relieved he had gotten over his infatuation with you."

"You noticed that too?"

"Hard not to."

GRACIE'S SURRENDER

She sighed. "I told him I wanted no more than friendship, and he hasn't spoken to me since."

"Sit." He waved at the chair. "I didn't know it was that bad."

She moved across the room and sank into the chair. "If it were just my feelings at stake, I wouldn't say anything. But it's affecting the children. The time we lead the games together has been sorely compromised. I don't know how to fix it. I wish all men could be like you."

His heart kicked at the walls of his chest. "Like me?"

"You're one of the few men I know who has always been a perfect gentleman. That goes right back to our meeting on the train when you clearly came to my aid yet paid me no mind."

How wrong she was. It had taken every bit of his will power not to stare.

"I was a little worried at first when you didn't want me here, but since we worked out those details, you've treated me with respect. It's been so refreshing to be treated as a business partner, not a woman on whose finger you would like to slip a ring."

Now, what was he to say to that? Most anything that came to mind would be a lie. He hedged. "You deserve respect. You're very gifted with the children."

"All I want is to live a life of service and to not hurt anyone in the process." Her eyes shimmered, brimming with tears. One splashed down her cheek.

"When you say a life of service," he said, "what does that mean to you?"

She brushed the tear from her face and sat up straighter. "Like I told you when I started volunteering here, I feel my work with the children is a calling. I don't ever see myself married, so why would I encourage someone like Max, as sweet as he is?"

Matthew's heart felt like a herd of buffalos had trampled through. "Never is a long time. Not all marriages detract from the goal. If you were to marry someone with the same passion and love for the orphaned—"

"Like Max?"

Of course, he did not mean Max. But how could he get himself out of the hole he'd dug? "Do you have feelings for Max?" He held his breath.

"Not in the least. I mean, I really like him as a friend. Or, shall I say, I *liked* him as a friend. He's not even that any longer."

"Well then, not Max. I would expect that, if you were to ever marry, you would have strong feelings for the person, and you'd both be on the same page regarding your calling."

A cute frown puckered her brow. "I've thought about marriage, but from what I've seen, it complicates life. I'm more than happy as a single woman who can come and go at will."

"You like that freedom?" He could certainly work with that.

She nodded. "Seems once a woman gets married, the husband takes the reins. To be perfectly honest, I like holding my own. It would have to be a very special man to make me change my mind on the matter." Her eyes brightened.

He smiled, but his heart sank. He must've heard God wrong. She wasn't mildly opposed to marriage. She had decided against it. Max's infatuation was not the only one that needed eradication.

He stood, signifying an end to the conversation. He needed time alone. "I'll speak to Max about remaining professional. And if you could give his broken heart a little grace, Gracie"—he smiled at his little play on words—"I believe time will work wonders in healing this little bump in the road. With this place busting at the seams, I need you both."

She stood. "I know you do. That's why I'm most eager to solve this problem."

He smiled through the words he was preaching to himself. "God is with us, great things we can do." He came around the side of the desk and looked down at her.

"I so agree. Thank you, Matthew. You're a true brother in the Lord."

Brother was the farthest thing from his mind. He placed a hand at the small of her back and ushered her out. He did not breathe until he closed the door behind her. His head fell forward and rested against the cold wooden panels. *Dear God in heaven, take this from me.*

CHAPTER 6

"She's not your everyday girl, Max," Matthew said. "Apparently, marriage is not on her list of priorities. But let's take this discussion into my office." They headed down the hall together.

"I admit, I've been rather mulish these past few weeks, but I'm working my way through the disappointment."

Matthew closed the office door behind them. Max had no idea how much he could relate to that. He could barely sleep at night, thanks to his wrestling with God. He kept agonizing over that day in his office when the message had been so clear. Only a very special someone would change Gracie's mind, and he doubted very strongly that he was the one.

"I've had a few of those same disappointments myself over the years." He clapped Max on the shoulder and entered the office. "But we have to remain professional and think about the children's wellbeing. Your smiling face and happy countenance play an important role in their day."

Max hung his head. "True."

"When the adults are grumpy or cruel—"

"I would never be cruel, sir."

"I know you wouldn't, but even your sadness affects them. Makes them feel insecure in a world that has already given them so much to worry about."

"I'm sorry. I'll make every effort to change my behavior."

"I'm sure you will. Now, how about we leave that subject. I've been meaning to go over the details you found out about the Orphan Train ministry when you were in New York." Matthew pulled the papers free of a file upon his desk. "This place is busting at the seams. If we could find some of these kids a real home with parents who love them, it would open room up for more. There are far too many kids still living on the streets in this city."

"That's it? You're not going to give me a lecture?"

"Not unless you want me to." Matthew looked up from his papers and gave Max a smile. "I've been there. The heart is a fickle beast. It can make a man truly miserable."

"Oh, and how."

No one had to convince Matthew. He'd been fighting off the doldrums in earnest. "About the Orphan Train. I read over the information you brought back from the Children's Aid Society, and it seems there is some real merit to this idea."

"Absolutely. I met with the founder, Charles Brace, myself, and he said they've been finding homes for children this way since 1854. They've worked out a lot of the problems."

"Is he willing to partner with us? No point in reinventing a process that is efficiently up and running."

"Yes. He'd be happy to share all the information needed, but we have to remain responsible for the children we place."

"Meaning?"

"If we send a train out under their recognized and trusted name, it will generate the crowds we need in the towns to find homes for the children. But each child we place will need a yearly check-up thereafter to be sure the pairing was a good fit.

Apparently, most are successful, but there are always a few who need re-placement."

Matthew sat back in his chair and ran a hand through his hair. "Hmm, I'll have to take this up with the board. Since you have firsthand information, I'd like you to prepare a proposal, including the potential costs. First, you'll share it with me and Gracie, and if we think it's something to pursue, then you'll share it with the board. Do you think you can manage that?"

"You trust me with such a—"

"You're ready for more responsibility. Plus, it'll get your mind off the other."

"Thank you, sir." Max stood with an added lift to his head. "I won't let you down."

~

Gracie waved hello to her grandmother as she walked toward the house at the end of a long day. Grandmother was perched in her parlor room chair that faced the street. She knew all the comings and goings of Church Hill Avenue and waited patiently for Gracie's return every evening. Gracie was barely in the door when she heard Grandmother's call.

"Gracie, dear. There's a letter from home. Do hurry down after you change out of your work attire."

"I won't be long." She headed to her room. Another exhausting day. The evening meal was long since passed and the children settled before she, Max, and Matthew, went over the information about the Orphan Train. Things would be much easier when she moved into the orphanage for good, but Grandmother would be heartbroken. Gracie had held off as long as Marianna was still there, but time was running out, and Grandmother kept hinting strongly that she wanted Gracie to stay.

She pulled her sensible skirt, blouse, and layered petticoat off, catching her reflection in the full-length mirror. Not one to give herself too much attention, the new soft cotton chemise with drawstring drawers trimmed in lace caught her eyes. Grandmother had insisted on fancy underclothing, stating that if a woman had to remain in sensible clothing on the outside as Gracie did, then something soft and feminine underneath was a must. Gracie smiled at the unnecessary luxury before pulling a muslin wrapper over her head and securing the belt around her waist. Grandmother would just have to accept her informality at the end of the day.

She made her way into the parlor, where an evening tea and a plate of her favorite biscuits sat waiting for her.

"You look tired," Grandmother said.

"I am. We had a meeting after we settled the kids."

"Goodness gracious. That sounds perfectly horrid at the end of a day."

"Not the best time, but more often than not it's the only free time we have."

"I can see why it would be easier for you not to have to go back and forth."

Gracie couldn't believe her grandmother was leading that charge. She breathed out a quick prayer. *Thank you, Lord.*

"Oh, don't look at me with those beautiful eyes popped out of your pretty head. I may be old and set in my ways, but I know when I'm being selfish. You came here to look after the children, and I need to let you do that. Whenever you find the time to visit will be a bonus I never had before you moved here."

"I am torn between—"

"Well then, I'll make up your mind for you. I'm so proud of the work you do, and whenever Marianna is ready to retire for good, you let me know, and we'll get you moved on over."

"If we get the new assistant Matthew is planning to hire, I'll be able to spend every weekend with you."

"Well, that is delightful news indeed." She lifted her teacup to her lips and took a delicate sip. "Now, how about that letter. I've been waiting all day to hear the news from the valley."

Gracie leaned forward and took the envelope from Grandmother's wrinkled hand. "It's addressed to both of us."

"Yes, I know. I was tempted to read it earlier but thought it best we read it together."

Gracie slit the envelope open with a thin decorative letter opener her grandmother had ready and pulled the paper out. Her eye slid to the bottom of the page. "It's from Jeanette."

"Go ahead, read it out loud." Grandmother waved her hand in Gracie's direction.

October 1, 1879

Dear Gracie and Grandmother,

I know by the time you get this letter, winter will be bearing down and there will not be much you can do until spring, but you need to know. I've sent a letter on to Amelia and Bryon, as well. Lucinda and Joseph, and of course Katherine and Colby have been apprised of the details. Ma and Pa asked if I would draft the letter, as I have spent considerable time with Doc Philips concerning Ma's health.

Grandmother gasped. "Oh my, this doesn't sound good." Gracie's hand shook slightly as she continued to read.

Ma is very ill. Doc Philips said he has seen this before. A person begins to lose weight, has little appetite...which we all know is not our Ma. Her energy has been steadily ebbing. She has quite a lot of pain in her lower abdomen, and the doc says he can feel tumors. Sadly, the outcome is rarely good.

So sorry to have to tell you this in a letter, but Ma needs your prayers. We are hoping and praying that she rebounds and we can all be together in the spring when travel will be kinder. She absolutely insists that no one visit this time of year. You all know how she is not a fan of train travel at the best of times, but she is terrified of it in the winter. With the stories of trains stranded in snowstorms and people freezing to death before help comes, she has made me promise I would communicate her desire that you wait to visit until next March. Now, I know I cannot make that decision for you, but that is her request, and Pa agrees with her. They do not want any family members taking undue risk.

If only she had not been so insistent in keeping this from everyone for so long, but that is between you and me.

May God bless you and keep you until we meet again, and may he grant us the blessing of all being together once again.

Lovingly, your sister,

Jeanette

Tears blurred Gracie's vision. She dropped the letter onto her lap. How could Ma be that ill? She had not noticed any decline before she left.

The settee dipped as Grandmother sat beside her. Warm wrinkled hands covered hers, and Gracie turned into her hug.

"My dear sweet Doris," Grandmother said. "How can this be?"

Her soft sobs filled the room, and Gracie could not hold back her own. Sorrow flowed out of the depth of her soul. Her and Ma had always been close. If she was *very ill,* as Jeanette wrote, then the thought of not seeing her again was unbearable.

"Makes me upset they don't want any of us to visit." Gracie's voice warbled as she tried to speak. "I need to see Ma. I simply must." She clenched squeezed eyes closed, and the tears suspended on her lashes broke free.

"I want to see her also, but I'm too old to travel. Can barely get from room to room."

"Grandmother, she wouldn't expect you to come."

"But I wasted so many years…my stubborn heart—"

"You two are finishing well, and that's all you should be thinking about right now. Ma knows you love her."

Gracie was a fine one to talk. She couldn't bear the thought of not telling her Ma how much she loved her. She had left on a colder, more determined note and didn't want that to be their last memory.

Gracie squeezed her hand. "I left in the spring with dreams and aspirations aplenty. Was I too self-centered to notice her decline? I knew she was slowing down, but Jeanette was there to help. I assumed it was age related." Gracie's head fell forward into her hands. "Even that wasn't fair, expecting Jeanette—"

"Best we both don't beat ourselves up about what we can't change." Grandmother patted her knee. "You're doing a good work with the children, and you're the farthest thing from selfish I have ever witnessed in a young person."

Gracie stood with a burst of energy. "Well, I want to see her, and I don't give a flying fig about winter travel." She paced the room.

"But dear, I tend to agree with your parents, and you're still under my care. They would never forgive me if I didn't respect their wishes. It's an unnecessary risk."

"Seeing my Ma before…before…" Gracie sank into a nearby chair. She couldn't even think the words much less say them. Was it really too much of a risk to travel?

"You seem to believe whole-heartedly in that God of yours. Surely He can keep your ma alive so that you can see her again."

"I wish life worked that way—that we got all our prayers answered in keeping with what we want. But after seeing Katherine's Josiah die, I know God does not work that way. His answers are often more complex."

"That does not sound at all reassuring."

"We must ask and pray in faith for Ma's healing, but at the same time accept God's will. No matter what the outcome, He's working things out for our growth and our good."

Grandmother shook out the crumpled handkerchief in her hand and dabbed again at the corner of her eye. "Seems your God has your allegiance no matter what He chooses."

"He does." Gracie's voice wavered. Did she really mean those words?

"'Tis mighty convenient for Him, I dare say."

"Grandmother."

"I know. I know. I tend to get a tad upset when God doesn't do what I want Him to."

And what if Gracie didn't get what she wanted? What if there was no way to see her Ma before it was too late? A shocking chill of agony ripped through her soul.

～

"You know how we've discussed hiring some help for you, Gracie," Matthew said. "You'll be run off your feet now that Marianna is leaving, and you need your weekends off. I know how important it is for you to spend time with your grandmother."

"It is." Gracie walked to the window and gazed out.

"I've done the preliminary interviews, and I've narrowed it down to the two best candidates, in my opinion." Was she even listening to him? She seemed lost in another world. Where was the focused girl he usually had in his presence?

She continued to stare out the window. "Thank you, Matthew."

"They're coming in tomorrow morning for another meeting, and I'd like you to be present to make the final decision, as you'll be working closely with whomever you choose."

"I'm sure you'll make a good choice."

She wasn't listening. "And then if she's really good, we'll keep her and let you go."

"Sounds reasonable. Whatever you think."

All right, what was going on? He joined her at the window. "Gracie." He waved his hand in front of her face.

She jumped. "Oh goodness, I didn't hear you get up."

"You didn't hear half of what I said. What's wrong? You don't seem your bubbly self."

"I…I…"

Her eyes clouded over. He couldn't read what lay within the depths, but he knew it wasn't good. "That walk you say you need at the noon hour, the one you haven't been taking lately? It's going to happen right now."

"But it's cold out today and—"

"Necessary." The truth was far more essential than the walk. In hopes of one leading to the other, he would weather the chill.

He directed the way out into the hall and removed her heavy cloak from the rack and held it open. When she slipped into the folds, the sweet fragrance of summer roses filled his senses. She secured a scarf around her ears and put on a pair of gloves while he grabbed his cap, and flipped it on his head.

She offered him a watered-down smile as he held the door open. He extended his elbow and she placed her hand in the crook of his arm. An instant rush of adrenaline shot through his body, but he willed it away. There were bigger things to worry about.

Outside, the air carried that fall crispness with a northern wind that whipped the last of the leaves from the trees. He pulled his cap a little lower to cover his ears.

"What happened to us both not leaving the premises at the same time?" Gracie asked.

"Every rule has an exception now and again. Plus, with the extra housekeepers we've been able to hire and Max being more than capable to handle an emergency, it's best I learn how to lighten up."

She arched one brow.

"Yes, Gracie Williams, I can lighten up."

They walked in silence down the block. Matthew was a patient man. He would give her time to collect her thoughts. A ceiling of rain clouds hung in an iron-gray sky. He held up his free hand. "Feels like I could touch the clouds today they're so low...much like you. Will you talk to me, Gracie? Tell me what's bothering you?"

She stopped and turned toward him, lifting her face up to his. It was the closest they'd ever stood together, and it took all he had not to encircle her within his arms.

"Ma is very ill, but she doesn't want us to visit because winter is bearing down. She's afraid of the train getting stuck in snow. Grandmother, Amelia, and Bryon all tend to agree. But I can't find peace with that decision. If she passes over the winter..." Her lips trembled as tears pooled in her dark eyes and splashed down her cheeks. "I'll regret..."

Against his better judgement he gathered her in his arms and said nothing, just held her close while she sobbed. His hands smoothed up and down her back as waters of love and desire swirled deep. His throat knotted and grew thick.

How could he help her?

"If you feel so strongly about this, you must go, and I'll escort you." The words were out of his mouth as if they had a life of their own. What was happening to his logical, methodical process of thinking everything through *before* speaking? And what if the board disagreed? Or what if winter came early and made the trip dangerous?

She pulled back, still in the warmth of his arms. Her face was smudged with tears, her eyes full of hope. She'd never looked more beautiful.

"You'd do that for me?"

The beat of his heart crashed against his chest. In that moment he knew he would do anything for her. He hurt because she hurt. There was this undeniable urge to protect, to help, to give her what she needed. "If the board agrees, we'll leave promptly, before winter hits. I can't promise more than a quick turnaround, but you'd get a visit."

"Oh Matthew, if it were only possible. I haven't been able to sleep at night thinking I may never see her again."

"I know what that feels like, and I don't want that for you." He lifted a thumb to dry the tears trickling down her cheeks, and a soft pull of air whistled through her upturned lips. Just one downward tilt of his head and he could satisfy the yearning to touch his mouth to hers. But that would ruin everything. He pulled free, offering his arm as they headed back.

"You never talk about your past. Why is that?" Gracie's voice was a soft whisper of concern.

"It's so long ago—"

"But you have memories that matter, Matthew."

The way she said his name melted the block of ice protecting that part of his heart.

"I just shared my heartache. Will you trust me with yours?" Her pleading busted down the wall he had erected. Why did he want to tell her what he had always successfully kept bottled up?

"Please," she whispered.

"My pa died on the boat over from England. Ma said she had friends in Richmond who would help her get settled, and we used the last of what she had to get here from New York. She never found her friends, nor the work she needed." He nodded toward their destination, just ahead. "I was only four when she left me on the steps of this very orphanage."

"You're an orphan?" Gracie gasped, and her eyes grew large.

"She said she'd be back for me, but she never returned. I have no idea what happened to her."

"Oh, Matthew, I'm so sorry." She pulled him to a stop a few feet short of the property.

He fought back the emotion clawing behind his eyes. "I never said goodbye. She wanted me to kiss her, but I was angry she was leaving." His voice graveled and choked.

She wrapped her arms around his waist. He didn't move, the scent of roses pulling him into her loveliness. Such closeness brought both the thrill and pain of unrequited feelings. His head knew she was offering condolences, but his heart kicked against the walls of his chest. Could she hear it with her ear pressed so close? He pulled free at the thought.

He cleared his throat, trying to hide the emotions and yearnings as well. "It's why I believe you should go see your ma. Things should never be left undone."

"Do you really think the board will allow two key members to be absent at the same time?"

"Marianna would stay and help, knowing the circumstances, and Max is biting at the bit for more responsibility. Tomorrow, we'll hire your assistant, so Marianna will have help." He nudged her forward with the palm of his hand on the small of her back. "Plus, you have me fighting for your cause."

They crossed the yard toward the main house, and she squeezed his arm. "You're the best friend any girl could ever have, Matthew Weston."

He looked down and smiled. Her cheeks were blushed by the wind, her mahogany eyes so trusting. The urge to brush her upturned lips with his once again burned hot. Startled by the powerful emotions he could barely contain, he twisted free. Friendship was the last thing on his mind.

CHAPTER 7

*G*racie called Ava into Matthew's office. They had already talked to Elizabeth, and Gracie was impressed.

"Have a seat." Gracie offered the chair next to her. Matthew sat across from them.

"Ava," Matthew said. "You've been called back for this second interview as the position has been narrowed down to either you or—"

"Oh, I was hoping I was hired."

Gracie didn't like the way she'd interrupted, but maybe she was nervous.

"Have you met Gracie? She's in charge of the girls and—"

"Yes, we met on the way in."

Again, she interrupted. How rude. And they had not formally met. Gracie had merely called her name and waved her in.

"Gracie will work directly with you. She's in charge of the interview this morning." Matthew nodded at Gracie.

"That will be just fine, sir."

Had she just batted her eyes at Matthew? Gracie was

instantly bothered. She took a deep breath. "What do you love most about working with children, Ava?"

Ava directed the answer at Matthew, smiling all too sweetly. "As I told you the other day, Mr. Weston, I've been around little ones my whole life. I come from a very large family, and being the eldest, I've been changing diapers since I was ten. I've had a lot of responsibility and gained valuable experience. I have no problem in an authoritative role. Mother always says I came out of the womb in charge."

Gracie couldn't keep her brows from standing at attention as she caught Matthew's eye. She had asked what Ava loved most about working with children, not how good she was at taking charge.

Gracie's guard went instantly up, though she wasn't sure why exactly. If Matthew had picked this woman out of a group, what was he seeing that she did not? Maybe it was the fluttering lashes and the hero-worship attention. Yet, Matthew had never struck her as that kind of man.

"Working Saturdays and Sundays is not a problem for you?" Gracie asked.

"Would there be some flexibility? If I had an emergency," she quickly added.

"For emergencies only," Matthew said, "and it would have to be authorized by either myself or Gracie."

"So, are you my boss, or is she?" She smiled sweetly at Matthew, still not giving Gracie the respect of her attention.

Oh, this was not going well. Gracie could tell this woman had no intention of following her lead. She hoped Matthew could see this.

"Why, Gracie, of course. As I mentioned the other day, she's in charge of the girls."

Gracie could've hugged Matthew in that moment.

Ava pursed her lips. Her expression gave away exactly what she was thinking—that she didn't like the sound of that.

Before Gracie could formulate her next question, Matthew said, "I forgot to ask you in our last meeting—the children are taken to church on Sundays and love the outing. Do you think you could handle that kind of responsibility?"

"Must I accompany them? I don't mind going to church, but prefer another denomination rather than the one affiliated with this orphanage."

Gracie spoke slowly, trying to draw Ava's attention for more than a fleeting second. "Yes, you'd be in charge of the girls, making sure they are rounded up after Sunday school. It's a huge responsibility to take them off site and bring them back safely."

Ava batted her hand in the air with eyes only for Matthew. "Not a problem. I have a way with children. They follow me around like I'm the Pied Piper."

"That's all." Gracie cut the interview short. Her mind was made up—Elizabeth it was.

Matthew's head snapped over. "You're sure? What about—?"

"I have all the information I need." She stood.

Matthew did also. "Thank you, Ava. We'll let you know one way or the other."

Ava lifted up from the chair and glided across the room as if she were a debutant at a ball, not interviewing to work with children. She turned one last time. Her eyelashes fluttered and her cheeks dimpled, surrounding a charming smile. "Thank you, Mr. Weston. I shall look forward to working with you."

Gracie understood why this woman had gotten so far along in the interview process, and she was about to take Matthew to task. When the door shut behind them, she turned back toward his desk as he slid back into his chair. "Elizabeth it is."

"Just like that, no discussion?"

"What's there to discuss? That woman will be very distracted from her work."

"What do you mean?"

"Come on, Matthew. She was making eyes at you the whole time."

"She was not."

"She was so." A tremble took to Gracie's hands, and she almost stomped her foot. Why was she getting so angry? "And she wouldn't even give me the courtesy of looking at me when I spoke to her."

"I did notice that, but I don't think it was because she was interested in me."

"Take my word for it. A woman knows these things."

"Well, what would be so wrong with that?" He said it with a laugh as if he were trying to get a rise out of her.

"First, she's no older than I am, and you haven't said a word about her age being a deterrent as you did with me."

"Ah…um…she's not taking over the lead role."

"Neither was I when I started. And I thought you were like me, that you didn't want the distraction of courting and marriage."

He shook his head. "I never said that. I want to marry someday. I believe God has the perfect woman for me. Don't mistake my patience in waiting for the right one to be a disinterest in women."

Heat swallowed her face despite her best efforts. "So…so you're attracted to Ava?"

"I didn't say that either, I was merely pointing out I'm not dead to the world around me."

"And I am?"

"You're entitled to your understanding at this moment."

"What exactly does that mean?" She moved closer to his desk looking down at him.

He stood and came around the desk, stopping far too close for her liking, so close she could smell a hint of mint and feel his breath fan her cheek. He looked as if he was about to say something but instead gazed down at her.

"So, you think plain Elizabeth is a better fit?"

"What she looks like has nothing to do with this." And why hadn't he answered her question?

He laughed and broke the spell his closeness had cast. "If you say so."

∼

"Put yourself in her shoes." Matthew said.

Twelve sets of eyes peered at Gracie from around the table in the board room. Matthew was fighting hard for her. She didn't know who to look at, so Gracie kept her eyes fixated on the grain in the wood of the table.

"Well, I happen to be in her shoes," Amelia said.

Gracie gulped back a knot-sized lump filling her throat. Of course, Amelia would want to see Ma, too. But would she argue it's not safe? Her eyes snapped to her sister. All she read was compassion.

"And I agree with Gracie," Amelia added. "If she feels she needs to go, then she needs to go. I would join her, but Bryon and I just found out I'm expecting another child, and travel is not possible with the amount of morning sickness I'm experiencing."

The place erupted in congratulations. Gracie ran over and hugged both her sister and Bryon before returning to her chair. Another baby. What a blessing.

Mr. Lewis raised his hand. "Best we return to the subject at hand unless we want to be here all night." The room quieted. "What I don't understand is why you feel the need to join her?" He stared over the top of his glasses at Matthew. "It's not as if you're personally responsible for her, bequeathed, or even courting."

Gracie's cheeks heated at the thought.

"I was on the train with Gracie when she arrived in Richmond. We hadn't met, of course, but I witnessed her being accosted by an unsavory character and had to step in. It's not safe for a young woman to travel unchaperoned, especially Gracie."

"I agree," Myrtle said.

"Indeed. Indeed." Matilda seconded.

"To be sure." Margot's head bobbed up and down.

What did Matthew mean by *especially Gracie*? And why was this the only point on which everyone agreed, even the stern Mr. Lewis?

Before Gracie could ask the question, Matthew continued. "Gracie is one of our hardest working and most invested volunteers. She has taken on leadership as if she'd been born for it. And need I mention that she donates all of her time? And, if you recall, I haven't requested any time off in years. The orphanage will do just fine without us for ten days."

"May I ask why you feel so strongly about this?" Reverend Peterkin asked.

Gracie cringed. This subject was very private to Matthew. She expected him to hedge, but he surprised her.

"My ma died young, and I never had a chance to say goodbye."

Melinda Preston looked with pure affection at Matthew across the room and smiled a knowing smile.

"Had it not been for the generosity of Melinda and Alex, who took me under their wing, giving me an education and believing in me I wouldn't be here today. Saying goodbye to loved ones is important."

The three sisters pulled out their handkerchiefs as if they were in each other's heads and dabbed at the corners of their eyes.

"Before we all get too teary eyed," Mr. Lewis said, "we could find someone else to escort Gracie. I don't believe it's a wise idea to have two integral leaders absent at the same time."

Most of the men nodded.

"Shall we vote on the matter?" Mr. Lewis asked.

Heads nodded around the room.

Gracie held her breath. She couldn't believe how much she wanted Matthew at her side for this trip. On the way to Richmond, Katherine and Colby had taken her to the train station in Staunton and her ticket had been pre-booked. This trip would be much different with winter bearing down and having to make arrangements for the stagecoach. But was it fair to ask this of him?

"Matthew and Gracie, please step out for the show of hands."

Gracie stood, and Matthew followed. They shut the door and walked down the hall.

"Whatever they decide, thank-you seems inadequate," Gracie said. "Without your support, I'm sure I would've come across as flighty having just been given the responsibility of the girls and then wanting time off."

He waved his hand. "Don't mention it."

"But, Matthew, I don't feel right having you sacrifice your days off. They should be used for a time of relaxation and a much-needed break. Are you sure?"

"I'm sure."

"And I don't understand why you all agreed that I shouldn't travel alone. What was the wording you used? *Especially Gracie.* What does that even mean?"

"For your safety. Remember the attention you drew on your trip here?" He stepped closer gazing down at her with a look in his attractive blue eyes she could not comprehend.

Now what made her think about how attractive he was? She never gave men a second look. Why, suddenly, was she noticing little things about him…like the smolder of blue flames dancing in his gaze?

"Don't you understand?" He stepped so close that their bodies were almost touching, his hand lifted to touch her cheek.

She held her breath. "What?"

"Just how lovely you are."

For the first time in her life, she had no inclination to run. The featherlight brush of his fingertips down the side of her face felt wonderful.

The door opened, and she heard their names being called. His hand dropped, and he jumped away from her as if he'd been caught doing something wrong. "You know it's not safe." He swiveled and marched back down the hall.

She ran to catch up to him. He wore an angry set to his jaw. "Why are you upset? What did I do?"

"We'll talk later." His voice was brisk and short.

She had not heard that tone in days. What had she done? She took her seat. She couldn't think about that now.

"The board would first like to thank you, Gracie"—Mrs. Preston smiled at her as she spoke—"for the amazing work and dedication you have given to the orphanage these past months. We unanimously support your decision to visit your ailing mother. We'll make this happen for you." She turned to Matthew, who sat across the table. "But as for you, Matthew, the decision was a tad more complicated. You more than deserve whatever time you request off, for whatever reason you desire, but to have you both gone at the same time is a challenge. In the end, we each decided to donate a day while you're gone to help support the orphanage. The two of you have twelve days with the hope you'll be back in plenty of time to help organize the Christmas Charity Ball. We cannot jeopardize that function as it is where we receive large donations for the year to keep the orphanage running. Do you think you can make that work?"

Gracie held back the little girl squeal she wanted to let out but instead squared her shoulders and made eye contact with each person around the room. "I thank you from my heart."

The three sisters nodded their heads in sync.

Mrs. Preston beamed.

"Give Ma our love, and our good news," Amelia said.

Bryon nodded.

"I will," she whispered.

The men smiled.

Mr. Lewis picked up his list. "Now on with the rest of the agenda."

Gracie waited until all gazes were glued back on the meeting outline before she caught Matthew's eye above his paper. "Thank you," she mouthed.

Whatever had upset him earlier, was no longer bothering him. Maybe it hadn't had anything to do with her at all. She was rewarded with a full smile, large enough to create those half-moon creases on both sides of his mouth. In an instant, she understood what Ava had seen…especially when that smile was aimed at her.

What was wrong with her? She'd have to give her feelings some deep introspection, but not tonight. Tonight was a victory, and she was going to see her ma.

"What's the urgency?" Gracie poked her head into Matthew's office. "Max came over to the girl's quarters and said you needed to talk to me immediately. Not a good day. Elizabeth didn't make it in this morning."

Matthew waved Gracie in. "That's what I need to talk to you about. A messenger just dropped off a note saying Elizabeth had a family emergency and won't be back."

"Won't be back, period? As in never?" Gracie moved into the room and sank into a nearby chair.

"That's what it says." He handed her the short note.

A needle of worry threaded its way from her chest to her throat. They were due to leave in two days. She scanned the short message.

"The timing couldn't be worse." Matthew ran a hand around the back of his neck, as he always did when he was bothered.

"I know, and Elizabeth was doing so well."

"This leaves me no choice but to call on Ava and see if she's still available."

"Ava?" Oh, how the thought rankled. But the woman was more than qualified, and Gracie did want to see her ma.

"We don't have time to go through the interview process again, and Marianna is going to need help with her health restrictions."

She couldn't argue with that.

"I know Ava's not your first pick, but contrary to your belief, she made my final cut not because of what she looked like but because of her experience and confidence."

Hmm, more like conceitedness. But what could Gracie say without sounding petty? Ava's qualifications on paper could not be argued with, and they did need her. "Whatever you think, Matthew."

"We need to do our best not to postpone our Thursday departure. The weather is changing quickly."

"I agree." Gracie gulped back her aversion to the woman she'd interviewed. Could have been nerves. Interviews were hard on most everyone. And maybe they had just gotten off on the wrong foot.

"Good," he said. "I'll send a messenger immediately. Marianna is very capable of directing, and Ava can do the heavy lifting."

Gracie nodded and smiled, but her gut churned at the thought of working with that woman when she got back. But what choice did she have?

∽

Early November 1879

The train rumbled down the track as they pulled out of Richmond two days later, so early only stray hints of light in the east gave hope of a new day. Matthew breathed a sigh of relief. Right up until the last moment, he'd feared something would go wrong and prohibit him from going.

The train's movement jostled Gracie's shoulder against Matthew. She reached out to steady herself by placing her gloved hand upon his knee. The pleasure brought pain. If only he could rein in his feelings and keep everything as platonic as she believed them to be. Which one of them was following the lead of the Spirit? Was he to pursue her or respect that she did not want to marry? Maybe he had misunderstood her comments. Maybe there was hope.

He looked down at her and smiled. It was going to be a long trip if his heart reacted to her every touch. This was where impulsive behavior got him. It had been so beyond his comfort level to offer his assistance on such a spontaneous and ill-prepared trip.

"If all goes well," he said, "we'll be in Staunton in time for the evening meal and a good sleep. Then, hopefully we've timed the stagecoach just right, and we'll be on our way tomorrow to Lacey Spring."

"Do you forget I've done this before?" She gave him a saucy grin.

"But didn't you have family take you to the train in Staunton from Lacey Spring?"

"Katherine and Colby's comfortable carriage. Indeed, I was spoiled. But Amelia's had to take the stagecoach at times, sitting on hard benches and bumping along crammed in tight quarters with people who haven't had a recent bath."

"That doesn't sound as agreeable as the carriage, but I'm sure we'll manage." He would not mention his worry that the stagecoach may not be running the usual three times a week in November.

"I hope you won't be sorry you offered to accompany me on this trip. Because the traveling is not fun." She removed her white gloves and adjusted a small pillow behind her back.

"You're making me want to get off at the next stop and reverse my direction." Matthew laughed when her eyes sprang open with what looked akin to fear. "Thought you said you could make this trip on your own?"

"Yes, with planning. But not without having my tickets for both the train and stagecoach in hand. Leaving on the spur of the moment does present unknown variables."

Matthew offered a calm smile. Did she have the same concern as he did? If they couldn't catch the stagecoach in a timely fashion, they'd never make it back in the twelve days the board had allotted them. The biggest disappointment would be to get as far as Staunton and have to turn back. "We'll be just fine." He patted her knee.

She reached toward his hand and gave a light squeeze. "Thank you."

He instinctively interlocked his fingers with hers. They fit so delicately inside his. Awareness thrummed through his veins. His eyes were on the hand he felt she would snatch free, but didn't. His thumb circled the inside of her wrist in a featherlight touch. Still, she didn't move. He dared a glance sideways, catching the most puzzled look on her face, her cute little brows knit tightly together. She was fixated on their braided fingers. He did what felt as natural as rain in spring and lifted the back of her hand to his lips. Her eyes followed until she was looking straight into his. He brushed his lips across the smooth skin, and her eyes widened. He longed to take that kiss across the small space that separated them and plant it on her lips. His heart bucked wildly. A desire like none he had ever known swept over him.

Her hand yanked free. "What did you do that for?" Her voice trembled, and she turned toward the window and shifted her back toward him.

"I thought only to comfort your worry." Liar.

"That didn't feel like comfort. That felt…I don't know what that was."

Wonderful. That was how it felt. She may not share his sentiments, but he couldn't deny what he had been fighting, a mixture of emotions inching ever larger by the day. And she was feeling something too. He was sure of it.

Why did he have so little control when it came to her? He wanted to respect her wishes but could not deny his growing affection. Was this what love felt like? *Dear God in heaven, I'm so confused. If she's the one, when will these feelings flow mutually? Please give me patience and wisdom.*

CHAPTER 8

Gracie gazed out the train window at the gathering morning light. What had just happened? Why had Matthew kissed her hand out of the blue? And why did it feel so…so strangely wonderful? She should've pulled her hand free the minute he interlaced hers with his, but she had never felt anything so exquisitely intimate in all her life. Emotions she did not understand churned inside. Her stomach still felt like butterflies were afloat. Whatever was happening, she had not been so affected before.

She must set this right. But how?

"Gracie."

She turned his way.

He dug his hands through his thick crop of hair. "I'm sorry—"

"No, it's me. I'm sorry for over-reacting when all you've been is caring. I'm not at all experienced with men, so I read the wrong things into simple kindness."

"I do care about you—"

"I know, but I've had men push their way into my life as far back as I can remember. By the time I was a teenager, I had boys telling me I was their future wife. I guess I've rebuffed men for so long, I don't know what the boundaries of true friendship between a man and woman look like." She could feel her face flush hot at the admission.

"Really?"

She nodded. "I don't think I've ever had a man who just wanted to be my friend and not want something more."

His blue eyes flashed a disturbed look, as if he were bothered. Then he threw her a winsome smile that kicked up the corners of his mouth. "Let's just work on being the best friends possible. How does that suit?"

That smile made her heart lurch in an unfamiliar way. "Yes. Indeed. That shall be a refreshing change." She looked forward to relaxing in his presence and him teaching her what friendship between a man and a woman could be like. Apparently kissing her hand was to be expected between friends. But then, why did the thought of that happening again cause a tingle in her chest?

~

The train rolled into Staunton ahead of schedule, and Matthew rose. With his height crammed into a space far too restricted for the length of his legs, the station could not come soon enough. His head was whirling with his carefully planned agenda.

Gracie stood beside him. "God is good. We've arrived safely."

He nodded, but his mind was already twenty steps ahead, considering all the things he had to do. He hadn't even thought to thank God. There was something so spontaneous about Gracie's faith. Oh, that his could have that kind of depth.

"First, we'll find a hotel for the night. Once you're tucked in your room, you can freshen up, and I'll secure our tickets for the stagecoach. When I get back, we'll have a hot meal." He pushed back the worry fermenting in his brain. What if the stagecoach —no, he would not let his mind wander there.

"Sounds lovely."

She looked up at him with such trust in her eyes. He didn't want to let her down.

"When I came through to Richmond," she said, "I stayed at the Waldorf. It's a clean and respectable establishment."

"Allow me." Matthew picked up both their bags with ease.

"Follow me," Gracie said. "The hotel is but a short walk."

"Good thing, since I don't know what you put in your bag, but it's twice the weight of mine."

"A girl has necessities." Her warm-hearted voice flowed over him like a beautiful melody.

"Necessities, you say. What would you have done if I weren't here to haul this for you?"

"Make do with a few less necessities." Her delightful laughter bubbled up and out.

"So, you're using me for my brute strength?"

"That and a whole lot more. Your protection. Your fine company and pleasurable disposition."

"That assessment has come a long way since we first met."

"It certainly has, Mr. Weston. You really are quite wonderful when you're not trying to get rid of me." She threw a grin over her shoulder as he followed a few steps behind. What a little imp she was. She flirted in a naively innocent way. No wonder men melted like butter in the hot sun in her presence. Him included.

"Surely, you're not done," he said. "Keep the compliments coming."

"I best stop before all this flattery goes to your head."

His laughter boomed across the street so that every head turned. Wrong thing to do. Once the men caught sight of her, their heads turned as if they were on a swivel. One cowboy lounging against the wall outside the saloon tipped his hat as they approached.

Gracie turned her head and Matthew caught the side view of her smile.

Now, why did she have to do that?

The cowboy spat out a wad of tobacco, straightened, and slid in beside her. "Where you headed, pretty lady?" His smile widened to show a missing front tooth.

She looked back at Matthew with wide eyes, and he moved in between them, stopping short.

"She's with me." He slid the carpet bags to the ground and straightened his shoulders to full height so he could look down at the wiry cowboy.

The man stepped back, a snarl on his face. "Mighty fine woman you have here, mister. If she were mine, I wouldn't be walking behind her like the chore boy. I'd be taking real good care of her, if you know what I mean." His beady eyes narrowed into a leer that plucked the clothes right off her.

Matthew towered over the smaller man. It took all he had not to wipe that look off his face. How dare he look at Gracie with such disrespect? "We don't want any trouble. But if you're intent on having some..."

The cowboy's hands shot in the air, and he shrunk back. "Relax. I meant no harm."

Matthew stared him down until he backed up and disappeared through the swinging doors of the saloon.

"Where's that hotel?" Matthew picked up the carpet bags. "Let's hurry. He may have friends."

"A couple buildings up the street. Follow me." Gracie picked up pace with Matthew shadowing her. She kept looking back furtively. "Don't be angry with me."

"I'm not angry, but you really must learn not to smile at everyone. Not every man has good intentions."

"I know. I'm sorry."

He hoped she did remember, or there may come a day when he would not be able to help her out of a situation. His gut churned at the thought.

~

"This time of year, the stagecoach does a mail run once a week, but they just left today." The thin man behind the wicket gave an obligatory smile that did not reach his eyes.

"We were informed they run three times a week."

"They do until the end of October. By November, not many visitors chance the inclement weather. So, there's no need." He stroked his thin mustache and went back to the book he'd been reading.

A muscle in Matthew's jaw tightened. How would he tell Gracie they had to return without her seeing her ma?

"Is there anyone who has a carriage I can rent and return in a week or so?"

Matthew was met with an empty stare. "Horses and wagons are not my concern. You'll have to check the livery for that. But for what it's worth, it's going to rain for the next few days. I can feel it in these bones. I wouldn't want to be doing that trek, especially with a woman in hand. They are, after all, so fragile and needy."

Matthew thanked him out of courtesy but couldn't get away fast enough. Some people oozed pessimism, and that man was one of them. Gracie would be waiting for him, but he wasn't going to return with bad news. He marched toward the local livery on the far edge of town. When no one could be found at the barn, he headed to the ranch house and hammered on the door.

"Whoa, hold your horses." A gray-haired weathered cowboy opened the door to his banging.

"Sorry to bother you at the end of your day, sir, but I was

wondering if you have a carriage to rent. I'll take it to Lacey Spring and bring it back in about a week."

"Ain't nobody called me sir in a long time." The cowboy waved him in. "No point in standing in the cold when it's about to rain." He stepped outside, and his eyes scoured the heavens. "Mark my word, it'll be raining cats and dogs by dawn tomorrow." He faced Matthew. "Now what's this about a carriage? I can tell you're a city boy through and through."

What did he mean by that? Why did asking for a carriage make him a city boy?

The cowboy waved at a chair in the large kitchen. "My missus has fixed some mighty fine grub. Ya want to join us?"

"I'm sorry I can't." Matthew removed his cap. "My friend is waiting at the hotel for my return. We're planning on eating there together."

"Well then, you better go fetch your friend. Nothing's open this time of year for food. They only run the restaurant from spring to the end of October. No one travels much after that."

Matthew couldn't believe his ears. No wonder Gracie's parents had advised against traveling.

"Run, get your friend," his wife chimed in. "I'm Lois, and this nitwit who's forgotten his manners is Noland. We're the Parkers."

The cowboy laughed. "I guess if I'm inviting you in for grub, you might want to know our names."

"I'm Matthew Weston." He held out his hand, which was engulfed in a hearty shake.

"If it's not too much of a bother?" Matthew ran a worried path over his knuckles with his thumb.

"None at all. The good Lord says to be kind to strangers and invite them in. And in our line of work, the opportunities are endless." Mrs. Parker laughed. "Plus, we quite enjoy the company now that all the kids are up and gone. Except Johnny, of course, but he's not much of a talker."

"I'll never turn down a home cooked meal that smells this fine. I'll be right back." Matthew slapped the cap back on and headed out the door. He gazed up into sky. The charcoal-gray canopy of clouds drooped heavy and low. Rain would complicate travel for sure. Hadn't he prayed for good weather? Was God saying no to Lacey Spring? He hurried down the street toward the hotel. How would he break the news to Gracie? Maybe they'd be able to make it work. There was still hope.

He rapped on her hotel door, and before he could lower his hand, she was in the hall.

"Did you get the tickets?" Her huge maple-syrup eyes were brimming with hope.

The words got stuck in his throat. The last thing he wanted was to immediately disappoint her. "The restaurant downstairs is closed."

"I know, I already inquired."

"We've been invited for a meal by the nice couple at the local livery. They're waiting for us."

"No coach. Right?" Her voice faltered, the usual lilt and bounce was missing.

Ahh she was too astute to let it go. "I'll apprise you of the details as we walk."

"Matthew, just spit it out."

"All right, there's no stagecoach for another week. But I have an idea." He kept his voice light and positive.

The corners of her drooping mouth lifted.

He looped his arm and offered it to her, and they walked down the hall and out the door.

"I visited the livery to inquire about a carriage. My idea is to rent it for a week and bring it back."

"You feel comfortable handling a carriage and figuring the way yourself?" Gracie's voice quivered. "I'm not sure I remember—"

"We'll talk to Noland, the livery stable owner, about it. Maybe I can hire some help."

"That could be expensive."

"I have some savings."

"But, Matthew, I don't feel right using your hard-earned cash so I can see my family."

"I can use my money in whatever way makes me happy, and you seeing your ma does just that."

Gracie leaned her head against his shoulder for a brief second. "Thank you."

She would never understand what the thrill of that simple touch did. To combat the hot blood racing through his veins, he pulled in the cool evening air. Why did the girl he finally fell for have to be an impossible quest? They walked in silence the rest of the way.

Matthew knocked at the door with much less vigor and ushered Gracie through when he heard the invitation to come on in. The entryway, large country kitchen, and sitting area with a roaring fire in a river rock fireplace were all contained in one cozy welcoming room.

"Mr. and Mrs. Parker, this is my friend, Gracie Williams."

Mr. and Mrs. Parker froze, their mouths hanging open. "We expected your friend to be a man," Mr. Parker said. "No one in his right mind would venture out this time of year with their little lady."

"I'm not his…"

"She's not my…"

"…little lady," they said in tandem. "I'm merely her overseer," Matthew said.

Noland cleared his throat. "Come in. Sit. We'll discuss over a hot plate of stew and dumplings." He motioned to the table where a large man was already seated.

Matthew and Gracie slid into chairs across from the bulldog

of a man. His shoulder width combined with his bulk almost filled up his side of the table.

"This here's our son, Johnny." Noland slapped the young man on his back as he sat down.

Johnny looked up and nodded.

The puzzled looks Mrs. Parker shot Matthew's way as she served up the plates caused his gut to clench. How hard could that ride be? Gracie had told him they made it from Lacey Spring to Staunton in one long day.

Lois set plates of stew and dumplings in front of Matthew and Gracie and then sat on her chair. "Noland, be honest. There's no way these city folks should be venturing out alone."

"We'll get to all that after we say our thanksgiving for this meal." With heads bowed, the old cowboy gave a quick blessing. Matthew did not miss that he tacked on the need for words of wisdom.

"Dig in." Noland took a large spoonful of stew, slopped it on a bun, and took a bite. Between mouthfuls, he pointed his spoon Matthew's way. "I'll be frank. First of all, there's no fancy covered carriages to rent in these here parts. The only people that own them are the extremely wealthy, and they're not inclined to share. Second, an old boxboard and our mule Blossom are all we have to offer. That means no protection from the elements. Third, the stagecoach only runs when weather permits, but your best bet is to wait for it. When the rain hits, the turnpike is a muddy mess. It's a two-man job if your rig gets stuck in the mud or ruts. And I do mean *men*. No disrespect, Miss Gracie." He nodded her way.

Disappointment clawed at Matthew's gut.

"And fourth, you best know how to use a gun real well. There are wild animals, and wild men. And this here purty little Gracie of yours is bait for the taking, if you get what I mean."

Noland took a whole dumpling and stuffed it in his mouth.

"Husband, must you rush through your food?" Mrs. Parker

shook her head. "You're no longer an orphan who doesn't know where your next meal is coming from."

Orphan?

"Old habits die hard."

"And don't talk with your mouth crammed full," she added.

Noland nodded and took a minute to finish his latest bite.

"Gracie and I run the orphanage back in Richmond. It's why we're short on time. There are many children and lots of need, as you can imagine. This trip is a huge concession on the board's part trusting us to go and return in timely fashion."

Mrs. Parker set her spoon down. "If you don't mind my asking, what makes this trip necessary? It's not exactly prime traveling season."

Matthew looked at Gracie.

"My ma is really ill, and I just have to see her." Gracie's voice cracked. "I don't know if she'll last until spring when the weather is kinder."

"Oh, dear." Lois patted Gracie's hand. "I feared it was something of great importance. As a mother, I sure would like to see my family if I were sick."

"I'll take them." Johnny said. "They can ride the stagecoach back, as long as they can put me up for a night of rest in between."

Matthew's head snapped up, but Gracie beat him to words. "You'd do that for us?"

"Yes."

Mrs. Parker gave her son an affectionate look. "Why, that's an excellent idea."

"I'd be happy to pay you for your time," Matthew offered.

Mr. Parker raised his hand in the air. "Wait a minute." He looked at Gracie and Matthew. "You two must talk this through. As I said, it would be far safer for a woman to be inside the coach, not out on display. Plus, it's going to rain, and traveling in the rain without protection is not for the faint-hearted. It makes that ten-hour trip twice as long."

Johnny's head bobbed in agreement with his father.

"Johnny here knows the valley inside and out. He's a bit of a loner, but you couldn't have a better guide and protector—"

"Pa, I'm quite capable of speaking for myself."

"Then why don't you?"

"Not much need with you around."

His parents laughed.

Johnny pushed back his chair and stood. His tall frame matched the breadth of his shoulders and his wide girth. Matthew was a big man, but this guy dwarfed him.

"If you want to go, be here at the break of dawn. We'll leave come rain or shine. I'll be ready." He strode from the room.

"He's gone to prepare." Noland said. "I suggest you two talk it over and have a good night's rest. If you decide to do this, you'll need it."

CHAPTER 9

Gracie slid from her bed and padded across the room to the window. Matthew was leaving the decision up to her. She pulled back the curtain and looked into the dim light of predawn. The rain had started in the middle of the night and was coming down in a steady pour. Could she really endure hours in those soaking wet conditions? Would it do any good arriving at her parents' sick from facing the elements? But she couldn't turn back after coming this far. She wouldn't.

She donned her warmest underclothing, a comfortable wrapper with a belt, and her thick wool cloak. Covering her head, she wore a sensible, warm bonnet, which she tied comfortably under her chin. Her cloak had a hood she could pull up over the bonnet to ensure rain did not drip down her neck. Her boots and a warm pair of gloves came last. She was as ready as she would ever be.

She dragged her carpet bag to outside Matthew's room and knocked lightly. He opened and stepped into the hall. She could tell by his clothing that he had known what her answer would be.

"Shall we?" He picked up the carpet bag.

"You knew I would choose to carry on?"

"You may be tiny, but you're strong, and you believe in a Mighty God, as do I. God opened a door last night, and we're walking through."

They stepped onto the street, and Gracie lifted her hood. How long would she stay dry? The thought brought a shiver to her bones. She shrugged it off. She could do this.

"Did you forget to pray for good weather?" Matthew asked.

"No, did you?"

"Nope. Seems the Lord felt like the earth needed water more than we needed to stay dry."

They headed down the street to the livery. "You sound a tad disenchanted," Gracie said.

"Aren't you? Be honest."

Gracie's heart had plummeted to her feet when she heard the rain start in earnest during the night. She couldn't lie. "Somewhat. But God must have a reason."

"I do appreciate your faith, Gracie, but I can't say I share your sentiments. One day earlier, and we would've made the stagecoach and missed the rain."

Gracie pulled at his arm, stopping them on the muddy street. "Are you sure you want to do this? You don't have to, you know."

"I'm not leaving you now. We're in this together." His voice had an edge to it. Was he angry?

He started walking, and she followed, tucking her hand into the crook of his arm.

"Thank you doesn't seem enough."

"I just hope we're making the right decision." Worry laced his words. "I'm not concerned about myself, but the last thing I want is for you to get sick, or worse if we meet danger on the road."

They angled toward the livery barn. "I thought this through and prayed," she said. "I'm at peace."

He put his arm around her for a brief moment and squeezed. "Good then. We go with God."

She smiled up at him. "We go with God."

When they entered the barn, Johnny was rigged up and ready. Blossom snorted her hello. Gracie smoothed a hand down the mule's nose.

"She's not pretty, but she's the best one in the muck and mire," Johnny said.

"Ahh did you hear that, Blossom? Johnny said you aren't pretty, but I think you are." Gracie hugged its neck. "Pretty little burrow."

"Nope." Johnny patted the animals' rump. "A burrow is a donkey, a mule is a cross between a male donkey and a mare. Blossom here has the smarts of a mule and the strength of a horse."

That was more words strung together than Johnny had spoken the previous evening.

"We should settle on a price that would be agreeable," Matthew said.

Gracie gulped back a knot gathering in her throat. She didn't feel right about Matthew using his own money. Maybe she could ask Katherine for the funds to pay him back.

"The buggy and mule go for five cents a day."

"What about your services?"

"I'm doing this unto the Lord."

Gracie smiled at them both. "See, the Lord provides in mysterious ways."

"You calling me mysterious?" Johnny leveled a stare.

"Only if you think it's a compliment," Gracie said with a dip of her head.

"Smart girl." Johnny laughed, the jowls on his cheeks jiggling as he hopped on the back of the wagon.

Matthew's brow rose in surprise. He leaned in. "Looks like

you've already charmed your way into his good books," he whispered.

What was she to say to that? He seemed disappointed, so all she did was nod.

"Ma has supplied us with enough food and water for a week. Now, all we have to do is get you both ready." He pulled an overcoat from the backboard and threw it down to Matthew. "It's an old one of mine. It'll be a bit big, but it'll keep you dry."

Matthew slipped the overcoat over his own. It hung on him. Johnny laughed but said nothing.

"Now for you, my lady. Best we make you look like a young boy rather than a woman. Take that bonnet off and roll your hair up into this." He handed down a man's wool hat. "And then put this on. It will hang to the ground and cover the bottom of your dress."

Gracie took the weird smelling coat and slipped it over her shoulders. She didn't much care what she wore as long as it kept her dry. "What is this? Smells like—"

"It's a rubberized Mackintosh. Best thing for traveling in the rain." He hopped over the backboard to the front seat and threw Gracie a cowboy hat from the seat.

She slapped it over her wool cap with attitude and smiled up at him. "Why, thank you, kind sir."

"All right. Climb on up here." Johnny held out his hand to Gracie. "You'll sit in the middle. It'll be tight, but it'll keep you warm and protected."

Seemed like a good plan, but when she glanced at Matthew, his frown surprised her.

"Hop on up here. Times a-wasting."

Matthew's seat barely hit the buckboard before Johnny slapped the reins. The buggy lurched forward out of the barn and into the pouring rain.

Gracie, sandwiched between two very large men, looked up into the heavens. *Dear God, please take care of us.*

Matthew wasn't accustomed to being the small man in the group, nor was he used to not being in charge. He didn't like it much. He squared his shoulders and sat up straight on the buckboard. He could at least look confident, even if he didn't feel it. And the way Gracie chatted away with Johnny, one would never think the man a loner. He was not lacking for words today.

"How long do you think this trip will take?" Gracie asked. "Seems we're moving slower than I remember."

"The stagecoach has four thoroughbreds, and we only have one mule," Johnny said.

"We'll make it today?"

"No way," Johnny said. "With the shorter days and muddy turnpike, if we can make it to Harrisonburg before dark, I'll be happy. But that's a good three quarters of the way."

Matthew had not thought about the fact that shorter days meant fewer hours of light. They would have to find lodging for another night. He formulated the math in his head… hotels, mule and buggy rental, train tickets, food. Had he brought enough money? Worry ticked like a clock, one relentless question after another.

"And how far from Harrisonburg to Lacey Spring?" Gracie asked.

"Another nine, ten miles…If all goes well, we'll make it by noon tomorrow."

Now, just what had Johnny meant by that? What else could go wrong? No stagecoach. Raining…no pouring, with water dripping down his neck.

"Matthew, do you know how to use a gun?"

That was one skill he hadn't learned living in an orphanage. Guns weren't exactly plentiful, and the women looking after him were not inclined to give that tutelage. But he wouldn't tell that hulk of cowboy any more than he had to know. "No."

"I do," Gracie said. "In fact, I'm quite good."

"What?" Matthew said.

Johnny chortled and slapped his knee. "Well, I'll be jiggered."

"I did grow up on a farm, you know." She looked up at Matthew with a mischievous sparkle in her eyes.

"This I have to hear," Johnny said.

"My sister Katherine is quite a crack shot, and when I was about eleven, I asked her to teach me. Thought it would be a fun way to get her attention. She was married with a baby, and I was feeling a little left out. So, we had a weekly sister time, shooting tin cans off fence railings. I got quite good, but never as good as her."

"Seriously, Gracie. You're not spinning one of those afternoon tales you tell the kids at the orphanage?" Matthew gazed into her intelligent eyes and knew she told the truth.

"Rifles or revolvers?" Johnny asked.

"Both."

"Well then." Johnny pulled a revolver out of his coat pocket "Take a look at this Colt six-shooter. Familiarize yourself and tuck it somewhere safe. Perhaps inside the top of your boot. It's loaded."

Matthew watched in wonder as Gracie handled the gun as comfortable as a toy. She flipped open the chamber, then looked down the barrel. "I see you have five loaded and the sixth empty." The hammer dropped on the empty chamber.

"And I see you know what you're doing. Keeping it on that empty chamber to prevent accidental discharge is the safest way to go."

"That's one of the first things my sister taught me. Safety."

Irritation nipped at Matthew's mind. He was clearly out of his element, and it looked like Gracie could protect him more than he could protect her. "May I ask why we need guns?"

"Pa told you last night."

"No more to add?" Matthew asked.

"Nope. If danger comes, I'm sure we'll all do what we can to thwart it, but there's no point in me carrying two guns when this little sharpshooter would indeed be a surprise attack to anyone or anything giving us trouble." He looked down at Gracie, who was smiling up at him. "But I'm praying for a peaceful trip."

"So am I, Johnny. So am I." She lifted the heavy coat and the bottom of her dress and slid the gun into the top of her boot.

"We don't need any more trouble. This dang rain is irritation enough." Matthew took off his hat and shook off the water, which continually dripped down his neck.

"I'm so thankful for this coat, Johnny," Gracie said. "Between this warm cowboy hat, waterproof overcoat, and my wool cloak, I'm surprisingly warm."

Why was Matthew so bothered by her sunny disposition?

He grudgingly admitted the truth. Her obvious admiration for the cowboy was clawing at him. Suddenly, all Matthew's business and management skills, and how good he was with money, and how much he loved the orphan children, paled in the light of this man's talents. Johnny was certainly the man of the hour.

Matthew clenched his teeth against the spike of jealousy that rode his spine. He looked out over the misty terrain. He could barely see through the driving rain, and it suited his dreary mood.

Oh God, help me. Here the man is kind enough to assist us out of the goodness of his heart, and I'm sitting here fuming at him.

Matthew looked over her head and caught Johnny's gaze on Gracie.

Scrap that prayer, God. Johnny was not motivated by the goodness of his heart. His motivation was no different from the one most men were inspired by when it came to Gracie. She was infectious, delightful, and all together captivating.

"So, how did your sister learn to shoot?" Johnny asked. "I do believe I'm going to enjoy meeting her."

Gracie laughed. "It's a long story."

Matthew could barely listen for the stick in his craw. They laughed and teased and were thoroughly enjoying each other's company, all the while he stewed in silence. The supposedly quiet one, Johnny, had found his tongue.

"We have nothing but rain and time." Johnny encouraged in a voice too gentle for the hulk of a man. "I'm all ears."

Matthew's hands fisted. This was supposed to be about him meeting her family and leaving a great impression. But how selfish even that thought was. He shouldn't be helping Gracie because he wanted to further his relationship with her. His hand ran behind the back of his neck as he brushed water and irritation away. It was time for honesty. What he felt was far more than attraction. He had fallen in love with Gracie, despite his best intentions to respect her wishes. Johnny's admiration for her had brought out the beast. One of Melinda Preston's favorite idioms came to mind. *Jealousy makes you feel just-lousy.* And boy, did he feel lousy.

Out of the driving rain, three horsemen suddenly appeared. Johnny pulled up on the reins slightly and directed the mule to the far right of the road. "Keep your head down, Gracie."

The men crowded in. Johnny reached down and grabbed the rifle he had at the ready. "Can I help you boys?"

The lead man moved closer to Johnny. The other two moved into position as if they were in a well-rehearsed play, one in front of the wagon, the other on Matthew's side.

"Well, who do we have here? A brute, a boy, and by the looks of that useless hat, a city rat." He grinned through rotten teeth. "It's our lucky day. Sure didn't expect to run across any fools in this downpour."

The other two laughed.

Matthew turned to the man on his right and realized he was the same one they had run into outside the saloon the day before. His blood ran cold. He immediately turned his face in the opposite direction. If he was recognized, Gracie's cover would be blown.

Matthew's hands bit into the buckboard. The last thing he wanted to show was the tremble that had taken up residence.

Johnny looked calm. His voice held steady. "If it's all right with you boys, we best be on our way."

The lead man sneered. "It's not all right. Now get down and leave that rifle right where I can see it."

"We'll do no such thing." Johnny's voice turned dark and menacing.

In a flash, three guns were cocked and pointed at them.

"If you want to see tomorrow, you will."

"Just tell us what you want. We'll gladly give you the little bit of money and provisions we have. But we're only passing from one town to another. Not much for the taking."

Matthew could feel the man beside him crowd in, the horse's breath hot on the back of his neck.

"Hey, boss. I think they're hiding something mighty fine and ripe for the pickin'." He poked Matthew's arm with his rifle. "This here's the city boy I ran into yesterday. No wonder we couldn't find him this morning. And smack dab in the middle is that purty little thing I was telling you about, all wrapped up like a boy."

"A beautiful woman you say." He turned to Gracie. "Lift your head."

Gracie kept her head down.

"Lift your head and take that hat off, or I'll kill your friend here."

Gracie slowly lifted her head and slipped off the cowboy hat.

Her long braid fell free, and panic edged up Matthew's throat. He would do anything to protect her.

But what could he do?

"Well, well, well," the leader said. "This day is getting better by the moment."

"Didn't I tell you she was a beauty, boss?"

The air sucked out of Matthew's lungs. His pulse spiked.

Gracie nudged Matthew, and Johnny must have got the same by the raised brows he sent Matthew's way. She stood and put both hands in the air. "Now boys, no need for those ugly guns. Why, they make my poor head swoon." Her voice dripped with honey and a drawl she didn't normally have. "Put down those simply horrifying weapons, and we'll gladly cooperate, won't we boys?" She looked first at Johnny, and he nodded.

Then she turned to Matthew, pleading in her eyes.

What was she up to? He glanced at Johnny, whose gaze told him he had no idea what Gracie was doing either. But they didn't seem to have a choice. Wherever she led, they would follow. But this one thing he knew—he was prepared to be a human shield if they came anywhere near her.

The boss lowered his gun to his lap, and the other two followed. "Anything for a cooperative lady." He licked his lips.

"See, there's no need for violence." She pulled out her handkerchief and waved it in front of her face. "But I do declare you have given me quite a fright." She swooned and dropped into the seat. "Oh my, give me just one moment. I fear I'm about to faint." Her body collapsed forward.

She bent down. Matthew and Johnny shifted in their seats showing concern to hide her movements. One look over at Johnny, and Matthew knew what to do.

"Now," Gracie shouted.

Matthew grabbed the rifle hanging loosely on the man's lap beside him. The startled horse bucked, and the rider went flying and lay sprawled on the ground.

Behind him, Matthew heard two other shots. He took a brief look to ensure Gracie was all right and jumped from the wagon. He trained the rifle on the man scrambling to get up in the mud. "Don't move."

The man froze.

Matthew kept the gun pointed at him. "Stay down or I'll put a bullet in your head." That reprobate didn't have to know he didn't have a clue how to use the weapon.

Johnny led one of the men around the side of the wagon. The outlaw had blood dripping from his hand. A length of rope was slung over Johnny's shoulder. "Bring him." He nodded to the reprobate in the mud. "We'll tie them both to the nearest tree. The next town isn't far, and the sheriff can deal with them."

Matthew lifted the scrawny one in the mud to his feet in one yank. "Not so tough now without a rifle in your hand, hey boy?" He glanced at Johnny, who was dragging the other to a tree. "Where's the other one?"

"Their boss wasn't so lucky." Johnny slammed the scoundrel with the bleeding hand against the trunk. "Count yourself fortunate Gracie only went for your hand and not your heart. She's much kinder than I am. With scum like you who like to prey on innocent women and everyday people, I have no qualms about killing in self-defense."

The bite in his voice shocked Matthew.

"If you hadn't dropped your gun, I would've finished you off. Make no mistake about that." Johnny tied knots that Matthew had never seen before.

Gracie led one of the horses their direction. "Why not take these boys to the next town? Seems a little harsh to leave them in the elements."

"Please, take us," one whined.

"Shut up." Johnny clenched the rope tighter and looked at Gracie. "Nope. I've done that before. All it takes is one mistake, and you have another battle on your hands. Too risky. And after what they had planned for you..." He shook his head. "It will be kind enough to tell the sheriff where to find them. I have a notion to let them rot out here."

For the first time, Matthew appreciated Johnny very much.

The younger man continued. "Let's round up the other two horses and tie them to the back of the wagon. I'll get some good money for them and probably a reward for helping get these outlaws off the turnpike. As you said, Gracie, the Lord provides in mysterious ways."

"Really? Money for these horses and a reward?" An unladylike whoop slipped from her dainty lips.

They all laughed.

"We'll share the profits three ways." He clapped Matthew on the back with his large hands. "You had the worst of it, with no gun in hand. I thought maybe you'd startle the horse, but you did way better. Takes a lot more courage to face the enemy without a weapon. I'm impressed."

Gracie looked up, her large brown eyes filled with wonder. "I second that. You were amazing, Matthew." She flashed him a smile, the kind that melts the heart into a puddle of mush. The kind no man ever wants to admit the full effect of. His chest swelled to full breadth. Suddenly, the rainy day no longer mattered.

They hopped back up, and Blossom resumed her plodding with one small crack of the reins. The old mule seemed unfazed by what had just happened.

Not Matthew. The tremble in his hands was only now starting to subside. All he wanted to do was draw Gracie close and never let go.

She is the one.

The message in his spirit sent a chill of excitement spiraling through his veins. He had not heard wrong. God was speaking in the pouring rain while Matthew sat on a buckboard next to the most beautiful girl in the world. That near-death experience took the question mark out of his head and replaced it with a solid exclamation point.

He loved Gracie. With all his heart, he loved her. And he was going to pursue her. His heartbeat thumped against the walls of his chest in crazy abandon.

Johnny looked down at Gracie. "I have to ask. Was that a lucky shot, or did you mean to shoot the gun out of his hand?"

"I couldn't kill a man. So, I thought if I got the hand that held his gun—"

"You are some kind of woman, Gracie Williams. If I didn't know you were already taken, I'd be in the lineup."

"But I'm not taken. I don't ever intend to marry."

"I think after all the daggers I've been on the receiving end of this morning, you'd better take that up with Mr. Weston there. Seems he has other ideas." Johnny laughed out loud.

Matthew wanted to thump him, but how could he refute the truth? That was exactly what he had been doing. But he wanted to woo Gracie slowly, not scare her away. He planned to follow through on what God had told him. She was the one for him. No more pussyfooting around.

Gracie looked at Matthew, her eyes covered by a furrowed brow. "Matthew and I are only friends. Tell him, Matthew."

The words got stuck in his throat, but he forced them out. "We're friends."

Johnny laughed all the louder.

Let Johnny laugh. He was right. They were friends, and a whole lot more. It wasn't Matthew who had the message wrong from God. It was Gracie. And he aimed to find out why.

CHAPTER 10

*G*racie couldn't help the smile that split across her face as they rolled up to her parents' house in the wagon. The air was crisp though a weak sun struggled through the overcast sky. They hadn't made it all the way to Harrisonburg the day before as planned, thanks to stopping at the sheriff's office in Spring Hill. But she had welcomed a good night's rest at an inn in Mount Crawford, and the remainder of the trip had been dry and uneventful.

She was home. She whispered a prayer of thanks and then grabbed the arms of the men on either side of her. "I can't thank you both enough. There are no words." She fought back the tears welling in her eyes as she turned first to Johnny.

He smiled down at her. "Don't mention it."

When she turned her gaze on Matthew, he squeezed her hand. "It's what friends do for friends." There was a wistfulness in his voice and a look in his eyes she could not untangle.

They pulled to a stop at the hitching post, and the door to the house opened. Jeanette ran out. "Gracie is that you? Oh, my goodness, am I glad to see you."

Gracie crawled over Matthew in haste, held up her skirt, and jumped to the ground. There was nothing ladylike about her actions, but she didn't care. Jeanette's warm arms encircled her in a desperate hug that wouldn't let go. She turned her head to see Matthew standing directly behind her with a wild grin on his face. Somehow, her joy made him happy.

Gracie pulled free and linked her arm into her sister's. "How's Ma?"

"She's resting. We made a bed in the parlor for her so she doesn't have to manage steps during the day. But you know her, as stubborn as they come. Every night, Pa and I help her up to her bed. But tell me, how on earth did you get here when most of the services are shut down?"

Gracie turned back toward Matthew and Johnny. "Oh, how rude of me. Jeanette, meet my very good friend and boss at the orphanage, Matthew Weston, and my new friend, Johnny Parker. Without his help, we never could've made it." She pulled Jeanette closer but noticed the decided frown on Matthew's face.

What had she said wrong now?

"Nice to meet you," Jeanette said, then quickly turned away. Her face flushed a crimson red.

Gracie felt a surge of pity. Why did Jeanette feel so uncomfortable around men? She'd love to have that conversation, but how did one ask something so personal?

Jeanette whispered to Gracie. "Before we go in, prepare yourself. Ma's lost a lot of weight."

Gracie's heart ached with sorrow. She had made the right decision in coming home, despite the risk.

"We'll go to the barn and settle the mule," Matthew offered. "Give you a little privacy before we come in."

"Good plan." Johnny clapped Matthew on the back.

Gracie could've hugged Matthew at that moment. He knew little about settling a mule, but he knew what she needed. "Thank you." Her words seemed so inadequate, but she looked him straight in his eyes and hoped he read the gratitude in hers. No, it was deeper than gratitude. It was something she could not define. What an odd thought in an untimely moment. She pushed the strange flutter in her stomach away and turned back toward the house.

"Ready?" Jeanette took her arm.

Gracie nodded.

The screen door squeaked as they entered. That familiar sound soothed the homesickness she had been fighting ever since finding out about Ma's illness.

"Hope the shock of seeing you won't send Ma into a dither. I almost fainted when I looked out the window and realized it was you arriving in that wagon."

They walked down the hall and turned into the parlor. Gracie took one look at the withered woman sleeping on the makeshift bed and turned away. Her hand flew to her mouth to suppress the cry. Her beautiful Ma with plump cheeks and a sturdy frame was no more than a shell.

Gracie stepped out into the hallway. Tears broke free. She was glad her ma had not been awake to see her reaction.

Jeanette's arms came around her, and they cried together.

"She's...she's so much worse than I imagined."

"I know," Jeanette whispered. "She's declining steadily, way faster than even Doc Philips anticipated."

Gracie pulled back to look at Jeanette. "But you told us not to come until spring and there's no way—"

"None of us could've known things were going to decline this quickly. It's shocking enough for us who see her every day. I can't imagine what it's like for you."

"When I left, Ma was fine. How can this be?" Gracie bit down on her bottom lip to still the tremble.

Jeanette shook her head. "I honestly don't understand any more than you do. But I'm sure glad you're here. Should've known you'd be the one to buck Ma and Pa's request not to travel. You've always had a penchant for doing the unexpected." Jeanette reached across with her handkerchief and dried tears that coursed down Gracie's cheeks. "Here, you need this more than I do. I've cried buckets already." She handed the lace trimmed hankie her way. "Take whatever time you need to collect yourself. It's best if you're not—"

"I understand." Gracie dabbed at her eyes. "I need to talk to Matthew for a moment. I'll be right back." She ran out the door not sure what she needed, just knowing she needed him.

Her feet carried her in an all-out run toward the barn. "Matthew. Matthew."

He hurried out of the barn. "What is it?"

"Ma is so…much worse…" She could not get the words out for all the blubbering. He opened his arms, and she walked in. Her shaking and trembling slowly subsided in the warmth of his strength.

He pulled back enough to look at her. "I wish I could take your sorrow and bear it." He brushed his hand lightly down the side of her face, thumbing away a tear.

That was one of the nicest things anyone had ever said to her. She had no idea how to tell him just how much that meant.

"Will you pray for me? Ma was sleeping when I first walked in, and I somehow have to compose myself enough to talk to her."

He closed his eyes and began praying. She had not meant for him to pray that instant, but again, he knew what she needed more than she did. The prayer was a soothing balm that calmed her from the inside out.

"Amen." He opened his eyes and planted a kiss on the top of her head. "Go, see your ma. You'll be fine now." He pointed to the heavens. "He is with you, and so am I."

"Thank you, Matthew." She looked up into blue eyes swimming with warmth and compassion so deep she dared not scrutinize the source. "I can do this now."

"Yes, you can." He gave her shoulders one last squeeze.

Gracie ran back across the yard and up the steps. When she entered the house, Jeanette was waiting. She held out her hand. "Ma's awake, and I told her you'd arrived. Thought it would be good for her to have a few minutes to process."

"Good idea." When Gracie entered the room, Ma was perched up against a stack of pillows. She ran a hand through her hair, smoothing the sprigs that stuck out in all directions. "I got Jeanette to cut my hair. Do you like it? Seemed the sensible thing to do when one's too weak to run a brush through the tangled mess." A forced laugh came through.

Gracie tried to smile, but no words surfaced. Her soul ached with sorrow, knowing the truth. Her mama was dying.

"Come, give your ma a hug." She held out arms that all too quickly dropped to the bed.

Gracie fell into her embrace, and they held each other and rocked back and forth.

"Now, what's this about you disobeying your ma and traveling at this time of year? I told Jeanette to make it clear that no one was to come running."

Gracie pulled back and sat on the side of the bed. "Yes, it's Jeanette's fault," Gracie said with her best attempt at a smile.

"What?" Jeanette smacked Gracie on the arm but focused on Ma. "Told you she was a rebel and wouldn't listen. Being the youngest and the spoiled one, I knew she'd do her own thing." Jeanette's eyes sparkled with tease.

Ma enclosed her frail hand over Gracie's and gave a weak squeeze. "Sure is good to see you, my child. How long do you have?"

"Only a few days, but I had to see you…" Her voice cracked, and tears filled her eyes.

"There, there child." Ma patted her hand. "Please don't cry, or I'll be blubbering alongside you, and you know how much I hate that."

Gracie attempted a smile. It took all she had to press past the ache in her throat.

"I'm sorry I don't have more time, but we made a promise to the orphanage board that we—"

"We?"

"Matthew, my boss, who is an amazing friend, came with me. And then when we couldn't get the stagecoach in Staunton, a nice man at the livery offered to bring us the rest of the way. His name is Johnny."

"Amazing friend?" Jeanette had apparently gotten hung up on the first part of Gracie's remark. She raised her eyebrows far above her glasses. "Looks like a whole lot more than friendship is simmering between you and this Matthew."

"Well, I do declare, has Gracie finally found a love interest after all?" Ma asked. "That kind of news would do my heart good."

"Both of you stop. We're just friends—"

"What I witnessed out in the yard was a whole lot more than friendship, but what do I know, the old spinster that I am?"

"Now stop that, Jeanette," Ma said, "always talking yourself down. A mother could not have better care than what you've given me. I'm blessed you're here. What would I do without you?"

Jeanette pursed her lips as if she were biting back words.

"Truth be told, I'd die a happy woman to have you both happily married and find love as wonderful as I've had with your father."

Gracie could not hold back the sting prickling behind her eyes. Tears rolled down her cheek. "Ma, don't talk about dying." She leaned forward and rested her torso against her ma's chest. "You have to fight this thing."

"I've been fighting, baby girl, but it's winning. And I'm getting tired." She smoothed her hands down Gracie's hair. "So tired."

*G*racie walked into the kitchen and joined Jeanette at the counter, and Matthew's gaze followed her movement. Awareness prickled, but he pushed it down. These past two days with her and her family had only heightened his acute responsiveness to her every need. Dark circles shadowed her beautiful eyes as she yawned. All he wanted was to get up and put his arms around her and give comfort. Clearly, she was suffering. She shuffled over to the stove in a huge pair of slippers and poured herself a cup of coffee.

"Sure enjoying getting to know your young man here." Her pa clapped Matthew on the shoulder as he walked by.

"I told you, Matthew and I are just—"

"While you're at it, bring me a warm-up." Pa lifted his mug.

She turned a delightful pink. Matthew could not help but like the way her pa kept her from repeating the word that was fast becoming his nemesis. If he never heard that word *friend* from her lips again, it would suit him just fine.

"Seems to me you two have a lot in common, with the most important thing being the good Lord. You both love children, you both work at the orphanage, you both—"

"Are friends." She filled his mug and snuck a peek at Matthew. Her eyes rolled, and she mouthed *sorry*.

"And that's the best place to start. Indeed, it is." Her pa gave a knowing nod.

Gracie blew out a hot breath of air, and Matthew hid his smile. *You go, Pa Williams. You tell her. You're preaching just what I want her to hear.*

Then again, why not take an opportunity handed to him on a silver platter? "So, if I were to ask for your daughter's hand in marriage, you'd be fine with that?"

Gracie nearly dropped the coffee pot as she slammed it back on the wood stove. Her body snapping around. "Matthew!"

Pa slapped his knee. "Darn tootin' I'd be fine with that."

"Well, your pa has got me thinking." He caught and held Gracie's pointed stare. "We do have a lot in common." He winked, and her brows shot up.

"Quit it, or Pa is going to take that as gospel, and the next thing you know the whole valley will be arriving for a wedding."

Matthew chuckled. "All right, enough teasing for the start of a day." He stuck a huge piece of flapjack in his mouth, wishing he could tell her that a wedding would make him the happiest man alive.

"Jeanette, you sure do make the best meals." He lifted his head and turned her way. "These flapjacks are divine."

Jeanette didn't turn from the stove where she was flipping a hot one, but he heard a faint "Thank you."

Matthew was determined to get her talking. He remembered only too well what it felt like to choke on most every word you tried to say in public.

Gracie slid into a seat at the table. "Where's Johnny?"

"He left at daybreak." Another reason it was a happy morning, but he couldn't tell her that. "He confirmed that we can take the stagecoach to Staunton on Wednesday, so he pushed on out."

"Without saying goodbye?"

"You slept in, sleepyhead, and he wasn't going to wake you. He asked me to pass along the message that if you're ever in Staunton again and need anything, to look him up."

"Do you think we'll have time to stop by the Parkers' on the way back? I'd like to thank him in person."

"I rather doubt it, but we'll see. It'll most likely be too late, and we board that train bright and early the next morning." He shouldn't sound so happy about that, but he was. In fact, he was pleased about the whole visit and so glad he had insisted on coming. He loved Gracie's family, the kind of family he had always dreamed being part of. Yesterday, he'd met her other sisters, Katherine and Lucinda, along with their husbands and children. Plus, he'd hit it off instantly with her pa. The only sadness was over her ma's health.

"Jeanette, can I take Ma something to eat?" Gracie asked.

"You can try, but I'm not sure she'll eat anything. Maybe some porridge with brown sugar and cream."

Gracie prepared a bowl.

"And I'm doing the dishes," Matthew said.

Jeanette twirled around from the stove. "Heavens, no. A guest does not do dishes, especially a—"

"A man?" Matthew laughed. "This man does. I was raised in the orphanage. Chores were a part of everyday life, and I learned how to do them well." He pushed from the table and stood, bringing his plate to where Jeanette stood. "Now take those last few hot flapjacks and make yourself a plate. You'll see just how good I am at this."

Jeanette blushed and looked down, unable to make eye contact.

"I can attest to his skills," Gracie said. "Besides, you do too much. Let us help while we're here." She picked up the tray with tea and porridge and headed out of the kitchen.

Matthew started stacking dishes.

Pa rose from the breakfast table. "Gotta check on the progress of the workers, but I'm hoping to have some more time to chat this afternoon, son. I want to maximize these last few days with my Gracie and her man." He grinned across the room at Matthew.

"Pa. Gracie's not going to appreciate your meddling," Jeanette said.

"Sometimes a father knows what a father knows." He flipped his cap on his head and headed out.

Matthew smiled into the sudsy basin of dishes and washed with vigor. Oh, did he hope her father was right. Because everything about Gracie felt like his future.

He jumped when Jeanette spoke from the kitchen table. "I can see…"

When her words trailed, he said, "See what?"

"Never mind."

"Come on, now, you can't leave me hanging."

"You love her, don't you?"

He had barely allowed his mind to think those words much less say them out loud. He worked on keeping his expression blank as he looked at her, but his heart pounded.

"Most every man who spends any time with her falls for her," Jeanette said.

His stomach lurched and fell. He nodded and kept washing. "I can believe that."

"She has something special far beyond her beauty, but men tend to see only the outward package."

He glanced behind him, but Jeanette wouldn't make eye contact. She pushed cut up pieces of her flapjack around on her plate.

"I'm beginning to see that everyone in this family has that something special. You included."

"Ha, now that's a laugh. I'm as invisible as they come."

He could not believe Jeanette, who was as quiet as Johnny had turned out *not* to be, was talking to him, especially about something so personal. Maybe it was because he was across the room and facing the other direction. He kept his eyes on the work.

"You may be shy, but you're hardly invisible," he said. "Everyone can see how you hold this all together for your ma and pa. Did you ever consider—?" Where did those thoughts come from? Was he supposed to repeat what was thrumming through his brain?

"What?"

"No. I'm overstepping my boundaries." He couldn't share

what he was hearing in his spirit. She would think him mad. And what if he was wrong?

Speak.

He recognized that voice. The same one that did not change the message that Gracie was *the one.*

"Oh, come on, you're going to be my brother-in-law as soon as my sister wakes up to the obvious. She may say you two are only friends, but who did she run to when she needed a shoulder to cry on?"

The thought of being part of this family and a husband to Gracie sent a thrill shooting through him.

Speak.

All right, Lord, I'll speak.

"What I was going to say is… is something I have no business saying but feel that the spirit wants me to. God's timing is not ours."

"God's timing is *never* when it comes to me. He doesn't seem to hear…"

When she didn't finish her sentence, he admitted his own issues. "I've been waiting for God too. Asking Him for the woman He has for me, and not just those who come calling."

"At least you have options. I've never dipped from that well, and I have no idea why I'm telling you this." Her voice came out in a stiff staccato.

"Maybe because we understand each other. I've never felt I belonged anywhere, and you somehow feel you don't quite fit into society because you're not married yet."

"Yet? Surely, you jest. There is no *yet* about it. I will never be married."

"I believe differently." He snatched a towel and dried the dishes that were stacking up, turning to face her. "The desires of your heart and mine are just a matter of timing. They're coming."

Her gaze darted down the hall as if she were making sure no one heard their conversation. A flush of red poured into her cheeks from either embarrassment or anger, he couldn't tell. "I won't get my hopes up," she whispered fiercely. "Done that one too many times. And I'd appreciate you not trying to get into this family so desperately that you'd use a so-called message from God."

"Jeanette, I'm not—"

"Enough." Tears filled her eyes. She pushed her glasses up, and droplets fell from below the lens. "I'll keep your secret if you keep mine."

He'd made her cry. He'd spoken what he felt he'd heard, and he'd made Gracie's sister cry. He longed to say something kind, something to undo what he'd done. All he came up with was, "Deal." And then he added, "As long as I get an invitation to your wedding, no matter what happens."

"Is your faith wavering so quickly? You just said that it's only a matter of time for the both of us, and I know what your desire is. She's in the room down the hall."

He smiled at her. "Right you are, on all counts. So, let me re-word that. I get an invitation to your wedding regardless of whether Gracie and I are married—yet. How does that sound for faith in action?"

"Well, at least it makes me feel you believe your own words." She lifted her chin and gave him a watery smile as she pushed up from the table. She crossed the kitchen. "Finish washing. I'll dry."

Apparently, he hadn't done too much damage. And maybe… just maybe God was speaking to both of them.

CHAPTER 11

"Why aren't you working, Jeanette?" Gracie placed the last of the dishes on the counter and wiped the crumbs off the table from their lunch.

"I've put my teaching on hold. Mrs. Beasley has graciously offered to come out of retirement for the rest of the school year so I can be with Ma."

"She looks…terrible." Gracie's voice hitched. It was hard to voice the truth when she was begging God for a miracle.

"I'm glad you got to see her. I don't think it's going to be long now." Jeanette's chin wobbled.

Gracie's heart lurched. Those words brought a storm cloud of sadness rolling in. "Should I stay?"

"Certainly not. Go back to the children where God has placed you."

"But why should you do this all alone?" Her heart felt torn in two. The children needed her, and yet Jeanette deserved help with Ma, too.

"I'm not alone. Katherine comes over every day, and Lucinda's been coming most every weekend."

"Has anyone talked to Ma about Jesus? Seems one by one we

all found our way, but not her." The thought of not seeing Ma in heaven crushed her heart. A heaviness had settled in over the past few days that she could not shake. She was praying almost constantly.

"I've thought about that a thousand times and prayed over her for hours while sitting by her bedside. But she's stubborn. The minute anyone mentions anything about God, she swiftly changes the subject."

"Even now, when time is short?" Gracie's throat grew thick, and unbidden tears stung her eyes.

"Especially now. She says she's lived her life without God, and she's not about to be one of those last-minute Christians that call on the Lord just in case He's real."

"She said that?"

"She did. It'll have to be a real leading of the Lord to breach that fortress."

"Oh my." No wonder Gracie had been so grieved in prayer. "I'll head in there now and sit with her. You take some time for yourself. Go for a walk in the fresh air or whatever fills you up."

"Fills me up? Now, that's a funny way of putting it, but I like the sound of it. I think a walk outdoors and then a nice long bath sounds wonderful."

"Go." Gracie snatched the dishtowel from her hand. "Scat."

"When did you get so bossy?"

"Looking after a bunch of kids does that."

"Don't I know it?" Jeanette laughed. "In a way, our days are quite similar."

"I never thought of that, but you're right. We are indeed sisters, loving children like we do."

"Where we differ is, I'd like to have my own family, but I can't find anyone to love me. You, on the other hand, have no such inclination, yet could have a dozen men at the nod of your head. Do you think God got something mixed up?"

Gracie smiled until she caught her sister's forlorn expression. She moved forward to give a hug, but Jeanette turned abruptly. "None of that feeling sorry for myself. Off I go for a long walk in the orchard. Thanks for looking after Ma."

Gracie watched her go. What could she say? It was true. Boys, then men, had noticed her for as long as she could remember. But from the time she met Rosina and made that promise, she had found men a nuisance and would've gladly traded places with Jeanette. She hung the dish towel on the hook and headed down the hall to Ma.

"I'm glad you're here," Ma said. "I just woke up. Don't want to sleep away your whole visit." Her hand lifted and motioned Gracie closer, but even that seemed an effort. She dropped her arm to the side of the bed.

Gracie had to choke back tears every time she entered the room. She pulled up a chair and sat down, taking her ma's hand in hers. "Are you hungry? Thirsty?"

"No appetite. But hungry for time with my baby girl."

Gracie squeezed her hand and held on tight. *Please God, give me words of love and wisdom. Redeem this time I have with Ma. Let her know how much I love her and how You love her even more.*

"I knew you'd be my last. Your Pa secretly hoped for a boy, but not me."

"Why? You had four girls already."

"Men have a penchant for war. And there was rumor and talk of war for years before it broke out. When you were born, it was a relief. My daughter would not fight in any war. Then my greatest fears were realized when the twins went off to join the Confederate Army. Losing both Scott and Jonathan nearly took me under."

Ma rarely talked of the twins. Her grief was intensely private. Gracie wished she could remember them, but she couldn't. "What were my brothers like?"

"I guess you were too young to remember. How handsome and full of life they were. And oh, how they doted on you."

"They did?"

"Oh yes, they loved their baby sister, and you loved them. Your eyes would light up, and you'd go running every time they entered the house. They would fight over who got to pick you up first. Then they'd take turns lifting you high in their strong arms and twirling you around. Your giggles and their laughter filled the house with love."

"What a lovely memory Ma. Thanks for sharing that with me." But why had her brothers been erased by the silence? She dared not ask. The clock on the mantlepiece ticked, carving off the seconds.

"They were far too young to die," Ma said. "The day I heard the news was the last time I believed there was a God in heaven who cared a whit about me." Her voice grew hard. "I had prayed and prayed for their safety."

What could Gracie say? "I'm so sorry." This conversation would be so much better had Ma had it with Katherine, who'd lost her first husband, or Lucinda, who'd gone through a horrific first marriage, but what did Gracie know about suffering and loss? She couldn't even remember her brothers. *Oh God, give me wisdom.*

The only thing she could think of was to change the subject. "Why did you and Pa name me Grace?"

Ma was staring at the ceiling, lost somewhere in deep thought. "Hmm?"

"Why is my name Gracie?"

Ma turned toward her. "That was all your Pa. He was obsessed with that hymn, *Amazing Grace*. Had heard it somewhere." Her brow furrowed. "Not too sure where. We never attended church back then."

"I'm named after a hymn?"

"Not exactly. He loved what grace meant, the favor of God."

"You know what my name means?"

"Of course I do. Back then, we were both open to God. But

then the twins died, and that was it for me. I'll never understand how Pa turned more toward God. It made me plum angry." Her brows knit together. "If there is a God, He's up there somewhere not at all concerned with the hell we go through down here."

"Jeanette and I were talking about how, one by one we all came to a believing faith in God except…" Oh dear, how could she say that?

"Except me?"

"Except you."

"Your Pa said even the twins…"

"How?"

"Some sergeant in the military was continually talking to the troops about being ready, not only to die, but to live beyond the grave. I guess one day all three of them prayed with this man. It gives your Pa comfort to believe the boys are up there somewhere with God."

"Don't you want to see them again, Mama?" Gracie bent her head to hide the tears that were forming.

"I can't get past the anger. If God is so big, why couldn't He have saved my boys? Why did He have to take both of them?"

"He saved your grandson. Remember you prayed that day Sammy was missing?"

Ma nodded.

Gracie felt so inadequate. Why had God chosen her for this conversation? "And I'm named Grace to remind you every day that God's favor is with us more than we even realize. He gave us this home after ours was burned to the ground by the Yankees. He brought Lucinda back to us alive after her husband almost killed her. He helped Matthew, Johnny, and me fight off some bandits on the way here, bringing me safely to you."

"What? You had to fight off—"

"Don't go worrying about that now, Ma, I was merely making a point. God's favor is all around you, all around me, despite the cruelties of this world. When I see the orphan children who did nothing but be born into their circumstances, my heart is twisted and tortured. And then I see all the people who give of their time and money to keep the orphanage open so these children have a chance. I lay on my bed at night after a long day of work, and I'm reminded of the grace I've been given so I can, in turn, freely give grace."

Ma reached out to touch Gracie's cheek. "You were named perfectly." Her hands were ice cold.

"Please, Ma. Accept God's grace just the way you are…anger and all. God is big enough to handle how you feel."

Ma clenched her eyes closed, and the tears on her lashes ran in streams down her sunken cheeks. "I want to, but I don't know how."

Gracie wanted to run and find Jeanette, or Pa, or Katherine. Anyone who could do a better job of this. *God, help me.*

Matthew's knock sounded on the open door. "I was walking by. I couldn't help but hear some of that conversation. I was going to turn and leave, but the Spirit of God wouldn't let me. Do you think I could tell you a bit of my story? It may help answer your last question?"

He stood respectfully back, and to Gracie's surprise, Ma waved him in.

Fresh tears filled Gracie's eyes to blurring as he entered and pulled up a chair beside her. She slowly let out a breath of air and squeezed his hand below her mother's view before letting go. She could not thank him now, but she could certainly thank God. *Oh Jesus, you are worthy of all praise. Thank you for sending Matthew. Thank you for loving my mama so much. Thank you for your forgiveness.*

"I was angry at God for years," he said. "My ma left me on the orphanage steps to look for work, promising to return. I used to sit there for hours wondering if that would be the day. I looked for her everywhere I went—in the streets, at church, in the faces of every woman who passed by."

What must that have been like for the child Matthew? She pictured him as a tiny lad, forlorn and lonely, waiting for his mama. It took all Gracie had not to weep.

He paused. "I was furious when I would see families, kids playing in their yards without a care in the world. Somehow, God had forgotten me."

Ma nodded. "I've felt that way."

"My anger grew. By the time I was twelve, I was running away from the orphanage at every turn. Self-destructing. But hunger always brought me back, and they always extended grace. Marianna, who is the sweetest of ladies…much like your Gracie here, who has a gift with children…"

He looked at Gracie, and his kindness burned through to her soul. Her heart tugged like he had looped a rope around and pulled tight. She drew in a pull of air. What was happening to her…to them?

When he looked back toward Ma, she could think again.

"Marianna took me back time after time, grace after grace. And Mrs. Preston, your Amelia's mother-in-law, she kept on encouraging my education, told me how smart I was, that I didn't belong on the streets. She paid for a special tutor for me. Even still, I believed God had forgotten me.

"At fourteen, I got in a street fight after running yet again. I almost died. The other guy pulled out a knife, and I have some good scars on my chest to remind me daily of my folly. I literally saw my life pass before my eyes, bleeding out in the street."

Gracie gasped and reached for his hand. She squeezed tightly and did not let go. Everything about their hands intertwined felt right, but somehow…more than friendship. But this went against her promise, against her understanding, against her plan.

She could not think about that now.

"I cried out to God, begging for one more chance at life, and I swore I wouldn't waste it. I'd serve Him and use every bit of potential I possessed for his glory. God spared my life, but when I healed and was ready to leave the hospital, the orphanage had made the tough decision to let me go and give my spot to a child more willing to comply. That could have been the end of me, of my future, but Mrs. Preston personally took me into her home, into her care. Grace after grace after grace."

"And your anger?" Ma asked.

"From the moment I said yes to God, willing to give Him my anger, I was given eyes to see grace, to see His favor. My anger vanished—at my mother, at the world, at God. I felt like a new person."

Ma rubbed a trembling hand on her temple. "Honestly, I'm so tired of being angry."

"Will you pray with us?" Matthew asked.

Gracie was shocked at his boldness, first to tell his story, which she knew he shared with no one, and then not to waste the moment.

Ma nodded, and Gracie almost jumped out of her chair in excitement. Her whole being trembled with emotion. She squeezed his hand, and he squeezed back.

Matthew reached out his other hand to Ma, and Gracie leaned forward and placed hers on top. The minute their hands folded together, a warmth seeped up her arm and into her heart. She bent her head, listening to the rich timber of Matthew's voice as he prayed. Everything about him being present in this moment felt like divine intervention. Everything about Ma whispering a prayer to God felt like a miracle.

How did Gracie get so blessed to be part of that moment?

Thank you, God, for Mama's salvation. Thank you that this world is not the end and I will see my Mama in glory. Thank you, God. Thank you.

CHAPTER 12

The train jostled and hummed. The steady rhythm of the movement of wheels on rail had lulled Gracie to sleep numerous times. This time, her head came to rest on Matthew's shoulder. He slowly eased his arm around her so that she fell into a more comfortable position against him. Now, this was heaven. The sweet smell of wild roses drifted up. He was able to take her tiny hand in his and hold it. What would his wedding band look like on her finger? With her snuggled so close, he could dream.

A sudden jolt snapped her eyes open. She popped to an upright position back into her seat, causing his arm to fling off. "I'm sorry, Matthew. You should've woken me."

"No hardship on my part. I didn't have the heart. Your head kept bobbing like a return wheel, so when it came to rest on my shoulder, it made sense to let you sleep." He worked hard to keep his voice steady and flat. Showing no emotion would make the incident seem matter of fact. She didn't need to know that her sudden withdrawal left him feeling empty.

"You've been asleep a while. We'll be in Richmond in less than an hour."

"An hour? How long was I leaning against you?"

"Long enough to make my limbs go numb." He laughed to lighten the dismay on her face.

"Oh my. How perfectly horrid for you. I'm so sorry."

"I'm not." The words came out before he had time to process them. They surprised even him.

Her brows knit together.

He could tell she was wrestling with his words, words she most likely didn't want to hear. He was going to have to be careful and take it slow.

"So, about this trip—"

"It was wonderful to see where you grew up. I love your family. They explain a lot about you." He laughed at his own remark.

"But—"

"And what a blessing to be part of bringing your ma to the Lord."

"That was incredible."

"Which reminds me, I have a big favor to ask. My story, about being an orphan." He could trust her, but he had to make her understand the difference between country and city folk. His neck and shoulders tightened.

"Yes."

"Only a handful of people know. Mrs. Preston and the board president, Mr. Lewis, and a few friends I trust, like Bryon and Amelia. But… could you keep that to yourself?"

"It's an amazing account of God's love and healing. Look how it spoke to Ma."

Tension pulled across his shoulders. He pressed them back against the seat. "Richmond society wouldn't understand. Their snobbery would never allow a mere orphan to rise up and become educated enough to run the establishment. If people knew my roots, giving would decrease, and it would negatively affect the orphanage."

"So how did you manage to achieve what you have?"

"I owe it all to Mrs. Preston. She could see something in me I couldn't see in myself. And when I turned my life around, she took me under her wing doing something fairly unconventional."

Her eyebrows raised in question.

His nerves corded tighter. He would tell her the rest of the story, come what may. He wanted no secrets between them. "We had to change my name from Matthew Wheaton to Matthew Weston in order to create a new life. I lived with the Prestons for four years as a distant relative of theirs who came to the big city for education. I received the best tutors and had a real aptitude for numbers. I learned how to act and present as a man born into privilege. It's the only reason I have the job I do today."

"That's quite the story. I'll for sure keep that to myself. It's just sad that we live in a world that is so bent on creating all these different classes when we're all God's children."

"So, it doesn't matter to you that I'm a mere orphan with no lineage to speak of?"

"Of course not, Matthew. How could you even think that would matter to me? I'm no more than a farm girl myself."

"But you have aristocratic lines. Your grandparents—"

"Are people like you and me."

His shoulders lowered, and he relaxed into his seat. "True. And now you've become one of my chosen few whom I've trusted with the deepest part of my story." He squeezed her hand. She slowly removed it from his grip.

"Which is what I've wanted to talk to you about. We've become too familiar with each other. Well…with the travel, the danger, then that amazing experience with Ma, not to mention Pa pushing us together. I want to apologize if I've stepped over the line of propriety."

What could he say to that? Everything she mentioned had

brought them closer. He had entertained hope she was beginning to feel as he did. "No need to apologize."

"Friends?" She cocked her head at a delightful tilt.

It took every bit of willpower he had to brush off what he really felt as no more than friendship. "Friends."

"And Matthew, I could never have done this trip without you. I thank you from..." She smiled sweetly and raised one hand to her heart.

"You're welcome."

"We had such a good working relationship, and I want nothing to jeopardize that."

"Nothing will."

"So, when we get home, things will be back to normal?"

He didn't want to answer. Why should he answer when everything within him wanted more, much more than *normal*? He looked straight ahead ignoring her question.

"Matthew?"

"I'm tired. Wake me when we roll into Richmond." He slouched, extended his long legs under the seat in front of him, and pulled his hat low on his head. He closed his eyes.

"I will," she said.

Another lie averted. But how long would he be able to continue pretending he didn't feel the crazy heart-stopping sensation he felt in her presence? And now that he had spilled his story, what was hers? Why was she so dead set against marriage when her parents clearly emulated a true love story? It made no sense.

~

*G*racie usually thrust herself fully into whatever was expected of her, but this ball preparation was her least favorite task. She had to meet Mrs. Preston, Eliza Whittle, and Dorothy Greenbrier that afternoon for a meeting on that fundraising project, and Myrtle, Matilda, and Margot were due any minute for the orphanage monthly inspection. She loved them, but that would take up most of the morning. To them it was a social outing. To her, it was time away from the children who needed her.

She rounded the corner swiftly and ran smack into Max.

He steadied her with his hands on her arms. "Didn't think you cared." He laughed but did not step back.

They had a peaceful truce and a good working relationship, but he still flirted. "Sorry, Max. So much on the agenda today that I'm not even watching where I'm going."

"Don't be sorry. The pleasure was all mine." He let go of her arms. "Let me know if the feeling is ever mutual."

"Max, you know—"

"I know. I know." He put up both hands. "But you can't blame a guy for trying."

She hated how his teasing had that element of truth…of longing. "Got to go. Don't forget the three Hampshire sisters will be here soon for the inspection, and I'll be tied up for the rest of the morning."

Max groaned. "Oh, yeah. I better double-check the boy's quarters. Forgot to read them the riot act this morning."

"Go. They'll be here soon."

Max shot off in the opposite direction, and Gracie headed down the hall to Matthew's office for a quick question.

She knocked on the open door and entered at the same time. He looked up and back down again without saying a word, as if she were an irritant. Ever since they returned from her parents', he had been quite distant. Rude almost. She sent a smile to warm his icy greeting. "Are you busy?"

"I'm always busy."

"I meant, do you have time for a quick question. I need the paperwork on that new girl, Emma. She's not adjusting very well, and I want to read whatever history we have on her."

He didn't look up but swiveled his chair to the cabinets behind him. Thumbing through a few files, he pulled one out, slid back to his position, and held the file out with his head back down on his ledgers. "There's not much on her. They found her alone in an abandoned shack down by the river."

She moved closer to take the file. "Are we all right, Matthew? Have I done something—"

"We're fine. Just have a lot to do."

Gracie took the file and walked toward the door. As she stepped out into the hall, she looked back. He was staring at her. His face held a peculiar expression. Sad? Disappointed? She could not be sure. He immediately focused back down on his work. She wanted to ask, but ask what? Instead, she hurried away. She had too much on her plate to worry about Matthew's odd behavior.

Gracie had no sooner returned to her desk in the girl's house and opened Emma's file when the three sisters walked in.

"Good morning."

"Good morning."

"Good morning."

Gracie put down the file and stood. She pasted on a smile and made her voice sound welcoming. "Come in, ladies. We'll get right at it because I have a meeting this afternoon as well, and the more time I'm tied up, the less time I have with the children."

"Well, good thing I'm not Eliza Whittle, or I'd be right put out," Myrtle said.

Matilda laughed. "Now, that was a no-nonsense approach, wasn't it, sisters? I think the girl is busy."

"Busy! Why, I do declare. If there's anyone who appreciates busy, it's us." Margot waved her handkerchief. Three heads nodded.

"What do you have on the agenda this afternoon?" Matilda asked.

"That meeting for the Christmas Ball Charity." Gracie rolled her eyes. "Not my favorite thing."

Myrtle twittered. "Let's go easy on the girl today. She'll need energy to deal with Eliza." The three of them laughed like a tea party of magpies.

"Indeed," Matilda said.

"We most certainly will." Margot clapped her hands. "We best get started."

Gracie shuffled them out of the office. "Let's check the sleeping area first." She motioned up the stairs to the girls' bedrooms. Following, she climbed the steps and eased out a heavy sigh. Why did the administration part of this job feel like such a waste of time? If not for people like the three Hampshire sisters, who gave freely of their time, this orphanage would be a whole lot worse off. *Lord, help me to be charitable and patient.*

"Good. Good," Margot poked her head this way and that.

The sisters moved through the two large bedrooms on both sides of the hall.

"All looks neat and tidy." Matilda nodded. "Just the way we like it."

"You're doing a fine job," Myrtle encouraged.

They were about to head back down the stairs when a sobbing sound came from one of the closets. They all stopped, and Gracie headed in that direction. She opened the door to find little Emma on the floor with her knees scrunched up to her body. Her hands covered her downcast head.

Gracie kneeled to her level. "Emma, darling. What is it?"

Emma's head lifted for a brief moment. Dark brown eyes filled with tears swallowed her face. They smoldered beneath thick lashes. In contrast, her hair, as pale as a field of wheat, framed her face in a riot of curls. Her head went back down between her knees.

Gracie looked behind her to see three heads poking into the closet. No wonder Emma wasn't talking. She stood and motioned to the door. Out in the hall, the three ladies gathered around. "Do you think you could go on with the inspection without me for a bit? I have a feeling this is important. Emma is fairly new and not adjusting well."

All three heads nodded.

"We'll be praying," Myrtle whispered.

"In fact, we'll go down to your office and do that promptly," Matilda said.

"That we will," Margot added. They turned and headed for the steps.

Gracie moved back to the closet and slid down to the floor just outside the door. She found if she joined the children where they were, they were much more receptive.

"Can you tell me what's troubling you, Emma? I'd like to help." She kept her voice soft and low.

Emma lifted her head to take a peek. Her cherubic cheeks were wet from tears, with her little bow mouth turned down. Could there be a more angelic looking child?

"You can tell me," Gracie invited.

"I miss my mama."

Gracie opened her arms wide, and little Emma scooted onto her lap. Gracie cuddled her close, rocking her until the sobbing subsided. She ran her hands up and down the little girl's back until her tiny body stopped shaking.

Gracie pulled back and raised Emma's chin with one finger. "I'm so sorry you lost your mama, Emma, but we're here to help, and we love you."

"You're not mad?"

"Why would I be mad at you?"

"I didn't listen. I hid in the closet."

"We would've been so worried if we couldn't find you, that's for sure. It's never a good idea to hide, but this is all so new. And I'm sure a bit scary."

Emma nodded.

"Do you think you can join the others now?"

Emma's head bobbed up and down. She stuck her thumb in her mouth.

"How old are you?"

Emma held up five fingers. She was too old to be still sucking her thumb, but kids with a whole lot of trauma found ways to soothe themselves. Gracie knew that over time, when Emma started to feel at home, she'd outgrow that. But for now, she'd have to read that file, get acquainted with her history, and make sure the other kids didn't tease her.

"How about we dry those tears?" She took a handkerchief from her pocket and gently cleaned the child's face before planting a kiss on her forehead.

A shaky smile peeked up as Emma lifted her full head of curls.

Gracie stood. When she held out her hand, Emma's small fingers folded into hers, and Gracie's heart lurched.

She was about to lose her mama after a lifetime of love. Poor sweet Emma, losing her mama so early in life… And where was Emma's father? Her story made Gracie's heart squeeze so tightly that she literally hurt.

But to have the privilege of bringing love into Emma's hurting soul? Well, this was what she lived for. These kids were everything to her. Rosina came to mind, and the promise Gracie had made to make a difference in this hurting world. Now she was doing it. She should feel fulfilled, yet deep inside, loneliness gnawed.

And why did Matthew keep filtering in? She could not eradicate memories of their more relaxed interaction, laughing with her pa, praying with her ma, him holding her while she slept until his limbs went numb. Why did those thoughts stir her as if they were calling her to a life she had not yet envisioned?

Truth be told Matthew was becoming the very distraction she had promised herself she would never allow.

CHAPTER 13

*G*racie picked up her cup of tea and sipped it slowly. She looked around Mrs. Preston's opulent parlor. She had tried to arrange the meeting in her office at the orphanage, but because it was just the four women, Mrs. Preston had pressed to have it in her home. Gracie could hardly make a fuss.

"Now, we expect the orphanage staff to lead the charge in drumming up volunteers," said Eliza Whittle. "After all, we can't do everything, and money doesn't grow on trees. Isn't that so, Melinda?" She had a hard edge to her voice.

In contrast, Melinda's answer was soft and gentle. "I think what Eliza is trying to say is that there's a lot of work in order to ensure this ball is the talk of the Christmas season. And we dare not disappoint, as we need to draw the crowd with the money in their pockets, year after year."

Gracie was just about out of steam for the day. The episode with Emma, and then trying to get the three sisters out the door, had exhausted her. She cared not a whit about dancing and balls and ensuring the who's who of society had a lovely evening so they would open their wallets. But she cared about the orphanage, and the Christmas ball paid for many of the services throughout the year. Somehow, she'd have to muster up the energy to do her part. "What would you like me to do?"

"Marianna knew her role. Can't you just confer with her rather than waste our valuable time?" Eliza lifted her head and jutted her chin. "Goodness, these young people nowadays, so inept."

Gracie bit down on her lip. That kind of criticism was harsh when everyone at the orphanage worked so hard. If these ladies had half the responsibility, they would crumble under the pressure. Their only concern was a Christmas ball. She almost spilled out a heated rebuttal, then remembered what the end goal was…help for the children. The more donations raised, the more children she could get off the street.

"I have pen and paper in hand. If you'd be so kind as to give me the outline of what you expect, I'd sure appreciate it. I'd rather not bother Marianna, as she's not been well."

Melinda Preston and Dorothy Greenbrier nodded, but Eliza looked down her nose with disgust.

"And just think, by next year I'll be a whiz at this." Gracie kept a lightness in her voice.

"We need enough volunteers to set up and clean up, do the decorating, and serve the food," Melinda said. "Months ago, I booked the hall, the caterer, and the musicians, and I'll make sure that all this follows through without a hitch. Eliza, if you don't mind doing what you did last year and overseeing the guest list and tickets at the door, and Dorothy, if you're still all right with handling the donations and processing the money, then we're set?"

Both ladies agreed.

"How many volunteers would a ball this size need? I really have no experience in organizing anything of the sort." Gracie hated that her voice trembled.

Eliza's eyebrows shot up. "So, you never helped your mother

host—"

"I grew up in the country. The only gathering that even remotely resembles what you're talking about—and on a much smaller scale—is my older sister's yearly Christmas gala. I would pitch in and help, but I organized nothing."

Eliza sat up in her chair, her back ramrod straight. "You don't say. A country bumpkin on our hands. This is going to be a disaster. At least Marianna came from some breeding. She knew what needed to be done." She turned to face Mrs. Preston. "Who, dare say, is going to be the face of the organization? How is this girl going to fill Marianna's shoes?"

"We'll give her a chance, now won't we?" Mrs. Preston said. "Look at all she's done for the children."

It took all Gracie had to take a sip of tea as if she was not fazed. "I can learn most anything—"

Eliza huffed. "Culture and breeding take a lifetime to learn. One does not just step into gentility. And why in heaven's name was this not brought to our attention sooner?"

"I went to visit my dying mother. Remember?" Gracie could not hold back the bite in her voice.

"Now, now, Eliza. Calm yourself," Dorothy said. "You do have a penchant for the dramatics. Gracie is a hard-working, intelligent young woman who will do just fine given a little coaching, and I'll offer my help." She turned to Gracie and patted her hand. "You ask me whatever questions you need, my dear. I'm at your disposal."

Gracie let out a breath of air. "Thank you, Dorothy."

The older woman nodded her gray head of upswept hair. She leaned close. "Never mind Eliza. We'll talk to Reverend Peterkin. He's wonderful at drumming up volunteers from within the church, and I'll coach you on how to present at the ball."

Eliza had a grim set to her lips. "Well, if you have the time to coddle, be my guest. I sure don't."

"Good then. That's settled," Mrs. Preston said. "We shall meet every week for the next three weeks until the ball to share updates and solve problems." She rose gracefully from the chair signifying the meeting was over.

Gracie was only too glad. "I best be on my way." She set her cup down ever so delicately. "There is much more to do before my day is done. Thank you for your hospitality, Mrs. Preston." She stood and dipped her head in gratitude.

"Do say hello to your grandmother for me," Melinda said.

Gracie smiled, but her insides churned. She had signed up to help with the children, not put on charity balls. Why was a life dedicated to serving the Lord and the children so much more complicated than she'd imagined?

Please God, help me.

~

"Why that obnoxious biddy." Grandmother stabbed her fork into a piece of chicken. "Eliza Whittle has met her match." She lifted her fork with the meat on the end and pointed it at Gracie. "If you're short of help, I'll hire whoever you need and pay their wages. This will be the best Christmas ball this city has ever seen, and I'll see to it." She popped the food in her mouth.

Gracie shook her head. "I was only telling you because I need your advice. I don't want to fall flat on my face and give Matthew a good reason to send me packing."

"I thought you and Matthew were on good terms?"

"I thought so, too, but he's been distant ever since we returned from the valley. Like he's angry with me about something. He barely says two words to me in a day. I'm waiting for…well I don't know what I'm waiting for. The bad news, I guess." Gracie pushed her food around on her plate. Just the thought of not measuring up and Matthew being disappointed in her made her lose her appetite.

"Sounds like unrequited love, if you ask me."

"What? No. You have that all wrong. This has nothing to do with love." But Gracie's heart kicked up speed. Could Matthew have feelings for her? How would she respond if he did? The thought brought a smile she had to stifle. For the first time in her life, the possibility did not bring dread but a bubble of excitement.

See this was what she meant by distractions that lapped up her energy.

"Are you sure?" Grandmother asked.

"I'm sure." Gracie was not going to give Grandmother an opportunity to run away with that idea. She would dissect her feelings in private.

"So, there was no discussion during your trip about keeping things professional or just being friends?"

"No. We've never crossed that line. Things got a little too familiar back home because Pa kept trying to throw us together, but I apologized for that."

"I knew it." Grandmother clapped her hands in glee. "He's ignoring you to stem off his feelings for you."

"That is not possible. Matthew is professional and respectful and—"

"So professional and respectful men can't fall in love?"

"Grandmother, I will not discuss this. Can we please get back to the problem at hand?"

"Pff." Grandmother waved her hand. "Just when the conversation was getting interesting. All right, child, we'll go over what you need to organize, but rest assured, this ball will be a raging success because my granddaughter is involved. And the best part"—she clapped her hands—"we get to go shopping for the most stunning dress of the Christmas season for you."

"No. I don't even want to attend, but apparently it's a must… to show the face of the orphanage to the people."

"And what a lovely face you have, my dear. You shall dazzle the money right out of their greedy little hands."

"That's not what it means."

"Oh, that's exactly what it means. You should've seen Marianna work that crowd. She had everyone from the oldest to the youngest opening up their pocketbooks."

A spike of anxiety scuttled up Gracie's spine. "Great. Now you've terrified me. The thought of trying to finagle money out of people scares me to death."

"Your technique will not be Marianna's. You will not have to speak a word, that'll be Matthew's role. But you will wear the dress I purchase, and you will dance." Her graying blue eyes twinkled with mischief. "And then, we shall see if your Matthew has a thing for you or not. I'll be watching his face as you twirl with the men who will be eating out of your hand. You do know how to dance, don't you?"

If there was one thing that came naturally to Gracie, it was dancing. She picked up every dance by just watching the steps. Her body instinctively felt the rhythm. "And if I don't?"

"Then we shall add dancing lessons to your schedule directly."

Gracie groaned. "I thought you were on my side."

She chuckled. "Oh, but I am. Remember Eliza Whittle's condescending country bumpkin remark, and you'll shine."

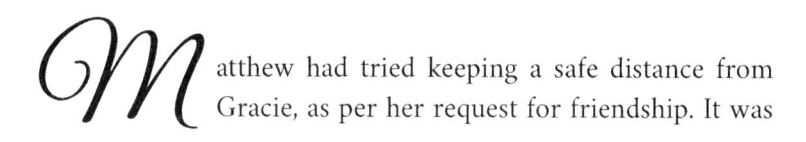

◈

Matthew had tried keeping a safe distance from Gracie, as per her request for friendship. It was not working. The constant ache he felt in trying to remain professional was killing him. Every time she showed up, he lost a good hour of work after she was gone for lack of concentration. When would this abate? When would she feel even a smidgeon of what he felt for her?

A short rap on his closed office door snapped his attention up. "Come in."

Of course, it had to be Gracie who walked in. He was already stewing about her. A bead of perspiration trickled down his back.

"Should we go over the plan for the ball this weekend?"

"What plan?"

"Well, the ladies said that you and I are the face of the orphanage, and we're supposed to make the rounds talking to people…trying to get them to donate. What exactly does that look like? I'm not much for that kind of thing."

"You and me both. Marianna used to be so good at that."

Grace looked pale, almost afraid, which was unusual for her bubbly personality. Her hands fiddled with the pleats in her skirt.

"Sit." He gestured at the chair. Now why was he encouraging her to stay? He had not done that since they'd gotten back.

She lit up at his invitation. The uncertainty in her face changed to a smile. "I'm so nervous."

"Why? You've never struck me as the shy type."

"I'm good one-on-one, but I hate a crowd, and I've never been to a high society ball."

"I struggle, too, when I'm thrust in those environments. But I'm learning to embrace the truth that we're all made in God's image, and He doesn't much care about class and status, even if we get caught up in it at times. He cares only about our relationship with Him. And a kind heart for the needy, like you have for the children."

She blushed a delightful pink and looked down at her hands.

Clearly, he had made her uncomfortable. He had better think fast. "Look how you're loving on Emma and bringing that little girl back to life."

"You noticed."

"Hard not to notice. She lights up whenever you're in the room."

"But I haven't seen you around very much."

Now what could he say? That he was spying from a distance? She need not know that detail. "Oh, I keep tabs on all the children."

"Where have you been? I thought you were avoiding me."

Her perception was a problem. "Just had a lot of work to catch up on after we got back." At least that wasn't a bold-faced lie.

She visibly relaxed into the chair. "Oh, good. I was so worried I had said or done something to upset you."

"No. No. Just busy."

"So, about the ball… Grandmother says all I have to do is dress pretty and look like I'm enjoying every person I dance with, and the donations will pour in. Dancing I can do, but please not the idle chit chat and asking for money."

The thought of her dancing the night away caused an instant knot of jealousy in his gut. "You don't mind dancing?" His voice came out raspy, and he coughed to clear the blockage.

"That I can do. Haven't had that much experience, but for whatever reason, dancing comes easily to me."

"Well good. Then you dance, and I'll converse. I've had some practice over the years, and I know how to fake it."

"That's wonderful." She slapped her knees and stood up with a snap. "Thanks for making this easy on me." She turned to go.

"On one condition."

She turned back around. "Yes?"

"You save the last dance for me."

"Oh, now that's a hardship." She laughed her way out the door.

Why did he just set himself up for more heartache? Memories of holding her on the train had kept him awake for days, and now he'd invited a dance. Had he gone crazy? If he had, it was a good kind of crazy. He could not wait for the weekend.

CHAPTER 14

Gracie stood before the mirror in her bedroom. "Is this all necessary?"

"But it is, my dear girl." Grandmother fiddled with a ribbon, ornamented with a string of pearls around Gracie's neck. The black velvet stood out against her milky white skin.

"Sarah. Come help out this old lady. My hands are not working well anymore."

Sarah tied the ribbon into place so that it hung down Gracie's back. "You look so beautiful," she said with a wistfulness in her voice. "Wish I could see you dance."

Gracie whirled around. "Would you like to come?"

"Oh my, but that is not done," Grandmother said.

Sarah's head dropped. "No, my lady. I don't need to come."

"Melinda Preston said I can invite whomever I please, and I'd like Sarah to come."

"Sarah, could you excuse us for a moment?" Grandmother waved toward the bedroom door.

Sarah nodded and scurried out.

"Gracie, my dear, Melinda did not mean the colored help."

"Whyever not? Delilah and Lizzie and numerous others come to Katherine's Christmas ball."

"But...that's the country, not the city. The class distinctions run deep in this town. Poor Sarah would be ostracized, and whatever would she wear? You must think of her before making rash decisions."

A spike of heat raced up Gracie's spine. How dare they be so uppity? Yet she knew what it felt like to be looked down upon. The likes of Eliza Whittle had done a good job of that. She would not want the same for Sarah. Sadness filled her soul. When would the world look beyond the color of one's skin, their social standing, what family and privilege they were born into? It all seemed so wrong. "I wish I didn't understand, but I do. Would it be all right to invite Sarah to come as a volunteer if she wants to? Then she could at least be there to see the extravaganza."

"Why, that's a splendid idea. Let's give her the choice." Grandmother went to the door and yelled down the hall.

Sarah was back in the room in a flash.

"If you like, you could see the ball," Gracie invited. "We have enough volunteers to give everyone some time off during the evening to watch, eat, and listen to the music."

Sarah's dark eyes sparkled with excitement. "I'd love that. Sounds mighty fine. I'll get to see you dance in that beautiful dress of yours."

"Then you shall come."

"Good, that's settled. Take a look at yourself, Gracie." Grandmother pointed into the mirror. "I told you this dress was perfect."

Gracie could not deny that the gown was stunning. Her dark hair, piled in a riotous array of curls on top of her head, contrasted beautifully with the creamy white of her bare shoulders. The soft rose-colored dress, with layer upon layer of ruffle and frill trimmed in black velvet, cascaded to the floor in a puddle of pink, which trailed behind her. The off-the-shoulder style with short, puffy sleeves accented the fullness of her figure. "Don't you think it's a little too low?" Gracie pulled at the top of her dress to cover more. It didn't help.

"Good heavens, no. What is with you Williams girls? You're stunningly beautiful, yet you'd rather hide it. In my day, if I had looked like you, I wouldn't have thought twice about showing off what the good Lord gave me."

"The Bible teaches modesty."

"Pff. God wouldn't make you that gorgeous and then tell you not to light up this dreary old world. Doesn't it say something about not hiding your light under a bushel?"

Gracie laughed. "You're stretching that message, Grandmother. It means not hiding the light of Jesus who lives inside us, not showing off this outward shell." She pointed at her body.

"Well, tonight you shall light up both. Talk all you want about how Jesus would have them help your poor little orphans, but mark my word, between your inner *and* outer beauty, the donations shall go through the roof."

Gracie gulped back a nervous giggle. All she wanted to do was get through the evening with a semblance of confidence until that last dance, when she could finally relax in the safety of Matthew's arms. He had a way of making her feel comfortable and protected.

She slipped on the gloves and touched a hand to the matching bow in her hair. "Are you sure—"

"That you're beautiful? Yes. Now off we go." Grandmother shooed her out of the bedroom.

∼

Matthew had never seen anyone more beautiful than Gracie dressed in all her finery, sweeping around the ballroom in yet another man's arms. The air squeezed out of his lungs. She made a vision of loveliness with those hauntingly beautiful mahogany eyes under sooty lashes, and glossy dark hair that picked up the reflection of light with every turn. Porcelain skin draped in a blaze of pink with an all too revealing neckline for his liking. If he were honest, he loved it, but the part he didn't like was that he was not the only one to notice. He should be moving throughout the crowd, talking up the good work of the orphanage. Instead he was watching the reaction she had on the men. His chest tightened. He fought against a shortness of breath.

The ballroom gleamed with sparkle, dazzling dresses, and the tantalizing smells of food to come, but Gracie gliding across the dance floor put his head on a swivel. It didn't matter who she danced with, she melted into his arms and complimented his lead. How did she do that—dance as if it took no effort, so fluid and natural? He had to think about every step. His frustration grew. He did not like the edginess nor jealous thoughts that filled his mind. *God, why'd you have me fall for the woman every eligible man in the room is falling for too?* His fists clenched.

"She is beautiful, isn't she?"

Matthew turned to see Francis Brunson at his side. "Yes, your granddaughter is truly the belle of the ball."

"So why aren't you out there, staking your claim?"

Was he an open book? "I-I'm not sure what you mean."

"You know exactly what I mean." She lifted her fan and waved it, laughter oozing from her gray blue eyes.

"All right. I'll play along. What if I were to tell you I'm madly in love with her?" He laughed to make it sound like the most ridiculous scenario.

"I'd say that most every man has fallen under her spell tonight, and you'd better not waste time. In the next few weeks, there'll be suitor after suitor coming to call."

Matthew's gut twisted into a knot. He had already been almost sick with jealousy…the way Gracie smiled so sweetly, and man after man gazing down, undressing her with their eyes. Was she that naïve? "Gracie's made it quite clear she's not interested in marriage. She's devoting her life to God and the children."

"Fiddlesticks." Francis waved her fan at him. "She's too young to know what she's interested in. But a strong man like you could remedy that confusion. Besides, last I checked, the Bible encourages marriage and procreation. Does it not?"

"I…ahh…can't speak for her, but I do agree."

"May I do you a special favor?" Her eyes sparkled with mischief.

He was interested now. No point in trying to deny how he felt. "Go on."

"As you know, Gracie is staying the weekend with me. I'm going to feel quite tired very soon and tell her that you'll bring her home, though I'd love nothing more than to see this evening to its end." She smiled up at Matthew and winked. "Don't waste the opportunity." Her laughter floated behind her. Though her steps were slow and measured, she gracefully walked away.

The evening continued in slow torture. He danced a number of dances. Talked until his head ached. And watched from the sidelines. Why did the men have to flock around Gracie? Was his species really that pathetic, driven only by beauty? At least he knew her. He'd taken time to learn the things that made her laugh, made her cry, made her get up in the morning. But then again, he had been attracted to her from the get-go as well. Hadn't he? He was no different from the rest.

The last dance could not come soon enough.

The three Hampshire sisters came flying his way. "Matthew."

"Matthew."

"Matthew."

"Did you hear?" Myrtle said.

"The great news." Matilda added.

He listened politely, knowing he could not get a word in edgewise even if he tried.

Margot cut in as if the conversation were choreographed. "Dorothy just confirmed, the donations this evening have never been higher, thanks to that girl right there." All three ladies looked at Gracie, who was whirling by on the arm of yet another man.

She waved, and they all waved back with smiles as wide as the ocean. Matthew wanted to scream, but he plastered on a fake grin.

"After every song, her dance partner beelines over to the donation table and opens his wallet—wide," Myrtle informed.

"'Tis true. And they're only too willing to sign up for monthly donations." Matilda clapped her hands. "We've never seen anything like it."

Margot leaned close. "Don't you wish we could hear what she's been saying? The poor dear must be exhausted dancing the night away, and yet look at that smile."

"And how gracefully she moves," Matilda said. "Get it? Grace…full." All three twittered and giggled like schoolgirls.

"There you go again, sister, making us laugh at your puns," Myrtle said.

"So, I get no credit for this fund raiser tonight?" Matthew forced a lightness into his voice.

Margot snorted. Matilda snickered. "With a beauty like her around? I dare say not. But we love you anyway," Myrtle said with a laugh.

Sophia was heading his way. His battered ego needed a boost. "Excuse me, ladies, but I have my own donation to work on." He nodded at the woman who'd seemed intent on slipping his ring on her finger.

He heard their cackling as he took Sophia by the hand. "Shall we?"

"We shall," she said with all too much eagerness.

Why couldn't he fall for her? She was educated, wealthy, and had the social standing that would elevate his reputation in the community to a whole new level. And surely he could convince her that his work at the orphanage was of utmost importance. He glanced down at her beautiful dress. "You look lovely tonight."

"Thank you, Matthew." She tucked in closer as they danced. "All for you," she whispered.

He gazed into her gorgeous blue eyes and felt…nothing. Not even a smidgeon of inner response. Gracie waltzed by in another gentleman's arms, and his heart kicked up speed as she smiled at him. How inconvenient.

At the end of the dance, he bowed and thanked Sophia, putting some distance between them.

"Would you like to catch a breath of fresh air out on the veranda?" Her arm linked back into the crook of his.

Had that been Gracie asking, he would've leaped at the chance. "Best I keep mingling."

Her pouty frown irritated him.

"Maybe later, then?"

What could he say to that? He was not about to encourage her. "This is the orphanage charity ball, after all, and I have to do my part."

Sophia's laughter tinkled like the sound of one too many wind chimes. "With all the attention she's getting"—she nodded in the direction of Gracie, whirling on the dance floor—"you could leave for the whole evening and no one would miss you—except me, of course."

He worked hard not to clench his teeth. "Please, excuse me." His voice sounded wooden even to his own ears. He turned and walked away.

"Matthew…" she called after him.

He ignored her as he headed to the men's dressing room. Once inside, he let out a deep breath and unclenched his fisted hands. A claustrophobic loneliness pressed in. This evening was going far too slowly. He took his time before re-entering the ballroom.

He pulled his watch from his pocket and fingered the heavy gold chain. The last dance would be soon. He could do this. A few more conversations, and he would have her in his arms.

He aimlessly walked the perimeter, smiling and nodding appropriately. At the start of each new song, his ear was tuned to the band's announcement. Ahh there it was, the announcement for the last dance.

Matthew's height made it easy to scour above the crowd. Where was she? He didn't want to miss one second. There, coming out of the ladies dressing room and heading his way. Three men stopped her, and she shook her head. Finally, she was standing in front of him.

"Would you be so kind as to whisk me out of here and take me home? I'm dead on my feet."

Matthew's stomach dropped into his nicely polished shoes. He had waited patiently all evening, and she wanted to go home. His heart skipped and skidded in erratic disappointment. Obviously, she felt nothing for him, or she would be longing for this moment as much as he was. Frozen in the weightiness of indecision, not wanting to surrender one moment with her that was rightfully his, he sighed. "You sure were popular."

"As were you. You danced a fair amount."

"Ahh, but not like the belle of the ball who made a promise and now is too tired to fulfill." He chuckled to hide his disappointment. "Come on." He took her hand. "In keeping with proper etiquette, we need to say our goodbyes to Melinda, the official host. Then I'll get you home."

"Glad you know all the rules of this uppity bunch. You're the best, Matthew." She squeezed his hand and rested her head on his shoulder for a brief second. "I knew you'd understand."

Understanding was not the word he would've used.

*S*ettled in Matthew's hired carriage, Gracie patted the seat beside her as Matthew entered. "I think I need your shoulder to lean on. I may be asleep before I get home."

He slid in beside her, and she lowered her head on his shoulder. The carriage lurched forward, and they were on their way.

His arm came around her, strong, warm, and protective. There was something about this man that felt different from all the rest, than all the men who had held her that night. Her insides fluttered with the movement of butterflies as she soaked in the closeness.

Suddenly, it felt too intimate, and she lifted her head and pulled away, leaving a respectable distance between them. Tiny prickles of awareness danced over every nerve ending. Why was she feeling this way?

She peeked up at him, and he held a look of disappointment…sadness even. She turned to the window and stared into the dark. The carriage came to a stop at a crossing, then lurched forward. His hand came out in front of her as her body pitched forward. He eased her back onto the seat.

"Thanks," she whispered.

His hand slid back and landed on top hers. "I think I'd better hold on. You're so tired, you may land up in a puddle on the carriage floor."

She nodded but was not sure what to do with the way his hand touching hers sent shivers skimming up her arm. She pulled her hand back and removed her gloves as an excuse to create distance. "Ahh nice to get these off, and it'll be even better to get out of this dress."

He laughed. "Not the thing you should say to a man, in a carriage, in the dark."

Her face flushed hot. "You'll have to excuse me. I'm so tired, I'm not thinking clearly."

"You're excused." His hand came out to hold hers again, but this time the contact was skin on skin. A sharp breath sucked the air out of her lungs. Never had she felt anything quite so exquisite in her whole life. His thumb caressing an unnerving path around and around the inside of her wrist. Her eyes flew up to his. Their gaze locked. What was happening? Why did she long to be closer, yet feel the urge to run at the same time? Her body instinctively leaned in, and his joined hers until she could feel his warm breath on her face.

"I'm going to do something I've wanted to do for a long time," he whispered. He lowered his head and brushed his lips across hers with aching tenderness.

Men had tried to kiss her before, but she had felt nothing. This time, her heartbeat quickened, a warm sensation curled in the pit of her stomach, and a ripple of delight ran a tremor from tip to toe. She pressed closer, and he deepened the kiss. She hadn't expected this…whatever it was, between them. All she knew is that she didn't want it to end. With tearing slowness, his mouth left hers.

Floating in a muddle of emotions, she hadn't realized the carriage had come to a stop in front of her grandmother's house. How long had they been stationary? She looked around confused, terrified of feeling so much. "I must go."

He lifted a hand to gently touch the side of her face. "You felt it, too, didn't you?"

Oh my goodness, did she feel it…whatever *it* was. She was exhilarated, excited, and scared at the depth of emotion. She had to get out of there before she begged him to kiss her again. She turned to the door, unlatched the handle, and almost fell out of the carriage, refusing to wait for him to help her.

"Gracie."

She heard him call her name, but she didn't turn around.

CHAPTER 15

"We need to talk."

Matthew looked up as Gracie walked into his office and slammed the door behind her. "You've ruined everything." She moved to his desk and glared down at him.

He leaned back in his chair. He'd been waiting for this for two weeks, but December had slipped uneventfully into January. She'd made a point of ignoring him, but he'd known that wouldn't last. It seemed, finally, today was the day. He aimed to find out why she was so opposed to marriage.

"Bothers you, doesn't it?"

"What bothers me?" She jutted out her chin.

"That you feel something you don't want to." He liked that she understood what he'd been fighting for months.

"I-I do—"

"So," he finished.

"We…you and I, we had a friendship—"

"We still do."

"I mean… I thought you were the one person—the one man I could trust."

"You can trust me."

"To not want more than friendship!" She spat out the words. "To not complicate my life."

"Your perfectly ordered life, where you tell God..." Were those tears filling her eyes? Now, what should he do? He had planned to push her into admitting that she had responded to his kiss, that she had felt something.

Wait.

That one word came into his spirit. A very inconvenient word.

"Where I tell God what?" A tear slipped down her cheek, and she sank into the chair across from him.

He could get up, go around that desk, and kiss her until she acknowledged the truth. But that one word...

Wait.

She was clearly not ready.

He kept his seat. "Can I ask you why you're so opposed to a deeper relationship with a man?"

"I told you, it would be a distraction to—"

"No. I mean where did this thinking begin. I want to understand how God led you to this decision." He could not tell her he'd been led to another conclusion, and that those conclusions were in direct conflict with each other.

"Rosina."

Her eyes stared blankly, as if she were in another place and time.

He waited, afraid that if he spoke one word, he would break the reverence of the moment. She was about to trust him with her story.

"I was twelve. Visiting my grandparents here in Richmond with my ma. We were out shopping with Grandmother, and she had just bought me a new dress—all frills and lace, in the latest of fashion. All I could think about was what I would look like wearing it to church when I got back home. We stepped out of the dress shop, and there she was, gazing into the store window with the most wistful look on her face. A ragamuffin, clothed in a tattered dress with stockings and shoes that had holes in them. I had never seen anyone so thin and in such need of a bath in all my life. Her arms and legs like mere sticks. Her paper-thin shawl hardly a deterrent to the blustery wind."

Tears slipped down Gracie's beautiful cheeks, and it took all Matthew had not to get up and pull her into his arms.

"Grandmother and Ma swept by, but I stopped. She jumped at the sound of my hello and blurted out, 'I never did anything wrong. I was only looking.' She seemed ready to dart, and my heart wrenched in a way that forever changed me. We didn't have street urchins back in the Shenandoah valley. Grandmother turned around and came back to grab my hand, but I pulled it free.

"Stupid me, all I could think about was how hungry she must be. We were headed for lunch, so I invited her. Grandmother gasped. Ma stood with her mouth open, and the girl, Rosina had nothing but fear in her eyes.

"Grandmother quickly opened her reticule and pulled out some coins. She pressed them into the girl's hand and she ran away. No words were spoken, but those coins clearly meant *take them and be off*. Grandmother then explained, on the way to the fancy hotel we visited for lunch, how street children would never be allowed in the establishment. I remember feeling furious."

Gracie popped up from the chair, her hands fisted as if some of that anger still lived. She made her way to the window and gazed out.

"So that's what led you to working with the children?" Matthew asked.

She shook her head. "There's way more."

Should he press for the rest of the story? That one word *wait* filtered into his spirit again.

"As only God could orchestrate, we came out of that hotel,

and there she was, sitting on the corner her hands stretched out, begging for money to feed her baby brother. She held a sickly child of about three in her arms. Nothing could have stopped me from going to her. I wanted to know her name. Where she lived. How I could help. Grandmother and Ma bustled after me, calling out, but I ignored them.

"I begged her to tell me her name, and she said it was Rosina. I was so naïve as to why this girl around my age would be on the street with her sick brother. My sheltered twelve-year-old brain couldn't comprehend. I asked her how I could help? One look in Ma and Grandmother's direction, and she said, 'you can't.'"

When I asked where she lived, her answer shocked me.

"'I live right here.' She pointed to the street, and I could not believe what I was hearing. Ma pulled at my hand. Her voice was stern, and I knew I'd better obey. In the carriage, I sobbed all the way back, completely inconsolable. It wasn't until my grandmother said that she could maybe talk to Bryon and Amelia about seeing if there was room in the orphanage for them that I stopped. I was relentless in the next few days until Ma agreed that I could go with Bryon and try and find Rosina and her brother. Best and worst day of my life."

Watching her pain, a knot twisted in Matthew's throat. The cruelty of the street he knew only too well, but to a sheltered girl, the realization must've been traumatic.

"We found Rosina in an entrance way shielding her brother from the pouring rain. When Bryon talked her into coming with us, I was so excited. That feeling of making a difference was euphoric. But it lasted only a moment. When she handed over her brother to Bryon's strong arms and we jumped in the carriage, I could tell something was terribly wrong. Bryon's face went white, and he did not speak all the way to the orphanage.

"Amelia was waiting to do an initial check. When she took the child from Bryon's arms, he shook his head."

Gracie's voice cracked. "Rosina's brother was dead."

The tears flowed freely now, her voice no more than a whisper. "I will never forget Rosina's wail. That day I made a promise to both Rosina and God that I would devote my life to helping these children."

He crossed the room and pulled her into his arms. She sobbed into his shoulder. Now was not the time to tell her that a childhood understanding of what it meant to help those children did not mean she could not marry. Holding her close was torture to his soul, along with that one word—*wait*—but it resonated with his soul.

He pulled back, and slowly released her from his arms. "I'm sorry, Gracie, for what happened the night of the ball." He wanted to promise that he would not kiss her again, but he could not.

She looked up at him with her doe-like eyes. "But you can't just change our whole relationship and say you're sorry."

"What would you have me do?"

"I don't know. Tell me why you jeopardized the special friendship we had."

He had to think fast. *Because I love you.* No, that wouldn't work. "Surely you've been kissed before." As pretty as she was, that had probably started at twelve.

"Of course, I have."

"It was a dance. You looked beautiful. I was feeling out of sorts."

"Out of sorts? Why?"

"Well, your popularity eclipsed my presence at the ball. It was as if I didn't exist. And...the truth? I was lonely."

"Lonely? But Matthew, you had women buzzing around you all night."

"I'm a twenty-six-year-old man who longs for something deeper. God is just taking His time..." He wanted to add *getting the right one to see she is the right one,* but he could not.

"Our friendship has been the best part of my life these past months," she said.

"And yours, mine." That much was true. But she had no idea how he really felt. How he read her every emotion. He knew what made her laugh and made her cry. He could list off her likes and dislikes. And the story she'd just told filled in a huge gap in his understanding of what made Gracie Williams tick.

Relief flooded into her expressive brown eyes, and sorrow into his soul. His wait was far from over.

"I'm sorry if my behavior jeopardized that. Friends?" He held out his hand.

She nodded as her fingers slid into his.

"What do you say we go join the kids for lunch?" He held out his arm. She linked hers into his, and they walked into the dining room hall with her believing they were no more than friends.

∽

JANUARY 1880

Gracie could not get Ma out of her head and prayers. The Christmas letter had been unsettling and the message clear. Time was short. She wondered how Jeanette was doing, ever the faithful helping hand. And Pa…how would he be managing? She longed to be with them…especially Ma.

She stood in the main house library, gazing out the window in a daze. Now what had she been doing? She'd best keep moving.

She entered the hallway as the door knocker sounded and motioned to Max to open it. "If it's another man from the ball, tell him that I'm working and do not take callers at the orphanage."

"If it is, that'll be the seventh one this week." Max snickered like he was enjoying her discomfort.

Drat the Christmas ball. It may have been a raging success according to the board, but it was a major inconvenience to her. "I'm sorry you have to manage this, but I dare not encourage them by showing up in person."

"It's amazing what one dance in Gracie Williams's arms can do." His tone held a sarcastic bite.

"Please Max. The board insisted I attend this Christmas ball and dance in order to encourage donations. If I had my way, I would've stayed home."

The door knocker sounded again.

"I know, I'm just teasing you. Seems you have no idea the impact you make on the male species."

"Trust me. I did not encourage them. When they said they would come calling, I told every one of them I was dedicated to God and the children only."

"Oh, that speech, I know it well."

"Max, I'm sorry—"

He held up his hand. "I'll go let the guy down gently." He walked off.

"What was that about?"

Gracie jumped at the sound of Matthew's voice behind her. She whirled around. "There has been a string of callers. I tell you, next year I'm not doing that stupid ball. I don't care what the board says."

"And I'll support you in that decision. I don't much like all these strange men on the premises."

Gracie's shoulders relaxed and she rubbed a hand behind her neck. "Good, because this is no fun. I don't go to social gatherings for this very reason. The distractions are unsettling. It's never pleasant to have to let someone down."

"I can imagine. I've had a few women who could not take no

for an answer. And it's not easy when you don't want to hurt their feelings."

"Exactly. And poor Max having to have to deal with this, but I'm glad they gravitate to the big house so I'm not answering the door."

"This too shall pass." Matthew squeezed her arm.

His touch caused her insides to roll and somersault. She smiled through the confusing reaction. If she wasn't wholly dedicated to God and the children, he was the one man who could tempt her to explore more. But she had made a promise, and she aimed to keep it.

She'd best get away before Matthew read her conflicting emotions.

~

Max's presentation to the board regarding the Orphan Train was going well. Matthew was impressed with how much work Max had put into gathering the information and how professionally he was communicating the details to the board.

"The Children's Aid Society has been doing this for how many years?" the board president, Carl Lewis, asked.

"Since 1854, twenty-six years," Max said.

"Twenty-six years of successfully placing the orphans from New York into rural areas in the West via the train, and I'm only hearing of this now?"

"Not just New York, but Boston and other east coast cities where too many orphans live on the streets and the orphanages can't keep up."

"The same problem we have in this city," Matthew added. "You see the little ragamuffins everywhere. Eating out of garbage cans, sleeping in doorways. The orphanage is filled to capacity, and the need is not met. There are still too many of them living on our streets, hawking newspapers, selling rags or matches, whatever they can find to eke out a living. Others are begging or stealing in order to eat. That's no life for a child."

Heads nodded.

"No life," Myrtle said.

"So sad," Matilda added.

"We have to do everything within our power to help." Margot looked at her sisters, and all three heads simultaneously bobbed.

Max flipped through his papers. "The Catholic Sisters in New York started the New York Foundling Hospital about ten years ago and have adopted Charles Loring Brace's idea. They, too, are sending children West in what they call Mercy Trains."

"So, if we join this ministry, we'll be responsible for exactly what expenditures?" Bryon asked.

"We can't afford any surprises where future financial needs cannot be met," Edwin added.

Matthew looked at Max and nodded. "Go ahead. You've done all the research."

He leafed through to find the correct page. "Children's Aid Society asks that we supply all traveling expenses and food along the way. Each child must have a sturdy pair of shoes, a serviceable cap, a good set of clothing, including a thick overcoat, and a recent haircut. Matthew has helped me work out the projected cost per child including the train fare. It comes to about ten dollars per child, a little more for those we take right off the streets who will have no clothing to speak of." He passed around a paper with the itemized expenses.

"What do you mean, those right off the streets?" Reverend Peterkin asked.

"We've decided to take ten children directly from the orphanage," Matthew said. "And ten who have been waiting to be placed, who are currently living on the street and coming to our soup kitchen for the supper meal."

"So that's twenty kids, a minimum of two hundred dollars." Mr. Lewis whistled through his teeth.

"We also have to send two agents out with the children for placement, preferably one woman for the girls and one man for the boys, so a bit more cost there."

"Where exactly are you proposing these children be taken? Not that I mind getting some of those urchins off our streets." Eliza waved her nose in front of her face. "They always have their grubby hands out begging." Her body gave a decided shiver.

"Since I visited New York last fall to talk to the society directly, we've been writing back and forth at what this would look like," Max said. "They've saturated the towns along the Pacific Railroad in Ohio and had great success in finding farming communities and cities alike where the children are well-fed, learning trades, and are finally part of a family that loves them. But because we won't be leaving from a northeastern city where jumping on the transcontinental train takes the children west, we have a new route in mind—Southern Ohio. The Society has had requests from families in that area but no sponsor to take it on."

"Pass the map around." Matthew prayed the board would be receptive. All he could think about were the children he had to turn away from the orphanage every day because there was not room. It grieved him greatly. This plan would make room.

Max pulled out his map and offered it to Mr. Lewis. "In short, we'll take the C&O Railway from Richmond to Huntington, West Virginia. From there, a forty-mile steamboat ride up the Ohio River to Gallipolis, and then board another train. From that point, finding the children homes at prearranged towns begins, until there are no children left. The furthest point north will be Marion, Ohio, if we have to go that far."

"But how is this safe?" Dorothy asked. "How do we know the families are good people?"

"The Children's Aid Society does the leg work. They've prearranged a committee in each town and will advertise the date of our arrival. This committee preprocesses the approval of all applicants. All the heavy lifting has been done." Max smiled proudly at the board members.

"Any ongoing responsibility after that placement?" Mr. Lewis asked.

"We'd be responsible for yearly check-ins," said Matthew, "which would mean a trip back. Also, we have to send in a yearly report to the Children's Aid Society."

Mr. Lewis scratched his bald head. "And if these placements are unsuccessful?"

"We'd be responsible to find new homes or take them back to the orphanage. In a case like that, the local sheriff would come along and assist in enforcing the agreement which the parent's signed, allowing the orphanage full authority to take the children back if needed."

"Who are you proposing would be the agents in this case?" Melinda Preston asked.

Matthew said, "Gracie and I are highly invested in our children's lives, and we—"

"You are suggesting that the both of you leave, yet again?" Mr. Lewis's brows raised.

This battle Matthew had to win. There was no way he wanted to leave Gracie behind. "It would be far different from the last time. We're better equipped for both of us to leave. Max here is biting at the bit to take on more responsibility. And as you can see by the work he put into this report, he is more than capable. And Gracie has an assistant who can—"

"Where is Gracie tonight?" Reverend Peterkin asked. "I always appreciate her insight."

"Max is with me this evening, and she felt it better that one of us remain on site. And as I was saying, we have two very capable up-and-coming leaders. Max here, and Ava, who has been with us a while, and we'd be taking ten of the children from the orphanage with us. It's a good way to ease others into management so we always have a backup without overwhelming them. Right Max?" Matthew clapped his shoulder.

"Yes. Absolutely." Max gave the group a charming smile.

"Orphan Train. Who would've ever thought of that?" Reverend Peterkin shook his head. "I wasn't convinced until you told me there would be yearly check-ups on these homes. And honestly, I fear a year in between is too long. What if one of the placements doesn't work out, or worse yet, is abusive? At least here in the orphanage, these kids are guaranteed good care."

"But there are so many more kids still on the streets," Amelia said. "I can't help myself, but I want to take all of them home. If this is a success, we could make a significant difference over time to the orphan problem on our streets."

"I think we have to trust the statistics, Reverend," Matthew said. "The Children's Aid Society says they have an eighty-seven percent success rate."

"There you go." Reverend Peterkin threw up his hands. "Thirteen kids out of every hundred are still at risk."

"I would argue that they are at far less risk than on the streets," Melinda Preston said. "But what if we checked after six months? Since we're paying for this out of our own funds, surely we can check more often if we want to."

"Absolutely." Matthew couldn't agree more. "I would feel better about doing a check sooner, for the children's sake." The thought of Gracie and him being thrown together into close quarters more often was also no hardship to him.

Mr. Lewis held up one hand. "Not so fast. We'll have to go over our financial obligations already in place and see if adding this to our budget is possible. At our next meeting, we'll have the financials, and the board can take a vote."

"In the meantime, is it all right if Gracie and I strategize over which children to take? Because if this is a go, we need to be ready to move quickly."

"Why?" Mr. Lewis knit his brows together.

Matthew took a deep breath. He knew Mr. Lewis, and if he had his way, he'd take a year to decide and then another to implement. "It's January, and if we convene next month to decide, and the Children's Aid Society needs at least two months to advertise and organize our stops along the way, that pushes us to leaving in early April."

"So?" Mr. Lewis questioned.

"I think we should take a vote on the idea tonight, because I'd like to leave no later than mid-March since everyone seems to be more comfortable with a six-month check-up. To beat the cold weather, we'd have to do that no later than mid-September."

Melinda Preston and Dorothy nodded.

"You're brilliant." Margot clapped her hands.

"So sensible." Myrtle said.

"Thinking so far ahead. What would we do without you?" Matilda added.

"I think we all agree the need is great." Amelia said. "So, to save time, I agree with Matthew, let's take that vote right now. If we agree on this ministry, then the finances can be scrutinized next week, and if we can afford to do this, it will leave more time for the Children's Aid Society to make their arrangements."

"All right, ladies." Mr. Lewis threw up both hands. "I know when I'm beat."

"Well, I tend to agree with you, Mr. Lewis." Eliza looked down her nose at the group.

"That's because you're tighter than a jack-in-the box ready to spring." Dorothy laughed.

"Well, I never," Eliza huffed.

Dorothy wasn't one bit sorry. "Come on. You just told me

last week you wanted to work on being more generous and to keep you accountable."

"That was private." She scowled at Dorothy.

Bryon took the lead. "Ladies and gentlemen, let's vote. If we can afford this new ministry to get more children off the streets... Raise your hand if you are in agreement with the Orphan Train project."

Of the ladies, only Eliza kept her fingers folded together on the table. The men took their time, but one by one, their hands lifted. Eliza's hand was last to join the unanimous vote.

Matthew's heart jolted with joy! He couldn't wait to tell Gracie.

CHAPTER 16

"Stop whining, Emma." Ava's voice was sharp. "It's breakfast, and I don't have time for your dramatics."

Gracie stopped short just outside the girls' bedroom, listening from the hall. She had noticed Emma's absence and thought to check the closet yet again. The poor girl was traumatized. With so little history on her, they had no idea what she had already suffered.

"Come here this instant. You may get away with being spoiled and coddled by Gracie, but not with me."

Emma sniffled, and Gracie's heart squeezed tight. The child was crying. Instinct told her to step in, but she wanted to see how Ava responded when she thought Gracie was not around. Ava had been borderline insubordinate with her from the get-go but a model of perfection in Matthew's presence.

"Get out of your nightwear immediately. You have ten seconds to get your clothes on or else."

Gracie gasped. Ava did not have to speak so harshly to poor Emma. These children had all suffered enough, and there were many creative ways to administer discipline that didn't involve threatening a child.

"Ten, nine, eight..." Ava's voice held a harsh unyielding tone. Emma was sobbing.

"One. You're lucky that you made it, and if I find you hiding in that closet one more time and have to leave the other children to come looking for you, I won't be so kind. Now tie up your shoes and stop your crying or I'll give you something to cry about."

"I... I can't. I have a knot." Emma's small voice was barely above a whisper.

"For crying out loud, give me that shoe and hurry up about it."

Gracie rounded the corner to see Emma scrambling to get at her shoe, Ava hunched over her with an angry scowl.

"That will be all, Ava. Go down to the dining hall immediately and tend to the other children."

Ava snapped up. "I was merely helping Emma with her shoes."

"Go." Gracie pointed to the bedroom door. "And you can rest assured there will be further discussion regarding what just happened here."

Ava's eyes grew large and then narrowed. "Nothing happened."

"I've been standing outside this bedroom door for five minutes."

Ava's face blanched, and she hurried from the room.

Gracie knelt down and opened her arms. "Come, Emma, darling. I can tell you need a hug."

Emma ran into her arms, sobbing on her shoulder.

"It's all right, sweetheart." She let the child cry and then pried her arms from around her neck. The child's dark brown eyes glittered with tears. "Sit here on my lap, and I'll help you with your shoes." Gracie cuddled the child, wondering how anyone could be so harsh, especially with a child who'd clearly suffered abuse.

∽

"*B*ut Matthew, Ava threatened Emma and made her cry," Gracie said.

Matthew let out a heavy sigh. He was trying to have all in place for the departure of the Orphan Train in less than a month, and they needed Ava. But they also needed to trust her.

"We'll give her a fair opportunity to tell us what happened before you mention what you overheard."

"Why are you so lenient with her?"

"I'm not lenient. I've observed her from afar very carefully, and she's been nothing but kind to the children."

"Yes, anywhere she knows you may crop up, that is true. And for the most part, she is good with the children. But she has a few I can tell rub her the wrong way, and Emma is one."

"Oh, come on, Gracie, be honest. We all have our favorites." He thought of Henry. He loved that kid, his intelligence, his sense of humor, and his mischievous but loveable spunk.

"I do not." Gracie's eyes flashed with indignation. She fidgeted with the folds in her dress. A sure sign she was agitated.

"Henry is one of mine, and Emma is clearly yours."

"I merely feel for what she may have already suffered, and don't want to add to it."

"You also give her preferential treatment."

"How?" Gracie sat in her chair with her back starched straight.

Matthew tapped his pen against the ledger he should be working on. He was way behind on his accounting. This was the last thing he needed.

"Well, for example, Emma receives way more hugs in a day from you."

"She's affectionate, and loveable, and ohhh, all right, she gets me right here." Gracie touched her heart and relaxed.

"Good. Now that we can both acknowledge we're less than

perfect in our approach, we'll handle this situation with the same amount of grace we need ourselves. Go get Ava."

Gracie stood and headed for the door. She turned before exiting. "I hope you'll consider the possibility that Ava is one person when you're around, and quite another when you're not. I've tried not to complain, but she questions everything I tell her."

"She doesn't follow your instructions?"

"She does, but reluctantly at best. Everything is a battle, and I'm exhausted. The children are easier to work with than her."

"She's most agreeable with whatever I suggest."

"That's exactly my point." She opened the door with more force than needed. "I'll be right back."

If Matthew were honest, he'd admit that he'd seen Ava's eyes lingering on him in a way that made him uncomfortable, and she did find every opportunity to interrupt his work. Though he had made it clear she was to take up her questions with Gracie, she refused to do that. But it was halfway through February, and he'd hoped to be on the train in a month—with Gracie. They didn't have time to hire and train someone else up to the level of proficiency needed in so short a time. And to find someone as qualified who'd work for what they could afford to pay would be almost impossible.

He bent his head down to the ledgers but couldn't concentrate. From the beginning, trouble had brewed between those two. He did not need it erupting now. There was an unspoken competition. If only it were for his love, he could put Gracie at ease and marry her on the spot, putting an end to Ava's obvious interest in him.

The ladies walked in.

"Have a seat." He waved his hand at the two empty chairs.

Ava slid into the chair closest to him with a generous smile. Gracie wore her stern, no-nonsense face. *Oh God, give me wisdom. Help me to put my agenda aside and deal with this objectively.*

"Ava, it has been brought to my attention that there was a concerning incident with Emma this morning. Before we begin discussing it, we'd like to give you the opportunity to give us your thoughts on the matter, wouldn't we, Gracie?"

Gracie nodded. But her chin was jutted out and her arms crossed. Not a great start.

"Well, I noticed that poor Emma was missing once again. Leaving all the other children behind put me on edge, and I admit I was pressing her to dress quickly."

"Did you threaten her in any way?"

"Of course not. I've never laid a hand on any child here."

Gracie's brows flew up like two startled birds. "So, telling her you'd give her something to cry about? That was not a threat?"

"Oh that, pff." Ava waved her hand in the air. "I would never follow through, but someone has to deal with her spoiled behavior. Discipline is certainly not coming from you. And her hiding in the closet has got to stop."

"We do not advocate threatening violence to make children adhere to the rules," Gracie said.

"I was not threatening—"

"Ladies. Ladies." Matthew held up his hands. They both turned his way. "Can we not find enough grace and love to talk this out civilly? We preach to the children all day about getting along and using respectful conversation in order to solve problems. Surely we can put that into practice right now."

They both had the decency to look contrite. That was a good sign.

"Ava, can I be honest with you?" Gracie's voice was now level and sincere.

Ava looked at her and nodded.

"I'm not saying this is all your fault, but I fear that, for whatever reason, you've had trouble respecting my leadership. We simply don't make a good fit working together."

Where was this headed? Matthew couldn't afford to lose either of them, but he knew in an instant who would be the first to go, and it wouldn't be Gracie.

Ava looked at her lap and pulled a handkerchief from her pocket. She dabbed at the corner of her eye, but he could see no tears. "And I fear that you have not liked me from the get-go."

"It's not that I don't like you. You're good with the children for the most part, but you question everything I tell you, all of which Marianna taught me. It's exhausting."

"I need this job. My family is in a bad way right now. Daddy can't find work, and Mama's not well." Ava's voice hitched.

Gracie's beautiful brown eyes instantly softened.

"Then do you think you can cease from threatening the children and try harder to work under Gracie's leadership?" Matthew asked.

"Oh yes." Ava reached out and grabbed Gracie's hand. "Please, give me another chance?"

"All right then," Gracie said. "Come to me if you have any problems with disciplinary issues and I'd be glad to help."

Matthew breathed out a relieved sigh and sat back. "All right, ladies, I'll let you work out the rest of the details. I have a ton of book work to finish." He tapped his ruler upon the page.

They stood, and Gracie headed out the door. Ava turned with a brightness in her eyes that had nothing to do with the tears she had supposedly just been wiping. She gave him a smile and a lift of her brows that sent an unnerving chill scuttling up his spine, then hurried out.

She was indeed flirting with him. He needed to put a stop to that immediately.

He got up from his desk and rushed to the door, but a flash of her skirt hem at the end of the hall was all he could catch.

The next time she made any overtures, he would be bluntly honest with her.

His heart was taken.

~

*M*atthew hurried across his private flat. His one afternoon off a week, and someone was hammering frantically on his door. Surely, whatever it was, Max and Ava could manage without him.

Ava was getting far too familiar. The past two Sundays, she had found something to panic about and had come running. It was one of the pitfalls of living above the orphanage.

He braced himself with a frown on his face. This had to stop. He opened the door with a swift motion to show his irritation.

Gracie stood with unchecked tears streaming down her cheeks. A gust of cold February air blew in.

"I can't believe she's gone. Ma is gone."

He opened up his arms, and she fell in.

Her body shook against him. Tears soaked the front of Matthew's shirt, but she needed his hug. He pulled her out of the cold into his private quarters and shut the door. She'd never been there before, and for propriety's sake most likely should not be now.

"Sorry…for interrupting… your only afternoon off." She hiccupped the words between her sobs.

"Shh… Let it out. It's all right to cry." He pulled her back into a hug but was careful to keep more distance this time. He soothed a hand up and down her back, resisting the urge to hold her close and never let go.

The only way for him to handle the headiness of her closeness was to pray. He whispered into her hair. "Dear Jesus, take Gracie's sorrow, carry the weight of this grief, touch her soul with your healing power. Help her to remember that she will see her Mama again on the other side. Oh, Lord, we ask for Your help. When we feel weak, You are our strength. Amen."

She would have no way of knowing how weak he felt, but the last thing he wanted to do was take advantage of her vulnerability.

She melted into his embrace at the sound of his prayer, and instead of feeling stronger, he felt weaker. Her sobbing quieted, so he led her to the settee and urged her to sit. He had to put distance between them.

"I'll make us a tea."

"No. I don't need tea." Her large dark eyes were a shimmering pool of tears. "Please, sit with me." Her voice warbled, and her lips trembled. She held out her hand, then let it drop to her lap.

He slid down beside her and cradled her against him. She collapsed onto his chest and rested. Why did this feel so much like home? Why could she not feel it, too?

They sat that way for a long time. The silence between them was peaceful even if what was going on inside of him was anything but. He could do this, be there for her and put his own need aside.

"I can't even get to the funeral."

He looked down, and her tears gathered afresh.

"I'm sorry. That must make your grief—"

"But how shallow of me to complain when I'm so grateful I got to see her in the fall? I don't know what I would've done now had I not had that time with her." She pulled back enough to look at him. "All because of you. I don't think I ever properly thanked you."

"Yes, you did—"

His words were cut off by her mouth on his, moving so deliciously over his lips.

This shouldn't be happening. She was emotional. But Lord, did she make his body sing. He longed to deepen the kiss and take what she offered, but she was not thinking straight. He would not take advantage. However, even God would understand a minute more.

His flat door flung open, and Ava and Max stood on his outside entrance steps with their jaws hanging open.

CHAPTER 17

Gracie flew off the settee, smoothing her hands down her rumpled dress and brushing the hair back that had slipped free of her braid. Goodness, what had she done?

"Well, I never." Ava moved into the room with her hands on her hips, scowling at Gracie. "I saw you sneak up here a while ago and throw yourself into Matthew's arms like a loose woman. When you didn't resurface, I went and got Max."

"There was no sneaking, I had something important to share with Matthew."

"Yes, we see how important it was." Ava shook her head.

"Who's looking after the children?" Matthew asked, a bite in his tone.

"The children are having their quiet time," Max said. "And there's enough other staff."

"And how dare you open up my private quarters without the courtesy of knocking." Matthew glared at the man.

"And good thing I did." Max stepped up, and Matthew stepped in. They stared eye to eye.

This was getting out of hand, and it was all her fault. "It's not what you think," Gracie said.

"So, what exactly is this, then?" Max's hands fisted, and his Adam's apple bobbed as he whirled her way. "You made it out to me that you're all pure and holy, never going to marry because you're given to God. And now, you're up here fornicating with Matthew?"

"I was not—"

"We were not fornicating," Matthew said. "Last fall, as you know, I went with Gracie to see her ma. She naturally came to me when stricken with grief with news of her mother's death. I was merely comforting her."

"Comforting her?" Max threw up his hands. "I've heard it all now. Inviting her into your private flat with your lips sealed on hers. Some kind of comfort."

Gracie flashed a look Matthew's way. "It was my fault. I was distraught. I don't know what came over me. I was the one—"

"You came here to tell me your ma died." Matthew lifted a hand to silence her, and she clamped her mouth shut. "I should have ushered you into a more public place." Matthew rose to his full height. "I take full responsibility."

Gracie could not let Matthew take the fall.

"Fine example this is for the children, especially the teens. Any number of them could've seen you sneak in here." Max's eyes were filled with disappointment.

"That's for sure." Raw jealousy oozed from Ava's voice.

They both stared Gracie down. And she was to blame. Whatever possessed her to kiss Matthew? All the closeness, the hugging, the connection, and suddenly she'd wanted to see if she felt the same way she had the first time he'd kissed her. Once she'd started, she hadn't wanted to stop. The pleasure had been mind-numbing.

"Wait until the board hears about this." Max said the words with a firmness in his voice.

"Yes, indeed," Ava added. "I'll be happy to give them a full report. Given the time they were alone in here, all measure of indecency could've taken place." She jutted out her chin and stomped off.

Max pointed at the door but looked at Gracie. "I suggest you leave—before I do."

Gracie nodded. "I'm sorry, Matthew." She walked out onto the landing and Matthew followed the group.

"Nothing happened. You have nothing to be sorry for. The board will be far more compassionate and open to the truth than these two were."

Gracie took the narrow metal stairs down to the ground, hanging onto the rail with care. Her knees were wobbly, and her legs felt weak. What a mess she had made of things.

She walked toward her grandmother's home. Her first instinct after getting that devastating letter had been to console her grandmother and then to run to Matthew. Not even Amelia, who would be suffering the same loss, had come before him. She had needed him.

"Wait up, Gracie."

She turned to see Matthew running after her and waited. Oh goodness, she did not want to face him. How embarrassing to have thrown herself at him like that.

"Thought I would walk you home. After all, it is my day off, and there is no one who can get offended by a walk." He smiled at her as if nothing were amiss.

They walked side-by-side in silence.

"I'm sorry…"

"I couldn't…"

They both spoke at the same time, then stopped.

"Ladies first," Matthew said.

"I wanted to say how sorry I am that I…"

"And I wanted to say I couldn't leave things the way they were, and that I'm not sorry."

What did that mean? Had he enjoyed the kiss as much as she had?

"I'm not sorry you came to me in your grief, and I'm not sorry that you kissed me. Things like that can happen when someone is overly emotional."

Was that all the kiss was, her being emotional?

"My fault lies in not suggesting a more suitable meeting place. We could've gone to my office, or for a walk, or—"

"The fault is not yours, but mine."

"You were not thinking straight. I should have been."

"So, what now?" Gracie's voice quavered. "What will the board say? And why would Max and Ava both be so angry."

"We know that Max has a thing for you, so his anger most likely comes from you not choosing him. And as for Ava, I haven't mentioned this, but she's been making some pretty obvious overtures to me."

"See." She hit him lightly on the arm. "I knew it."

"Seems they both have the same emotions they're battling. Maybe they've found strength in one another."

"And the way they burst through your door without knocking—who does that?"

"I'm sure they felt they were justified after what Ava thought she saw. It's unfortunate they burst in at that moment, as it confirmed their suspicions. But even if they had believed us and decided not to tell the board, I'd tell them the truth. We overstepped the boundaries of propriety, and Max is right. It's not a good example, and I won't have that hanging over my head."

Gracie stopped and grabbed his arm. "I need to meet with the board to tell them it was my fault. Your work is too important to be jeopardized."

"Your work is just as important, and I could've stopped kissing you, but I did not." He offered her his arm and she placed her hand in the crook and they kept walking.

She didn't have the nerve to ask him why he hadn't stopped,

but oh, how she wanted to know. Had he enjoyed it as much as she had? And if so, what did that mean? She now understood the pull, the attraction between a woman and a man. Suddenly, her childhood promise to Rosina faded in the light of this very adult emotion. And how did God view this attraction? She was still fulfilling her promise to the children...or was she? What she had done jeopardized her job and Matthew's.

"What do you think they'll say?"

"Everything will be fine. Don't worry. Nothing much happened."

Nothing is not the way she'd describe the turmoil inside her head. Was he a man who kissed girls but believed it meant nothing? To brush that off, he obviously didn't feel the earth-shattering emotions she did.

That thought both comforted and agitated her.

∼

Matthew rubbed his hand around the back of his neck, squared his shoulders, and entered Mr. Lewis's private office. He had been summoned before he could arrange a meeting himself. Max and Ava had wasted no time.

Reverend Peterkin and Melinda Preston were also there. It surprised him to see the others, but having this conversation in the company of three was a lot easier than all twelve, and he was grateful Melinda was there. She protected him like a mother bear over her cub. He took a deep breath in and slowly let it out. He had prayed and felt a calming peace.

"Matthew, good morning. Have a seat." Mr. Lewis pointed to the empty chair.

Matthew sat but did not relax.

"As I'm sure you're aware, Max came to see me yesterday with a story of something both he and Ava witnessed."

Matthew nodded.

"I've called in Mrs. Preston and Reverend Peterkin, as I do not like to handle things of this nature alone. I felt the whole board did not need to be privy to what we discuss."

"Thank you."

"I've already discussed with them the information given to me by Max and Ava and their concerns. Now, I'd like to give you a chance to tell us your version."

Matthew cleared his throat and shared what had happened. He finished with, "And so you see, it was nothing more than comfort, but I agree I did err in the location of this meeting. The whole thing caught me off guard." All three of them had listened respectfully without interrupting, but Matthew couldn't read their reactions.

"All right. Now each of us will respond," said Mr. Lewis. "Reverend Peterkin, would you please go first?"

"To be honest, Matthew, I disagree that this was no more than comfort. I have comforted many people of the opposite gender in the throes of grief and have not ended up kissing them. I believe your first bit of hard work is to acknowledge your feelings for each other."

Matthew swallowed an instant knot that choked his throat. *Really, God? I ask for Your help, and this is what comes back at me?*

"I agree with you, Reverend," Melinda said.

Even Melinda? She's my support in everything.

Melinda continued. "Gracie is an attractive girl, and you two have been working very closely together. You have many of the same passions and aspirations. It's quite natural to assume this closeness would lead to a mutual love for one another. In fact, I'd champion so wonderful a match for you." She smiled as if she were thoroughly delighted.

Matthew's gut twisted. Could he admit to them how much he loved Gracie without knowing how she felt?

"We didn't discuss our opinions on this matter because we wanted to hear from you first, but it seems we're all on the same page," Mr. Lewis said. "And if you two have genuine love and affection for each other, which is all right with us, then we can assume the boundaries of propriety will become increasingly hard to keep. Have you discussed marriage?"

Matthew let out a nervous laugh. "Marriage? She doesn't even know I love her." Now, why had that spilled out? He could feel heat spread around the back of his neck and up into his face.

"You'd better tell her, son." Reverend Peterkin laughed. "You don't want a gem like Gracie to slip through your fingers."

Melinda clapped. "Yes. I agree."

Mr. Lewis put his hand up. "How ever this love story unfolds, we still have business to discuss. I expect each of you to write an apology letter to Max and Ava, as well as promise you will not meet inside your flat under any circumstances. As leaders, we must remain upright, a good example at all times. You showed a lack of wisdom on your part."

Matthew nodded. "Absolutely, and I'm truly sorry."

"Also, going forward, any time you meet in your office, the door will need to remain wide open."

"What if there's something of a private nature to discuss? For example, a conversation on a particular staff member."

"Then you'll go for a walk or meet at a restaurant for a coffee."

He didn't appreciate the constraint, but he understood. "That makes sense."

"And lastly, any part of your relationship with Gracie that is of a personal nature must take place off site until such a time as you two are married and all question of your conduct and respectability is beyond reproach. That means no signs of affection at the workplace."

They all nodded, assuming that he could simply go and ask Gracie to marry him. If only they knew. A terrible dilemma crossed his mind. "What about the Orphan Train?"

All three shook their head. "Out of the question," Mr. Lewis said. "Ava must go with you, or Max with Gracie, but not the two of you together."

What a mix-up. They had no idea that Ava and Max would love nothing more—for reasons as complicated as his. And he was not about to jeopardize the opportunity these kids had for a family because of his behavior.

"Unless"—Melinda smiled as if she had the most delightful solution—"you two married in the next month. I'd be more than pleased to help arrange a lovely celebration."

Matthew felt his eyebrows shoot up. "I'll have to talk to Gracie."

"But of course, you will, my dear." Melinda leaned over and patted his arm. "Be sure to propose in a romantic spot. She'll relive the moment many times over her life. Make it count."

Reverend Peterkin rose and came over to stand in front of him. "Let me know the date as soon as possible so that I can fit you in." He clapped Matthew on the shoulder.

Mr. Lewis beamed. "I'm not what you'd call the romantic type, but even I like the sound of this."

They were assuming Gracie would be thrilled at his proposal, acting as if their engagement were as good as done. He had to say something. "I-I'm not sure—"

"Don't you worry," Melinda said. "We can keep a secret until you find the perfect moment. Our lips are sealed." She sewed her lips closed with her fingers. "But need I remind you—that train leaves in a month."

CHAPTER 18

"We need to talk privately. Let's walk." Matthew rose and came around the side of his desk, pointing to the door.

"It's cold out there," Gracie said. "Why don't you just shut the office door and—"

"Not possible. I'll explain. Come on, now. Bundle up and you'll be fine."

"Oh, all right." Gracie reluctantly followed him into the hall, where they put on their winter wear.

Once past the orphanage gates—and the chance of any listening ears—Matthew began. "I met with Mr. Lewis, Mrs. Preston, and the reverend. They assume we have feelings for each other, since we were caught kissing." He waited for her reply. Did she even comprehend that she had initiated and quite enjoyed that moment, or had that been lost in her grief and the shock of being caught? "It's why they asked we keep our personal relationship off site."

Gracie buried her neck further into the nape of her cloak to ward off the February chill. She didn't respond.

"Now that the door has to remain open, the last thing I want is for big ears—meaning Ava or Max—standing outside my office door hearing our conversation."

"I'm sorry I brought this on you—"

"And that's not the worst of it." He might as well get it all out. The troubled waters of his soul rippled with apprehension.

"There's more?"

"We're no longer allowed to go on the Orphan Train together."

"What?" She stopped and grabbed his arm.

Just that simple touch sent shivers spiraling up his arm.

"But I want…no, I need to see where the children will be placed. I'm not even sure about this whole Orphan Train idea. Their safety means the world to me."

"I know."

Her eyes held such disappointment he could not continue looking at her. He turned forward and kept walking.

"Then who will go?"

"That's complicated, too. They suggested either you and Max, or Ava and me. We know how awkward that would be."

"I can't go with Max. He's still all puppy-eyed with me."

"And Ava's even worse. She thinks this whole thing has put a stop to our relationship, leaving the door wide open for her."

"What is this exactly? This…this relationship?" Gracie asked.

He knew what it was on his part, but she wasn't ready to hear the truth. He would have to take this slowly. "It's friendship and…the meeting of two people on the same path in life."

"And that's all?"

"I can't answer that for you."

"But what about for you?"

He pointed across to the German bakery. "Let's stop and warm up with a coffee before we head back." They crossed the street, and he held the door open, hoping she would forget her last question. There were definitely sparks between them, but he doubted she'd be ready to hear his declaration of love. They chose a table for two tucked in a far corner and he pulled the chair out for her to sit.

"I'll be right back. I know exactly what I want you to try."

He returned with a pastry and coffee for each of them. "It's called a Franzbrötchen, originating from Hamburg, Germany. I know I'm not saying that right, but I think it'll be to your liking."

"Thank you," Gracie lifted the plate to her nose and inhaled. "Hmm, I detect two of my favorites, cinnamon and, by the flakiness, a lot of butter."

"Wait until you taste it." Did she even realize he paid attention to every nuance?

She bit into the warm pastry and closed her eyes. "Oh, my goodness, butter, cinnamon and caramelized sugar wrapped between layers of croissant pastry, all melting in my mouth at the same time. Matthew, this is simply divine."

"It is."

She opened her eyes and laughed. "You haven't even taken a bite of yours."

"I wasn't referring to the pastry."

Her eyes widened beneath lifted brows.

That was too forward. He'd better think fast. He shook free of her gaze and looked out the window. "With all the grief of losing your ma and this latest drama, it's nice to see you enjoy something, even for a brief moment."

"You're always thinking about me with such kindness."

It wasn't merely kindness he felt. Would she agree to what he was about to offer? If so, it would open the door to a lot more. A bead of sweat trickled down his spine. He was more than a little nervous. "There's one more suggestion made by the board that would ensure our plans to travel the Orphan Train together stay in place."

Gracie dropped the pastry on her plate. "Why didn't you start with that? Here I thought all hope was lost."

"Because I'm not sure you'll be interested."

"Of course, I'm interested. We want to share in this experience, and I thought I had ruined everything. What can I do to make it right?"

She picked up her coffee.

What must she think it is? Certainly not what he had in mind by the way she was sipping her coffee as if she hadn't a care in the world.

"Marry me."

She lowered her coffee cup with a thud. The hot liquid splashed free. She grabbed her napkin and frantically dabbed at the stains on her dress and on the table. Her fingers trembled until he placed his hand over hers. She met his gaze.

"It's a reasonable solution." What a stupid way to put it.

"What? You can't be serious?"

"I know this is a shock, but I've had time to think. It's not a bad idea."

"Except for the fact that I don't ever intend to marry, and you want to find love."

He'd found someone to love and to love him, if she'd open her eyes to the obvious. "So, we meet in the middle and agree to a pairing that could not be more suitable."

"I don't want to be paired."

"Are you sure?" His thumb circled on the inside of her wrist. He could feel her shiver.

She pulled her hand free. "I-I made a promise to Rosina, to the orphan children—"

"Which you are fulfilling."

She turned away and stared out the window.

He had to resort to his least desirable plan. It was either that or lose her. He would never love another, so something was better than nothing. "How about we commit to a marriage of convenience—in name only. No one would be the wiser. We'd go on helping the children at the orphanage, live our life in ministry to God and to them. Nothing would change except we'd have more freedom. We'd be able to travel together, and complications like Ava and Max and the many other suitors you've had calling since the Christmas ball would end. I see a lot of advantages to this idea."

Her brows knit together, and she kept twisting and untwisting her braid around her finger.

He waited in silence.

"I can see that your suggestion has merit for me, but what's in it for you? You told me you were lonely and wanted to find someone to share your life, to love, to—"

"I'd hardly be lonely if I had my best friend around. And we care about all the same things. Who knows where that might lead?" He knew where he hoped it would lead, with her walking right into his arms.

"Lead?"

"Let's just leave this conversation for now. I've had time to think this through, but you have not. Marriages have been arranged with far less in common than what we share, but I can see you need time to process."

Gracie rubbed her temples. "I can't think straight."

Dark shadows were painted beneath her pretty eyes, and her cheeks were pale. This was all too much, especially after losing her ma. Though he clearly knew what he wanted, it wasn't fair to expect she would. "Take your time. Under the circumstances, it's not reasonable to expect a decision too quickly. You could be part of the next train. It wouldn't be the end of the world for me to take—"

"No. Ava wouldn't care which home Emma landed in. Emma's sensitive and needs somewhere special."

"Then either Emma waits for the next train or—"

"No. The sooner that child is placed in her forever home, the better. She's not adjusting to community living."

"Then you go with Max. He'll be thrilled."

Gracie groaned. "That's just it. He'd be too thrilled."

So would Matthew be thrilled to join her on a train ride to Ohio, but he dare not admit that. "I was going to say that Max would be thrilled because he's done so much work on this project, but I get what you're saying."

Matthew wouldn't go to the board with all these complications, or they'd lose faith in his leadership. The thought of not being able to solve this problem caused an instant clench in his gut. He had slept little in the last few nights. The board had been so good to him, giving someone with his humble beginnings a chance at management. The thought of failing them washed in like constant waves lapping on the edges of his mind.

"And the board is all right with our sudden marriage?"

"Like I said, they assume we've grown close over the months and fallen in love." Even saying the words made his heart slam against his chest. How he wished she felt the same.

"So, if we decide to get married, they won't question it?"

"No. In fact, Melinda Preston offered to help arrange a special day. But think and pray about it. I know this must be a shock."

"I still don't get why you'd sacrifice finding a love relationship for what we have."

"Maybe what we have is not a sacrifice to me."

Her head tilted adorably to the side. "I don't understand."

"You don't have to. I'm fully aware of what I'm suggesting. Just sort out what you want. Now eat up. We have to get back."

He bit into his pastry, hoping he looked as if he didn't have a care in the world. "Yum. So good."

"What do they call these things again?" she asked.

"Everything's in German, and I've already forgotten what the owner told me. I point and order it as the cinnamon pastry, and he knows exactly what I mean."

"You sure do know what I like."

"Now, if only you'll trust me with more than a pastry selection." He gave her a slow, easy smile.

Her smile blossomed like an unfolding flower. "I just might, but I need time to pray."

∽

Gracie had knelt beside her bed every night for a week, but no answer was forthcoming. So, she knelt again. A pang of deep regret sliced into her heart. She deserved this turmoil. She'd broken her own rule and put herself and Matthew into this mess. That kiss had been a failure on her part, one not to be repeated. She'd been overly emotional, distraught at the news of her ma, and somehow weakened.

"Dear Lord, You know how much I love You and want to please You. And I can't believe I'm even asking this question, but should I marry Matthew? You know I've dedicated my life in service to You and the children. I wouldn't want to let anything that is not Your will side-track me from that goal."

Would you be side-tracked from the orphan children if you married Matthew?

Now, that was a peculiar question, but at least she was hearing something. She thought about it for a moment. Matthew had the same goals as she did. The children were everything to both of them. No, she wouldn't be distracted, as long as they maintained a platonic relationship. But then was that really marriage?

Gracie got up and paced the room. She didn't need to dissect that question when all week long she had been counting the ways in which a marriage in name only would be a satisfactory solution. She walked back and forth in the light of a lone flickering candle. The shadows on the wall mirrored the shades of self-doubt she had in her soul.

"But, God, Matthew suggested this, and it's a solid idea. No more uncomfortable advances from men. No need for a chaperone traveling with Matthew at my side. We could carry on as we have been, enjoying friendship and the bond of ministry without the romantic complications. And the best part, God, we could go on the Orphan Train together and personally place the children we love so much into the right homes. Surely, this sounds reasonable?"

What about what Matthew needs?

She paced some more and then smiled as a perfect solution came to mind. Yes, that's what she would do.

What God has brought together, let no man put asunder.

Now, where did that Scripture come from? God knew this would not be a real marriage, so it didn't apply. She blew out her candle and pulled back the covers, slipping beneath the cozy blanket. As she snuggled down into the comfort of her bed, she let out a long full breath. A decision had been made. She'd be doing something tomorrow she never would have anticipated, accepting a proposal of marriage.

She drifted off to sleep thinking of a man with laugh lines crinkled around his eyes and dimples on both sides of his mouth. Those eyes so blue. Dancing with shadows of laughter, serious intent, and something she could not quite decipher.

CHAPTER 19

Matthew laid down his pen and leaned back in his office chair. Gracie wanted to meet with him. She apparently had her answer. He could not concentrate on his work and could barely wait until the children were settled for their afternoon quiet time so they could have their conversation.

He closed his eyes, determined to discipline his thinking onto the orphanage and the children. The younger ones would sleep during this time. The older ones would read. He was proud of the fact that every child was learning to read and receiving basic arithmetic skills. His orphanage was a standard far above the normal. He had high aspirations to be groundbreaking in his techniques and efforts, so much so that he would revolutionize the way things were being done, not only in his orphanage but across the country. His goal was to become a leader from whom other orphanages would glean information, like Charles Brace and his Orphan Train idea.

And if he could enter into marriage with the woman he loved, everything in life would be heading in the right direction.

There he was, back to thinking about her. Everything circled around to her. If he could get her to agree to the marriage, he didn't care how long it would take to woo her and help her realize that marriage in the fullest sense would not jeopardize her calling to God or her childhood promise to Rosina. He'd not change a bit of what she had now…freedom to lead, his support and friendship, her involvement in the decisions for the children.

But the best part—she'd be wearing his ring. Would-be suitors would vanish, and he could relax and let his love unfold like a bud into a rose. Her beautiful scent.

But first he had to get her to say yes.

His eyes popped open, and he sat up straight at the sound of her heels clicking down the hardwood hall toward him. Gracie's head poked into his office. "I'm ready now."

He was on his feet in an instant. If her smile was any indication, he was going to be one happy man by the end of this conversation. "Coming." He pulled his coat and hat from the coat stand by the office door.

She was already down the hall, slipping into her cloak. "I have a craving for that cinnamon thing. Do you think we could head back to the German Bakery?"

"Absolutely. I knew you'd like that one."

"You seem to know me better than I know myself most days." She laughed as he held the door open for her, and she waltzed through.

If only she could comprehend that he knew her far beyond her penchant for cinnamon and sugar croissants. "Hold that thought, and this conversation will go really well."

"Now, now, don't jump to any conclusions. We have a lot to discuss." She placed her hand in the crook of his arm, and they started down the street.

The late February afternoon was bright and sunny. A balmy warmth teased the buds on the barren trees, beckoning them to break forth. Matthew could feel the joy of new beginnings on the horizon. His hopes soared. His feet held a lightness akin to dancing, and he didn't even care for dancing all that much. He held his tongue, though he wanted to shout *tell me already.*

"Look, there's a robin." Gracie pointed to a nearby bush. "I always know when spring is right around the corner as they seem to come out of hiding. Where do you think they go in the winter?"

He could barely concentrate. The last thing he wanted to discuss was the weather or the local bird population. But he would humor her. "Hmm, I read that they stay in the state but forage in the moist woodlands, feeding on berries and other fruits during the winter months."

She squeezed his arm. "I love that about you."

His heart kicked up speed.

"You seem to remember most everything you read. So, rather than hopping around the lawn looking for juicy worms, they eat berries?"

She was killing him. "Yes."

Silence followed. It was anything but comfortable. He kept reminding himself that he was a patient man.

"Do you think it'll be warm enough for the children to travel come mid-March?"

"Does that mean you're planning to go?"

"I'm hoping to, but there is much to discuss."

"Well then, discuss." It could mean she wanted to go with Max.

"I want to be in our spot at the bakery."

So, they had a spot now. That was promising. They crossed the street, and he held the door open.

"Oh good. I see our table is free." She smiled as if she were stifling a grin. "Please, get me the same as last time." She headed to the corner.

"Good morning, Mr. Weston" The portly man with a thick

German accent smiled, showing off a wide gap between his two front teeth. "How are the children?"

"They're good, Helmut, thanks to people like you who continually give so generously."

"The good Lord blesses me"—his hand flew out over the busy establishment—"so I can bless the children. Now what can I get for you and your lady?"

"She's not my…well I'd like her to be my lady." A wash of heat spread onto his face. "She loves the Franz…botch…in."

Helmut's booming laughter matched his burly stature. "You mean the Franzbrötchen?" The word rolled off his tongue. "Coming right up. And it's on the house today. We have to help your cause in any way we can." His head nodded in Gracie's direction, and he chuckled.

"Here you are." He placed the coffee and cinnamon swirls on a tray and slid it across the counter to Matthew. "Enjoy."

Matthew walked across the busy room to their table in the corner. He liked the sound of that—their table.

"Here you are." He unloaded the tray and returned it to the counter before slipping into his seat.

"You're the best, Matthew." She smiled sweetly and took a huge bite and washed it down with a sip of coffee. Her hands trembled as she gripped the sides of her cup.

"Are you nervous?"

"Of course, I'm nervous. Never thought I would be accepting a marriage proposal from anyone."

His adrenaline spiked. He wanted to jump up and kiss her on the lips, but he dared not. "So, it's a yes?" he asked as calmly as he could.

"It makes sense."

Not the most romantic answer he could think of, but it was a yes.

"However, I have some concerns."

"Yes?"

"Will I maintain my freedom to come and go as I please and make my own decisions?"

"Of course."

"And this marriage is in name only?"

He took a sip of his coffee. He had to gulp that one back. "If that's what you want."

"Isn't it what you want?" Her eyes flashed darker than usual.

"Whatever makes you comfortable."

"Look Matthew, it's all I'll ever want. Are you sure—?"

"I'm sure." He said the words firmly so she wouldn't question his sincerity, though his hope fizzled. This was going to be a long road.

"And, in case this doesn't work out, I've come up with an idea."

"Hmm?" He sipped his coffee with one hand splayed around the mug, his spirits plummeting.

"We'll stay married for six months, long enough to complete both Orphan Train runs, then we can reassess. If either of us does not find the arrangement to our liking, we can get an annulment. After all"—she lowered her voice—"this won't be a marriage in the realest sense of the word."

He didn't know what to say. One hand went into his pocket to finger the ring he had purchased in hopes she would agree, but he had not expected her easy out. The sense of security he hoped marriage would bring turned as lukewarm as his coffee. Maybe this was not such a good idea after all. Was he pushing open the door of marriage when he should have let God open it slowly?

"Matthew, did you hear me?"

He shook his head. "Sorry, my mind was…"

"I asked you if you still wanted to go ahead?"

He was about to say no when a spark of genius hit. The affection he intended to shower on her would break down her walls of resistance. She didn't know it yet, but anyone who initiated and kissed him like she had was in love, even if she was in denial.

"You do understand that we have to make this look like a love match to the world?"

"Meaning?"

"A marriage ceremony with guests. Affection in public. Even the odd kiss when necessary."

Her big brown eyes shot wide. "I hadn't thought of that."

"How else would the board agree? Melinda is waiting to pounce on the arrangements for hosting the wedding, and your sister and grandmother will no doubt insist on being part of the celebration. Not to mention, we want people like Ava and Max to believe we're in love. And all this in a matter of three weeks until that train pulls out. Are *you* sure?"

She did not hesitate. "I am."

Then we start now. He rose from the table and bent down on one knee in front of her. "Make this good," he whispered. He pulled the ring from his pocket and spoke loudly and clearly. "Gracie Anabelle Williams, will you marry me?"

Every eye in the room turned, and there was a hush in the waiting. Then, as if she finally understood what was happening, she jumped from her seat. "Yes."

He rose and she threw her arms around him.

The whole place erupted in clapping and hooting. Matthew stood to his feet with her still in his arms and swung her around. He lowered his head to kiss her solidly on the mouth as he eased her feet back to the floor. When he pulled free, a very dazed girl looked up at him. She was as affected as he was. With renewed confidence, he slipped the ring on her finger. There would be some definite advantages to their little arrangement.

Helmut raced over. "Praise the good Lord, my prayers worked. I make you da most delicious wedding cake." He kissed the tips of his fingers throwing his hand into the air.

"You have two weeks," Matthew said.

"Ah, you're not wasting time. A man after my heart." Helmut clapped him on the back. "Congratulations."

~

Gracie stood before the bedroom mirror in her grandmother's home. She poked a few more pins into the twisted braid at the nape of her neck, catching the wayward strands. Her hands trembled as they smoothed down her pink gown...her Sunday best. She swiveled the engagement ring on her finger. How would she begin to find the words to tell Amelia, Grandmother, and those back home that she was engaged after she had made such a fuss about never getting married?

Oh well, the shock of this news would die down fast, and she'd go on as before. They need never know the rest of the story.

Dear God, give me the words. Allow me to humbly admit that You work in mysterious ways. The thought that she had been proud and wrong to be so dogmatic about a promise made as a child had been haunting her daily. *Lord, I'm sorry if I've come across as prideful. Thank You for teaming me up with Matthew so the children on that orphan train will have the best care—something I cannot do without him. Thank you, God for Your provisions and Your love.*

Familiar voices filtered up to her room. Amelia and her family had arrived. Gracie slipped the ring from her finger and slid it inside her pocket. She squared her shoulders and took a deep breath in. *I can do this.*

She turned the corner into the hall where they were removing their outer wear. "Hello." When she crouched down, Jenny and Pearl hurdled themselves into her open arms. She hugged them close. "How are my two special girls?" Gracie kissed both petal-soft cheeks and stood with a tiny hand in each of hers. "Shall we have tea?"

"Yes please," Jenny said like a little lady.

Gracie nodded her head in approval. "Very good manners."

"Tea. Tea. Tea." Pearl shouted, jumping up and down.

"Pearl." Bryon's voice was sharp, and Pearl quieted.

Amelia rolled her eyes. "She's not about to be outdone by her older sister. A real firecracker that one."

"Grandmother's waiting in the parlor. Let's join her." Gracie looked down at Amelia's decided bump. "How are you feeling?"

"The end of April can't come soon enough. This pregnancy has been so different, with way more sickness. You'd think at seven months I'd be done with that. But no."

"Maybe it's a boy."

"Bryon would love that," she whispered. "He pretends another girl would be just fine, but he has all boy names picked out."

Grandmother waved them in. "Sit. Sit. I'd get up, but these old bones are a crackin'."

"Mama calls me a fire crackin' too." Pearl said, plopping herself beside Grandmother.

They all laughed, and she beamed.

"So." Grandmother rubbed her hands together. "We're all accounted for. What's the big surprise? I love surprises."

"Me too. Me too." Pearl's little bottom bounced up and down on the settee.

Oh dear. Where was Matthew when she needed him? He was supposed to be there. The door knocker sounded. "I'll be right back." Gracie raced out.

She opened the front door with flourish and dragged Matthew in. "You made it in the nick of time. Grandmother was starting in. And all of a sudden, I'm so nervous. I don't know how to present this."

"Good afternoon to you too." He laughed and dropped a light kiss on her cheek.

"What did you do that for? There's no one around."

"Getting you used to it. It's what people in love do."

She rolled her eyes at him. "Glad you're the expert on all of this because I'm sure not."

He hung up his coat. With his hands on both her shoulders and looking straight into her eyes, he whispered, "Breathe, and let me do the talking."

His confidence brought calm, but his hands on her shoulders and those twinkling blue eyes caused a stirring she could not understand.

"Where's your ring?"

She pulled it out of her pocket, and he slipped it back on her finger. Then he took her by the hand. Instinct demanded she pull free before entering the parlor, but he shook his head and held on tight. They entered holding hands, which was enough to send eyebrows to the ceiling and shock to their faces.

"Why, Matthew, it's you," Bryon said. "We were wondering who the mystery guest was when Gracie ran out."

All of them had their eyes on the interlocked hands. Gracie could feel fingers of heat spread from tip to toe.

"We'll pull the bandage off my awkward appearance and show you this." Matthew held up her hand. The ring sparkled for all to see.

Gracie watched as if in slow motion. Bryon's smile turned into laughter.

Amelia squealed and jumped to her feet, scaring little Pearl, who started to cry. She bent to console her.

Grandmother's head came forward as she tried to focus on Gracie's hand, and then she let out a loud chortle. "Why I do declare." She tried three times before she could get her body out of the settee. "Come here and give your grandmother a hug."

They all gathered around, laughing and hugging.

"What? How did I not know?" Amelia asked.

"When did this happen?" Bryon clapped Matthew on the shoulder.

"I knew. I knew it. Was I not right?" Grandmother smiled as if she'd won a prize.

"Mind if we sit?" Matthew asked. He guided Gracie to the two empty chairs, held the back of her chair as she sat down, and brought his closer.

He reached out his hand to take hers, and she almost grimaced. How awkward. Yet as soon as she felt the warmth, she relaxed into the chair. He would handle this.

"So, I heard a few different questions, and I know this must come as a shock, so how about I tell you our story."

They had a story now? This should be interesting.

"I fell in love with Gracie almost from the day I met her. Honestly, I think it was the day I met her. But as you all know, Gracie here had an aversion to courting, love, and especially marriage. So, I took things very slowly."

He sounded so believable that she could almost take the story as gospel. How did he do that?

"It was that trip in the fall to see your family in the Shenandoah Valley when I knew I had to be part of this family. What I felt for her was far more than a passing infatuation. In fact, I was downright jealous when the cowboy Johnny who helped us on the last leg of the trip took a shining to Gracie." He looked over at Gracie and winked. "I even asked her pa for her hand in marriage, hoping that day would not be long in coming."

Her face flooded hot. Wow, he was convincing. Gracie could not believe how effortlessly he spun the tale.

"But still, she held me at bay. At the Christmas ball, she promised me the last dance, and then when it came my turn, after agonizingly watching her float around the floor for hours in the arms of another, and another, and another…"

They were all laughing at Matthew's eye roll and antics.

Gracie forced a smile.

"Do you know what she did? She begged me to take her home. Her poor feet were tired."

If this was to be convincing, she had better say something. "They were tired," Gracie said.

"So, I packed up this lovely girl who almost fell asleep in the carriage, keeping in mind what you said." He looked at Grandmother.

She had a mischievous glint in her eyes and a knowing grin pulling up the corners of her mouth.

"What? I don't know this part of the story. What did Grandmother encourage?"

"Ahh, that is for her to tell." He leaned close and lifted Gracie's fingers to his lips. He kissed the back of her hand, all the while staring into her eyes. Her head knew it was just for show, yet her heart was responding. She could not break his gaze.

"Uh-hum..." Bryon coughed. "The rest of the story."

Matthew broke their connection, turning to the others. "Where was I?"

"The carriage," Jenny answered. She sat cross legged on the Persian rug directly in front of them, hanging on to every word.

They all laughed again.

"You know what I did, Jenny?"

Jenny's eyes grew wide, and she shook her head so that her curls bounced from side to side.

"I kissed your auntie right on the lips."

Jenny covered her mouth with her hand and giggled.

"Why did you tell them our secret?" Gracie pretended to look horrified, but she was quite enjoying a side of Matthew she rarely saw. Spirited. Smiling. Spontaneous.

"Sorry, my dear, but it was the day I knew..."

"Knew what?"

"William Shakespeare said it beautifully, 'My lady doth protest too much, methinks.'"

Gracie pulled her hand free and hit him playfully. "Oh, really?"

"Yes, really." He leaned in and wrapped his arm around her with a squeeze before relaxing back into his chair.

"From that day, our friendship, our mutual respect for the work we do and the different talents we both bring, have developed into an ever-deepening love. And being that we're very busy people and the Orphan Train is scheduled to leave in three weeks, we want to be married immediately."

"Before you go?"

They looked at each other, and she grabbed his hand as if it were the most natural thing to do. "Yes." Gracie squeezed, and he squeezed back.

"Goodness gracious." Grandmother looked at Amelia. "We have a lot to do."

Matthew held up his hand. "We want only a small gathering, and Melinda Preston has offered her house."

"Melinda knew before me?" Grandmother sat up straighter like a dog raising its hackles.

"Not officially," Gracie added quickly.

Matthew caught on fast to the potential rivalry. "Melinda knows me too well. I couldn't hide that I loved Gracie. She encouraged me to ask for her hand in marriage, but you're the first to formally hear that she has agreed to be my wife."

Grandmother let out a sigh of relief. "Well, that's good. I quite like Melinda Preston these days and want to keep it that way." She laughed with a charming tinkle to her voice.

Gracie tried to hide the nervous energy behind her smile. Matthew had masterfully filled in all the blanks to her questioning family, but it created a storm of questions in her head. What had Grandmother encouraged? Did Matthew think she was just protesting too much? But most important of all, had he fallen in love with her? Her hands tingled and her heart crashed against the sides of her chest.

That thought sounded so beautifully complicated.

CHAPTER 20

The black of night still cloaked the room in darkness, but Gracie could not sleep another wink. It was her wedding day, of all things. Who would've ever thought? She threw her covers back and slipped out of bed.

Her insides were aflutter with a mixture of emotions she had never entertained before. An element of excitement tumbled alongside the other variables of the unknown, all frolicking in her head. Theirs would not be a real marriage, of course, but how would they navigate the waters of living together in close quarters? The reality of the complicated intricacies was sinking in, and her pulse quickened at the thought of such intimacy. His flat was tiny, and they'd be returning there together after the ceremony. She nibbled at her baby finger until the nail was a jagged mess.

She padded across the room and pulled back the curtain. The first faint blush of dawn hugged the eastern ridge. She was not sure how long she stood there praying. By the time she moved from that spot, the strengthening light danced across the cloud-scattered horizon, splashing the sky in hues of pink, red, and splattered gold. As the promise of a beautiful spring day unfolded, her prayers brought inner peace. Somehow, this crazy decision felt right.

In the past, if she had contemplated marriage, Matthew would never have been the type of man she would've considered. The brusque and serious attitude she'd come up against in the beginning would've sent her running. But there was more to him, much more—a man with a softness beneath his commanding mannerisms that encompassed a deep kindness and gentleness toward the hurting children. They shared a bond few couples would ever realize…a passion and goal of helping the poor waifs of their city.

Truly, she loved the way he had taken the time to get to know her, from sharing her love of cinnamon to sharing her last moments with her ma. He made her feel happy, cherished, protected. What more could a girl ask for?

What if she was falling in love? Would she want something more in the relationship? How would he react to that?

Would she experience another heartbreak, first Rosina's sad story, then Ma, and possibly Matthew? A raw and haunting pain filled her being. No, she couldn't take more loss. She would ensure she kept things platonic, safe, secure. It was all right to love him like a brother, but no more kissing. There was no way she would let anything jeopardize her work at the orphanage, and unrequited love on either side would do just that.

She busied herself making her bed and packing her carpet bag. As soon as the staff started moving about, she would request some bath water.

~

Matthew barely slept. Excitement hammered in his chest. It was a marriage in name only, but his insides felt like they were doing backflips. She may not know it yet, but she was going to be his—mind, soul, and body. He was a patient man, but annulment was not a word in his vocabulary. Once he slid that wedding ring on her finger, it would never come off.

He whistled a tune as he pulled his best suit from his wardrobe. The day was much too young to put it on, but he could prepare. He looked around the flat he had cleaned the day before. Everything sparkled, small and perfect. The thought of bumping into her at most every turn caused his heartrate to accelerate from a walk to a full-on gallop. He prayed she'd see the insanity of keeping their marriage platonic as unnecessary as he did. They could be man and wife and still do everything and more than they were doing now. His bones quivered with excitement.

He didn't feel he was misleading her. Rather, he was leading her to a wonderful place she had yet to discover. From the way she had responded when they kissed, she was not as unaffected as she'd like to pretend. And he'd take great joy in slowly awakening her to the world of love, where the desire of a woman for a man and a man for a woman felt as natural as the continual flow of the James river. He pressed back the urge to laugh out loud and then realized he was too happy to contain the joy. A man did not get married every day. Full-bodied laughter filled the room.

∽

A small group was gathered in the Preston's beautifully appointed parlor awaiting Gracie's arrival. There was no aisle to walk down, no fanfare beyond the dress Grandmother insisted upon. Gracie had been planning to wear the gown she'd worn at the Christmas ball, but Grandmother would not have it.

"Every girl needs her own special wedding dress, no matter how small the gathering, because what you're committing to is huge." She had winked and opened up her pocketbook. When they couldn't find what Gracie wanted, Grandmother had her seamstress come in and work tirelessly to create the perfect dress. Gracie could not be more pleased.

She glanced in the mirror as Amelia fussed with the veil, pinning it in place below the swath of hair swept to one side. A thick braid cascaded down her torso, like she wore it most days, but Amelia twisted and folded the hair into a stylish, coiffured look. A few fresh flowers added that special touch.

The dress had simple lines with an elegance that made Gracie feel feminine. The rage was to wear a huge bustle, but Gracie had insisted on the opposite with no long train or miles of crinoline. She was excited to spend the best part of a day wearing this gown rather than dreading the confinement. The soft layered silk fell in ruffled folds from her sculptured waist to the floor. Adorned with a bouquet of pretty yellow daises from Mrs. Preston's glasshouse, she was ready.

"So, you never confided anything to me about falling in love." Amelia made a pout.

Gracie fought back a grimace. What could she say?

"If I didn't know how busy you both have been, I'd feel offended. Imagine, your sister being the last to know."

"Yes, too busy, and now with the arrangements that have to be made for the children traveling on the Orphan Train, we've been run off our feet." At least that much was the truth. She couldn't confide in her sister. The ever-romantic Amelia would never understand.

"I would've never thought of Matthew as your type, with him being more on the serious side, but you know what they say. Opposites attract."

"He's not all serious. Not once you get to know him. You should see him with the kids. He's loving, kind, and he has a sense of humor beneath that stern—"

"All the things I would expect a woman in love to say." Amelia chuckled as she tucked another daisy into Gracie's hair.

Gracie's face flushed with heat. A woman didn't need to be in love to know the many wonderful qualities Matthew possessed, but she could hardly argue that point.

"Look at you. You're so beautiful." Amelia placed her hands on Gracie's shoulders and swiveled her body back toward the mirror. "This dress is everything that reflects your personality, functional, yet elegant. Unusual, yet stylish. Simple design, yet stunningly beautiful. You may have just created a new trend."

"With only a handful of guests, I rather doubt there will be a following."

"In any event, you do look stunning. Matthew is going to have a tough time waiting all afternoon to sneak you away."

"Goodness me. You're going to make me blush. We women do not talk about such things."

"Well, we should. Just you wait. You're in for the most delightful surprise of your life." Amelia made her eyebrows dance.

Heat climbed from her neck to her face. Just the thought of what a husband and wife did in private was cloaked in mystery, and she wanted to keep it that way. If she were honest with herself, she had given little thought on the matter until Matthew's lips had touched hers. Since then, a desire to know more had crept in on more than one occasion.

A slight tapping at the door, and Melinda poked her head in. "Everyone is seated, and the groom and Reverend Peterkin are ready and waiting."

A needle of concern stitched its way up Gracie's spine. How had she arrived at this moment? So many little steps, woven together. Would they be all right, or was she making the biggest mistake of her life? Ah, but this was not a real marriage, and they did have the plausible solution of an annulment if they weren't happy.

As she entered the parlor, she gripped the yellow daises so tightly that her knuckles turned white. All eyes were fastened upon her. But the moment she lifted her head and looked at Matthew, she felt a tingle in her chest. His easy smile broke free, lifting the corners of his mouth, deepening the half-moon laugh lines. And his eyes were warm and dreamy, pulling her closer with a softness she wanted to drown in. But what was that look on his face? It was no ordinary gaze, but that of a man for a woman…a man in love.

The room tilted and spun. What was she doing? She should run.

If he was in love with her, she would break his heart, and he didn't deserve that. But step by step, she moved closer until she stood in front of him. He gathered her hands in his. Instant awareness danced up her arms.

Reverend Peterkin began to speak, but Matthew's intense blue eyes held her gaze so powerfully that she had to look away to concentrate on the Reverend's words.

Her focus faded in and out until it came time for the vows. With the rich timber of his voice, Matthew recited his vows with firmness and confidence, not one waver.

Reverend Peterkin turned her way. "Gracie, repeat after me."

"I, Gracie Annabelle Williams take thee Matthew Timothy Weston…" She had not even known his middle name was Timothy.

"To be my lawfully wedded husband, to have and to hold from this day forward, for better, or for worse, for richer, for poorer, in sickness and in health…"

This was wrong. She was making a commitment that she would have and hold Matthew from this day forward.

"To love and to cherish," the reverend said.

Gracie could not repeat his words.

She stared down at her bouquet tongue-tied until Matthew squeezed her hand. She tripped over the words. "To…to love, and to cherish till...till death do us part, according to God's holy ordinance. And thereto I pledge thee my faith."

She was making a vow before God, yet all the while she had an *out* tucked in her pocket. There was something terribly wrong with what she was doing. A tremble took to her fingers.

Words dimmed, along with her integrity. They exchanged rings. The ceremony could not be done soon enough. She was a liar and a fraud, yet Matthew looked composed and unflustered. She didn't understand.

Unless he meant every word.

In which case, this whole charade wasn't a charade at all in his mind. Making this a terrible mistake.

Unrequited love in either direction would ruin their working relationship, and she was not prepared to risk that.

"I now pronounce you husband and wife. You may kiss the bride."

Too late. The deed was done.

His head bent, and the minute his lips touched hers, all confusion calmed. She could think of only one thing. How wonderful it felt to be in his arms. She was startled by the powerful emotions surging inside her. A sigh shuddered through her body as he pulled away, and her eyes popped wide open.

Oh, goodness, she had lost focus on everything else.

The small crowd clapped and cheered.

Mrs. Preston stood. "Ladies and gentlemen"—she waved her hands, and the crowd quieted—"tables are set up in the dining hall for a lovely meal, and you are all invited to stay and share in this most joyous occasion." She looked at Matthew with such love in her eyes. "Matthew is like a son to Alex and me, and we feel privileged and honored to be part of this wonderful celebration. We also welcome Gracie with open arms. Having already had the pleasure of welcoming one of the Williams' girls in our family"—she smiled at Amelia—"we feel doubly blessed to welcome Gracie. I could not think of a more perfect partner for Matthew. God is indeed good."

Matthew bent his head and whispered in her ear. "You're my perfect partner. Did you hear that?"

Gracie felt a tingle scuttle up her spine—half excitement, half unease. Was it true? The best she could do was smile up at him.

"Follow me." Melinda stood at the door of the parlor and pointed toward a room down the hall.

Matthew looked down at Gracie. "Shall we, Mrs. Weston?" He offered his arm.

"We shall." She smiled up at him and slipped her hand into the crook of his arm.

CHAPTER 21

Steady. Matthew reminded himself on the carriage ride back to what was now their small living quarters. *Keep calm.* This may have been his wedding day, but it was by no means going to be *the* night. He pulled in a deep breath and let it slowly out, willing his shoulders to relax and his neck to stop tensing.

Gracie had been silent from the moment they'd stepped into the carriage. He didn't try to hold her hand, and she didn't reach for his. During the ceremony and continuing into the afternoon and evening, he could feel her unease. At one point in the ceremony, he'd thought she might bolt. He sensed this was another such moment. Her fingers trembled, and the one leg that was crossed over the other bobbed up and down.

"Mrs. Preston put on a wonderful spread for us, don't you agree?" He tried to break the mounting tension.

Gracie nodded, but kept her face turned to the window, gazing out into the growing darkness.

Conversation was not what she wanted.

The Prestons had offered to pay for a night's stay in the prestigious Ford Hotel on Shockoe Hill, but Matthew had declined, saying they wanted to keep things simple. Circumstances were complicated enough without throwing in a romantic location.

He jumped from the carriage the minute the wheels rolled to a stop and hurried around to help her out. She took his hand but ripped it free the minute her feet touched the ground.

"Are you going to be all right navigating those steep stairs with that dress?"

She nodded. "But maybe you want to follow and catch me if I stumble."

He laughed but she was not smiling.

"You're serious?"

"Of course, I am. Any kind of fashion wear is ridiculously impractical. Matched with your steep entrance, anything could happen."

The lilt to her voice was gone. In fact, she sounded edgy and tense.

He felt like sweeping her up into his arms and carrying her upstairs and across the threshold, but he did no such thing. He followed as close behind as her dress would allow. After unlocking the door, he held it open. Inside, he lit a lamp. The soft glow of light cast shadows around the room and evoked an intimacy he knew would make her even more uncomfortable.

Gracie's eyes took in the room as if it were her first time in his flat. She poked her head into the small galley kitchen, then the two doors off the main room—the bedroom and the water closet. She stepped back into the main area. "Where's the second bedroom?" Her hands trembled, and she grabbed the doorjamb for support.

"There is only one bedroom. You've been here before."

"I didn't exactly get a grand tour, plus I was distraught and not thinking straight. I thought for sure, in light of our agreement, when you suggested we live here, there would be two bedrooms."

"I'm prepared to sleep on the floor."

"You can't sleep on the floor. With the strenuous jobs we have, we both need our privacy and our sleep. What were you thinking?"

What had he been thinking? That he may have to sleep on the floor for a short while, but when she realized how wonderful sharing life with him could be, she'd melt into his arms, and they'd share the bed.

What a fool.

He had not thought of her need for privacy. "I'm sorry. You can have the bedroom. I'll make myself at home out here."

Her eyes swept the small room, and she perched onto the edge of a nearby chair like a bird ready to take flight. "What have you done? There is no way we can live in these tight quarters. I'm going back to my room in the girls' house."

"Then this getting married business was all for nothing."

"What do you mean? We're still married."

"Word will get out. The board will know this was a ruse. Newlyweds do not live apart. Besides, Ava has already moved into your old room."

"Already?"

"Her parents' home is busting at the seams. She asked me this week if she could move in immediately, and I agreed. We did discuss this."

"But I thought I'd move in slowly. Where are my personal things?"

"Why, here of course. The last few days while you stayed with your grandmother, I had the maids move everything over. I've given you most of the wardrobe, and the bureau in the bedroom, and there are some empty shelves if you need—"

"No. I-I can't do this." She buried her head in her hands.

"Then we'll get a larger place when we get back from the Orphan Train run."

"But you like to be on site. Close to the children. We should've thought this through."

He wouldn't tell her that he had thought it through very thoroughly, and he had no problem with sharing his flat with her.

She popped to her feet and began pacing.

He wanted to console her, to ease her angst, to find the right words, but they were lodged in his throat like a splinter of wood. "You take the bedroom. I'll sleep out here on the settee—"

"The settee. Matthew, that's about half as long as you are. I'll sleep on the settee. You keep your bed."

"The settee is too short even for a petite woman like you." He tried a bit of humor with a smile, but she didn't respond.

She stopped, placing her hands on her hips. "Then what were you thinking?" Her eyes grew large. "Were you thinking we'd share the bed like a married couple?"

"No."

"Then what?"

"I hadn't considered the privacy issue very well, but I did prepare a makeshift bed on the floor. With comfortable blankets—"

"Really. You're going to sleep on the floor?" Her arms folded across her chest. "And I'm going to be selfish and take your bed?"

"I never had much growing up. Truly, it's not a hardship." He moved close enough to pull in a whisper of her perfume. That small feminine nuance caused an uptick in his heartbeat. He had better be careful. She was fragile. "Gracie, we can make this work. Whatever you need, we'll figure it out together. But you're exhausted. It's been an emotional day. Will you please take the bed tonight?"

She stepped closer.

His eyes found hers.

"Matthew, if I asked you to share the bed with me, as a wife with her husband, would you?"

His heart skipped and skidded in erratic desperation. Was she offering? Or was she testing him? *Oh God, give me wisdom.*

He looked deeply into her soulful mahogany eyes. A troubled light stole in, and wisdom was given. "I think if that was ever an option, words would not be necessary."

She visibly relaxed. Her hiked shoulders dropped, and her hands, which had been twisted into the folds of her beautiful wedding gown, fell to her sides.

She was definitely not offering.

"Can you trust me?" He held out his arms and she walked in. She rested her head against his chest, and he smoothed a hand down her back. "We'll be all right. And I'll see to whatever makes you comfortable. Now, why don't you slip into bed, and I'll wait a respectable amount of time before coming in? The bed I made for myself is on the far side of the room, out of the way." He gently kissed the top of her head.

She disappeared into the bedroom, and he plopped down on the chair. Wow, that had been a close call. With every fiber of his being, he wanted their marriage to be real, but they had an agreement, and she would have to initiate a change in their understanding before he did anything. But he was hopeful. Another kiss today, and it had been better than before. There was no way she could hide her response. She felt far more for him than she yet understood.

Dear Lord, I know you told me she is the one, and I may have pushed this door open, but help me now respectfully wait for her to know it too.

∽

What was wrong with her? Gracie pulled the wilted daisies out of her hair and threw them on top of the bureau. One minute she was angry at Matthew for thinking they could share such a small flat, and the next she was in his arms wishing she didn't have to leave. She undid the braid and the twisted coiffure and picked up her brush that had been placed where she could easily find it. With quick, sharp strokes, she pulled the hair free and flowing. She brushed with vigor.

Now for the dress. Could she get out of it herself? No. Most of the buttons down the back were out of her reach, and the few she got undone did not begin to loosen the fabric. And then there was the corset. Why had she not thought of this problem? She really would have to put that trust Matthew offered into action.

She opened the bedroom door to find him sitting forward in the chair with his head in his hands. His torso snapped up, and as she approached, his blue eyes grew intense and smoldering. The cords in his neck tightened, and he swallowed hard.

"I was hoping you could help me get out of this…" Goodness that was not what she meant to say. "I-I mean undo the buttons and untie the corset."

She turned her back away from his penetrating stare. The chair squeaked as his large frame lifted.

"You have beautiful hair." His breath tickled her neck as he lifted her hair out of the way. "I've never seen it down." His voice sounded hoarse and raspy.

What did she say to that? "Thank you."

The touch of his hands sent a shiver akin to delight spiraling down her spine. He worked the buttons slowly and methodically, and then the corset stays. She held all in place at the front. Never had this process taken quite so long or been quite so pleasurable. Each touch of his fingers upon her skin sent a tremor coursing through. Whatever was happening, she could not deny the powerful urge to turn in his arms and invite more. Whatever *more* was.

"There you are." He backed away. "I need some water." He marched into the kitchen galley without turning his head.

She moved back into the bedroom and undressed, hung up her wedding gown, and slipped into a sensible night gown. The thought of the frilly sheer chemise Grandmother had purchased for their wedding night, which she had safely tucked in her carpet bag, made her cheeks feel like they were on fire. She could not imagine wearing that in front of Matthew.

She hurried into bed, worried he might catch her in a state of undress. The crisp clean smell of fresh laundry wafted up. Matthew had gone to great lengths to prepare. Not one thing was out of place. Everything was sparkling clean. But, to not think of the privacy matter. That was a man for you.

Should she leave the candle burning so he could find his way? She snuck a peek over the far side of the bed. Some blankets were piled, but it was sure to be a hard surface. A pillow and checkered blanket lay on top. She felt bad. A grown man, and a big one at that, sleeping on the floor while her tiny body was dwarfed in his bed. She snuggled beneath the covers and closed her eyes. She was so tired, yet sleep would not come.

There was a soft rap, and the hinges creaked as he opened the bedroom door. She kept her eyes closed. A soft blowing sound, and she ventured a peek. The room was dark. Some rustling as he undressed, and a thump as his big body hit the floor harder than he obviously meant to. A soft groan, and all went quiet. She was afraid to breathe. After an hour of listening to him toss and turn, she whispered into the dark. "Matthew."

"Hmm."

"I can't fall asleep while you're suffering on the floor."

"Neither can I sleep with me on the floor."

She giggled first, and his chuckle joined hers. It was ridiculous for him to endure when she had a comfortable bed clearly large enough for them both.

"Do you have extra pillows?" Gracie asked.

"Why?"

"Bring a couple, and we'll put them between us and share the bed."

"Hmm."

What kind of answer was hmm? Had she been too forward? She was so inexperienced with men. "Well?" she prodded.

"I'm thinking."

Why wasn't he moving?

"You know what? I'm going to go for a brisk walk. I need to clear my head. But thanks for caring."

"A walk at this hour?"

"Yeah, I do that often. It helps me unwind and sleep."

"Well, don't say I didn't offer."

"Maybe without me tossing around, you'll drift off."

Relieving her guilt did wonders. Before he was even out of the flat, her eyelids felt heavy. When she woke in the early morning hours, she heard a faint snore from the floor below her. He had not joined her. An unexpected surge of…what? An emptiness in a little corner of her heart ached. She rolled to her side and fluffed her pillow, but sleep wouldn't return.

The niggling inched deeper. Dare she name it?

Loneliness.

There it was again. Now a married woman with a man she could not deny she was attracted to, sleeping within reach, yet she'd chosen loneliness. Something felt wrong with her decision.

The promise she'd made at twelve years old she was indeed fulfilling. She loved the children. She loved God. The only question that remained…would marriage to Matthew hinder or help that promise?

CHAPTER 22

Morning could not come soon enough. Matthew flipped over to his other side to relieve his aching hip. The hard surface had him awake again. He lay there with his tangle of thoughts. The last two weeks had passed in a flurry of activity preparing for the Orphan Train run. The blessing to his crazy schedule was that he could flop on his makeshift bed on the floor and get to sleep quickly. It was usually his discomfort that woke him by early morning.

Numerous times, Gracie had invited him to share the bed. Being the innocent, she had no idea the great amount of willpower it would take to be a mere arms' breadth away and not touch her. What a fool he had been to suggest marriage and sharing his small flat. She took him at his word and seemingly had no problem with the arrangement. He, on the other hand, suffered most every night both in mind and body.

If his pride weren't so fierce, he would cart in a mattress, but he didn't want anyone to see or know they did not sleep together. The best he could do was add a few more pillows, but they separated and bunched when he tried sleeping on them. His bed would be better placed against a wall in the main area, but there again, others may see, and so he suffered in silence. They even decided to do their own cleaning in order to keep their secret from the eyes of the staff.

He sat up and slipped on his day-old clothes for the sake of modesty, then rose as quietly as possible. The days were getting longer, and dawn came earlier. The pearl-gray threads of sunrise filtered in through the small window, casting enough light to allow him to gaze upon her beauty. A curtain of dark hair fanned across the white pillow. The ebony tangle of splendor caused his fingers to itch at the craving. What would it feel like to run his hands through and bury his head in the glossy mass?

Her petal-soft cheeks beckoned. That button nose and those delicate earlobes. Everything about her was feminine and petite. His eyes rested on her full mouth. An ache fresh and powerful took over. He had to get out of there. He pulled some clean clothes from the wardrobe in the corner and tiptoed out of the room.

He would do best to keep his focus on business. They were leaving the next day, and he wanted all record of expenditures caught up to date and every detail of the trip checked and rechecked. He set to lighting the stove so he could make his coffee.

"Good morning."

He jumped at the sound of Gracie's voice. After living by himself for so long, it was an adjustment to have someone else in his space. He loved his early morning quiet and took his time waking up. He found she was the opposite, instantly awake and chatty. If he didn't adore her so much, he'd find that challenging.

With no need for a mirror, she brushed her long hair and made her usual braid as she stood talking to him. "I'm getting excited. Only one more sleep, and tomorrow we head off bright and early."

"You and the kids, both."

Her smile lifted the corners of her pretty mouth. "Last night, it was hard to settle the ones that were going, and I suspect tonight will be even worse."

"No doubt."

"I'll double-check all the clothing today. Make sure each child has their own cloth bag with their few favorite things and their new set of clothing for tomorrow."

"Sounds good." Matthew put the kettle on to boil. She liked her tea first thing. He set to roasting his coffee beans on the wood stove in a cast iron pan and then ground them for the pot.

"You really are good in the kitchen." Gracie came up beside him and patted him on the back.

That small touch set his heart bucking.

He poured the boiling water over her tea leaves in the teapot and over his coarsely ground coffee. He worked hard to calm the reaction to her nearness. "I'll be heading down to get at my books as soon as this coffee is done. Can you call me when breakfast is served?" He had to put some distance between his beautiful wife and his weak will this morning. He desired to kiss her into awareness. Maybe then, she'd understand the turmoil he suffered every day.

"I'll call you. And thanks for making my tea each morning. You're the best." She leaned into him letting her head rest on his shoulder.

The sweet smell of wild roses wafted up. What did she use… a specific soap? He stood very still until she raised her head and reached for the tea pot. He almost threw his best intentions to the wind and kissed her soundly.

"I'll see you later." His voice sounded harsher than he'd intended. He moved swiftly away.

"Matthew, your coffee."

He stopped and turned with his hand on the doorknob. "I don't have time to wait for it."

Gracie moved across the room. "Have I done something to offend you? You seem so distant."

There was no way he could admit that his distance was the only way to manage their closeness without overstepping the boundaries. "I have a lot on my mind with the Orphan Train run."

"You'd tell me if I did anything to bother you, wouldn't you?" She looked up at him with her soulful brown eyes, so full of concern. "Grandmother warned me there'd be some adjustments to living together and encouraged talking them through."

"Your grandmother is a wise woman, and I'd tell you if there were anything I needed to change." Yeah, not likely. What he needed was the farce of this arrangement to change into a real marriage.

She nodded and stood on her tippy toes and kissed his cheek lightly. "You are an amazing man."

She was killing him.

He opened the door and took one step out onto the landing. Ava was climbing the steps toward him. "I arrived early this morning hoping to go over some things before—"

Gracie's head popped out. "Good morning, Ava. He'll be right with you."

Ava stopped her ascent.

Gracie grabbed his hand and stepped close. "Don't miss me too much, darling." She reached up and planted her mouth directly over his.

Matthew was shocked—but not a man to waste a gift sent from heaven. He kissed her with all the pent-up feelings he had stored the past two weeks, noting in the back of his mind that she was in no hurry to escape his arms.

Ava breathed out a heavy sigh. "Really, must you two?" She never got an answer, but Matthew could hear her stomp back down the stairs.

He didn't want to leave at all. He wanted to take Gracie back inside that flat and show her there was more...much more. With tearing slowness, his mouth left hers. She looked dazed, her lips deliciously ripe. Her arms were still wrapped around his neck.

"Hmm, now that was an enjoyable start to my day." He smiled down at her.

"Got to keep up the pretenses," she whispered and then slipped out of his arms. The door shut behind her. He stood there. Why did she have to say that and spoil the most incredible start to a day—ever?

~

Gracie pulled herself out of bed before Matthew. Their normal routine had been for her to wait for him to get up and leave the bedroom so she could dress in private. But today, she was far too excited to sleep another wink. She pulled her wrapper around her body. It would suffice until Matthew woke.

"You're up early." His deep voice resonated from across the room.

"Sorry, didn't mean to wake you."

"Not to worry. It's almost time to get moving anyway." He sat up and squinted into the gathering light. "Too excited to sleep?"

"That, and a little apprehensive, as well."

"Why?"

"I'll let you get dressed. We'll talk over our morning coffee and tea?"

He nodded and ran a hand through his hair, which was sprouting in every direction.

"That didn't help." Gracie laughed as she slipped out of the room. She started the fire in the wood stove and put the kettle on to boil.

Matthew came out of the bedroom, dressed in his traveling

clothes with his hair neatly watered down and tamed into submission. "You clean up well." Gracie threw him a grin and turned back to the stove.

"And you're very sassy this morning." He came up behind her, so close that when she turned, she was almost in his arms. She gasped but did not move. Her heartbeat quickened.

"Just in case Ava decides to show up early again, we could practice so that our presentation is more natural."

She could see the dare and the teasing in his bright blue eyes. "Matthew, you're incorrigible." But everything within her came alive. She had never been so aware of a man, his nearness so palpable, the pull so strong. The heat of his body radiated through her thin wrapper. Shivers of delight skimmed over her flesh. She longed to put her arms around him and feel the wonder of his kiss on her lips.

Yesterday, it had made her stomach somersault every time she thought of the impulsive kiss she'd given him.

Now, a mixture of pleasant scents pulled her closer, the clean smell of soap, forest pine, with a hint of his own earthy essence. Her eyes flickered up to catch his gaze. A longing and a question were held there. She dropped her eyes from the intensity of his stare.

He moved aside to the boiling water on the stove. "I'll make your tea. Get dressed." His withdrawal from their close proximity left a cold void. She entered the bedroom, her limbs shaking from the urge to run back and fling her body into his arms. What was happening?

She shook her head. See, this was the distraction and tension relationships brought. They had so much to do to get ready, and the children came first. Today was not the day to sort such a conundrum. She washed, dressed, and joined him.

"You were going to tell me about your apprehension." His voice was back to matter-of-fact and professional. She let out a deep breath as he handed her a cup of steaming tea. Good, he wasn't upset with her.

"I have an idea, a way the children can let us know if something is wrong in their new home. But would that scare them to talk about that possibility?"

"What were you thinking?" He took a sip of his coffee.

"Give each child a blank piece of paper with an envelope, postage, and our address, so they could write a letter if they needed to."

"I'm sure if the circumstances weren't favorable, the new parents would sensor the letter."

"Not if we told the kids we have a secret code, a way to communicate without words."

"A secret code?" His eyebrows rose.

"Children love that kind of thing."

"All right, explain."

"We'll tell them that, if things are wonderful, they can write us and let us know about their new life, but if things are not going well, rather than put that into words and offend their new family, they could draw a picture, any picture, but it would have a sun with a smile on it. The smile being the opposite of the way they feel. That sun is not to be put on the letter unless they need help. A secret code to let us know."

"Hmm, what about the kids who can't read or write?"

"Those kids will only use the letter if they're not happy. They can draw a picture and make sure the sun with the happy face is somewhere on the picture."

"You're one smart lady. I like that idea a lot."

"Great. I'll have those envelopes ready to tuck into every bag."

Matthew took the last swig of his coffee and stood. "For that you get a kiss."

Her head snapped up as he came closer. He placed a kiss on her cheek and moved toward the door. "See you in a half hour downstairs in the breakfast hall. We'll go over the last-minute details with the children and board that train by nine o'clock sharp."

She nodded. As the door closed behind him, she felt an overwhelming sense of disappointment. She wanted a real kiss.

～

"Children." Matthew's hands went up. The chatter faded in the eating hall, and all heads turned his way. "Today's an exciting day but possibly a hard day for those of you who are staying behind and must say goodbye to a friend. To the ten of you who are new to our group and stayed overnight in preparation for this trip, you'll be saying goodbye to a hard life."

A group of those boys let out joyous *whoops.* Matthew could not contain his smile. He remembered the horror of the streets. He waited a moment for them to settle.

"To those of you left behind, most of you have chosen to do so, but if you're one of the few who wanted to go and were not chosen, we're hoping that this will be the first of many train runs. Do not lose heart."

Gracie went to Nellie, who was weeping profusely, and put her arms around the child. Matthew couldn't hear their whispers, but in no time at all, Gracie had her calmed. What would it feel like to see her caring for one of their own children? He shook his head free of that thought. Fat chance when she trembled at the notion of a kiss.

"If any of you have problems while Gracie and I are gone, please know that Ava and Max are here to help you." He looked at the two of them, and they smiled at the children.

"Any questions?"

Johnathan's hand shot up.

"Yes?"

His voice wavered. "What if we don't like our new homes?"

"We'll have lots of time when we're on the train to go over that question. But don't you worry. Gracie and I have a plan, and we'll be back in six months to visit you." He was so proud of Gracie for coming up with that great idea.

Another hand lifted carefully.

"Yes, Annie?"

"Will I ever see my friend Martha again?"

"You know how to write a letter?"

She nodded.

"Then we'll make sure you have all the writing materials you need to write to Martha. Won't it be exciting to tell her about your new life?"

"But…but will I see her again?" Annie's big brown eyes filled with tears. The two girls sat side-by-side, clinging to each other.

"If you keep up that letter writing, I bet when you're both adults you'll still be friends. Then, you can arrange to see one another."

"You won't see me crying to leave the streets of this city," Lee shouted.

"Me neither," Jessie said.

"You here in this orphanage have it too good. We're headed for a better life." George let out another whoop.

All three boys who had spoken were street urchins, and their life had been hard. "Boys. Boys." Matthew held up his hand again. "I'm glad you're excited, but we don't belittle how others feel." He lifted the chain of his pocket watch. "You have five minutes for your goodbyes, and then I want all twelve boys lined up behind me, the eight girls behind Gracie."

Gracie moved to the front beside Matthew and waved at the girls.

The ten children who had lived on the street, instantly lined up. The others milled around hugging and saying goodbye.

There were some tears, but most of them had known this was coming for a while and were prepared.

Matthew took a moment to wrap his hand around Gracie's and give a squeeze. At least she was beyond the flinching stage.

She looked up, smiled, and squeezed his hand back, leaving it folded within his grasp.

Now, this was progress. His heart galloped in response.

CHAPTER 23

"Can you believe this boxcar?" Gracie whispered to Matthew as they all crammed in. She looked around at the space, which was no more than a cattle car with hard wooden seats fastened to the perimeter, a wide-open spot in the middle, and a makeshift bathroom. "No wonder the price given was so reasonable."

Matthew nodded. "Good thing it's only twenty-four hours. Hopefully, the train on the next leg will be better."

The children scrambled for the windows and stood on the wooden seats to peek out, oblivious to the long journey ahead.

"Thankfully a few of the windows open," Matthew said. "We'll need that as the day heats up."

"I thought the railway was being sensitive to the children's plight and giving us a discount. Now I can see why the tickets were so affordable." Gracie gulped back her frustration, and Matthew swung an arm around her shoulders with a squeeze.

"Keep the faith. We can do this."

Gracie's heart sank at the thought of the hours ahead. With all the stops, this first leg of the trip from Richmond to Huntington, West Virginia would be slow. Thankfully, the last twelve

GRACIE'S SURRENDER

hours on the train, the children would be tired and hopefully sleep. Gracie's grandmother's group, The Ladies of Relief Society, had kindly made each child a small pillow and a drawstring cloth bag for the trip.

From West Virginia, they'd board the river steamboat and travel another eight hours before an overnight sleep in Gallipolis, Ohio at The Garden Inn.

"Before the train takes off," Matthew said, "let's take a final head count, and I'll pray over our trip."

Everything about him exuded calm. Gracie took a long pull of fresh air deep into her lungs. He had a way of centering her.

Matthew counted the boys, and Gracie counted the girls. She picked up four-year-old Charlotte, and Emma slipped in beside her. Gracie gathered her close. She had to admit, she was most excited about taking Emma. The thought that a loving family could make all the difference in this little girl's life brought a surge of joy.

Matthew stilled the group for prayer.

"Dear Jesus, we come to You. We know You are with us on this adventure, and we ask for Your protection. Let our hearts be filled with joy and wonder as we set off today, and Lord, help us find the perfect family for each child. Amen."

"Amen," William repeated. He was their oldest at fourteen and a recruit off the street. He loved animals of all sorts and dreamed of living on a farm. Now that they were heading to Ohio, his dream might come true.

Echoes of *amens* filtered around the boxcar as even the younger children joined in.

William lifted his head proudly, and Matthew nodded his approval. He beamed.

Matthew's prayer reminded Gracie that God was in control and eased the shadows of doubt that haunted her mind about whether they were doing the best thing for the children. If they found loving families, there was no better life, but if the children ended up in abusive situations… She looked down at sensitive Emma and shuddered. No. She wouldn't let her mind go there.

The blow of the whistle and the slight jerk on the railcar had the children hooting for joy. They were off.

~

Matthew smiled across the boxcar at Gracie, who now had five-year-old Emma in her arms and four-year-old Charlotte sleeping beside her. The woman was beyond beautiful. He could look at her all day and never tire of the scenery. In the still of the fading daylight, she looked weary but serene.

The day had started out with excited, hyper children, fighting over their turn at the window. Their eyes bulged as they traveled through the darkness of their first tunnel and rattled over a trestle high above a river. The street kids, used to their independence, were the hardest to control and prone to wander. When Matthew allowed them to stretch their legs at a stop, he had to have his head on a swivel in order to keep track of the twelve boys. A headache was bearing down.

He'd allow one more hour of freedom, and then it would be dark. He got up and walked around to the older ones, who were still awake. "We'll be bedding down as best we can within the hour. I suggest you find your pillow in your bag while there's still some light, your warm coat to cover up with, and a spot where you'll stay until morning."

Eight-year-old Thomas immediately went to his sister, Charlotte. He was used to looking out for her. Helmut had found the two sleeping in the covered doorway of his bakery when he came into work in the wee hours of the morning and had taken them to the orphanage. With no room there, he'd opened his home temporarily until the train left. The two were almost inseparable.

"She's sound asleep, Thomas," Gracie whispered. "Why don't you find a comfortable spot close by to lie down, and I'll watch over her. If she wakes, I'll bring her to you."

Thomas looked uncertain but did as he was told.

Hours passed. The dark and the rhythm of the wheels on rails lulled them to sleep, all except Matthew. He brought his hands to his temples and kneaded. His headache was not abating. He lit a candle to take one last look around.

The flickering light revealed that Gracie's head had fallen forward. She had one child cuddled against her side, while another had laid her head on Gracie's lap. Poor Gracie would be in pain by morning if he left her like that.

Matthew lifted Charlotte and placed her on the floor in the crook of her brother's arm. Thomas instinctively reached out, and she snuggled closer. Matthew covered them both with his blanket. No matter what happened, they would have to keep those two together.

He then slid Emma down on the seat and placed his pillow under her head. He slipped in between the child and his wife and pulled Gracie against his torso, cradling her in his arms. She snuggled up against him as if it were the most natural thing to do. Would she ever fall as madly in love with him as he was with her?

Dear God, the God of miracles and blessings. Step by step You've orchestrated my life, from when I was a young boy on, bringing me grace after grace. Seems fitting you would bring me a woman with that name to remind me every day of Your goodness. Help me to be grateful and thankful, and to praise Your name instead of worrying. Right now, the children and finding good, safe homes for them is the most important thing. Help the two of us to work seamlessly in Your power and love. Amen.

He dropped a soft kiss on her head.

"The children are so resilient." Gracie stretched her arms and rolled her shoulders back. "They don't even notice the hard bench or floor. Seems they can sleep most anywhere and start the day fresh."

"Oh, to be that nimble." Matthew looked around the boxcar at the children playing.

She moved her head from side to side, trying to work out the kinks and wake herself fully. "I need to stand up for a bit. All I want is a hot bath and a comfortable bed. I think I could sleep all day."

"Instead, we have an eight-hour steamboat trip, during which we'll have to ensure twenty kids are accounted for at all times. Don't want to lose one of them over the side."

"Are you trying to cheer me up?"

Matthew winked at her. "Just kidding." He stood and pulled out the chain of his pocket watch, flipping it open. "One blessing. We're almost to Huntington, and it looks like we'll have lots of time to find the right dock and steamboat."

"I can think of another blessing."

"What?" His brows knit together.

"Sleeping in your arms was a whole lot more comfortable than the alternative. Thank you. You're so giving." She reached up and kissed his cheek lightly. Her insides fluttered at the nearness, and she stepped back. "I bet you're feeling it this morning."

He brushed his knuckles against her upturned face. "Anything for my lovely wife."

He said the word *wife* like a soft caress. Shivers of excitement ran up her spine. What would it feel like to truly be his wife?

The train shook and shimmied its way to a stop. She stumbled forward, and he reached out to support her. For a brief moment, fully awake and aware, she rested in his strength. A longing to touch his face and smooth her hand over the laugh lines surrounding his mouth came over her. The urge to explore the contours of his chiseled chin and run her fingertips over the day-old stubble on his cheek brought a tremble to her limbs. It took all she had not to lift her hand. Her fingers tingled at the thought, but that would open the door to the very intimacy she had decided against.

He leaned close and whispered in her ear. "If you keep looking at me like that, Mrs. Weston, I will not be responsible for the consequences."

The tickle of his breath against her ear made her pulse weak and thready.

He straightened and gave her a knowing look.

Heat flooded her face.

Matthew pulled free, and she felt the void.

"All right, children." He clapped and waited for the group to hush. "Adventure number two is about to begin, but everyone must promise to listen and obey. As I explained to you yesterday, we'll be boarding a paddle steamer, and the water is dangerous."

"Not for me," said twelve-year-old Lee with his chest puffed out. "Before my dad passed away, he taught me to swim. All summer long, we'd swim in the James river."

"Well then, Lee, I expect that you have a great respect for the river and its currents."

"I do, sir."

"So, the rule on our walk to the docks and on the boat is that the girls will hold a rope behind Gracie, and the boys will hold a rope behind me. William, you're the oldest boy and will take up the responsibility at the rear and make sure everyone stays together. Teresa, you're the oldest girl and will do the same on the girls' side."

Teresa's hand went up.

"Yes."

"What if someone lets go of the rope?"

"Then you'll call to Gracie and let her know. And that person will be excluded from privileges for the day."

Teresa nodded.

"Once we board the boat, we'll head up the steps to the second level. We'll have our own room, thankfully bigger than the boxcar. Under no circumstances will anyone go out of the room or onto the deck alone. We hope, if the weather is nice and everyone cooperates, that we'll be able to take small groups out to the deck, but that all depends on your behavior."

"What's the name of our boat?" Lee asked. "Pa and I used to love reading the names."

"I know the answer to that one," Matthew said, "because I booked the whole trip around it. Heard the captain runs a safe steamboat. It's called the *Kate*..." Matthew scratched his head. "Hang on a moment." He removed a piece of paper from his pocket. "It's called the *Kate Adams*."

Lee hit William's arm playfully. "See, I told you it would be a girl's name. Most of them are."

Matthew swung the door of the boxcar open, and the children spilled out.

Gracie kept Charlotte in her arms and held Emma's hand. The rest formed a line behind her from youngest to oldest.

Matthew held five-year-old Frederick's hand and carried both their carpet bags in the other. He led the way.

Gracie smiled at all the heads that turned at their procession. They must look quite the sight, one couple with that many kids. The children carried their own small bags in one hand and the rope in the other.

The shimmering gold of early morning light brushed across the Ohio river like a thousand sparkling diamonds. The *Kate Adams* floated stately in the gilded water with a wooden ramp running to her deck, welcoming travelers. Her two steam stacks in the front reached toward the heavens, and a gigantic paddlewheel dripped water in the back. The children oohed and aahed, standing small against its backdrop. The triple decks were stacked onto each other, with each narrower than the one below. It looked like a tiered birthday cake.

The captain in his hub at the very top waved and gave a short toot on the horn.

The children laughed and waved back.

Gracie led the way onto the gangplank. The smell of livestock assaulted her senses, and little Charlotte pinched her nose with her skinny fingers. Barrels of goods and cotton bales took up most of the space. Heat from the boilers sent a blast of warm air cascading over them as they walked by.

A number of scruffy fellows turned their way, and Gracie looked away. She had learned not to make eye contact or smile at unknown men. She found the steps off to the side and began the ascent.

"Hey, pretty lady. Wanna leave the kids behind and—"

Gracie was glad she was out of earshot before he finished his suggestion. A knot of uneasiness curled in her stomach. She had heard rumors of unscrupulous happenings on the riverboats, but Matthew assured her this leg of the trip would be safe because Helmut personally knew the captain, and he ran an honest boat, unlike many others.

They left livestock, hot boilers, freight, and everyday ruffians on the first floor and rose to the second, where ornately decorated rooms were filled with music, fine dining, bars, and gambling tables. The differences between the two classes could not be starker. Gracie walked past to the end of a long hall and found their room number. It was small, sparsely furnished with one table and a couple chairs, but once they were all inside, a sense of relief flooded her. A large window looked out over the water on one side, and the children pasted their noses to the glass.

Gracie's arms ached from carrying Charlotte most of the way, and she was only too glad to put her down and let her run.

Thankful to have a moment to relax her worried mind and tired body, she moved across the room to the chairs.

Matthew walked over and sank into the chair next to her. "After seeing those decks below, I'm sure glad Helmut knew the captain and that this room was secured."

"Me too. If that had been all we could afford—"

"It was, but Helmut knows a lot more about traveling on a steamboat than I do, and I listened to his advice." Matthew ran a hand through his hair. "I have a feeling he paid for a good chunk of this ride as he secured the tickets for us, but he wouldn't say."

"That's generous."

"I can see why the Children's Aid Society was dubious about this route when they heard it required a river run. But it'll bring us into southern Ohio, which, Lord willing, we'll see this evening." Matthew stretched his long legs out in front of him and interlocked his fingers behind his head. "Can't tell you how much I'm looking forward to a good night's sleep on a real bed."

"You haven't had a bed for a while. Even though I've offered to share." Just the mention of them sharing a bed flooded Gracie's face with heat.

"True."

Now what did he mean by that? True, he hadn't had a bed and was noticing the fatigue, or true she had offered to share? She glanced at him but couldn't read his expression.

"How will the sleeping arrangements work tonight?" Gracie couldn't imagine getting a good night's rest with all the kids.

"We've booked all four rooms at an inn. The proprietor said we could divide the rooms up however we like, and they'll have them sparkling clean for those sleeping on the floor."

Gracie was so tired she could barely think. "Any ideas?"

"How about a good mixture of the older kids with the younger ones to help out? Two rooms for the girls and two for the boys, but the adults get the bed."

"My weary bones like the sound of that." Gracie put both

hands on the back of her waist and arched. The stretch to her lower back felt wonderful. "And you asked about the food for the next day's travel?"

"All arranged," Mathew said. "The innkeeper will have a hot supper tonight, breakfast tomorrow, and some fresh biscuits and cheese for the rest of the trip."

"It will be slim pickings today. Yesterday, the older boys ate more than I counted on. I didn't have the heart to stop them. Speaking of which, I'd better get the children settled for some breakfast, if you can call it that." Gracie stood and picked up the larger of the two carpet bags. She opened the wrong one that shared their clothing, then reached for the one with the food.

Now where were those canteens of water the older boys had carried?

Gracie set out the meager fare. "Come, children." They lined up as they had done the day before, from the youngest to the oldest. Gracie handed each child a dry biscuit, a piece of cheese, and a handful of walnuts from the bag that Grandmother had sent along. The ladies had spent hours shelling them in preparation.

The room grew quieter as everyone ate. "May I have some more?" William asked.

Gracie looked in the bag and shook her head. "I'm sorry, but we have to get through all our meals today with what we have left."

The lanky boy nodded but looked longingly at the biscuits.

"Here," Gracie whispered. "You can have mine. But don't show the others." She snuck him her biscuit, and he slipped it in his pocket. "Go eat it over there facing the window, so others won't notice."

She watched as William did as she asked.

Matthew whispered in her ear. "I saw that."

"He was hungry. Look at him, all that height. Probably has hollow legs."

"But you have to eat too."

"I'm fine. I'll just be glad when we're off this boat."

"Why?"

"Maybe it's the water. Even though my sister Katherine taught me to swim, I know if something went wrong, I could help so few."

Matthew slipped an arm around her shoulders, and she leaned in. "We'll be fine. God is with us."

The paddleboat's whistle pealed, setting the children to jumping up and down at the window with shouts of, "We're off. We're off."

The boat inched away from the bank, and they cheered.

CHAPTER 24

Matthew took a second group of boys out onto the upper deck. They basked in the morning sunshine, their eyes as bright as the glistening water. There was something so peaceful about drifting along, as if time had slowed. "Look." He pointed out an eagle gliding overhead, and the boys squinted into the sun. "If you pay attention, boys, you'll see all kinds of life. The water will give up a splash of a fish, a turtle sunning on a log, or a muskrat along the banks."

"What kind of fish will we see?" Charles asked.

"I read the biggest fish is the blue catfish, but there are bass, pike, perch, and many more. And if you keep your eyes focused on the banks, you may see white-tailed deer, red fox, cottontail rabbits, raccoons, or even a mink. However, the last two are largely nocturnal."

"Noc…trunal?" Seven-year-old Edgar tried to say.

"That means they come out at night," Art explained, his chin lifted.

"Very good, Art," Matthew said. "You were listening last week during your lessons."

Art told the boys other facts he remembered, and Matthew took a moment to daydream.

Slowly, Gracie was getting used to his spontaneous touch—his hand holding hers, an arm around her shoulder, his help into the train or out again. At first, she allowed a brief connection, but now she relaxed in his embrace. Earlier today, she had melted into his arms instead of pulling away. Hope flowed through his veins.

"All right, boys, time to head back in and give the girls a turn."

"Can't we stay out one more moment?" Edgar's eyes were big and pleading.

Matthew pulled out his pocket watch and flipped it open, reminded of what he had learned from Gracie, that children loved games. "I'll tell you what. I'll give you one more minute, but you have to point out some type of bird, fish, or mammal. And I need to see it, too. If one of you is successful, you'll earn five more minutes for your group. Ready. Set. Go."

The boys had their eyes bugging out and their heads turning this way and that.

Matthew smiled at their concentration. They were down to ten seconds, nine, eight... A bird swooped in and hopped along the deck. "A crow, a crow," they screamed.

Matthew laughed. "I was hoping for something a bit more exotic than a common crow, but a deal's a deal. Enjoy your last five minutes." The look on their faces, filled with joy, warmed Matthew's heart. He lifted his head up into the heavens with gratitude. He was doing the work he loved with the woman he loved. God was good.

"Matthew, come quick." Gracie's voice was high-pitched and frantic. She waved to him from the deck door, then disappeared back inside.

"Boys, we have to go." He herded them into their room and found Gracie. Fear radiated from her eyes.

"I left the older teenagers in charge and went across the hall to take Charlotte and Mary Jane to the privy. When I returned and did the head count, Henry was gone. No one saw him leave."

Matthew's pulse kicked up. "Well, he can't have gone far." He managed to keep his voice steady, though a knot of nerves twisted in his gut. "I'll go find him."

"But Matthew. The water."

"Good thing he's twelve and not four. He'd have more sense than to go too near the edge." The confidence he was exuding was a far cry from the chill of concern spreading through his bones. He raised his voice and got the group's attention. "Under no circumstances is anyone to leave this room until I return. Understood?" His words boomed across the small space in his most authoritative voice. Heads nodded up and down.

"Don't worry, I'll find him." He squeezed Gracie's arm and left.

He quickly searched the upper deck outside, checked the privy, and scanned the dining area. Henry had been living on the street, so he may have decided to steal some food. But the dining room was near empty, and Matthew saw no sign of him.

He flew down the steps, praying all the way. The railing on the lower deck was not nearly as secure, and there was a large section up front that had no railing at all. But when he asked around, no one had seen the boy, which most likely meant he had not ventured down there.

There was only one other place left to check but he couldn't imagine the child going into the bar or sidling up to the gambling tables.

Where was he?

Matthew raced back up the stairs, taking them two at a time. He poked his head into the door at the end of a large room. Men and women sat around the bar and in booths, but no sign of Henry. The next door fed into the gambling area. Scantily clad women with trays of drinks weaved among the tables crammed with men. The smoky light forced Matthew to enter to take a better look.

His eyes had barely adjusted to the dimness when an attractive blonde with painted ruby lips and a very low-cut dress approached. "May I assist you in finding your game, handsome? Possibly Faro, or poker? Or do you prefer the dice… High-low, Chuck-a-luck—"

"No, thanks. I'm looking for—"

"Perhaps a dancing partner would be more to your liking, or some company over a drink?" She batted her long thick lashes at him. Clearly, many a man had been led down the garden path by her, but he was not about to become one of them.

"I'm wondering if I could have your assistance in—"

"I'm at your service, sir." Her long, painted fingernails danced up his arm.

He wanted to rip free but needed her help. "I'm trying to locate a young boy. I'm transporting a large group of orphan children, and we seem to have misplaced a twelve-year-old. Did you happen to see him?"

"Well now, that all depends on your generosity."

Matthew fished in his pocket and pulled out a dollar. *Hurry up and tell me what you know.*

Her eyes lit up, and she reached for the coin.

Matthew snapped his hand closed. "After I find the boy."

"Fine then." She put on a pout. "Follow me."

They wove through a maze of tables to the far corner of the room. Thankfully, the piano music and singer drowned out most of the yelling and cussing. He was shocked to see some woman playing at the tables. Being led down a dark hall off the main room, a trickle of sweat ran down his back. Was she thinking he wanted something he did not?

"Have a peek, then let me get out of here before you enter. I want nothing to do with this." She opened the door just a slit.

Matthew peered in. Around a table were three men—plus Henry, all deep in concentration. A game was underway with a few men on the sidelines. Packed holsters hung around their waists as they intently watched. Every man wore a gun except vulnerable Henry. Panic edged up his throat.

Matthew pulled back.

"You might want to shut your mouth before heading in." The woman stifled her laughter, but her smirk said it all.

A spike of raw fear scuttled up his spine.

"My dollar." She held out her hand.

Matthew held out the coin but did not let go. "If you feel good about taking food out of the mouths of orphan children."

With one hand on her voluptuous hip, she glared at him. "Fine then. Only because I was once one of them."

"May God bless your kindness."

"Pff, keep your blessings for yourself. You're going to need it in order to get that kid out of there." Her head nodded toward the door. "They all have loaded guns, and they're not afraid to use 'em. The stakes are always high in there. Very high." She turned and flounced away.

Now what? *Oh God, have mercy, give wisdom.* Should he hurry back and tell Gracie what was going on? Should he try to find the captain?

No, the situation was volatile. He had to get Henry to safety. He hated to risk his life and feared leaving Gracie to fend alone, but he could see no other option. The hair on the back of his neck spiked.

Do not be afraid. I am with you.

An unexplainable sense of calm came over him, and his heartrate settled. Without further thought, he flung the door wide open.

"Henry. Come here at once."

Every head snapped up. Every eyeball pierced through him.

Henry shot up, eyes wide. A look of relief flooded his face.

"Not so fast." A wiry man with a black horseshoe mustache stood directly behind Henry, gripping his shoulder. He pushed the boy back into the chair. "We're in the middle of a game here. No one is leaving until we're done."

A hulk of a man caressed his gun, sending an all too readable message. The cigar hanging from the side of his mouth tipped and dipped as he spoke but somehow stayed in place. "Jessie's right. We ain't stopping nothing."

"Henry is with me, and I demand that he be returned." Matthew spoke with strength, though nerves twisted and knotted in his gut.

The large man slid his gun from his holster in one smooth movement. He pinned it on Jessie. "Thought you said this was your kid. Maybe I should use this gun on you." He swiveled it on his finger.

They all looked at Jessie holding the boy in place. "He's an orphan, Kean. I swear. And I've taken him in."

Matthew swallowed hard against the knot in his throat and found his voice. "You have no right to take—"

"You want me for your new pa, don't ya? Isn't that right, boy?" Jessie clapped Henry on the shoulder.

Henry's eyes darted from Jessie back to Matthew. He nodded but the look of fear in his eyes sent a different message.

Mathew's shirt stuck to his flesh as sweat trickled down his spine. "Henry is an orphan under the protection of my orphanage, and I demand he be set free."

"How old are you, kid?" Kean asked.

"T-twelve." Henry choked on the word.

"Twelve is old enough," Kean said. "Let the lad decide."

The other men nodded in agreement.

"Henry, remember what we talked about?" Matthew held out his hand. "We love you and want the best for your life, a far better life than what this man offers. He'll use and abuse you—"

"We'll have nothing but adventure," Jessie said. "You and I

make a hell-of-a team. With your talent, why waste it workin' on some stinkin' farm somewhere. What do you say, boy?"

Henry's face drained of color.

Matthew prayed desperately.

Do not be afraid. I am with you.

"I-I want to go with Matthew."

"I ain't no kidnapper," Jessie said. "But this kid entered into this game using my money, and I ain't about to take a loss because he decides halfway through he no longer wants to play." Jessie spit a glob of his chewing tobacco toward the nearby spittoon but missed his mark.

"And I'm not about to fold," Kean said.

"Nor am I," another added.

"I'll allow Henry to finish the game on one condition." Matthew couldn't believe he was suggesting such a thing, but concessions had to be made.

Jessie's eyes narrowed on him. "What?"

"I stay, and no matter who wins, you let that boy leave when the game is done."

"How do I know he won't throw it?" Jessie said.

"He won't. Will you Henry?"

"No, sir. I'll do my very best."

"Come on in and shut the door, then." Kean slid his gun back into his holster and picked up his cards with both hands.

Stale acrid air bit at Matthew's nostrils as he moved into the room. He knew little about poker, so he stood against the wall praying for the souls of each man and praying that Gracie would stay put upstairs. This was taking much longer than he'd anticipated.

The other two players folded and only Henry and Kean were left. Henry's brows knit together in concentration. His knuckles turned white. One would think he had a terrible hand until he laid down three aces and a pair.

Jessie let out a whoop. "A full house." He bent forward to scoop up the winnings.

"Not so fast." Kean laid his hand down slowly, displaying an eight, seven, six, five, and four of clubs. "Now, that's how's it's done."

"A straight flush. You cheatin' son-of-a—" Jessie went for his gun, and Henry dove to the floor as if he'd been in that situation before. He scrambled toward Matthew, who yanked him up by his shirt.

They ran.

A gunshot rang out, but they didn't slow as they entered the gambling area, continued through the bar, and raced down the corridor. They kept up the pace until they burst through the door of their room.

Matthew slammed it shut.

Gracie shot forward and grabbed his arms. Her eyes were popped wide, and her whisper was fierce. "I was terrified."

He threw an arm around her shoulders. Her shaking body collapsed against him, and he took a few moments to catch his breath.

The other children crowded close with all eyes on him.

"God was with us, but…" He turned toward Henry with his arm still around Gracie's shoulder. "What were you thinking? You put us all in danger."

Henry slid down the wall to the floor and dropped his head into his hands. He looked up with tears in his eyes. "I-I planned to take a quick peek and come back right away before anyone missed me."

"But why?"

"Thought maybe I'd see my dad. Before he left me, he'd been talkin' of hittin' the riverboats to make it big."

Ah. That explained a lot. "So, he's the one who taught you how to gamble."

Henry nodded. "Been doing that as far back as I can remember. I have a knack for remembering cards."

"He teach you to dive for cover like you did?"

"Pa taught me to read expressions and situations."

"But how did you get mixed up in that game?"

"He was gambling?" Gracie looked up at Matthew, clutching his side. Her eyes formed wide circles.

"I was lookin' for Pa when a game drew my interest. That Jessie guy was standing beside me when I shook my head and said the guy playin' wasn't gonna win. Jessie asked how I knew, and I recited what cards had already been played. The next thing I knew, he had me in his clutches and wouldn't let go. He promised money and adventure, and I thought maybe it would be a way to live until I found my pa. I'm sorry, so sorry." His voice broke and he put his head back down on his knees.

Gracie knelt beside Henry and wrapped him in a hug. "It's all right. I'd want to find my pa, too, if I were you."

"Why did he leave me?" Henry sobbed into his knees.

Gracie waved away the children who were crowding in. "Go on now, give Henry some room."

They wandered back to what they'd been doing.

Matthew bent down beside him and clasped him on the shoulder. "Maybe your pa left you because he wanted you to find a better life than what he could give you. Gambling leads to what you witnessed today…cheating, angry men, gunshots."

Henry looked up and swiped tears from his eyes. "Well, I ain't lookin' for him ever again."

"We'll find you a good home, Henry," Gracie said. "There's nothing wrong with still loving your pa. But there's hope for a much brighter tomorrow. Do you believe that?"

"I want to."

A knock hammered at the door, and Matthew marched across the room and spoke through the door. After what just happened, he wasn't letting anybody in until he knew what they wanted. "Who is it?"

"Lunch. Compliments of the captain."

Matthew cracked the door and peered out. Sure enough, a man with a cart full of food stood on the other side. He opened wider, and the man rolled it in. Sandwiches, apples, sweets, and lemonade. The children gathered around, laughing and jumping up and down. Their eyes sparkled with joy.

"Give the captain our sincerest thanks," Matthew said.

Henry pulled himself up, and his eyes brightened at the sight.

Matthew smiled at him. "Hey, Henry, you want to help me serve?"

As Henry stepped forward, with a crisp "Yes sir" on his lips, Matthew breathed a prayer of thanks. God had not only protected Henry and helped him bring the lad back, but He'd supplied a feast to a very hungry group. The heavy weight of responsibility lifted from his shoulders, as he stretched his neck from side to side. He did not have to carry the load. God was with them.

CHAPTER 25

"No. I insist." The matronly lady of The Garden Inn folded her hands together on top her rounded abdomen. "You must have a room to yourselves and a good night's rest so you have energy for the remainder of your trip."

Gracie met Matthew's gaze. The thought of sharing a room with him—with only one bed—set her heart aflutter. And the need for a good night's sleep was very tempting. "I think we should be with the children as planned. Don't you?"

"Nonsense." Mrs. Brooks said. "The children will be fine. They're exhausted and tucked in. And your group takes up all our rooms, so there's no one else on the premises but you. They are perfectly safe, and you need some sleep."

"But you only have the four rooms for rent."

"Yes, but when I heard what you two were doing for those poor orphans, I talked to my George, and we want to do our part. At no extra cost, we're offering one of our personal rooms at the bottom of the steps. It's ready and waiting. That way you'll be able to hear if any child needs you." That was true, they would not be far, and the children were worn out.

"I agree with Mrs. Brooks. Even the older children have

settled down," Matthew said. "And I could really use some decent sleep."

Gracie's eyes flew up to his.

"Of course you could," the woman said. "Come. I'll show you the room."

Matthew took Gracie's hand. "Shall we, my dear?"

She could not believe he was agreeing to this. There would only be one bed, and they'd both want it. She squeezed his hand hard, hoping he would understand her message, but he followed Mrs. Brooks as she waddled back down the hall, taking the steep and narrow steps with care.

"These used to be a whole lot shorter." She laughed. "Just you wait until you get to be my age. Without my dear sweet Mary to help with the cleaning, I'd never be able to keep this place running."

At the bottom of the steps, she turned to them with a smile across her wrinkled face and swung open the nearest door. "There's a hot bath prepared behind that dressing screen," she said proudly. "And the bed is ever so comfortable. One of the best we have. This room is usually only given to close friends and relatives."

Gracie could see extra care had been taken to make the room ready, from the fresh flowers in a vase on the washstand, to the pile of clean towels stacked on a chair beside the screen. A warm sensation curled in the pit of her stomach. The room exuded romance.

"What a wonderful gift." Matthew moved into the space, pulling Gracie along with him. "May God bless your kindness."

Mrs. Brooks beamed. "I'll leave you now." The door clicked shut behind her.

A warm fire glowed drowsily. The candle on the bedstand cast wavering shadows across the room, and the steam from the hot bath beckoned. There was nothing Gracie wanted more than to melt into its warmth and soak the grime from her body. But how could she with a man in her room?

"You take the bath first," Matthew offered, as if they were an old married couple completely comfortable with what was unfolding.

She gasped. "But Matthew—"

"There's a privacy screen, and I'm not about to join you—unless you invite me, of course." His eyes twinkled with humor.

He was enjoying this. How dare he? A rush of heat filled her cheeks.

"All right, then," he said. "I'll go first. I'm not about to waste a hot bath." He started to undo the buttons on his shirt.

"No, no." She scurried behind the screen. "I'll hurry so it's still warm for you."

As she undressed, a hand reached around the screen. "Here, you might need this." Matthew held the carpet bag with their few pieces of clothing.

"Thank you." She snatched it and pulled out her comfortable chemise and night jacket, placing them on the nearby chair. Undressing with Matthew just on the other side of the screen felt awkward and decidedly intimate. She hurried to rid herself of the clothing and slipped into the deliciously warm water.

"Take your time," Matthew said. "I want you to relax. We've had a tough couple of days, and we have a few more ahead of us."

With his voice husky and warm, and with only that screen between them, her imagination was heightened. What would it feel like to invite him into this space…into this tub? Her face burned hot. Goodness, she had to get her mind elsewhere. This trip was about the children…

"It'll be so emotional saying goodbye." A knot filled Gracie's throat the minute the thought crossed her mind. Maybe thinking of Matthew was a better choice. She smoothed the water over her skin and scrubbed with a bar of soap that smelled like spring lilacs.

"It will indeed."

Gracie wanted to linger but pulled herself from the tub before it cooled too much. "Matthew?"

"Hmm."

"Do you think we'll find good homes for all of them?" She hurriedly dried her body with the towel and slipped into her nightwear. She trusted Matthew explicitly, but there was something about bathing in such close proximity that had her pulse racing.

"That is my prayer."

"Mine, too. When you're done with your bath," she asked, "do you think we could pray about it together?"

"Sure."

That was, if she could keep her mind on prayer rather than on this intimate scenario. Gracie rounded the screen. "The bath is still nice and warm, but go quickly. Don't waste a moment." She worked hard to keep her voice level and nonchalant. "How thoughtful of Mrs. Brooks."

Matthew disappeared behind the screen. "We've been blessed on this trip so far."

In record time, Gracie heard the splash of water.

Prayer. She was going to keep her mind on prayer.

"Ahh, this is nice. The only thing missing is someone to wash my back."

Prayer went out the window, and her cheeks felt on fire. "Matthew Weston, you're incorrigible."

"Well, you can't blame a husband for trying."

She laughed but didn't know what to say.

Did he wish for a real marriage? Of course he did. What man wouldn't? How unwise this marriage was proving to be.

She had a promise to keep. She had children to care for. She did not need the distraction of a very handsome man. And how would they manage the sleeping arrangements for the night? She was not about to make her exhausted husband sleep on a hard floor. But the thought of him lying next to her caused tiny pricks of awareness to dance over every nerve ending.

She slipped beneath the covers on one side of the bed, thoroughly exhausted, but there was not a chance she would sleep.

She heard him pull from the water, and in a matter of moments, he emerged wearing only a pair of pants. She could not take her eyes from his firmly muscled chest, which slimmed to a trim waist. It was the first time she saw the scars he'd mentioned getting as a wayward teen. They made him look far too rugged and masculine.

He rustled through the bag and pulled out a brush, pulling his full head of hair into submission.

She forced her mind to a safe subject. "Men are so lucky. I didn't bother washing my hair. It would take hours to dry."

"Hmm, men have other things to worry about." His voice sounded strained.

Something was bothering him. Maybe he didn't want to sleep on the floor. "I want you to have a good night's sleep," she said. "You must share the bed with me tonight."

He gazed at her. For a moment confusion and something she failed to identify filled his eyes, but he averted them and he walked across the room. He blew out the candle and slipped into bed beside her.

"Let's pray," he said.

The shadows of the dying embers in the fireplace danced on the ceiling. The closeness of his body radiated heat, and a deep desire to curl into his arms overwhelmed her. She slid close and placed her head against his chest. She wanted to run her fingers down the length of each scar and kiss away the horror they represented, but she didn't dare. His arm slowly came around her. The intimacy made her hands tingle and her throat tighten, but somehow the nearness felt right. She listened to the rapid beat of his heart beneath her ear and the deep rumble of his voice as he prayed for each child by name. When he was done, he asked. "Is it all right if I hold you?"

Gracie could barely breathe. Though she had little knowledge of the way of a husband and wife, she wanted him to do a lot more than hold her. "Yes," she whispered.

"Turn the other way."

She did, and he moved behind her and drew her close until she was pressed into the curve of his body. She sank into the warmth and protection of his arms. She had never experienced anything so divine.

"Matthew?"

"Hmm."

"Are you happy? I-I mean with the way our marriage is."

She heard a sharp intake of breath and felt the slow release of air against the back of her head. "Go to sleep, Gracie," he said. "We're both too exhausted for this conversation."

He kissed the back of her head, and she relaxed in his arms. Sleep came fast.

～

Matthew looked out the train window at the rolling hills of Gallia County, Ohio. Soon, the first bunch of kids would be given away, hopefully to happy homes. As much as he knew Gracie was preparing her heart, he knew this would be harder for her than she could anticipate.

Just the thought of her brought back the torture of the night before. Sleep had come slowly, very slow. It had taken every bit of strength to stick to their agreement and not take advantage of her exhaustion and the perfect setting to woo his bride. He could've turned her in his arms and kissed her into oblivion. She may be innocent, but he could feel the way her body responded to his merest touch. She had not pulled away but burrowed closer. And he had kissed her enough times to know she felt every bit what a woman feels for a man.

But he wanted more. He desired her love.

The train was quickly approaching their first stop, Evergreen. He checked his notes. The farming community was known for raising hogs and livestock. And one glance out the window confirmed that corn and tobacco crops were planted as far as the eye could see.

Matthew whistled between his pinky fingers to get the children's attention. "Remember, if you're not chosen this time, there are many more stops, so do not despair. And do all of you remember the letter in your bag and how you can send a secret message to the orphanage if things are not going well?"

Emma's little hand shot up. "We draw a picture of a sun with a happy face and ask our new family to mail it off."

"That's right." Gracie said. "And is this a secret?"

"Yes," the children called out.

"We don't anticipate any problems, as the families have already been screened by a local committee," Gracie said. "Use the letter only if you're being harmed. This doesn't mean not getting your own way. Could someone give me an example of what I mean when I say being harmed?"

Art put up his hand, and Gracie nodded at him. "It's like when my ma used to beat me until I had bloody welts and bruises all over my body."

Matthew's neck tightened at the thought, and he swallowed against the knot in his throat. "I'm sorry that happened to you, Art. But yes, that would be an example."

"We'll also be back in September to visit and see how you're doing," Gracie said. "That's only six months from now. If you're not happy, we'll take you back with us, but our hope and prayer is that you'll love your new family."

Thomas raised his hand. "Will I be able to stay with my sister? I promised Ma I'd take good care of her."

Gracie looked at Matthew, and he nodded. "That's our hope, Thomas. It'll be harder to find a home for two children, but we'll certainly try."

"Is there a chance we could be separated?" His little chin quivered.

"I won't lie to you, Thomas." Matthew crouched down to his level. "We're going to try our utmost to keep you together. But you want the best for your sister, don't you? And living on the streets of Richmond was not the best, right?"

He nodded and blinked. Two fat tears rolled down his cheeks.

Matthew opened his arms, and Thomas fell in.

Charlotte followed, and Matthew's heart constricted with their little arms wrapped so tightly around his neck. *Oh God, please keep these two together. No child should ever have to go through this.*

He prayed silently as the train slowed and screeched to a stop. The whistle blew. After Thomas stepped away, Matthew stood, Charlotte still in his arms. Most of the children had excitement in their eyes, some looked afraid.

He whispered to Gracie, "Here we go."

Her guarded smile spoke volumes. "I'll take up the rear."

He stepped off the train, where he was met by an elderly man. His bespectacled and kind eyes set Matthew at ease.

The man held out his hand and gave a firm shake. "My name is Walter Krone, and I'm the pastor here. My wife, Martha, and I were asked by the Children's Aid Society to screen the families who would like to adopt a child." He waved the children closer as they piled out of the train car, Gracie being last. "We don't have much time, so we're going to do the selections here at the station. A platform is set up, and some very excited mamas and papas await inside. Follow me." His smile was wide and genuine.

Matthew thanked him, and they followed the man inside.

"If you could arrange the children from youngest to oldest

on our makeshift platform?" Mr. Krone said, pointing to the front of the room.

A group of adults split apart, making room for the children to pass through.

Gracie arranged the girls and Matthew arranged the boys, placing Charlotte and Thomas together in the middle. Thomas was holding on so tightly to Charlotte's little hand that it was turning white.

Matthew held up his arms, and the room quieted. "We thank you for coming today, and our hope and prayer is that you'll find the perfect child for your family. You may walk by and have a conversation with any child you think might be a good fit. If you are interested, please come to either my wife, Gracie, or myself, and we'll get you the appropriate paperwork. Keep in mind that we retain the right to decline any application. We're heavily invested in the lives of these children, first and foremost, will do what is best for them." He stepped behind Charlotte and Thomas. "These two are brother and sister, and we'd like to keep them together."

The crowd of adults moved in quickly. Two women began to argue over twelve-year-old Annie, an attractive girl with her big brown eyes, and wavy dark hair.

"I got here first."

"No, I did."

"Ladies, please," Matthew said. "Both of you may have a few minutes with Annie, and then we'll let her decide. How does that sound?"

Annie's eyes had doubled in size.

Matthew squeezed her arm and whispered in her ear. "If you're not comfortable with either of them, let me know."

She nodded.

"Get your hands out of his mouth." Gracie's voice cut through the din, and Matthew's head snapped around in her direction. He hurried over.

An old farmer pulled his dirty fingers out of ten-year-old Charles' mouth. "I was jus checkin' fur bad teeth is all."

"He's a child, not an animal," Gracie said. "You may ask him to open his mouth, but you may not touch him."

The farmer huffed and stomped away.

"Can you believe that?" Gracie's big brown eyes rolled.

"Take a deep breath," he whispered. "Who knew we would have to announce not to treat the children like horses?"

One by one, couples came forward, and by the time the whistle blew signifying it was time to board, four boys and three girls had found homes. Emma, with her blond curls and dark eyes, drew a lot of attention, but she shook her head at every couple who expressed interest in her. Matthew would have to get Gracie to talk to her, but there was no point in pushing the child at the first stop.

"Let's get the kids loaded," he said to Gracie.

They worked together rounding up the remaining thirteen and headed outside. "Can you take them to the train?" Matthew asked. "I want to say good-bye to William."

"By all means."

He darted from the group to fourteen-year-old William, who was climbing into a wagon. "I hear you got your wish." Matthew said.

The boy beamed. "Yup. Mr. Grier says I'll be able to learn everything about ranching there is to know. And I get my own horse too. Isn't that right?" William looked to the man beside him, who wore a wide cowboy hat.

"You betcha, son. You can't be a rancher without a horse, but the first thing you need is this." Mr. Grier reached to the back of the wagon and pulled out a cowboy hat identical to his.

William let out a whoop. "For me?"

"All Grier men wear them."

William took off his cap and slapped the new hat on his head. He turned toward Matthew with a wheedling smile.

"Thanks for getting me off the streets. I shall always be grateful." He held out his hand like a man.

Matthew gave a hearty shake. "I'll miss you, William." His voice caught, and he swallowed back the lump in his throat. "But I couldn't be happier for you." The train whistled a second time. "I've got to go." He turned before the young man saw the tears misting in his eyes.

CHAPTER 26

The train chugged to a stop in a thick forest with only a few shanties in sight. "We're in the middle of nowhere," Gracie said. "Why ever are we stopping here?"

Matthew looked at his notes. "This must be Moonville, in Vinton County." He stuck his head out the window and pulled it back in. "Yes, there's a couple waiting."

Gracie took a peek. The two stood under the protection of a slanted roof, which Gracie deduced was the extent of the town's train depot. "What do people do here?"

"There's a coal mine. The woman is the schoolteacher, and her husband is in charge at the mine."

"But there's nothing much here, no community to speak of. Has this couple been screened?"

"They have. They've written about ten times asking for a child because they can't have one. A boy or a girl—they don't care."

Gracie looked out at the heavily wooded area. There was something about the place that felt oppressive. "No point in unloading the children for one coupe. Let's go talk to them outside and see what we think before bringing them in to meet the children."

"Good idea," Matthew said.

They put Teresa in charge and stepped down off the train. Gracie took in the greenbrier, wild roses, and tall trees. Why didn't she like this place? Maybe it was the dark dreary day and the thick vegetation that gave her that claustrophobic feeling.

"Mr. and Mrs. Shirstein?" Matthew asked.

"That's right." Mr. Shirstein opened an umbrella for his wife and held it for her as they stepped out from the covering of the lean-to shed into the spitting rain.

The conductor stuck his head out of the window. "The engineer says you have ten minutes."

"Where are the children?" Mrs. Shirstein's voice sounded strained. She stared down her long nose at Gracie. The narrow visage of her face made her look stern and unfriendly, but Gracie didn't want to make a snap decision based on her appearance.

Matthew stepped forward. "This is my wife, Gracie, and I'm Matthew Weston."

"We only have ten minutes," she snapped. "Can we skip the pleasantries and see the children?"

Was there a bite to Mrs. Shirstein's voice, or was she merely nervous about the time constraints?

"We like to meet the parents, and we don't consider it a pleasantry but rather a necessity." Gracie kept her voice level but firm. "Being that we can't see much of this town, can you tell us about it?"

Mr. Shirstein lifted his head proudly. "Why, it's a booming little town growing in number every day. The coal mine is the main source of work. I manage the laborers." The short bulldog of a man puffed out his chest. Corded muscles pulled at the material in his upper arms and across his wide shoulders. The light in his blue eyes twinkled kindness, the direct opposite of his wife.

"And we have a schoolhouse, thanks to my insistence," Mrs. Shirstein said. "And a saloon, a store, and all the essentials."

"Is there a church?" Gracie asked.

"But of course—"

"Ethel." Mr. Shirstein raised his brows at his wife.

"Nearly. It's the next thing our town will build." Her beady eyes darted to her husband as if she dared him to disagree. "And I'm a teacher, so I can teach the Bible with or without a church." She blinked, and her voice softened. "Please, can we see the children? I'm sure you have no idea the pain caused from being a barren woman. I so want to give my husband the desire of his heart—to be a daddy." She pulled a handkerchief from her pocket and dabbed at her eyes.

He put his arm around her bony shoulders. "Either a girl or a boy would be fine with me, but Ethel's decided on a little girl, if that's all right?"

Gracie wanted to get in that train and keep going, but how could she convey that to Matthew without being rude?

The conductor stuck his head out the window again. "Five more minutes, and the train pulls out."

"Follow me." Matthew walked over to their boxcar. He helped the two women up.

Mrs. Shirstein took one look around the boxcar. Her eyes slowed as they passed over Emma and then came back to her once she had gone around the circle of children. "That little girl will do just fine."

Emma's dark eyes grew large, almost swallowing her face. She was about to shake her head but took one look at Matthew and Gracie and glanced down at the floor.

Gracie gulped back the knot in her throat. No, not Emma. Not to this woman. But they had just talked to Emma and explained how she was not to be afraid, and how they'd be back to check on her. Gracie was so proud of Emma in that moment for being strong.

Even still, she wanted Emma to decline.

Mrs. Shirstein moved toward the child.

"Just one moment." Gracie held up her hand. "Matthew, I need a word with you." Gracie hurried out of the boxcar.

Matthew followed.

"Emma's too soft for the likes of that woman."

"You're not being rational," he said. "Emma is special to you. No one will be good enough."

"You don't understand. I have a bad feeling…" The blast of the train whistle drowned out her words.

"Time's up," Matthew said. "What do you want me to say to them?"

"I don't know."

"I'll follow your lead. You know Emma the best." Matthew held out his hand to help Gracie back into the boxcar.

Mr. Shirstein was crouched down talking to Emma. His beefy hands and arms were stretched out wide. "If you want a daddy who will love you to the moon and back, I'd like to be the one you choose."

Emma intently looked into his eyes, then nodded and stepped into his embrace. The large man had tears running down his face when he stood, holding the child gently in his big arms.

"Why you sad?" Emma touched the tears with her small fingers.

"Those are happy tears, Emma. You've made me the happiest daddy alive."

She smiled at him, and he beamed.

Matthew looked at Gracie. As much as she wanted to snatch Emma back, she couldn't deny the love in the man's gaze.

She nodded.

"Let me sign the papers," Mrs. Shirstein said, "before this

train takes off with us in it." The bite was back in the woman's voice.

Unease flooded Gracie's heart.

~

Matthew stood beside Gracie as the train pulled out of the station. She waved out of the window at Emma, still held in Mr. Shirstein's arms. His wife had a dour expression on her face, hardly the look of a happy mama.

A knot twisted in Matthew's gut.

"I don't feel right about this," Gracie whispered. "Everything was so rushed. I couldn't ask the questions I wanted to."

Matthew's heart sank. He had a feeling it would be this way for Gracie when Emma was chosen, but now was not the time to talk about it. He didn't want the children to pick up on their misgivings. "Can we talk about it later?" He nodded to the left, where thirteen-year-old Teresa stood.

Gracie nodded, but a troubled light stirred in the depth of her soulful eyes.

"Mr. Weston, is this Emma's doll?" Thomas held up the rag doll.

Gracie whirled around. "Oh dear, it is." Gracie took the doll and turned it over in her hands. "Emma carts this doll everywhere. Now I really feel…"

Matthew caught her gaze and shook his head. She stifled her words.

Every child was listening. He wanted to take Gracie in his arms and let her cry, but he dared not give too much empathy or she would do just that.

"We'll mail it to her, and it'll be a lovely surprise." Matthew forced an upbeat tone into his voice for the sake of the children.

A mist of tears veiled Gracie's eyes, and she turned toward the window and stared out, the rag doll dangling at her side.

It was her pain, yet it felt like a hot stone had lodged in his chest. She was trying to find her composure. He'd best give her some time alone.

He slid into a padded seat, glad that their private boxcar was much more comfortable than the last one. It had a row of seats and an open area at the back to walk around, where the children could play or look out the window. He closed his eyes for a moment, succumbing to the lull and gentle rocking of wheels on rail. *"Oh God, help her."*

"Matthew." Gracie's hand tugged at his shoulder, and his eyes popped open.

"Did I fall asleep?"

"You did, and you needed it. But I'm starting to see houses, and I think our next stop is near."

Matthew flipped through his notes and moved toward the window. "This is Logan, in Hocking County." The sprinkling of houses thickened. A church steeple, numerous stores, and a bank came into view as they rolled into town.

"This looks much better," Gracie said.

"That's for sure."

"May I talk to you?" Henry stepped forward.

Matthew stepped away from Gracie. "Of course. What is it?"

"I've been thinking. The reason I went with that gambler was my fear of being stuck on a farm. I'm not much for country living. Do you think I could be paired up with a family that has a business of some sort? I'm real good with numbers."

"I could see that." Matthew said. "The way you could remember those cards was amazing. I think your idea is splendid."

"You do?"

"Absolutely."

The brakes screeched as the train pulled into the station. He looked down at his notes. "Let's see. This town boasts of an iron and steel company, two banks, numerous manufacturing businesses… Yup, we should be able to do just that. And if not here, then in the bigger centers like Lancaster or Columbus."

Henry let out a big breath. "Thank you."

Matthew ruffled his short hair, which stood on end, and threw his arm around the boy. "I'm so glad you chose to continue on with us."

Henry's lopsided grin warmed Matthew's heart.

They stepped from the train and were mobbed by a group of excited parents-to-be who crowded around. Matthew was thankful when the local preacher called order to the enthusiastic group.

"Wait." The man held up two arms. "Stand back and give the children room to disembark. There will be plenty of time to complete this process, and we don't want to overwhelm the children, do we?"

Matthew caught the look of one man in particular. He was impeccably dressed. Wealth oozed from the tip of his top hat to his shining shoes. His eyes were pinned on Teresa, but it was the way the older businessman looked her up and down that sent a shiver spiraling up Matthew's spine.

Matthew squeezed Gracie's arm to get her attention and leaned close to her ear. "If that man in the top hat wants to adopt Teresa, or any girl for that matter, let me handle it." The man's eyes were still pinned on Teresa.

Gracie's brows raised, and she nodded. "I understand."

Good. He wasn't imagining what was going on, Gracie picked up on it too.

The children were excited, more relaxed knowing what to expect. Numerous people wanted either Charlotte or Thomas, but no one wanted both. They clutched each other's hands as the activity whirled around them.

Matthew could barely keep up with the interviews and paperwork. He sent a happy couple and child on their way, then turned to see Teresa and the well-dressed man approaching.

The man stopped in front of him. "I'm Edgar Weans, and I'd like to adopt…you said your name was Teresa?" Edgar turned toward her and smiled.

"Yes," Teresa whispered, though her gaze didn't lift from the floor.

"Your wife said I needed to talk to you."

"That's right, Mr. Weans. Where is *your* wife today?"

"She's very ill and can't leave the house. That's why I want to adopt an older girl as a companion for her. We have all the maids we need, but I want my dear wife to have a daughter and a friend, something we've never been able to have."

"What is your occupation?"

"I'm a railroad builder. Finances are not an issue. As our daughter, Teresa here will have a fine opportunity to become a lady with upstanding prominence in the community."

Matthew looked into his dark eyes. He was saying all the right things, and he no longer had that lustful gleam. Had Matthew read him right? He prayed for wisdom, and the knot in his gut returned.

Matthew tried to smile at the man. "One moment please. I'd like to talk to Teresa privately." He waved her over to the corner of the room.

The minute they were out of hearing range, Teresa begged, "Please don't make me go with him. Mama's boyfriend used to have that look before she ran off with him, and he'd do things to me—"

"No need to say more. I understand."

"I'd much rather go to a big family on a farm, where I can help with the young ones and learn how to be a wife and mother."

"Well then, we'll do everything in our power to make that happen. But the best thing we can do is pray." He pointed heavenward.

"Thank you, Mr. Weston. I have been praying." Teresa gave

him a big hug. "I hope I find a pa just like you. Someone I can trust."

"That is our prayer for you too. Go join the others. We'll be leaving shortly."

She smiled and hurried away.

He walked back to the table.

"Where is she going?" Mr. Weans followed Teresa's progress across the room before he turned back to Matthew, a scowl on his face.

"We let the children decide if they're comfortable with the pairing, and Teresa has her heart set on a big family on a farm somewhere."

Mr. Weans's hands fisted. "Or she has her eyes set on you," he spat.

"I will ignore that disgusting comment, Mr. Weans." Matthew slapped his book shut and picked up his papers. "Good day."

"What about another girl then?"

Matthew kept walking. He did not feel comfortable spending one more moment in that town. If Mr. Weans was as influential as he looked, there could be trouble.

When he reached Gracie's side, he said, "Quickly, let's gather the children." He nodded in Mr. Weans direction.

Gracie took one look and flew into action. They had the remaining orphans on the train in minutes.

Matthew's breathing did not return to normal until they were miles from that town. He shuddered to think what would've happened to Teresa had God not allowed him to see that unguarded stare.

He looked out the train window. *Thank You for Your protection. Thank You that You love each child so much. Please shield these precious children. Help us to find not only a safe home, but the right family for each of them. We cannot do this alone.*

"Are you all right?" Gracie touched his arm. She leaned into him, and he put his arm around her.

"I was thanking God for His protection and asking for continued wisdom."

"Me too." She put her head on his shoulder.

"Well, Mrs. Weston, with both of us praying, God will not let us down."

"Winifred and Mary Jo found wonderful homes. What about the boys?"

"Henry went to a banker's home. You should've seen his excitement."

Gracie smiled. "That could not be more perfect."

"I agree. And Richard to a local newspaper man and his bubbly plump wife, who informed him he was way too skinny and that she was going to fatten him up with whatever foods tickled his fancy."

Gracie laughed. "Now, how did she know that the way to Richard's heart is through his stomach?"

"Isn't that the truth?"

"Only eight left, and we're not even halfway. I feel good about all the placements except—"

"I know, we'll talk about her tonight." Matthew entwined his fingers in hers and gave a light squeeze. "I promise."

CHAPTER 27

"Where is the next stop?" Gracie worked at keeping her voice from sagging like her spirits. Letting these children go was far more emotionally exhausting than she wanted to admit.

Matthew flipped through his book. "Three stops in Fairfield County, Sugar Grove, Lancaster, and Carroll."

"Sugar Grove?"

"It's a small community with a special request for a child directly through the Society."

"The last small community didn't go that well. I didn't like the pressure and time constraints." Poor Emma in that dark dreary forest with nothing but shanties and a stern looking mama. That was not what Gracie had imagined for the child.

Matthew's focus was on the paper. "In reading this, I was thinking of Teresa."

"Did I hear my name?" Teresa twisted around in her seat to face them.

"Says here that our next stop is a family who owns a sugar maple grove. They have four young children and a set of newborn twins—all boys. They want an older daughter to be a companion and help for the wife. Do you think you'd like to meet them?"

"The sugar grove sounds lovely," Teresa said. "And I do love children."

"Hope they're not looking for a slave," Gracie whispered. Her insides churned at the thought of any one of the children being used or abused. Loving these kids as much as she did, the responsibility weighed heavily.

Matthew looked at Teresa. "The three of us will go out and meet them. You're old enough to make up your own mind, and if there's even a hint of hesitation, we'll decline and move on."

Teresa nodded.

The train chugged and lurched, chugged and lurched—a now familiar rhythm to the children. "We're stopping again," Edgar said. "Maybe this time I'll be picked."

Gracie went over and sat beside the young boy. "This time there's only one family, and they're looking for an older girl. Teresa is going to go meet them, but the next stop will have more people waiting."

"Nobody wants me." Edgar's eyes filled with tears.

"No, that's not true." His words crushed Gracie's heart. Someone was going to be picked last or possibly not at all. How was life fair for these little ones to have to go through such turmoil so young? How could she reassure him? Edgar was small and skinny, and his one eye crossed into the middle. There was nothing that stood out about him unless you knew his affectionate, giving personality. He had tried to give his food away numerous times to the older boys who were still hungry. "Edgar, you're kind and—"

"'Cause I have bad teeth." His six-year-old smile revealed two missing front teeth.

Gracie put her arms around him and gave him a hug. How many things did these kids miss living on the street with no one to teach them? "Those are not bad teeth. Every child your age loses their baby teeth so your adult teeth have room to come in." Her heart felt like a leaden stone, weighty and weary, but the train had stopped. She had to get up and meet yet another couple.

Matthew and Teresa were heading out of the boxcar.

"How about we play a game when I return?" she said. His eyes brightened, and she kissed the top of his head. "You're a special boy Edgar, and don't you ever forget that."

He grabbed at her hand as she stood to go. "Will you be my mama?"

She fought back the tears and hugged him close. "There's a mama and a papa out there for you, Edgar. We just need to find them." She hurried out of the train before she burst into tears.

Teresa and Matthew were already talking to the couple, whose four boys were horsing around. The woman held a baby. The other twin was already in Teresa's arms.

"Meet Mr. and Mrs. Rubel," Matthew said as she joined them.

Gracie forced a smile through her tears.

"This little one has already stolen my heart." Teresa gazed down at the baby. "Look how he's hanging on to my finger."

Mrs. Rubel laughed. "Oh, and I think you've already stolen my heart." She gave Teresa a hug with her free arm. "To think I'm going to have a daughter to talk to and share girl things with. In a houseful of boys, you'd truly be a gift sent from heaven, if you'll have us." She looked upward into the blue like she was saying a prayer.

Mr. Rubel gave his wife a hug before turning to Teresa. "See how happy you've made my dear Alice. If you agree, we'd be honored to welcome you into our family. And we make the best maple syrup candy in the world."

Teresa's smile burst wide. "I'd love to be part of your family."

Gracie's heart melted as she gave Teresa one last hug. She took Matthew's hand, and they turned and boarded the train.

"This is the longest day ever," Gracie said. "We're only hitting Columbus, but it feels like we've been on this train for days. Hard to believe we left Gallipolis this morning with all the children, and now there's only Charlotte and Thomas and Lee left." She sank into the seat beside Matthew, and he put his arm around her. Funny how that no longer felt foreign or scary. In fact, she welcomed it. She felt protected in his arms. "I couldn't have done this without you." She leaned her head against his shoulder. Her words brought a stark realization. Could it be that God was showing her that they were better together?

"That goes the same for me." Matthew kissed the top of her head, and that simple touch made her long to lift up her face so that his lips could meet hers. She peeked up at him, and he caught her eye.

"What?" he asked.

"Oh, nothing." How could she tell him she wanted him to kiss her in broad daylight, on a train, with children who may be watching? Maybe fatigue was getting the best of her.

"Mrs. Weston, if you keep looking at me like that, I'm not going to be held responsible for the consequences."

Her gaze dropped to her lap. Her fingers clasped and unclasped. She would have to wrestle this through with God… her promise, her marriage, and her future.

His hand came over hers, stilling the movement. "Not that I'm complaining. I'd love to give you what that look invited."

She looked back into his eyes. "I wasn't inviting—"

"Oh, but you were, and you know it."

She pulled away and bounced across the seat, putting distance between them.

He had the audacity to laugh. Was she that transparent?

Could he read her thoughts? Heat crawled from her neck to her face.

"Has anyone ever told you how beautiful you look when you blush?" The tease in his voice annoyed her. This was no laughing matter. What was wrong with her, wanting to snuggle, practically begging for a kiss?

"I'm having an emotional day, that's all," she said through pursed lips.

"Fair enough. But someday soon you're going to come to terms with what is happening between us."

"That's not even gentlemanly to talk about."

"Oh, but it is, my dear." He lifted her hand and lightly dropped a kiss. "I'm your husband."

That slight touch sent tremors racing up her arm, and she snatched her hand away. His obvious invitation unearthed a tangle of emotions she was trying her best to keep buried.

"Have it your way," he said. "Let's talk about the children."

Gracie took a deep breath and willed her racing heart to quiet. This conversation she could handle.

"Today has been very successful," he said. "Wouldn't you agree?"

"It has. All except—"

"Don't worry about Emma. I have an idea I'll discuss with you tonight. Do you trust me?"

She did trust him. Implicitly.

He must've read the truth in her expression, because he said, "That's good." He squeezed her hand. "We only need to find two more homes, and we're headed to Columbus, a big center."

"I prayed all the way from Sugar Grove to Lancaster for Edgar as we played games, and I was thrilled when the doctor and his wife picked him first. They were headed for Charles, but I overheard the wife say, 'The Lord is saying this one,' and she walked straight to Edgar."

"What a faith builder this trip has been." Matthew looked

upward. "To see God in action and the way He loves these children. It's like He's hand-picking these homes."

"I believe He is. Who took Charles?"

"A family with three older girls picked him out. The father was a real humorous man, making everyone laugh. He asked Charles if he'd be willing to help him even out the household and add some more man power. You should've seen Charles straighten up tall, and the 'Yes, sir' he gave was priceless. Didn't know a ten-year-old could look that proud."

Gracie laughed. "Wish I'd seen that."

"And Oscar went to a dairy farmer just outside of town. He was eager to learn how to milk a cow. His new parents said they had a litter of puppies waiting for him to pick one out for his own and name it."

"Ah. Oscar loves animals. Remember how he begged to keep that wounded bird he found?"

Matthew nodded: "You should've seen that kid's face. That alone made this trip worthwhile."

"What about our shy Jonathan?" Gracie asked. "That must've been hard on you leaving him behind in Carroll."

"It was. But I feel good about the farmer and his wife who took him. They were a soft-spoken couple of German descent with very broken English. To my amazement, Jonathan could understand them better than I could. He was interpreting what they were saying as we filled out the paperwork. When I asked him, he said he has a faint memory of someone older in his life who spoke German."

"That's heart-warming. God is good."

"So good. It doesn't look like we'll have to do that second leg tomorrow up to Marion, if we can find a home for Lee and those two." He nodded at Charlotte and Thomas. "I refuse to separate them."

"I agree." Gracie held her hand over her heart. "This day has been tough. My poor heart couldn't take those two being separated."

"Lee has been quite picky, and at twelve, I want to give him a choice. But I think I finally understand what he's looking for. He likes to build and fix things. Maybe in Columbus, we'll find a home where the father is into manufacturing or building."

"I pray so."

"Now, come back here." Matthew lifted his arm, and she snuggled in close, leaning against him. "Hmm that's better."

If only he knew how much she enjoyed the closeness, he would be very pleased with himself indeed. His charm and attraction were wearing her down. The thought of being his wife—really being his wife—made her hands tingle and a warm knot curl in the depth of her being. There was not a hint of aversion to the man, but she needed time to hear from the Lord. If her promise was that of a child, what did the adult version look like?

CHAPTER 28

Columbus brought a crowd of people, more than they could supply with only three children left. The church building, with its soaring roof and bell tower, was busting with curious people. Some were just spectators wanting to witness the novelty of an orphan train coming through, but many were eager couples hoping to adopt.

Gracie and Matthew did the interviews together and then decided to make the decision privately with the children. Many offered to take either Charlotte or Thomas, but no one wanted both, and that weighed heavily on Matthew's heart.

Many boisterous voices echoed off the rafters. Matthew stood up tall and held up his hand to the crowd. The room slowly quieted. "My wife, Gracie, and I"—he loved saying that—"thank you all for coming today and the generosity of your hearts in wanting to give these children a good home. Please, give us a few moments to talk to the children and decide what is best for them. We'll let you know shortly."

He waved the children over. "Lee, what did you think of Mr. and Mrs. Martinez?"

"That's the one with the buggy-making company. Right?" Lee asked.

"Yes. They have no children and desperately want a son to leave their business to. You'd be working with your hands and building, as well as learning the business. I think you'd be great at both."

Lee's head bobbed. "They sound wonderful, though I quite like the Brannum's, and he builds houses, and I'd have a younger brother. I quite like the thought of that."

"The choice is yours."

Lee looked over the crowd, and his eyes landed on the Martinez's. They waved at him, and the woman smiled sweetly and mouthed, "Please." She held out her arms, and Lee marched across the room and into her hug. He looked a little uncomfortable at her show of affection, but his smile spread wide when Mr. Martinez shook his hand like a man.

Matthew smiled down at Gracie. "I think he's chosen."

"He has."

Two women hurried toward them. They were obviously sisters, both with the same prominent chin and deep-set eyes. "Before you decide on little Charlotte and Thomas, we have a proposal."

Two men trailed the women—their husbands, Matthew assumed. All four stood before them.

"Go ahead," Matthew said.

One of the women said, "We know you don't want to break up the brother and sister, and as sisters we understand that completely."

The other one added, "I couldn't imagine not having my sister in my life."

"Ladies," one of the men said, giving Matthew an amused look over their heads, "perhaps you want to introduce yourselves before launching in."

"Oh, my yes, we're just so excited."

He stepped forward. "I'm Jacob Snider, and this is my brother-in-law William O'Hearn." He gestured to the man beside him. "These two lovely ladies are Mary and Noelle."

"We were born on Christmas day, paternal twins," Mary said with a soft laugh.

"As I was trying to say," Noelle interjected, "we'd each like to take a child. We live on the same street, and the children would be able to go back and forth and see each other as much as they want." Excitement flowed from her voice.

"We're together more than apart anyway," Mary added.

"That's no word of a lie." Jacob looked at William, and they both nodded.

"Those two are tied at the hip," William said. "But we knew that before we married them and love them all the same."

"But of course you do." Noelle said.

"What's not to love?" Mary nodded.

Gracie whispered into Matthew's ear. "I love them too." She bent down to Thomas and Charlotte. "Do you think you could go into different homes if you lived on the same street and still got to see each other often?"

Charlotte bit at the nail on her thumb, and she looked at her older brother.

"That would mean one of these couples would be your mama and daddy," Gracie said, "and the other your auntie and uncle. And you'd all be family. Do you understand?"

Thomas nodded at Gracie like a little man. "Would I still be able to see Charlotte every day and watch over her like Mama told me to?"

Noelle and Mary crouched down, so Gracie let them field the question.

"Absolutely," Noelle said. "And you'll have sleepovers—"

"And outings that we all do together. It'll be so much fun." Mary smiled and clapped her hands.

"And every weekend, we have Sunday dinner together after church," Jacob added. "That's our favorite part, isn't it William?"

William's eyes twinkled. "Our ladies know how to cook, and how." He rubbed his protruding middle.

Thomas looked up at Matthew, and Matthew nodded. "This is a good choice, Thomas. Your mama would be proud."

Thomas turned to his sister, his eyes bright with excitement. "Charlotte, we're going to be all right. We found family together."

Charlotte took her thumb out of her mouth and hugged her brother.

Noelle held out her arms. "Charlotte, could I give you a hug, too? I'm going to be your new mama." Charlotte did not hesitate, and Noelle lifted her up. Charlotte's tiny head nuzzled in and rested on Noelle's shoulder. "I think I've died and gone to heaven," Noelle whispered to her husband.

Mary crouched down. "I know you're a big boy, Thomas, but our family believes that no matter how big you get, we all need hugs." She held her arms out, and Thomas walked in. She wisely hugged him for only a moment before releasing him. She stood and held out her hand. "Come meet your papa. He's the kindest man you'll ever know, and he's wanted a son for many years."

Matthew's eyes welled up, and his throat constricted. He looked heavenward. *Thank you, God.*

~

Gracie took the hand Matthew offered as they left the church. The soft approach of evening was brushing over the city, and a cool breeze rippled the surface of the nearby river.

"Let's find our hotel," Matthew said. "Shouldn't be far."

Gracie stopped. "Goodness, I forgot. Where are our bags?"

"Reverend Hopkins delivered them right after we arrived

and told me the church wanted to pay for our room. He said it's a short walk along the river and around the corner."

The thought of spending a night in a hotel with Matthew brought a flutter of awareness that tingled up Gracie's spine. She had so enjoyed sleeping in the safety of his arms.

"A meal and a good night's sleep are in order." Matthew squeezed her hand. "And being that we don't have to go any further, I suggest we take tomorrow to rest before heading back. Let's see this beautiful city."

"Do you still think there'll be time to stop and see my family on the way back? I need to see Pa."

"We'll have extra time from not having to go farther north, plus I received permission from the board to stop in the valley to see your family, since we never had a honeymoon."

"And you're comfortable leaving the orphanage?"

"They'll be fine." Matthew said. "It's good to let the others take the lead, and that never happens if I'm around."

"Really? I can't believe the take-charge Mr. Weston is learning to let go."

Matthew stopped walking and snatched her into his arms. "Are you mocking me, Mrs. Weston?" His blue eyes sparkled with humor.

"I am, indeed."

"Well then, that bad behavior demands retribution."

"What did you have in mind?" She knew she was flirting but didn't care. He pulled her off the cobble-stoned walkway and behind a large oak tree.

"This." He lowered his head slowly, so close his breath fanned her cheek.

Her breathing shallowed as she lifted her lips in invitation. His mouth covered hers, warm and pliant, then grew needy, seeking out a response. She melted into his embrace and kissed him back. Delight rippled from tip to toe. Whatever was happening, it was beyond wonderful.

His mouth left hers with a tearing slowness and he dropped his arms from around her.

An ache, a loss, a desire for more consumed her. She wanted to pull him back.

"Hmm, hope you get sassy more often if payback is that enjoyable." He laughed as he took her hand and resumed walking.

She could not speak. It was time to be honest with herself. Everything about Matthew drew her, from his intelligence to his kindness to his love for the children to…to whatever this physical attraction between them was. And to where it was going. Despite the men who'd shown her attention and stolen kisses in the past, she'd never felt anything even remotely as powerful. And the way Matthew fit into her life so perfectly when she had promised a life dedicated to the children—that was divinely providential, was it not?

Night's first pale stars flickered in the purpled sky. Gracie was thankful for the thickening darkness. What was this jumble of emotions crashing in on her heart? Was she falling in love?

"The hotel should be right around the corner." Matthew said. "And I have my own money for an extra room tonight and tomorrow. We can't expect the orphanage to pay for them. Nor would they understand why a husband and wife would need two rooms."

"About that." Gracie swallowed against the knot in her throat. How could she admit she'd had the best sleep of her life lying next to him? She wanted this time together to test her feelings and see if they grew stronger. "I don't mind sharing a room with you. We've been doing that for weeks now."

He stopped short. "Not in the same bed."

His bluntness sent heat rushing to her face. Good thing it was almost dark. "We did last night."

There was a sharp intake of his breath. "And that was not a good idea."

He must not feel the same as she did. A lump rose in her throat. "But—"

"Look, Gracie. We've had a few very long emotional days with little sleep. It's best we don't make any decisions based on this moment. I'm going to get two rooms. I need some sleep tonight." He took her hand and walked on.

She had slept just fine in his arms. Had she squirmed too much? Had he not enjoyed the closeness as much as she had?

If not, then why the sweet spicy kiss just a few moments prior? She was so confused.

∼

She was killing him. Her presence burned his discipline to ash.

How could she not feel Matthew's love and desire for her? At the inn the night before, he had been awake most of the night with her curled in his arms. Yet she had gone promptly to sleep. Numerous times in the night when she'd brushed against him, he had almost succumbed and turned her in his arms and kissed her into awareness.

Now she was suggesting more of the same. It would be sheer heaven and absolute hell wrapped up in one.

They walked down the hall to their respective rooms. "Go freshen up," he said, "and we'll have supper together downstairs. Knock on my door when you're ready."

She nodded but had said nothing since he'd told her they would not share a room. Should he be honest? Was now the time to admit his feeling, to tell her he was madly in love with her and had been from the moment he met her? Or should he keep hoping and praying she would fall in love with him and make it known?

He shut the door behind him and walked to the wash basin. Pouring the fresh water from the pitcher into the bowl, he caught a glimpse of himself in the mirror above the washstand. The man staring back at him had dark circles under his eyes. He needed sleep, and he needed her. He slammed the pitcher down and bent to wash up. What was he thinking, imagining that she would fall for him? She had made her thoughts on the matter clear. What an innocent offering to share the hotel room with him. He dared not risk another night sleeping side-by-side and think he could keep things platonic.

He grabbed a nearby towel and rubbed furiously at his face. He fumbled with the buttons trying to change his shirt, and finally ripped the last few open. He flung the dirty shirt on the bed.

God, was I wrong to believe she was the woman You had for me? Was I arrogant and willful, determined to have her as my wife at all costs?

Truth rushed in. His jealousy and need for control had spiked to an all-time high, especially when the men came calling after the Christmas ball. He deserved every bit of the agony he now felt. "I'm so sorry, Lord. I have a habit of getting ahead of you."

A slight rap at the door hurried along his maudlin pace. He slipped on his clean shirt and worked the buttons. Imagine that, a woman getting ready faster than he could. He had to stop daydreaming and live in the real world.

"Be right there."

He threw on the only tweed jacket he'd brought overtop his clean shirt. His striped trousers had many traveling creases, but they'd have to do. He opened the door with a bit too much gusto and offered her his arm. "I'm starving."

"Me as well," she said, the remark stiff and formal.

An awkward silence followed them all the way to the dining room. They were never at a loss for words, and Matthew hated the shift that had taken place. He knew her well enough. She was upset with him.

The waiter in the hotel dining room took them to a private corner, most likely assuming they were having a romantic evening together. How Matthew wished that were true. He pulled her chair out, and after she sat, he joined her.

They looked at the menu in silence and ordered. More silence.

"All right, Gracie. Out with it."

Her beautiful dark eyes widened. "Out with what?"

"I know when you're upset with me."

"I'm not upset, I'm confused." Her brows knit together.

"About what?"

"Do you want an annulment?" Her voice quivered.

An annulment? *Oh, dear God in heaven, please give me patience.* How did he answer this? "What I want is the opposite of an annulment and most likely not something you're prepared to give."

"I don't understand. The opposite of an annulment is marriage, and we're already—"

"Are we?"

She blinked several times. "Aren't you happy?"

"Are you? Do you like things the way they are?"

"Why do you keep answering my questions with questions? Grandmother says that is most rude."

"Does she?" He smiled.

"Matthew, stop that." Her dark eyes flashed, and she sat up straight, starch in her spine.

"I know this is another question," he said, "but I've told you that I don't want an annulment and desire the opposite. Do you not understand what I mean, dear wife? Do you still question why I can't lie in bed next to you without wanting more?" He watched her eyes widen as understanding dawned, and then she quickly looked away.

The waiter brought their food at that most inopportune moment.

Gracie chatted with the young man. The little imp was stalling. He'd let her, though. He had all night. And considering she'd pressed this conversation; he was not going to bed until they finished it.

The waiter left, and she dug into her food. "Hmm, this is delicious. Try my beef, it's divine." She cut a piece and slid it on his plate but would not make eye contact. Silence filled the space and she tackled her food like she had not seen a meal in weeks.

He knew just the thing to bring her back from her forced politeness. "About Emma."

Her head snapped up. "Oh yes, how could I have forgotten?"

The façade dropped, and Gracie was back. Matthew suppressed a smile.

"She's the only one I'm worried about," Gracie said. "Mr. Shirstein looked kind and loving but that woman—something about her makes me uneasy."

"I agree. Do you want to hear my idea?"

She finished her bite of food and motioned with her fork. "You know I do."

"We're headed back that way. I say we stop and make a surprise visit. We'll say that it was all so rushed, and we want to drop off Emma's doll."

"Oh, Matthew, that's a wonderful idea. Turns out it was a blessing that the doll got left behind." She took a sip of water. "But the train isn't going to wait for us. Is there a place to stay overnight?"

"We know there's a schoolhouse. We could bunk there if we had to."

"Do we have an address?"

"Only a box number at the store. I'm sure the store owner will know where they live. It's not a big town."

She held her hand out across the table, and he placed his into hers. She squeezed tight. "That would make me so happy."

"Thought it might." He smiled into her hauntingly beautiful dark eyes. They swam with compassion and kindness and something else as his thumb caressed the inside of her wrist.

"You know me better than any other person ever has." Her voice was low with a husky quality. "Why is that?"

He knew the answer, but was she ready for the truth? "I pay attention because…I care."

She pulled her hand free and picked up her fork to an empty plate.

"Want some of mine?" he teased. She had been so intent on ignoring him, she had rushed through her food.

"Dessert would be nice."

Ah, again, she was stalling. He would let her have her way—for the moment.

CHAPTER 29

"Gracie."

There was a forcefulness to Matthew's voice Gracie had not heard before. She turned from inserting the key in the lock of her room.

Matthew stood across the hall with an intense look on his face. "I won't get any sleep tonight unless I spell this out." He marched over, took the key from her hand, and opened her door. His hand swung across his body bidding she enter.

Why was he so intense? Had she disappointed him by not knowing how to answer him earlier? She needed time to think if she was going to take this marriage further. She stepped into the room.

He followed her and closed the door with a commanding click. As she turned toward him, he hauled her into his arms.

Her hand found his chest. The beat of his strong heart rapidly vibrating beneath her fingertips sent a tingle up her arm. "Yes?" Her voice came out in thready tones, and she stared at his chest rather than meet his gaze.

The tips of his fingers cupped her chin, and he gently lifted her head to stare into her eyes. His other hand slid down her temple. Like flames dancing in the fireplace the searing sensation of his touch shook her to the core. She caught his hand to stop the overwhelming wonder.

The smell of pinewood soap, the nearness of his body brushing against her, and the intensity in the blue of his eyes sent desire thrumming through her limbs. She had never experienced anything like this before.

"Gracie, I love you."

His words confirmed and enraptured a knowing that had been fermenting in the depth of her soul. He loved her. But for the first time those words from a man did not bring dread, but excitement.

"I've loved you from the moment I met you. Everything I shared with your family the day we told them we were getting married was the truth."

That's why he could spin that story with so much sentiment. She wanted to both hit him and hug him. No wonder his wedding vows had resounded with conviction, while hers had been weak and fearful. Why had he not told her? She would've run, that's why. But now, she did not feel like running at all. He knew her better than she knew herself.

"I'm going to kiss you, Gracie, with nothing between us except the love I have stored in my heart for you."

He started with a light kiss to her throat, to the pulse fluttering like the wings of a hummingbird.

His touch felt heavenly, and she willingly melted into him.

He slowly worked up over her chin and brushed a whisper of a kiss across her waiting mouth. She couldn't resist and pressed her mouth against his. The kiss lit her as if she were bone-dry kindling and he the fire. Heat crackled and flared between them. Never had anyone affected her so fully that she found clothing a hindrance to her wandering hands. Consumed by a feverish heat, she could not get enough of what he offered.

What was happening? The strength of emotion that seared

through her both captivated and terrified her. She could no longer deny its power.

He groaned and pulled away.

She gasped, fighting for control. She wanted to throw herself back in his arms. The loss of his closeness brought instant loneliness, and the room seemed to shrink in the aura of his presence. Why did he have to take up so much space—in body, in spirit, and in her heart? This was no passing attraction. Everything about him pulled her in. But she needed to wrestle with God…to be sure before speaking.

"I'll leave you to your privacy," he said. "But I intend to pursue you, Gracie Anabelle Weston, until you admit what is going on between us and are my wife in the fullest sense."

Heat rushed to her face, and her hand reached out, but he had already turned and walked away. He did not look back. The door clicked shut behind him.

Gracie threw herself on the bed. Her body ached for his return. Matthew could've had her had he just kept going. Why hadn't he? She had been pliant in his hands, responding to his every touch.

But he was too respectful. He wanted her to be sure.

She slipped out of her clothes, into her nightwear, and between the cold sheets. Everything within her wanted to curl up against Matthew and have him take her places she had never gone before. But was this mere physical reaction or did she love him as much as he loved her?

Sleep would not come. Gracie finally rose and paced. She went to the hearth in her room and threw on another log. The hot coals spat and sputtered, then ignited into a fiery glow. The room shimmered in the dancing light of the flames.

"Oh God, I've been so blind." She resumed her pacing. "Matthew loves me. How long have I tortured him with my response to his kisses and saying yes to marriage when deep down a part of me knew it was more than a convenient arrangement for him? What do I do now?"

Be honest with yourself.

"How am I not being honest? I admire Matthew. I respect him. For the first time in my life, I feel a genuine attraction, but is this love? And if it is, what does this mean to the promise I made to Rosina, to You?"

When you were a child, you spoke as a child, you thought as a child.

She had made that decision when she was twelve. Could God be widening her understanding? She was still dedicated to the children, and Matthew was indeed a helpmate, a partner, a friend. The final invitation to make their marriage real were three needed words spoken from her lips.

Gracie clenched and unclenched her hands as she moved around the room. A bead of sweat trickled down her spine. She was drawn to Matthew, to everything about him. From his serious, astute side to his outward expressions of love for the children. His charming smile with laughing moons on either side to his thoughtful preparation for every detail of this trip. From his fierce protection of her to the way her heartbeat kicked up when he looked at her with his kind, dreamy blue eyes. She loved it all.

Oh, goodness, she loved him. She truly loved him.

Should she go to him now?

No, he needed his sleep. Tomorrow, they would have the whole day, and she would tell him then. She slid back between the sheets and turned toward the glowing fire.

But she couldn't force her eyes closed.

Why waste one more minute apart? She threw off the covers, slipped on her wrapper, and headed for the door. She padded across the hall and lifted her hand to knock on his door. Her fist stalled and wavered, then fell to her side.

No, she could not be that bold. Maybe she should pray some

more, make sure this was not merely a response to a very emotional day.

She crept back to her room, slid under the covers. Sleep would not come.

~

*M*atthew's night had been anything but restful. Two times he had dreamed of Emma, and both had been more like nightmares. God was trying to tell him to go get her. Of that, he was sure. At the first blush of dawn, he rose and dressed, then crossed the hall and knocked on Gracie's door.

She opened with a blanket strewn across her shoulders and her hair hanging long and free in a curtain around her. "Matthew?"

He almost forgot his urgency.

"I'm so glad you came." She smiled and tried to pull him into the room. "About last night—"

"Don't worry about last night. We'll discuss that another time. But can you get dressed quickly?"

Her dark brows knit together. "What is it?"

"I know I suggested we stay here for the day, but we need to get Emma, today. I want to be on that morning train back. I have a bad feeling—"

"I'll be ready in a flash."

He went back to his room, gathered his few things, then stood outside her door. She did not make him wait long, joining him only a few minutes later. How could anyone look that good in so short a time?

He took her carpet bag, and they headed to the foyer. "They serve a complimentary breakfast. Do you think you could pick up a few things that travel well while I check out? And I'll ask if I can pay to take a little extra food for the day."

She nodded. "Give me my bag. I'll see what I can get."

He paid and was about to go after her when she returned, smiling. "I explained the situation, and the chef brought me a loaf of bread, a brick of cheese, apples, and some peach tarts. We'll be more than satisfied."

He took her hand, and they headed in the direction of the train station. "It's that smile of yours. You could charm a beggar out of his last penny."

"Ha, a lot you know. The chef was a woman. She asked me if the food was for that tall good-looking man who brought the orphan children into town. When I said, 'Oh, you mean my husband?' She laughed and said, 'Should've known a fine man like that would be married.'"

"You're spinning that story," he said. "But I like the tall, good-looking part."

"I tell no tales, and… We *are* married." She squeezed his hand.

Now, what did she mean by that declaration? He looked down at her, but she had a determined look on her face as she marched forward.

CHAPTER 30

"Gracie."

Matthew shook her shoulder, and she sat up straight. The late afternoon sun slanted through the car windows as she yawned and stretched, fighting to lose the drowsiness from her nap. "Goodness, I must've slept a long time."

"You did. We're almost to Moonville."

"Sorry about that. I hardly slept last night." She patted her braid to make sure it was still intact and tried to smooth the wrinkles out of her skirt.

"I talked to the conductor, who assured me they'll be back through and heading to Gallipolis around the same time tomorrow. They'll be looking for us. But I was thinking…and you're not going to like this, but it's for the best."

"What?"

"I want you to go on to Gallipolis and stay at the inn until I get there."

"No."

Matthew kept talking as if he hadn't heard her. "I'm sure,

even if the inn is booked up, they'll take you in and give you that guest room downstairs."

"Matthew, no. We're in this together. Please don't ask this of me."

"I'm worried about what I'll find, and I don't want you in any kind of danger."

She clutched at his arm. She had to make him understand. "I'll go crazy not knowing what is happening. I can't agree to what you're asking."

Matthew's eyes closed as if he were praying. The train slowed. The deeply wooded area and shanty station was now in view.

Oh God, please let Matthew agree to us doing this together.

His eyes opened. "I have my misgivings, but I did promise you your independence when we married, so you decide."

Gracie threw her arms around his neck and kissed his cheek. "Thank you."

He hugged her tight. "Does that mean you're coming?"

She angled out of his arms. "Of course. Besides it would look very suspicious if we didn't arrive together. It would alert them to your unease."

"I sincerely hope I'm wrong about this feeling I have."

The train screeched to a stop. "So do I." She stood, her hands tightening to white on the back of the seat in front of her.

As they stepped down off the train, Gracie got the same feeling she'd had when they arrived the day before. Though the sun was still shining in the western sky and it was clear, there was something dark about the place. She shivered. Her eyes followed a tangled wall of hickory and oak up to the sky, where a small patch of blue above the cleared railbed fought for dominance. The underbrush took over the rest. But for a few feet on both sides of the track, walking would be nearly impossible in her long dress.

Matthew took her hand, and they followed a path into a

small town built close to the tracks. Gracie's heart sank at the shanties and rundown feel of the place.

"There." Matthew pointed to a sign dangling in the breeze, held precariously by one rusty hinge. The sign read General Store. "We'll see if we can find out where the Shirsteins live." The steps up to the building looked as if they'd been slapped together in a hurry with rickety old boards.

"Careful." Matthew pointed to a broken plank.

She held onto his arm, and they entered the store, where the same sense of disrepair and disorganization followed through. "I wonder if the Children's Aid Society has any idea how rundown this town is?" Gracie whispered.

Matthew squeezed her hand. "Hello," he called.

A gray-haired man with a bushy beard halfway down his chest shuffled in from the back. "What can I do you fur?" he asked.

"We're looking for the Shirstein residence."

"We don't see city folk 'round here much." He spat a piece of chewing tobacco behind him. The blackened patch on the wall proved that was his pattern.

"They live further down the road that-a-way." He pointed.

"Could you be a bit more specific?" Matthew took a dollar out of his pocket and held it out, and the man's eyes lit up.

The old guy let out a crusty laugh. "Closer to the coal mine. There's the haves and the have-nots in this here little town. Take a walk past the schoolhouse and the graveyard, and you'll see a fancy arch over a gravel driveway on that next property. That's the Shirstein place. Ain't nobody round here is far from the noise of the tracks 'cept them."

"Thank you, sir." Matthew lifted his hat respectfully.

"Ain't nobody called me sir in a very long time. Are ya friends of the Shirsteins?"

"No. We're here on a private matter."

"Well, I wasn't goin' ta say anything, but most of us are

barely eking out a living 'cept the Shirsteins. They're in tight with the owner of this here land, and the rest of us get the dregs, if ya know what I mean?" His voice took on a bitter tone.

"Much obliged, Mr...?" Matthew held out his hand across the counter.

"I'm William Whitfield, but most folk jus' call me Billy." His grubby fingernails and yellowed fingers clasped around Matthew's in a hearty shake.

"Nice to meet you, Billy. This is my lovely wife, Gracie, and I'm Matthew Weston."

"So, what you here fur?"

Matthew looked at Gracie, and she nodded. There was something about this man she trusted, grime and all.

"We're from the orphanage."

"Yup, I was out on the porch, sitting in me chair when that sweet little girl came by. Old biddy Shirstein made her husband put the child down and insisted that tiny thing keep up to her march. That man is as hen-pecked as they come, and that woman... Well, I wouldn't trust me dead dog into her care."

"Isn't she the schoolteacher?" Gracie asked.

"She was, fur about a minute, until all the chil'ren came home cryin'. Meaner than a cornered badger, that one."

"Thank you for your honesty," Matthew said.

"If'n you need a place to stay overnight, Rosie, two houses back takes in guests. Nuttin fancy, but it's clean. Not like this place." He looked around the room, and his smile vanished. "Sure do miss my Annie. She up and died a year ago." Shadows of grief spread over his face.

"I'm so sorry," Gracie said. "That must be hard."

"I jus' haven't had the will since." His graying eyes misted. "She'd turn over in her grave if'n she saw this place now."

"That must be tough, losing the woman you love." Matthew looked at Gracie, with love in his eyes.

Her heartbeat increased.

"I can't imagine," he added.

"Bin together for thirty-five years, raised our girls, and then she was gone. I didn't even get a chance to say goodbye." A tear dropped free and rolled into his wiry beard. "With the landowner demanding so much and now the Shirsteins talkin' bout building a better store, I'll soon have nuttin' left." He sank into the chair behind the counter.

"Is there anything that can be done?" Gracie asked.

"Don't have the gumption to fight. I'll go live with one of my daughters, I suppose, till the good Lord feels fit to take me home to my Annie." He brushed the tears from his eyes. "Don't much know why I'm tellin' you folks all that. Guessin' it's 'cause not too many here-abouts care to listen."

Gracie went around the counter and leaned in to give the old man a hug. "I'll be praying for you. I wish I could do more."

"You jus' made me day." He smiled. "Bin a long time since anyone hugged the likes of me. Now go. Git that sweet little girl out of the clutches of the Shirsteins, cause I'm guessin' the good Lord done brought you back to do jus' that."

"He did," Matthew said. "And if I could bother you with one more question, where's the sheriff's office?"

"Moonville ain't got no sheriff. The nearest one is in Mineral, the next town over."

Matthew looked at Gracie, and her insides roiled. What may they face without the help of a sheriff?

"God will be with us." Matthew nodded with a show of confidence.

"Well then, I'll be prayin' fur you. Go slow and be wise. That woman's as slippery as an eel."

Gracie walked beside Matthew. She didn't want to add to his worry, but never again would they consent to dropping a child off in a town that did not have a sheriff. What if the Shirsteins refused to let Emma go? "If Mrs Shirstein lied to the agency about being the local teacher, then who knows what else she was deceitful about."

"Exactly, and that alone is cause to take Emma back. But we won't let on to anything we just heard," Matthew said. "We'll pretend that we're merely returning Emma's doll and doing a home inspection. If they invite us to stay the night, we will do so. I want to remain as close to Emma as possible."

"There's the school." Gracie pointed to the one room log cabin with a sign that read Moonville School.

Matthew nodded as they trudged by.

"Should we wait and try to arrange a ride to the next town to get the sheriff?" Gracie's voice was thin and trembling.

"Let's assess the situation. If Emma is doing fine, then we won't need the extra help, but if she's not, then we'll be on that train with Emma tomorrow one way or another."

"I agree." She squeezed his arm. "The graveyard and the driveway." A chill ran up her spine.

They turned off the main path into a heavily wooded area on the gravel driveway Billy had described. The ornate gilded arch with the name Shirstein hanging from a sign on a gold chain looked completely out of place. The crunch of gravel beneath their feet added a calming cadence, which fought the needle of dread stitching its way from Gracie's stomach to her heart. The road twisted and turned for a good ten minutes and then opened to a grand clearing in the woods. Sweeping lawns, manicured gardens, and a large house with white columns and an extensive veranda came into view. The place looked idyllic. A feeling of hope for the good life this couple could give Emma should have prevailed. Instead, a dark foreboding crawled over her skin. She shuddered.

Matthew put his arm around her shoulder. "I know. I feel it too. We'll tread lightly and go with God."

Panic edged up Gracie's throat as Matthew knocked on the

door. She hung onto his hand so tight her knuckles turned white.

"Relax," he whispered. "We have to look as natural as we can."

A man with dark skin and a serious expression opened the door.

"Is Mr. and Mrs. Shirstein in?" Matthew asked.

"Come in." The man held the door open. "Mr. Shirstein is at work, but I'll have you wait in the parlor while I go in search of the lady of the house."

He led them into a nearby parlor and disappeared. The show of opulence, ornate gilded moldings, and formal furniture made the room feel cold and unwelcoming. Even though Gracie was exhausted, she wouldn't dare sit with her travel clothes on the pristine white overstuffed chairs and settee. Not a speck was out of order.

The click-click-click of heels on hardwood alerted them to Mrs. Sherstein's approach. She whirled into the room like a tornado with a scowl on her face and stopped short. At the sight of them, her countenance instantly changed to a fake smile. "Oh, I thought it may be that bothersome neighbor of mine always looking for a hand-out. Whatever are the two of you doing here?" She smiled, but it did not reach her beady eyes.

"We were traveling back after the great blessing of finding the children homes and thought we would deliver this." Matthew pulled the rag doll from his coat pocket and held it out. "This is Emma's favorite doll. She takes it everywhere."

Mrs. Shirstein's eyes widened. "Goodness, that filthy thing? She won't be needing that." Her pointed nose crinkled in disgust. "You should see the room full of dolls she now has." She refused to take it from Matthew's outstretched hand.

"I don't think you understand," Matthew said. "It's from her past, from before she came to us at the orphanage. It's very important to her."

"She was going on about that thing last night. Wouldn't touch any of the new dolls she has in her room. Most insolent indeed."

"Children crave the familiar," Gracie said. "And so much has changed in her little life."

"Very well, but at the very least that thing must be sanitized before she touches it."

Mrs. Shirstein clapped her hands, and a dark woman in a black dress and sparkling white apron entered the room straightaway. "Yes, ma'am?"

"Take that." She pointed at Matthew. "Make sure it is washed and sanitized at least twice before bringing it back to me. And wash your hands after touching it."

"Yes, ma'am." The woman took the doll and disappeared.

"I would ask you to stay for tea"—her eyes flickered over them and to her immaculate furniture—"but I'm in the middle of a large undertaking at the moment. With no notice whatsoever of your arrival… Surely, you understand. Walter will show you to the door." She turned to go.

"We do not need tea, Mrs. Shirstein"—Matthew's voice was firm—"but we'd like to see Emma after coming all this way."

She whirled around.

Gracie plastered a wide smile on her face. "We could take her for a walk or sit out on your porch for a visit and not bother you at all." She forced lightness into her voice. "Give you time to finish up your…undertaking."

"She's having her afternoon nap at the moment. Children need structure and discipline, and you popping in when we're trying to help her adjust to her new surroundings will be most upsetting. I don't think a visit is a wise idea."

"I disagree." Matthew said. "Our surprise visit will bring joy to her little heart and"—he pulled his pocket watch out—"it's four in the afternoon."

"Fine, I'll check on her." She turned toward the parlor door.

Matthew and Gracie moved to follow.

She stopped and faced them. "Please wait here."

Gracie filled her voice with sugar, hoping to sweeten the bitter shrew. "One of the forms we must fill out for The Children's Aid Society reports the environment these children live in. If we do it now, we won't have to return in six months." When the woman only glared, Gracie added, "You know how it is…paperwork that must be done."

Mrs. Shirstein rocked on her feet. Her hands balled into fists. Finally, she said, "Very well, follow me."

"Why, this is a beautiful home, Mrs. Shirstein." Gracie poked her head into different rooms as they walked by. "You must be so proud."

That remark brought a decided lift to Mrs. Shirstein's shoulders, she turned with her sharp chin jutting out. "We didn't have things handed to us on a silver platter, either."

Matthew nodded. "You have indeed been blessed—"

"Blessing has nothing to do with this. It's the result of hard work." Mrs. Shirstein pointed out a few more rooms, showed them the back yard, complete with fountains and sculptures that looked hideously out of place in the surroundings, then marched them up the stairs.

She stopped at the first door and slowly opened it wide enough for them to peek in.

Little Emma was curled in a tight ball upon a frilly canopied bed. Her back was toward them, and she didn't move.

Mrs. Shirstein shut the door. "See, I told you she was sleeping," she said in hushed tones.

"That's all right," Matthew said. "As you said, structure is necessary. And having a child sleep too long during the day is not recommended." He pushed open the bedroom door, and Gracie rushed past him, not waiting for permission. She hurried across the room and sat on the bed. "Emma, sweetie."

Emma's body was shaking, but she wouldn't turn around.

"Am I allowed to move?" Her tiny voice was high-pitched and strained.

"But of course. It's me, Gracie."

Emma rolled to face her on the bed and sat up. Her eyes flitted between Gracie and Mrs. Shirstein.

Gracie glanced up at the woman, whose beady eyes were pinned on Emma. The child remained motionless.

"Come," Gracie said. "We'll go for a walk in your new gardens out back."

Still Emma did not move.

"Run along child. Don't just sit there." Mrs. Shirstein motioned at the door.

Gracie held out her palm. When Emma placed a shaking hand in Gracie's, she knew something was terribly wrong.

The child was dressed in an expensive-looking frilly dress. A pair of impractical shoes were handed to her by a lady who introduced herself as Lillian, the nanny.

Thankfully Mrs. Shirstein disappeared.

Gracie helped Emma slip into a jacket and noticed some bruises on her arm. When Emma bent over to put her shoes on, bloody red marks welted her upper legs. She looked up at Matthew to see if he had noticed the abuse, but he was making small talk with Lillian.

Gracie bit her lip to still the barrage of words that ached to be unleashed. In order to be successful, they would have to be very careful about how they extracted Emma from this situation. They headed down the stairs and out into the gardens.

Lillian followed.

"We decided to visit you before heading back to the orphanage because the exchange was so fast, and we never got to say a proper goodbye. Plus, you left your doll behind."

"You brought my dolly?"

"Sure did. Mrs. Shirstein is having it cleaned. It should be dry by tomorrow."

Emma looked up with eyes that were so forlorn and lost. A sting prickled behind Gracie's lids. *Oh God, help me not to start crying.* She looked at Matthew, who put his arm around her.

They walked the whole garden without finding one thing a child could play with. Gracie had to lift the child's spirits somehow. "How about a game of hide-and-seek?"

Emma's eyes brightened. "Hide-and-seek?"

Lillian shook her head. "That would not be a good idea. Mrs. Shirstein has prize roses from England and sculptures from Rome. If anything were to be stepped on or broken, she would not be happy."

Matthew's brows rose in Gracie's direction. "Well then, how about we go inside, and you draw us a picture, Emma. Remember how we said we'd love one in the mail? You can draw it for us now."

Emma's eyes grew large, and she nodded.

"That's an excellent idea," Lillian said. "We have some paper and pencils in the drawing room and a desk set up for her."

"Best we stay out here, at this table." Gracie pointed to the outside courtyard table. "Our traveling clothes are a tad dusty."

Lillian's eyes narrowed. She looked furtively to the house and back again. "Emma, come with me, and I'll show you where your drawing supplies are."

"We have such a short time with her. There'll be plenty of time for that when we're gone." Gracie waved her on.

Lillian scurried away.

As soon as she was out of earshot, Grace dropped to the child's level and touched one of the bruises. "What happened, my dear?"

Emma looked toward the house.

"You can tell us." Matthew bent down to her height. "We're here to help."

"Mrs. Shirstein dragged me out of the closet and slapped me across the face, then she—"

Lillian came flying out of the house, Mrs. Shirstein on her heels.

"It's best you leave now," Mrs. Shirstein said. "Evening is almost upon us, and these forest roads with all the wild critters are not safe after dark."

"We were hoping to say hello to Mr. Shirstein," Matthew said, "and thought perhaps you could put us up for the night in this fine home of yours."

Gracie was impressed at the nonchalance in Matthew's tone.

Mrs. Shirstein sputtered and stammered. "My…my husband comes home very tired from the coal mine. The last thing he would want is… is unannounced company. There's a lady down the road who will give you a room for the night. I'll get Walter to drive you."

Emma was squeezing Gracie's hand as if she'd never let go. Gracie bent down. "We'll be back tomorrow morning, I promise. You draw us a nice picture, you hear?" She wanted to snatch that child and never look back, but the train didn't come through until the next day and they had to make sure they had a fighting chance of getting Emma away.

Emma nodded, but huge tears filled her dark eyes soaking them in sorrow. Her thumb slipped into her mouth.

"Get that thumb out of your mouth," Mrs. Shirstein ordered. "That's a disgusting habit for a girl your age."

"We didn't have time to tell you about the trauma Emma has already suffered," Gracie said. "Sucking her thumb and hiding in the closet are her ways of soothing her pain. But as she grows more comfortable, those habits will diminish. This is another big change for—"

"And that kind of coddling is precisely why she's still doing it." Mrs. Shirstein jutted out her chin. "Life is hard for all of us. Emma will have a life she never dreamed possible, so the sooner she lets go of the past, the better."

Gracie ignored her prattle and gave Emma another hug. "See

you tomorrow, sweetie." Everything within Gracie recoiled at the thought of leaving that child in the Shirsteins' care for even one more night, but she rose and leaned into Matthew.

"Walter, why are you still standing here? Get the buggy ready to go." Mrs. Shirstein's voice was cold and demanding. She waved the man away. "Help these days. So dreadfully inept. You have to tell them every little thing."

Emma took the paper and pencil from Lillian's hand and sat on the courtyard bricks.

"Get up child. You don't sit on the ground with your lovely dress," Mrs. Shirstein barked.

Emma ignored her and drew a big sun with a happy face. She popped up and handed it to Gracie.

It took everything Gracie had not to burst into tears. Thankfully Matthew stepped in.

"Thank you, Emma. We shall treasure this picture." He crouched down to her level and whispered in her ear. She smiled from ear to ear.

Mrs. Shirstein's shoulders lifted, and her head bobbled back and forth with an I-told-you-so look. "See, the child is happy. I dare say, no other street urchin found so favorable an outcome as to be brought up a Shirstein with all of this." Her hands flew out, and she surveyed the courtyard with superiority emanating from her eyes.

Gracie wanted to scream that love was all the riches any child needed. She held her peace. All Mrs. Shirstein's possessions were nothing but a cold, harsh burden. There was no way she and Matthew were leaving Emma to grow up in an environment where she'd be constantly afraid of damaging Mrs. Shirstein's precious valuables. And worse yet, being mistreated in the process. Not a chance.

CHAPTER 31

Gracie and Matthew were escorted to the front entrance where Mrs. Shirstein opened the door. "There's no need to come tomorrow. Your inspection is done, and I'm sure we can agree it has been a raving success."

Matthew straightened his shoulders to full height. "We will come back to see Emma tomorrow morning because we love her and want to spend time with her. Won't we, Emma?"

Lillian held firmly onto her hand, but the child looked up and smiled bravely.

"It will not be for the purpose of an inspection. That has already been done and our decision made." His firm voice brooked no room for argument.

This was why Gracie had fallen in love with him. As if he'd read her mind, word for word, he voiced what she would have said. She squeezed his hand before bending to hug Emma one more time.

Walter drew the buggy up to the front, and Mrs. Shirstein waved them out. The door was shut firmly behind them. Everything within Gracie wanted to snatch Emma and never turn back. The thought of leaving her another night in this woman's clutches made her insides shudder. She reluctantly settled herself on the buggy seat.

As they rolled down the drive, they met Mr. Shirstein coming the other way. He pulled his wagon to a stop beside theirs. "What a surprise to see you so soon."

"We found homes for the children fairly quickly." Matthew said. "So, we decided to stop and say a proper goodbye to Emma. That transition happened so quickly, and she left her beloved doll behind."

"Well, isn't this a pleasure. But where are you headed at this late hour?"

"Apparently, there's a woman up the road who takes travelers in—"

"Why would you do that when we have a house full of empty rooms?"

"I fear our unannounced visit was a tad too much for Mrs. Shirstein." Matthew's wording was a lot kinder than Gracie's would've been.

"Nonsense. We have a houseful of servants, and I won't have you two spend the night elsewhere. With the happiness you've brought to our home, it's the least we can do." He smiled with genuine warmth.

"I'm not sure your wife—"

"I insist. Walter, please turn that buggy around and bring our guests back immediately. I don't know what Mrs. Shirstein was thinking in being so inhospitable. See you at the house." He lifted his hat and rode off.

"The closer we are to Emma, the better," Gracie whispered to Matthew.

"I agree."

Walter turned the buggy around. By the time they reached the house, Mr. Shirstein was waiting for them on his veranda. "I can't tell you the joy Emma brings. I've been looking forward to hugging my little girl all day. Makes the hard work worth the effort."

A heavy cloud of sadness rolled into Gracie's heart for this man, but he could not protect Emma. That much was clear by the bruises and welts on her skin.

They entered the house with Mr. Shirstein's loud voice booming out. "Ethel."

"How many times have I told you not to make such a racket? Gentlemen do not bellow…" She came around the corner. Her beady eyes narrowed, and she stopped talking.

"What were you thinking sending these two to Rosie's for the night?"

"Thought you'd be too tired after working all day," she said through pursed lips. The sharp lines around her mouth deepened.

"You know I love company any old time, and these two will always get the royal treatment from us. After all, they brought us our daughter. Where's my little girl?"

"She's washing up for supper."

"I asked you yesterday to have her available for her daddy's hug the minute I get home. She makes my hard work all worthwhile."

Mrs. Shirstein's lips flattened.

"Will you please go get her."

"Seems you might be interested in giving me a hello, but all you care about is seeing that girl." She stomped off.

Mr. Shirstein chuckled. "I see we have a little adjusting to do. In future, I must remember to kiss her first."

Did he laugh his way through life? Was that how he got through? Mrs. Shirstein was clearly jealous of Emma. Another reason this adoption would not work. Gracie was glad they had this peek into the Shirstein's private life, which revealed so much and further confirmed the Spirit's leading.

"I'll take you into my den," Mr. Shirstein said. "The only

place I'm allowed to sit down while I'm still in my work clothes."

Matthew nodded. "That would suit us fine."

Emma rounded the corner into the den, and her smile broke wide. "You're still here." She only had eyes for Matthew and Gracie.

"I brought them back for the night," Mr. Shirstein said. "Does that make you happy, my little Emma?"

She looked up at him and nodded.

"Come give your papa a hug." He crouched low, and she willingly went into his arms. He picked her up and whirled her around until she was squealing with laughter.

If only he had been married to a different woman. Gracie swallowed against the ache that rose in her throat.

~

Matthew was beyond exhausted. He blew out the candle, glad to shut out the world. Tomorrow was going to be a difficult day. Snatching Emma from this home without the help of a sheriff and somehow getting her safely on the train without an all-out war with the Shirsteins would be a miracle. Mr. Shirstein was clearly enthralled with his new daughter, and Mrs. Shirstein equally appalled. She was not mother material, but with her controlling personality, she would surely fight to keep the child.

He crawled into the bed next to Gracie. She was a complication he could not deal with tonight. "Good night." He turned away and shifted to the farthest edge of the bed.

"Matthew, should we talk about tomorrow?"

"No. I think we should each pray for wisdom and talk in the morning. It's been a long day."

He was almost asleep when she snuggled close and put her arms around him. A jolt of heat shot through his body. What was she doing? It took every bit of strength he had to ignore her and feign sleep.

"I'm afraid," she whispered. The soft warmth of her breath tickled the bare skin of his back. Oh Lord, this was not a temptation he needed.

"Will you hold me?" Her hands moved slowly over his chest.

He sucked in a deep breath and grabbed her hand, holding it tightly in his, then flipped onto his back. With his eyes adjusted to the dark and a soft glow coming from the few coals left in the fireplace, he stared at the ceiling and prayed. *Dear God, give me strength to be what she needs and not take what I want.*

"Roll the other way," he instructed. He wrapped his arms around her, keeping a scant distance between them. Obviously, she was not going to sleep until they talked. "Don't be afraid. God loves Emma—"

"But poor Mr. Shirstein. My heart weeps for him too."

"We have to trust Mr. Shirstein to God and do what's best for Emma. I'll leave a letter explaining our decision in his den. It's the best we can do. They're not willingly going to let Emma walk out of here."

"No, they're not. And we have to make sure that, in the future, this kind of situation never happens again."

"You have that right, but I have a plan…" He took a few moments to tell her what he was thinking.

She turned and threw her arms around his neck. "Matthew, what would I do without you?" She kissed the pulse beating rapidly out of control on his neck. "I've come to realize—"

He silenced her with his mouth, not wanting to hear about her admiration when all he wanted was her love. The kiss was sweet, tender, controlled. She pressed her body into his and opened her mouth.

He pulled away with aching slowness, not sure how he was going to manage his desire yet hold her close. But this was not the time, nor the place.

A small knock sounded outside their door.

Gracie sat up. "I told Emma that, if she was scared, she should come get me. I'll go sleep with her."

He grabbed her hand. "Tell her our plan."

"I will." She slid from the bed. The door opened and clicked shut.

He flipped onto his stomach. With a punch to his pillow and his covers thrown off his overheated body, he groaned into his pillow. *Thank You, God. I think.*

~

"Where is Emma's doll?" Gracie asked the nanny sweetly. Lunch had been served and, once again, Mrs. Shirstein had tried to get rid of them. Getting the doll back was the last thing that needed to be done before they left.

Lillian's eyes rapidly surveyed the area before answering. "Mrs. Shirstein thought it best she get used to her new dolls."

"Well then, could you go get it for me. It'll be fine for another orphan child back home."

Lillian shook her head. "I am instructed to watch Emma at all times."

"Emma can go with you," Gracie offered.

"It's most likely been thrown out, but I'll ask Bertha. She'll know."

"Go with Lillian. And bring me back that dolly." Gracie winked at Emma once Lillian turned to go. Emma hurried off.

Matthew pulled his watch out of his pocket for the hundredth time that day. "Just about time," he said.

Gracie nodded.

Emma returned with Lillian and her doll in hand.

"Are you all right with giving this to another child who does not have a dolly?" Gracie asked.

Emma nodded, playing along beautifully. She handed the ragdoll to Gracie, who placed it in her carpet bag.

"Well, my dear child, it's time for us to go, but how would you like to walk with us a bit down the road?"

Emma's head bobbed up and down. Gracie was so thankful for those moments in the night when she'd whispered their plan.

Lillian's eyes filled with fear. "Let me ask Mrs. Shirstein."

"No need, Lillian. We already said goodbye to her, and you know she doesn't like to be bothered unnecessarily. Besides, you're coming along, aren't you?"

"Emma needs her nap."

"She can have a nap when you get back. These are our last few moments with the child. You're not going to deprive us of the pleasure, are you?" Gracie smiled as sweetly as she could and prayed fervently. From that point on, timing was everything. There were so many things that could go wrong, the first being Lillian's refusal to allow Emma to come along. "A little fresh air is good for a child," Gracie encouraged.

"Well, I suppose that would be all right."

"Wonderful." Matthew said. "Emma will need her coat and a good pair of walking shoes, perhaps the ones she arrived in."

"Mrs. Shirstein said those were horrid, but I agree. They're far more suited for a child's play time."

Both Gracie and Matthew nodded their approval.

Lillian came back with the shoes and the practical coat Emma had worn on the train from Richmond.

They slipped out of the front door and down the drive. Gracie's heart was beating out of her chest as they hurried out of sight. If Mrs. Shirstein saw them walking away, she'd be sure to send someone after them. It wasn't until they rounded the bend that Gracie breathed more easily. Still, so much was at risk.

Matthew handed the carpet bag to Gracie as planned, having

purposely left one behind for the sake of ease and swung Emma up onto his shoulders. She squealed in delight. They picked up the pace and made it all the way to the railroad track before Lillian challenged them.

"This is far enough." Lillian said. "Come, Emma, we must get back."

Matthew didn't stop walking but faced the woman. "Lillian," he said firmly, "Emma is coming with us. She has bruises on her arms from Mrs. Shirstein's abuse, and welts on her legs from whatever the woman whipped her with, all within the first twenty-four hours."

"But—"

"No buts, you and I both know Mrs. Shirstein is not capable of being a mother."

"But Mr. Shirstein—"

"We feel truly sorry for him," Matthew said, "but it's not fair to put a child in harm's way just to please him. His wife doesn't even like children. He's going to have to face that reality. I've left him a letter on his desk, explaining our decision."

Gracie prayed as Matthew talked.

"Give me that child at once." Lillian's voice was louder, a command.

"No, we cannot."

Lillian looked between them, then swiveled and sprinted back toward the house.

"Let's go." Matthew started jogging. They slowed down as a woman and child approached—so as not to appear too obvious—but as soon as the strangers passed, they picked up pace again.

Gracie's lungs hurt by the time they piled into the General Store. They were wheezing and gasping for air when Billy came out from the back.

Matthew quickly relayed the story. "Can Emma and Gracie hide here until the train gets here? I don't want them involved while I wait to flag down the train. I pray we can be gone before Mrs. Shirstein summons help, but I can't be certain."

"Darn tootin', you can stay," Billy said. "Imagine that battle-ax beating this poor child." His blackened fingertips reached out to pat Emma's blond head. "Besides, the thought of having someone take that Mrs. Shirstein down a button-hole or two pert nigh makes me sing."

"We're not sure if anyone saw us come in here."

"The way that woman looks down her nose at everyone, ain't nobody in this town 'bout to help her out. Don't you worry none about that."

"I'll come get you the minute that train stops," Matthew said.

"No." Billy shook his head, his tone firm. "You stay put, and I'll bring 'um as soon as I hear the train. I know how to sneak 'em on. Then I'll come let you know which car they are in."

Matthew shook the man's big hand, kissed Emma and Gracie on the cheek, and headed out the door.

"Come into the back." Billy waved them in.

To Gracie's amazement, his living quarters were far more organized than the store. The small kitchen and sitting area were clean and presentable.

"I keep this part up in memory of my dear Annie. Just don't have enough in me to do the rest." His hands pointed back into the store. "I'm a thinkin' I best hide the two of you until I hear the train arrive." He pulled a ladder out from underneath his bed and placed it against the wall.

Gracie's eyes gravitated to the top of the ladder, where a hatch in the ceiling was visible. Billy climbed up first, opened the hatch, and stuck his head in. "There's some cobwebs fur sure, but if'n you can handle that, I feel it would be safer."

He went all the way up, and Gracie could hear some moving around before he came back down.

"Take a gander."

Gracie climbed the ladder and poked her head into the attic. Light filtered in from a small dirty window. Dust an inch thick, but no sign of cobwebs. Billy must have seen to that. She looked back down. "We can make this work."

"I'll follow the child and make sure she gets up safe."

Emma slowly climbed. Her eyes flicked down and then up, widening.

"Don't look down, Emma. Come on, you can do it." Gracie kneeled and held out her arms. Emma's little hands were white against the ladder rungs until Gracie pulled her safely in.

"I'm goin' close the hatch and take this ladder out back so they don't think to look on up," Billy said.

"Like a game of hide-and-seek." Gracie winked at Emma.

"This here's the best fun I've had in a long time." Billy's chortle could be heard all the way down the ladder.

Gracie wiped the thick dust from an old rocking chair with her traveling glove. The white turned a decided gray. She sat and opened her arms.

Emma cuddled in.

"Soon we'll be on the train," Gracie whispered. She smoothed her hand over Emma's blond curls and said nothing about the child's thumb in her mouth.

The longer she waited, the bigger the knot of unease tightened inside her chest. Why couldn't she hear the train?

Suddenly, the door downstairs slammed, shaking the building.

Emma jumped in her arms. Gracie stopped rocking and put a finger to her mouth.

"Where are they?" Every word of Mrs. Shirstein's screech could be heard clearly.

Billy took his time answering, "Where's who?"

"Don't you play smart with me. That couple who stole our child."

"Have you gone plum batty?" Billy answered. "What would I have to do with any of this?"

"People talk when I wave coins in their face. And they were seen hurrying in here."

"What do ya think you're doin' in my private space?" Billy's voice was nearer. "You have no right."

"You have no right helping those two steal our child. Walter, search the place."

The voices grew louder. They were right below. Doors were opened and slammed shut, and furniture pulled across the hardwood.

"Check the privy," the woman said. "Under the bed. The armoire. Hurry up, Walter, we have to find that child before the train gets here." Mrs. Shirstein was huffing and puffing, she was clearly in on the search.

"See, I told ya," Billy said. "And I'll be taking this up with the sheriff from Mineral next time he visits…bustin' in here is against the law."

A far-off whistle echoed through the town.

"Come on, Walter. Take out your gun. They must be in the woods behind the station. And I'll be darned if I'm going to let them take that child."

Gun? Oh, dear Jesus, help us.

The door slammed out front and then out back. Gracie stood and put Emma down with a finger to her lips. Emma's terrified expression told her she understood.

Noise below sounded like the shuffling of Billy bringing in the ladder, but she could not be sure. She didn't want to open the hatch for fear it would draw attention to them.

"Gracie," Billy whispered.

She slid the hatch open.

"Quick," he said. "My neighbor will help us. We both know how to use a rifle better than that there butler they brought in from the city. You'll be on that train, or I'll die tryin'."

Gracie dropped Emma into Billy's arms and then climbed down after her.

"Stay close." Billy grabbed his gun, and they headed out back. He looked both ways and hurried them to the next house. Billy hammered on the back door.

"Hold your horses. I'm coming." The door opened swiftly. A big burly man with a long gray beard looked down at them. His eyes flicked over Gracie and Emma.

"You ready, Jimmy?"

The man held up his gun. "As ready as I'm ever gonna be." His smile revealed a missing front tooth. He stepped out to join them and followed Billy's lead into the nearby woods onto a well-beaten path.

At the screech of the train wheels rolling into town, Billy turned back and nodded. "Good, your Matthew must be flaggin' 'em down. Now, we jus' have to git you and the little girl safely on board. This here path comes out on the opposite side of the station. The train will block us from view."

Just as Billy predicted they came out of the woods facing the train. He hurried them down the side checking in between the cars until he found what he was looking for. "This will do." He slid a boxcar open. Wooden crates and boxes filled the space with a little room at the front. "Plenty of room for the two of you itty bitty ladies, jus' until we git this sorted. Hop in."

"But Matthew—"

"I promised to git you on the train, and I'm aim to do it."

She wanted to argue, but Billy was right. She needed to think of Emma first.

She lifted Emma in, and Billy helped Gracie up. The door rolled shut behind them.

Gracie sank onto a crate. She held out her arms and pulled the trembling Emma onto her lap. "God is with us, Emma. It says in His word He will never leave us nor forsake us."

Gracie wanted to believe those words, but her heart

hammered, and her breathing felt strangled. A freight train of fear gathered speed and careened down the rails of her mind. What if they harmed Matthew? What if Billy did not get to him in time? She had not even had the chance to tell him how much she loved him. And oh, how she loved him. She didn't want to live one more day without telling him she desired to be his wife in every way. She couldn't imagine life without him.

Mrs. Shirstein had probably sent for reinforcements. What if Mr. Shirstein and other men arrived before the train started moving? Billy and Jim would be no match for a group of them.

Her hands trembled.

Emma's small fingers curled around hers. "Should we pray, Miss Gracie?"

Out of the mouths of babes came wisdom. "Yes, darling, we should pray." Gracie kissed the top of Emma's head. "Dear Jesus…"

CHAPTER 32

Matthew talked briefly to the conductor and was given ten minutes. He closed his hand into a fist to hide the tremble. Why had he agreed to let Billy bring them from the store? A hundred things could go wrong. If Mrs. Shirstein and her helpers found Emma, what would Gracie do? Would she fight? He had to go get them, now. He jumped off the platform.

"Stop right there." Mrs. Shirstein's shrill voice pierced the air.

Matthew turned slowly around.

Walter had a gun pointed at his heart.

A thin chill slithered up his spine. If they were trying to stop him, that meant they had not found Gracie and Emma. Thank God for that. Matthew held up his hands. "Look, we don't want any trouble. But let's face it, Mrs. Shirstein, you don't even want to be a mother."

"I will not let you ruin this for my husband." Her voice was cold and clipped.

He could see Billy and his friend sneaking up the rail behind

Mrs. Shirstein and Walter. They carried rifles, both raised. Matthew had to stall. Just a few steps closer.

"We have to do what is right for the child," he said. "Surely you understand?"

Billy and his friend leveled their guns. "Let em go," Billy growled.

Mrs. Shirstein and Walter whirled around. Walter wisely lowered his gun as Billy and his friend moved beside Matthew.

"You won't get away with this," Mrs. Shirstein warned. "Burton and his boys will track you down."

Billy leaned close and whispered. "Tenth car, other side. Jimmy and I will hold em here until the train pulls out."

"Can't thank you enough," Matthew said.

"Go, before Shirstein comes with his posse."

"What about you two?"

"I saw the bruises on that little girl," Billy said. "I'll tell Mr. Shirstein. He may be livid to see the little girl leave, but he's no fool."

Matthew focused on the conductor, who watched from the window. "Give me one minute, and let's roll out." He grabbed the carpet bag and ran, counting down to the tenth car. Heart racing. Hands pumping. He looked up to see a group of men on horses barreling down the side of the track.

He shouted back at Billy. "Tell the conductor to go. Mr. Shirstein's coming."

He ducked between the cars to the opposite side just before the slow movement of the train jerked forward on the rail. Matthew rolled back the door of the boxcar. Inside, he saw Gracie and Emma. They both looked terrified.

There was no time to switch them into the passenger section. He jogged to keep up with the train's movement, throwing in the carpet bag. The train was gaining speed. He leaped, landing on the cool wood boards. He jumped to his feet and slid the door closed.

Mr. Shirstein and his men were too far behind to know which car he was in. But if their horses were fast enough, they could jump on the train as it took time to gain speed.

He barely had time to brace himself before Gracie collapsed in his arms. "I was so scared you wouldn't make it. What happened?"

Little Emma hung onto them both.

He ushered them back to the wooden crate where they'd been sitting and settled in beside them. Gracie's shaking body melted into his and Emma crawled up onto his lap. He put his arms around them both.

"Mrs. Shirstein was there with Walter." He bent his head and whispered so Emma couldn't hear. "And his gun."

Gracie's fingernails pierced into his arm as she hung on.

"Thankfully, Billy and his friend came to my rescue. All is in God's trusty hands." Gracie looked up at him and he nodded down at Emma.

They sat silently, for a long time swaying to the lull of wheels on rail. When Emma's eyes drifted shut, Gracie whispered. "Do you think they'll be on the train?"

He hated to be so blunt, but he would not lie to her. He nodded. "Mr. Shirstein and his men were in hot pursuit. They may have jumped on the train. We won't know until the next stop."

"What will we do?"

"First and foremost, we have to keep the faith. God is protecting us. If we were in the main passenger area, they could easily find us. But this is perfect, there's no access to this car until we stop."

"But Matthew. They could take Emma by force. And the trauma she would experience before we could get back with the sheriff would be horrific."

"I'm going to get off and find them before they find us. Hopefully, I'll be able to reason with Mr. Shirstein. He's not a hardened criminal, just a man who desperately wants a child."

"But not knowing what is happening to you is—"

"I wouldn't like it either, but we have to do what's best for Emma. And right now, you keeping her calm and safe is the most important thing." He kissed the top of Gracie's head. "Can you trust me?"

"I do, with everything that is within me."

Her gaze held a softness that pulled him in. What was that in those trusting doe eyes? His throat felt tight and parched. He glanced away. He was not thinking straight. All the tension was getting to him.

Late afternoon light sliced through the cracks around the sliding door. As they traveled, that light grew dim. All that lay between them and Mr. Shirstein's group was the miles of rail to the next station, a fast-moving train, and time to pray. At the thought of arriving in the next town, muscles in the back of his neck constricted. His hand worked to rub the pain away.

"We've come too far to hand her over now," Gracie said. "I believe God will make a way." She tucked her trembling body into his arms, and a surge of protectiveness and responsibility flooded over him.

"Me too." He said the words with all the confidence he could muster. Only God knew how his gut churned with each passing mile. Without being able to see outside, he had no way of knowing where the men were. His faith was not being merely tested; it was stretched nearly to the breaking point. Yet, at the same time it was his lifeline, his peace.

The cadence of wheel rocking on rail slowed to a chug.

Emma stirred in Matthew's arms. "Here." He handed the child to Gracie. They were likely in Vinton. The stop would be short. "I'm getting out," he said. "If I don't get back to you—"

"What do you mean?"

Matthew stood. "Stay right where you are. There'll be a stop in Evergreen and then Gallipolis. I plan to talk to the conductor right now and make sure he knows where you are. He'll help you off the train when it's safe. Go to the inn at the second stop. I'll meet you there."

Gracie set Emma on her feet and stood. "But Matthew—"

He touched her lips with a quick but urgent kiss. "I need to go now so they won't know where you are. I hope to talk some sense into Mr. Shirstein, but if they hold out, then you'll need this backup plan."

"But if they use force... What's *your* backup plan?"

The train lurched to a stop. "As long as they don't know where you are, we're all safe. I have to go." He slid open the freight door and jumped out. The gathering dusk was a blessing. He purposely dodged in between the cars from one side to another, running toward the middle, where he knew the passenger cars and the conductor would be. He jumped back on board.

First things first. He had to talk to the conductor and let him know which car Gracie was in and beg him to help her get to the inn in Gallipolis, in case things got ugly with Mr. Shirstein. He found the man in the second passenger car, and they were barely done talking when Mr. Shirstein and his group crushed through the door.

"Where is she?" Mr. Shirstein demanded. "Where's my daughter?"

He faced the man, shoulders back, and kept his voice calm. "She had to be removed. She was not safe in your wife's hands. And you won't find her because I'm the decoy."

The man's eyes narrowed. "You mean Emma's back in Moonville?"

"I have no intention of telling you where she is."

"Why would you take her? I love that little girl." The large man's eyes misted with tears and his voice broke.

"I believe you do, but your wife has already left bruises and welts on her body, and it's been less than twenty-four hours." Matthew's hand swiped at the sweat beading on his forehead.

Mr. Shirstein's eyes looked down.

"You saw the marks, didn't you?"

"Ethel said the child fell."

Matthew felt the passenger's gazes on them. He didn't want to humiliate the guy in front of so many people, but Mr. Shirstein hadn't given him much choice. "You wanted to believe her, didn't you? But given her past, you know the truth."

"What do you mean?" Mr. Shirstein's eyes shifted. He couldn't make eye contact.

"Your wife didn't last as the schoolteacher because she was cruel to the children."

"That's town gossip. She stopped working because we don't need the money."

He leaned close and lowered his voice. "I doubt you believe that. You must know better than anyone that your wife is not suited to be a mother. We took Emma back because your home failed our inspection."

"How could our beautiful home fail inspection?" His eyes bulged, and the muscles across his chest tightened as he crossed his beefy arms.

"A house is not a home without love. Mrs. Shirstein is far more concerned with keeping everything perfect than she is in being a mother."

His arms dropped to his sides, and his head drooped. "Why didn't you talk to me? Why sneak Emma away?"

"I left you a letter, but after seeing the signs of abuse, I couldn't trust you'd willingly let us take her. And I wasn't wrong. At your wife's command, your servant held a gun to my head." Truthfully, they both seemed unbalanced in their approach. Mr. Shirstein showed signs of wanting the child too much, and his wife, not at all, but there was no use speaking what would only hurt the man more. "I'm truly sorry, but Emma is our foremost concern."

"I'll make sure Ethel never lays a hand on her again." Mr. Shirstein's voice grew desperate.

"How are you going to do that when you're at work all day?" Matthew asked.

The whistle blew. "If you boys are getting off, now is the time," the conductor announced.

"You know I'm right." Matthew clasped a hand on the other man's shoulder. "Think of little Emma living in fear and pain, every time she makes your wife angry. And your wife with all her treasures that no one dare touch. You can't even sit on your own furniture. What would that be like for a child?"

Mr. Shirstein hung his head. "Blast that woman." He hit the back of the seat nearest to him so hard that his meaty fist squirted blood. He whirled around. "Let's go, boys." He pointed to the door.

Matthew watched him depart. The man's head was down, and there could not be a more dejected looking man. A pang of sorrow hit his heart.

~

Gracie could not contain her joy. They were safe and almost to her beloved Shenandoah valley. Only one more day of traveling to go. She would be so happy to be off the swaying, rumbling, endless miles of track and able to sleep in her old bedroom at the farm...with Matthew in her arms. Her heartbeat quickened at the thought.

Emma had not left their side. Each night, she had slept curled in Gracie's arms, her thumb in her mouth. During the day, she was fixed on one of their laps. It was Matthew's turn.

Gracie grabbed his hand and squeezed tight. She couldn't wait for a moment of privacy so she could pour out the words of love burning a hole in her heart, but for now she would show it. She looked up at him with unguarded eyes, hoping he could see her adoration.

"What?" he asked.

"You're amazing. That's what. Organizing that I get to see my family and—"

"If you keep looking at me like that, I'll have to kiss you right in front of Emma."

Emma giggled, pulling back on Matthew's lap to look at them. "Kiss her. Kiss her," she said, bouncing on his knees.

"Yeah, kiss me." Gracie invited.

"Oh, you're so brave when we have an audience," he whispered, dropping a quick kiss on her lips that did not satisfy at all.

She laid her head on his shoulder. Soon, he would see that she was brave enough for a lot more.

They were approaching Staunton. The beautiful Alleghenies rose majestically in the background as they rolled toward the valley floor. "We're so close to Pa and my sisters that I'm getting excited. I guess there really is something called homesickness." She touched her heart.

He put his arm around her shoulder.

"I can't wait to see Pa. Losing Ma must be so devastating for him. He loved her so much."

"Love has a way of doing that...devastating a man." He turned to look out the window.

Was he talking about her pa or himself? She wanted to kiss him, really kiss him. And wipe away all doubt as to how much she loved him. But Emma was watching their every move.

CHAPTER 33

"Well, I'll be." Pa slapped his work cap on his dusty overalls and dropped his shovel.

Gracie ran down the freshly planted row right into his arms.

He pulled back. "Is that really you, baby girl?"

"It's me." She gave him a wide grin.

He threw his arm around her shoulder. "This calls for a celebration. And where's that good-looking man of yours?" They walked from the field toward the house. "Didn't I tell you he'd be the one you marry?"

"He's in the house with one of the children we didn't find a good home for on the Orphan Train."

"Orphan Train?"

"Long story, but I'm here for a few days, and we'll have plenty of time to talk. How are you, Pa?"

He stopped and turned her way. "Been sadder than I have words to say." A muscle jerked in his jaw as tears gathered in his pain-filled eyes.

Gracie fell into his arms, and they wept together.

He pulled back and smiled through the sorrow. "But you

coming to visit has just made me happier than a hippo in a hammock."

Gracie swiped at the tears running down her face, half giggling and half crying. "Where do you come up with those, Pa?"

"Have lots of time in the fields to think. But tell me, girl, are you happy?"

"I am so happy, Pa. Doing what I love with the man I love."

"Ah, there he is now." Pa waved at Matthew, who was heading their way.

The two met and hugged. "Thanks for bringing my girl."

"My pleasure." They stepped apart.

"Gracie was telling me how happy she is, doing what she loves with the man she loves. I suppose she was talking about you?" He chuckled and clapped Matthew on the shoulder.

Heat rushed into Gracie's cheeks. She had not said those words to Matthew yet, but there was Pa spilling the beans.

"Sure hope so." Matthew teased as if her declaration was nothing new.

He must think she was playing the part.

"You did the impossible, son. I tried to tell her, but nothing doing."

"The impossible?"

"You convinced her that loving God, loving her orphan children, and loving a man, all at the same time, was possible. There's no way she was going to take that advice from her old Pa."

"Where's Emma?" Gracie had to turn the subject in another direction. "She hasn't let either of us out of her sight."

"Jeanette is amazing," Matthew said. "Emma's in there learning how to play checkers with her."

"Pa, do you think we could have a family gathering with Katherine's and Lucinda's families tomorrow?"

"Darn tootin', we can. I'll send one of the hands over to

Lucinda's to let them know you're here. She'll be thrilled. Something to cheer her after…"

"After what?"

"Not sure it's my place to tell, but another miscarriage. Been praying hard, but sometimes God just don't answer the way we'd like."

"That must be so difficult for them." How had Gracie gone on with her own life in all the busyness and somehow missed her sister's pain? That had to be her third miscarriage. Yet, no one talked about the babies lost before they ever entered the world or the sorrow that must bring to a couple. Why was that?

"And then with losing Ma too. It's been real hard on that girl. Real hard."

They climbed the steps into the farmhouse. A wave of grief crushed in at the thought of not seeing Ma moving within those walls. Tears bit behind her eyelids. "I'm going up to my room for a little rest before supper." Her voice quivered.

Matthew seemed to understand. "I'll help with supper and watch Emma. You go." His eyes softened, and he dropped a kiss on her forehead.

"You're so good to me," she said.

"You're easy to love," he whispered in her ear.

She wanted to melt into his embrace and never let go, but instead she climbed the steps to her old room. Collapsing on her bed, she prayed, thanking God for His protection and for Emma, safely in their care. She asked for help with the pain of grief, each one of them missing Ma in their own way, and Lucinda's sorrow on top of sorrow.

Oh, God, heal Lucinda's pain. And God, please bring Emma a family who will love her.

They will bring healing to each other.

The thought came like a feather floating landing softly—a sister for Sammy and Tommy, a little girl for Lucinda and Joseph, a family for Emma, where she'd be part of something bigger. The Williams clan. Gracie rose from the bed with one swift action. She excitedly paced the room. Could this idea be from God? There were no people she would trust more than Lucinda and Joseph with Emma. They would be wonderful parents to that little girl.

Dear God, if this is Your will, give me a sign and speak this into Lucinda and Joseph's spirit.

~

*E*mma skipped alongside Gracie and Matthew as they walked from the farmhouse to Katherine's. Gracie pulled a deep breath in, loving the familiar scents of home. Emma's cherub cheeks, kissed by the sun, and her wide smile brought tears to Gracie's eyes. Oh, how she would love this child to stay in her family.

"Do you like it out here in the country where I grew up?"

"Yes, yes." Emma pulled at her hand as they passed through the orchard. "Flowers." She pointed to the trees.

"These are cherry blossoms." Gracie swung her up into her arms and carried her closer. "Look at how pretty they are, just like you."

Emma's little hand reached out to touch a silky petal.

"You'll have some new little friends to play with today. They're all my family, nieces and nephews, who are lots of fun." Gracie put her back down.

"But will you be there?" A tremor filled Emma's voice.

Matthew stopped and crouched down. He took Emma's hands gently into his. "You're safe now, Emma. And Gracie's family love children. You can run and play, and no one will hurt you. I promise."

Gracie bent down. "And we're so sorry for leaving you with the Shirsteins. That decision happened all too quickly."

"I draw a happy sun…when I sad."

BLOSSOM TURNER

"You sure did, sweetie. And that picture told us just what we needed to know."

"I did good?"

"You betcha." Matthew swung Emma onto his wide shoulders. "Now, off to supper we go." He galloped like a horse making neighing sounds, and Emma's laugh trailed behind her.

Gracie smiled into the heavens. What a great daddy he will make. *Thank You, God for Your mercies, and thank You for a wonderful man who loves children as much as I do.*

~

Gracie sat beside Matthew around the large table in Katherine and Colby's grand dining room. Her gaze traveled slowly around the room, stopping on each member of her family. What did they feel? How were they really doing? From the moment she'd met Rosina, her life had been centered on children and that promise. How much had she missed going on around her? How insensitive had she been to her own family, especially negating marriage in front of Jeanette in such a self-righteous manner.

Katherine and Colby emulated love. The soft touches between them and the shared discipline of their four rambunctious children spoke of true teamwork. Twelve-year-old Seth looked like a little man next to his three little sisters, Jillian, Georgia, and Geena, who continually pestered him.

Jeanette spoke only when spoken to. There was a deep sadness to her. Did she feel fulfilled being the local schoolteacher? She'd talked of marriage and family her whole life, and Gracie had been the one to balk at the notion. Yet here she was married, and still Jeanette waited. What must that feel like? Gracie would commit Jeanette to prayer more often.

Gracie's eyes affectionately landed on the gray heads of Abe and Delilah. How slowly they had moved with canes in hand, helping each other to the table. Between the two of them, they only caught half of the conversation, Abe asking Delilah to repeat what was being said. It was so endearing to see them help each other, such a testimony of life-long love.

Pa looked as if he'd aged ten years since she last saw him, the gaping wound of losing the love of his life was evident. The fact Ma was not at the table brought a lump to Gracie's throat, but that would be ripping Pa apart. Still, he smiled. Still, he gave the most beautiful prayer of thanks to God before the meal. Still, he was her hero.

Her eyes passed on to Lucinda and Joseph, obviously crazy in love. Joseph's arm was almost always around Lucinda's shoulder, but for the first time, Gracie paid attention to the nuances—the pain in her sister's eyes when she looked at Katherine's girls giggling one moment and fighting the next.

Six-year-old Sammy sat on one side of Emma, and four-year-old Tommy on the other. They were listening with rapt interest as Emma told them about the steamboat, the Orphan Train, and the parents she almost had.

A small miracle unfolded right in front of Gracie's eyes. Shy little Emma relaxed. Her story took over the whole table as everyone started asking her questions. Lucinda reached over Sammy and smoothed a hand down Emma's back.

"You are the bravest little girl I have ever met."

Emma's smile creased her rosy cheeks.

The only family missing were Amelia and Bryon with their three. They would've loved to share in this moment.

How blessed Gracie was to have such a beautiful legacy, and to think Matthew had no memories, no history, no joy of family to fall back on. The realization that Gracie had taken this all for granted pulled at her heart. A burning desire crashed in, not only to share her family with him but give him one of his own.

"Where are you?" Matthew bent and whispered in her ear. "You look a million miles away."

She turned to him and smiled. "I'm actually more here than I've ever been."

His brows knit together.

"I'll tell you later."

"Unlike you folks, we have an hour ride before we get home." Joseph pushed up from the table, "and—"

"—farming takes no holiday," Lucinda finished for him.

Joseph laughed. "I guess I do say that a lot."

"Can Emma come with us?" Sammy asked. "I want to show her our baby horse. She's never even *seen* a baby horse." His chest puffed out like a little man on a mission.

"Why don't we go too?" Gracie asked. "When was the last time I visited your home, Lucinda?"

Matthew's brows rose in surprise.

Gracie focused on Emma. "What do you think? Would you like that?"

Emma vigorously nodded her head.

"Can she ride in our wagon with us?" Sammy asked.

"Of course, she can if she would like to." Lucinda smiled at Emma. "You're more than welcome."

"But you're coming too?" Emma looked up at Gracie.

Gracie nodded. "Is that all right with you, Matthew?"

"Whatever you wish. I'd love to see Lucinda and Joseph's place."

"Hey, what about me?" Pa bantered. "I get to see my Gracie once in a blue moon, and you expect me to share?"

"We'll all ride out tomorrow," Colby offered. "After all, one of the perks of having help is that we can leave them to it once in a while. What do you say?"

"I'd love that." Katherine said.

Gracie turned to Jeanette. "And you must come, too, so the four of us have more sister time."

Heads were bobbing up and down all around the table.

"This will be a wonderful experience for Emma, to play and

have some fun on the farm," Gracie added. Her heart squeezed at the notion that maybe, just maybe, divine intervention was unfolding without her saying a word.

"Can we come tonight, too?" Katherine's girls begged.

"Why not?" Lucinda's eyes brightened. "The cousins can have a sleepover."

"Yes. Yes. Yes." The girls jumped up and down.

"Do you want to come, Seth?" Lucinda asked.

"Nope. A whole day without the girls bugging me sounds like heaven."

Laughter filled the room, and Geena stuck her tongue out at her brother.

Colby's brow knit together. "Geena, do you want to stay home?"

"Sorry, Seth." Geena offered a quick apology, then lifted her chin in such a way at her brother that it took everything Gracie had to hold back a laugh. She was a feisty one. A little Katherine for sure.

"Do you have room to put us all up?" Matthew asked Joseph.

"The kids can all sleep together, but I won't subject you to the bedroom next to that. I have the perfect spot for a little privacy for you newlyweds."

"I like the sound of that." Matthew's eyebrows danced.

Everyone laughed, and Gracie's face heated.

"We just finished building Nigel a cabin on the property to work on his inventions rather than take up the barn all summer, or the kitchen table all winter," Joseph said. "It's clean, has a bed, a nice fireplace. What more does a couple need?" He winked. "I'm thinking after the ordeal you two just had on the train, a little time alone would be nice."

"And you can sleep in as long as you like," Lucinda said. "It'll be my pleasure to spoil the kids." She looked at Emma. "You can help me make little bear hotcakes smothered in maple syrup with peppermint eyes and a chocolate smile. How does that sound?"

Emma's eyes lit up, and she nodded.

The other girls ran around the table and gathered together. They danced in a circle. "We're going to the farm. We're going to the farm."

Gracie smiled at Matthew. "That sounds perfect."

The sides of his mouth turned up, but the way the chords tightened in his neck revealed he wasn't as calm as he projected.

Her heart tap-danced in excitement. The privacy and setting would be the perfect opportunity to tell her husband just how much she wanted to be his wife.

CHAPTER 34

Matthew swung the door of the cabin open and entered in the light of the candle. The smell of freshly hewn logs filled the air. A fire crackled in the fireplace with the flicker and pop of hungry flames. Joseph must have lit it while they were tucking Emma in for the night. Everything looked so romantic and all too dangerous. And Gracie had been way too cuddly in the wagon for the past hour. His desire burned as hot as that fire, and his discipline far too distant to be of any help tonight. He offered up a quick prayer, but it felt like it hit the roof and bounced back down.

"This is lovely," Gracie said.

Her beautiful brown eyes swirled like melted chocolate as she surveyed the one-room cabin. She nibbled at her lower lip, and he ached to kiss that nervousness away. The urge to make sure she never entertained the notion of an annulment again ran through his veins like liquid heat. Why did he have to be so honorable and hold out for love? *He* loved *her*. Wasn't that enough?

She pulled the carpet bag from his hand. "Glad Lucinda gave

me some fresh clothing. But since there is no privacy screen, be a gentleman and turn around while I slip into my nightwear."

He wanted to snatch her into his arms and show her she would have no need for nightwear, but he didn't dare. Instead, he slid into a chair at the kitchen table and gazed at the chink in the log wall like a perfect gentleman. *Oh, Lord, help me.* He listened to the splash of water at the washstand, the rustle of clothing, and then the quiet.

"Done," she said.

He turned, expecting her to be under the covers, but there she stood in a lacey gown with her hair hanging to her waist, gloriously free. His eyes devoured the secrets that the gown did little to hide. "What are you doing?" His voice came out low and raspy. A stupid question, but he couldn't think clearly. His heart skipped beats at the magnetic energy surging between them.

She slowly walked toward him. "What does it look like I'm doing?"

The pulse in his throat thumped so rapidly there was no hiding the effect she had on him. Was she really inviting him…? Her eyes danced, and her lips smiled, and she was standing but a hairs breadth away instead of cowering under the blankets. The smell of roses tickled his nose. He had to look elsewhere, not focus on her gently curved mouth and full lips, or there would be no return.

"Kiss me," she offered, pressing against him.

"You understand that, once I start…"

Her arms circled his neck.

"…there may be no turning ba—"

She brought his mouth down to meet hers.

He crushed her close. A blaze of intensity ignited. Explosive. His fingers dug into the luscious feel of her hair, and he kissed her with months of pent-up desire. The tips of her fingers found a way to his chest. He groaned. Dragging his mouth from hers, he ran a kiss from her forehead to chin.

"Do you feel what you do to me?" He crushed her hand against the pounding of his heart. "I want you more than I can say, but are you sure?"

"I once told you it would take a very special man to make me change my mind on the matter of love and marriage. You are that special man. I love you, Matthew." She kissed his lips. "I love your intellect"—another kiss—"and your bravery." The kisses continued between each declaration. "Your kindness. Your generosity. I love how we both love the orphan children. And I want to give you a family of your own."

Was he hearing right? Was she really in his arms offering him love, family, everything his lonely heart had always craved? The necessity for air in that moment was no greater than his need for her. Words got stuck in his throat.

"Say something." Her eyes collided with his. Thick lashes blinking above smoldering eyes.

He swept her up in his arms. Gently, he lowered her to the soft bed.

She landed, hair splayed beneath her, gaze never leaving his. Her fingers played in the curls at the nape of his neck. She knew instinctively how to drive him wild.

His breathing turned ragged as she mimicked everything he did. A jolt of heat shot through his body. He wanted to savor the moment he had dreamed of for so long. Fingers interlocked, he slowed the pace, and she melted against him. His eyes drank her in. "You're so beautiful. How is it that God saw fit—?"

"I ask the same about you, my handsome husband."

He rolled on top of her and gazed down. "I love you, Gracie Weston, more than life itself."

Senses exploded as she wrapped her arms around his neck and pressed her body against him.

*G*racie rolled back into Matthew's embrace in the early morning gray of dawn's first blush. She smiled into the dim light. There was no hurry. No rush. No duty to bid she climb out of bed. How perfectly delicious to be lazy for one glorious morning.

The thought of what they'd shared the night before brought a heated flush to Gracie's face, but also a stirring, a longing for more. Had she known a love between a man and woman could be so incredible, she would not have fought it so valiantly. She had indeed been thinking as a child, not a woman. But it was more than just the physical. There was power in the unity of marriage, of not going it alone. She did not need to be so fiercely independent. She could trust Matthew to look way beyond her outward shell. The way he took notice of her every nuance and desired to protect, to help, to draw closer. What a remarkable man he was in every way. She turned in his arms and kissed the pulse beating on his throat.

His eyes slowly opened. "Good morning, beautiful. It seems I wasn't dreaming." A smile split across his handsome face. His husky voice made her heart skitter.

"I didn't mean to wake you."

"Never be sorry for kissing me awake."

"I should be sorry when the opportunity to sleep in comes… practically never." She kissed a path from his whisker-stubbled jaw to just below his mouth.

"Sleep is overrated when you're in my arms."

"Do you think we could hide out here for a week and no one would notice?"

"Hmm, that sounds wonderful."

He kissed her lips, and her whole body tingled. Awareness blossomed. He kissed her long and slow—a whole new pleasure in the world of delights to explore.

She lifted her mouth from his, and he groaned.

"Before we get side-tracked, I want to run something by you."

"How about we take the road we're on, then circle back?" He kissed her lips invitingly. Everything but pleasure faded…

It was some time later when, exhausted, they fell back to sleep in each other's arms.

Gracie stirred. She sat up and rubbed her eyes. Goodness, what time was it? That sun shining through the one window looked awfully high in the sky. She pushed at Matthew's shoulder.

"Hmm?" He rolled toward her, reaching out. She batted his hand away with a giggle.

"Check your pocket watch. What time is it?"

He leaned toward the night table on his side of the bed, flipped the watch open and squinted at the hands. "Can't be." He put his watch to his ear. "Yup, it's still ticking. If this is right, we've slept through breakfast and lunch."

"Goodness gracious." Gracie flung the bedcovers off, grabbed her night jacket, and hurried to the privy.

Matthew's laughter followed her. She came back out and rushed through her morning ritual. Matthew sat in bed in no apparent hurry, watching her every move.

"Do you mind?" Her voice sounded sharp even to her ears.

"Don't mind at all," he said, amusement in his voice.

"Really, Matthew, give a lady a bit of privacy."

"After what we shared last night and then again this morning—"

"A gentleman would not talk of such things." Heat raced from her neck to her hairline.

His laughter filled the room. "I guess I'm not a gentleman then."

The nerve of him to laugh when Pa, Colby, and her sisters would've arrived already, and they were going to present so late in the day. She was mortified.

She yanked at her chemise and pulled on her skirt. Her hands were trembling so much that she could barely do up the buttons on the front of her jacket.

She had not heard him slip from the bed, but Matthew's hands folded over hers. "Relax. They all understand the way of newlyweds."

"What about Emma?"

"Emma's fine, or they would've come for us long ago." He lowered her hands gently to her sides and did up the rest of her buttons. "Let's just enjoy this tiny window of free time. And when we see them, we'll laugh at their joking and relish the fact that, for the first time, the teasing will be justified."

"Matthew. You are truly incorrigible."

He kissed her mouth quickly. "No. I'm happy. Now sit while I get dressed and tell me what you wanted to talk about earlier before we got so deliciously sidetracked."

"Not another word." She smacked his bare arm, and he turned toward the wash basin with a grin. The way he was splashing water on his muscled torso was most distracting.

"Go ahead."

"I wanted to talk about Emma."

"Why? Is something wrong? She seems so happy here." He rubbed a towel over his body, then pulled out his toiletries to shave. She was mesmerized by the deft movement of blade on skin without one nick, and the attractive body that had been hidden by clothing. How wonderful to just enjoy the beautiful creation he was. He caught her eyes in the mirror above the washstand and smiled.

He'd been watching her eye him up and down. "Emma?" he prompted

Gracie purposely gazed out the window. She couldn't think straight. "What do you think about asking Lucinda and Joseph to adopt her? Sammy and Tommy seem to love her, and she's relaxed here. They didn't have to come get us, which is a miracle after what she's been through."

"Hmm, that would be wonderful for Emma, if they're in agreement, but it's not exactly something you can put on a couple. Especially after the loss they've just experienced."

"I know, that's why I hesitate to say anything, but this idea came when I was praying for them both. Suddenly their names came together. I don't know how to explain it."

"You don't have to, Gracie. I know how much you love the Lord and how He speaks to you. How about we watch their interaction and see what today brings?"

"I knew I could count on you." She smiled up at him.

"Are you ready, Mrs. Weston, to start the day at"—he pulled out his pocket watch—"precisely one fifteen in the afternoon?"

Gracie stifled a grin. "I guess all we can do is join in the teasing."

"That's the spirit." He offered his arm, and she stepped in beside him.

They were halfway across the yard when the children bombarded them. Everyone talking at once. Emma the loudest of all…

"The baby horse is chestnut with a white patch on his nose…"

"You missed the best breakfast. Aunty Lucinda made…"

"Come see the colt. Colt is another name for a boy horse…"

"Whoa." Matthew held up his hand. "One at a time. And after I have my coffee."

"Coffee," Pa called out. "You're way too late for that." He sat with Colby and Joseph's Pa on the porch. "Came to visit with my daughter but seems she plum forgot about her pa with her handsome husband around."

Gracie climbed the steps. "We were so exhausted after all those hours on the train—"

"Exhausted? Is that what we're calling it now?" Colby said with a laugh.

The others joined in, with Matthew's laugh the loudest.

Gracie scurried indoors. Katherine, Jeanette, and Lucinda stood at the sink peeling potatoes for the evening meal.

"Glad you decided to join us." Lucinda said with a smirk. "So much for sister time."

"Don't start. The men are already having a hoot out there."

"Glad you got a good night's rest…or did you?" Katherine winked.

"Can't help yourself, can you?"

"Nope." They all giggled.

"For a girl who said she was never going to marry, she sure has something figured out."

Gracie could feel the heat pour into her face. "Jeanette, you too?"

"I had to listen to you lament about the shallowness of men and how the only thing that mattered was helping the orphaned children of Richmond, so I figure I have the right to tease, wouldn't you say?"

"You do." Gracie put her arm around Jeanette's shoulder. "Indeed, you do. And by the way, I was wrong. When you find the right man, he'll champion your dreams, and he'll love you from the inside out."

"I'll take your word for it."

An awkward silence filled the room. Gracie wanted to assure Jeanette that the right man was out there, but at twenty-eight those words would fall flat.

Lucinda gazed out the kitchen window. "That Emma is a doll. Look at her helping Sammy and Tommy brush the dog."

Gracie stood on her tippy toes and glanced out. "Ah, isn't that adorable, all of them together?"

"We were hoping for a girl the last three times." Lucinda placed a hand on her abdomen.

Gracie slid a hand around her sister's shoulders and gave a hug.

"Emma needs a home, and the boys would love a sister," Katherine said in her matter-of-fact way. "And quite frankly, I can't think of a better mama."

Gracie could have hugged her oldest sister. Her forthrightness spoke the words in Gracie's heart. "Neither can I."

Lucinda's eyes widened, and she turned to Gracie. "Joseph and I actually talked about this last night, but we weren't sure that you and Matthew would be willing to give her up. Seems she has quite a bond with you two."

Gracie flew into Lucinda's arms and hugged her tightly. "You would be the perfect mama, Lucinda. We have so many children to care for, and all we ever wanted was for Emma to be loved and cherished. And to think she could stay in my family? Well, that'd be the icing on the cake."

"You're serious?" The potato in Lucinda's hand dropped into the sink. "I'm going to go find Joseph this instant. This is the best news we've had in…" The rest of her words were lost as she bolted out the door, her red hair a flame flying behind her.

EPILOGUE

Fall 1880

"After hearing all the excitement from Ava and Max, do you wish you'd been the one checking up on the orphan children?" Gracie asked.

Matthew turned from the bureau in their tiny bedroom. "I meant every word when I said I'd much rather be home with you. But I'm relieved to know the children are happy. Except for Art, who missed his friends and the city, and what initially happened to Emma, the Orphan Train gave those children a way better life than they would have had otherwise. Nice to know Max is happy to take that part of the ministry over so I can concentrate on the rest."

"You're gifted, Matthew, and I'm not just saying that because I'm your wife. With your ideas and innovations, you're making quite a name for yourself."

"It's because I grew up in the institution and know what *doesn't* work. And I've learned to relax in my role because a certain dark-haired beauty has helped me understand that God put me here, so I need to stop worrying about what others think."

"See what marriage does?" Gracie laughed and sank into the pillows on their bed. She rubbed the ever-growing mound and held out her hand to Matthew. "Come quickly, she's moving."

Matthew crossed the room and sat on the bed beside her. "So, the baby is a girl?"

"Yes, and a mother-to-be is never wrong." She guided his hand to the left side of her belly. "Can you feel her?"

His eyes widened as the baby gave a good poke. "With that kick, I think we have ourselves a spicy one, just like her mama." Matthew rested his head on her abdomen. "I love you, wee one, before I even meet you. And I can't wait to be your daddy."

Gracie leaned forward and kissed the back of Matthew's head. "I'm so blessed. God knew me way better than I knew myself. What a revelation to find I could love the orphans and commit my life to their wellbeing yet somehow have abundant love for this coming child and her daddy. The more God gives, the wider the portals of love swing open."

"All I know is that you've made me the happiest man alive." Matthew shifted and brushed his lips over hers with aching tenderness. "I love you, my darling. You complete me."

His lopsided grin, with those adorable accompanying dimples, made her heart gallop. She was happy, so fiercely happy that she could barely contain the joy. "And you complete me. But who would've thought it was possible when first I met the serious, somber Matthew who wanted to send me packing?"

He laughed. "I was falling in love from the first glance on the train, and the thought terrified me. There was no rationale, and the fact you were dead set against marriage complicated the message I thought I heard from God."

"Message from God? You've never told me about this." Gracie turned toward him, propping her arm under her fist.

"I'd been praying for years for the right woman, and then

you came like a mini-tornado upsetting my day with fun, laughter, and this attraction I could not control."

"Go on." She smiled.

"I thought God said you were the one, but then every guy seemed to feel the same way. How was I any different?"

"So, you wanted me gone?"

"Yes, but thankfully God had other ideas. For reasons unknown to me, he picked the most beautiful woman in the world for my bride."

"Ah, that talk will get you everywhere." She lifted her lips to his, and they kissed long and slow, enjoying the wonder of each other.

She lay back and smiled into the heavens. How obstinate she had been in her thinking, but God had whittled away her presumptions one stubborn idea at a time. Once she embraced Matthew's love, no longer fighting the current or where it desired to flow, she was amazed how the surrender was part of the beauty. Their love carried its own language and took her to faraway places where only perfect soul mates could travel.

Did you enjoy this book? We hope so!
Would you take a quick minute to leave a review where you purchased the book?
It doesn't have to be long. Just a sentence or two telling what you liked about the story!

∞

Receive a FREE ebook and get updates when new Wild Heart books release: https://wildheartbooks.org/newsletter

Don't miss the next book in Shenandoah Brides Series!

Jeanette's Gift

SPRING, 1881
SHENANDOAH VALLEY

Twenty-nine felt like ninety-nine. Up until this birthday, Jeanette had held a smidgeon of optimism that she would someday marry and have a family of her own. All hope was now gone. God had somehow forgotten her. The cheery frosted cake that sat on the table seemed to mock her dreary existence.

"Auntie Jeanette?" Her four-year-old niece, Geena, pulled on her hand. "Can I help you blow out the candles?"

She could blow them all out for all Jeanette cared. She nodded and Geena jumped up and down, her smile the spitting image of her beautiful mama, Katherine. Seemed everyone in the family from the youngest to oldest was attractive except for her.

"Not until it's time, Geena," Colby said. "Quit bothering your auntie."

Jeanette lifted Geena into her arms. "You're not a bother, are you pumpkin?"

Geena wrapped her chubby arms around Jeanette's neck and pressed in a hug. Oh, how she wanted one of these little ones of her own.

Jeanette gazed around Katherine's parlor at those trying their best to give her a birthday celebration and forced a smile. Tears bit behind her lids. She pushed her glasses higher on her nose, glad she could hide behind Geena to cover the watery sheen she could feel building. Pa, Katherine and Colby and their brood of kids, Lucinda and Joseph with their family, Gracie and Mathew visiting from Richmond with their four-month-old baby, all conjured up one feeling—loneliness. She stooped down to let the squirming Geena go, then stood with her shoulders squared. She'd best get used to the fact. She had a lot of living yet to do.

Gracie moved beside her and gave Jeanette's shoulder a quick squeeze, as if reading Jeanette's mind. That hug made her eyes fill once again with unwanted tears, and Gracie perceptively steered the conversation away from matters of the heart.

"How are the students this time of year?" Gracie asked. "I bet with the warmer weather of spring they're not too focused."

"So true." Jeanette gathered her emotions and tucked them deep. "This next stretch until the end of May is the hardest to keep them learning. We lose a lot of the older boys to the necessary farm work this time of year."

"But I heard enrollment has never been higher," Katherine said. "Crazy how Agnus keeps sending disparaging remarks about your teaching style into the county superintendent. Little does she know that Colby is good friends with him, and we can counter the untruths."

Jeanette batted her hand in the air. "Agnus has always wanted my job. She's been beating the *it's not fair a married woman can't still teach* drum ever since she wed. And I don't disagree with her, I just don't like the way she's trying to push me out. She thinks if I'm not teaching, the school board would be forced to hire her."

Lucinda's brows arched. "Well, you're more charitable than I would be. Besides, the county couldn't find a more admired teacher than you. Those children love you."

"Yes, you were born to teach," Pa added.

"I don't know about that. It's what one does when they can't find a husband to have a family of their own." The words slipped off her tongue with a bitter tone. She hadn't meant to be that transparent. The room fell silent.

Jeanette bit her lower lip and turned to her niece. "Geena, I'm ready for my birthday cake. Are you going to help me?"

Geena's head popped up from her play and she squealed in delight.

∼

Jeanette lifted her head and her spirits, determined to fight off the depressing effects of yesterday's celebration. God's mercies were new every morning, and it was up to her to find the truth in that passage. The mile-long walk to school gave her time to ruminate about the lessons and offer a short prayer over the day. If nothing else, she was dutiful in her faith.

The fragrance of lilacs filled the air. She paused at the array of blooms hanging heavy over Helen Donovan's white picket fence and fingered a panicle. Dipping her head, she breathed in deeply. Ahh. Now this was the closest thing to heaven she would get all day.

"Do you want a few for a bouquet, dearie? It would brighten up that schoolroom."

Jeanette looked up to see Helen rocking on her veranda. "Goodness, you're up early."

"Don't know how many more beautiful spring mornings I'll have. Seemed a waste to spend it in bed." She beckoned with a wave of her hand. "Come, I'll get you some scissors. I know how much you love those lilacs."

Jeanette strolled up the cobblestone pathway toward the small but cozy home.

Helen tried three times to pull herself from the rocking chair, but to no avail. "Either this chair is getting smaller, or my behind is getting wider." She chuckled as her plump bottom flopped back down.

"Sit. I know where they are. I'll help myself." Jeanette pulled the screen door open and walked into the familiar kitchen. Funny how at twenty-nine, an eighty-year-old woman was her best friend. Helen had picked up the pieces of Jeanette's broken heart when she lost her ma, and from that time forward, she popped in regularly.

Jeanette loved her company but also understood loneliness, and she cared to ensure the widow was managing fine. She pulled the scissors from the drawer and hurried outside. She couldn't dawdle. Having plenty of time to organize her day down to the last jot and tittle was important to her. She snipped at a few clusters and returned the scissors to the rightful drawer.

Back on the porch, she moved close to Helen. "Thank you. I'll stop by again soon."

"You're such a dear." Helen lifted her spotted hand to squeeze Jeanette's arm. "How is it some fine man hasn't snatched you up already?"

How indeed? Ugly was not what any man was looking for snuggled up next to him in bed. Jeanette ignored the question. With a kiss on Helen's papery cheek, she set off.

She refused to think any more about men, or the lack thereof, in her life. Teaching was her reprieve from the monotony, the only place she contributed to the world and had some purpose. She took joy from doing it well.

The door to the one-room log schoolhouse squeaked as it

swung open. She would have to get Pa to oil that for her soon. She hung her cloak on the first hook in a row that lined one wall and placed her lunch pail on the bench directly below. No need to start the pot-bellied stove in the far corner on such a warm spring morning. She let out a breath. *One less thing to do.* She straightened the few rows of benches facing the front.

Now where was that mason jar? It would be perfect for the lilacs. There. She moved across the room to the washstand and dipped water from the drinking bucket to fill the jar. She plopped her lilacs inside, took a moment to arrange them before setting them on her small desk. The school board could afford only a table, but thanks to Katherine and Colby's generosity, she had both a desk and a bureau to store the children's records.

She'd best go over her preparations for the days lessons. With grades from one to eight and ages from five to eighteen, there were a lot of wheels turning. She pulled her outline from the small carpet bag she toted to and from school and sank onto the hard wooden chair. The door creaked opened, and her newest student, eight-year-old Laura Wallace, poked her head in.

"I know I'm early, but the others aren't coming today." She smiled. "May I help with something?"

Jeanette waved her in. "Your older brothers won't be here again?"

"Papa says he needs the boys around the farm this time of year."

"Even Benjamin? He's only seven."

"Papa says its time he learns how to feed the chickens and muck out the stalls."

"And the other girls?"

"Little Tessie isn't feeling well today, so Sarah had to stay home to look after her."

Jeanette sighed deeply. She couldn't blame the father, with six children to care for and having lost his wife, he must be overwhelmed. News was buzzing around town about the handsome widower and his big family who had moved into the area, buying the old run-down Reiner place.

All available women were a-twitter. All except her. She heard he was a city boy with hopes of giving his family the farm life. Pa had mentioned how the soil was fertile and, with a few bumper crops, he would be on his way. She prayed for the sake of his little ones that it would be so.

"Could you clean off the blackboard?" She handed the cloth to the blonde curly-haired child with cherubim cheeks. "I'll do the top and you do the bottom."

Laura's smile split wide.

"And how about I walk you home today? It's time I make my acquaintance with your pa."

Laura stopped swiping at the chalkboard. "I, uh, don't think Papa would like that."

Jeanette sat in her nearby chair so as not to tower over the child. "Why ever would you think that?"

"He's not much for talking to strangers, and he tells us to stay clear of the town folk."

Now that was odd. He brought the children to church. But come to think of it, he never interacted with people. The most anyone could get from him was a lift of his hat. Of course, the women loved the mystery. She, however, was his children's teacher and had no qualms about visiting their home as she did with all her students. Nor did she fancy herself an eligible woman, so there would be no room for misunderstanding. Plus, it was Friday evening and she wouldn't be missed at home. Pa went over to Katherine's for the evening meal. It was her one night off from cooking for him.

Jeanette stood. "Well, I'm not a stranger or one of the town folk. I'm your teacher, and I make a point of meeting all the parents. So, we'll walk together, and I'll have the delightful pleasure of getting to know you better. How does that sound?"

SNEAK PEEK: JEANETTE'S GIFT

Laura smiled and flung her body at Jeanette. Her little arms wrapped tightly around her waist. Startled at the reaction, Jeanette bent to give her a proper hug. Laura melted into her arms and wouldn't let go. Soft sobs broke out and Laura hiccuped.

Jeanette's chest tightened. "What is it, my dear child?"

Laura muffled into her shoulder. "I miss my grammie so much."

"Ahh, sweetie, you go ahead and cry. Missing those we love when we move away is normal." Jeanette held her until the sobs subsided. Funny it wasn't her mother she said she missed. Just how long had Mr. Wallace been a widower? There was certainly more to this story than met the eye.

Get JEANETTE'S GIFT at your favorite retailer!

BOOKS IN THE

SHENANDOAH BRIDES SERIES

Katherine's Arrangement (Shenandoah Brides, book 1)

Word Guild Semi-Finalist

Amelia's Heartsong (Shenandoah Brides, book 2)

Lucinda's Defender (Shenandoah Brides, book 3)

Gracie's Surrender (Shenandoah Brides, book 4)

Jeanette's Gift (Shenandoah Brides, book 5)

ABOUT THE AUTHOR

*I write because I can't **not** write. Stories have danced in my imagination since childhood. Having done the responsible thing—a former businesswoman, personal trainer, and mother of two grown children—I am finally pursuing my lifelong dream of writing full-time. Who knew work could be so fun?*

A hopeless romantic at heart, I believe all stories should give the reader significant entertainment value but also infuse relatable life struggle with hope sprinkled throughout. My desire is to leave the reader with a yearning to live for Christ on a deeper level, or at the very least, create a hunger to seek for more.

Blossom Turner is a freelance writer published in Chicken Soup and Kernels of Hope anthologies, former newspaper columnist on health and fitness, avid blogger, and novelist. She lives in a four-season playground in beautiful British Columbia, Canada, with gardening at the top of her enjoyment list.

She has a passion for women's ministry teaching Bible studies and public speaking, but having coffee and sharing God's hope with a hurting soul trumps all. She lives with her husband, David, of thirty-nine years and their dog, Lacey. Blossom loves to hear from her readers. Visit her at blossom-turner.com and subscribe to her quarterly newsletter.

Don't miss Blossom's other book, *Anna's Secret,* a contemporary romance and Word Guild semi-finalist.

WANT TO JOIN BLOSSOM'S SUPPORT TEAM?

If you enjoyed this book and love reading and would like to be a part of my Support Team as the next book launches, contact me through my web page at https://blossomturner.com, under the "Contact" heading.

A Support Team member will receive a free advance copy of the next book *before* it is released and promises to support in the following ways:

• Read the book in advance and have it completed by release date.
• If you enjoy the book, leave a review on Bookbub and Goodreads before release date as soon as you are done reading. Right after the release date, copy that review onto the other retailers, Amazon.ca, Amazon.com, Kobo, Barnes and Noble, and Apple Books. I will send you all the links so it is super easy.
• Promote ahead of time on social media, FB, Twitter, Instagram, or where ever. (I will send you memes to post before release date so everything will be easy. I will not inundate you with too many.)

WANT TO JOIN BLOSSOM'S SUPPORT TEAM?

I will have numerous prize draws for the support team members, in which your name will be entered to win gift cards from Amazon. I will try and make the process as fun and painless as possible, and hopefully you will enjoy the read. Those of you who have joined my team before and left such wonderful reviews, I thank God for you and consider you a part of my writing family.

I thank you in advance for joining me on this journey!

(Sorry, open to residents of Canada and the USA only.)

ACKNOWLEDGMENTS

To put in words my thank you to the amazing team at Wild Heart Books is next thing to impossible. To publisher/final editor Misty M. Beller and edit team Erin Taylor Young and Robin Patchen you have my sincerest thanks for elevating my work way beyond its original first draft. Wild Heart Books is a pleasure to write for, the company is well-run and the professionalism second-to-none.

To my critique partner Laura Thomas who spends hours fine-tuning my story, thank you from my heart. And to my amazing support team who read the book before it hits the market and then encourage others to read by your wonderful reviews, as a new author your gift of time is invaluable. I thank you.

And as always, but by the grace of God go I. Without His outstretched hands of help each day when I sit down at the keyboard, I could not accomplish half of what I do. Thank you, Jesus, for being a living, breathing, wonderful part of my every day. Thank you for the gift of imagination.

Want more?

If you love historical romance, check out the other Wild Heart books!

Rocky Mountain Redemption by Lisa J. Flickinger

A Rocky Mountain logging camp may be just the place to find herself.

To escape the devastation caused by the breaking of her wedding engagement, Isabelle Franklin joins her aunt in the Rocky Mountains to feed a camp of lumberjacks cutting on the slopes of Cougar Ridge. If only she could out run the lingering nightmares.

Charles Bailey, camp foreman and Stony Creek's itinerant pastor, develops a reputation to match his new nickname — Preach. However, an inner battle ensues when the details of his rough history threaten to overcome the beliefs of his young faith.

Amid the hazards of camp life, the unlikely friendship growing between the two surprises Isabelle. She's drawn to Preach's brute strength and gentle nature as he leads the ragtag crew toiling for Pollitt's Lumber. But when the ghosts from her past return to haunt her, the choices she will make change the course of her life forever—and that of the man she's come to love.

Marisol ~ Spanish Rose by Elva Cobb Martin

Escaping to the New World is her only option...Rescuing her will wrap the chains of the Inquisition around his neck.

Marisol Valentin flees Spain after murdering the nobleman who molested her. She ends up for sale on the indentured servants' block at Charles Town harbor—dirty, angry, and with child. Her hopes are shattered, but she must find a refuge for herself and the child she carries. Can this new land offer her the grace, love, and security she craves? Or must she escape again to her only living relative in Cartagena?

Captain Ethan Becket, once a Charles Town minister, now sails the seas as a privateer, grieving his deceased wife. But when he takes captive a ship full of indentured servants, he's intrigued by the woman whose manners seem much more refined than the average Spanish serving girl. Perfect to become governess for his young son. But when he sets out on a quest to find his captured sister, said to be in Cartagena, little does he expect his new Spanish governess to stow away on his ship with her six-month-old son. Yet her offer of help to free his sister is too tempting to pass up. And her beauty, both inside and out, is too attractive for his heart to protect itself against—until he learns she is a wanted murderess.

As their paths intertwine on a journey filled with danger, intrigue, and romance, only love and the grace of God can overcome the past and ignite a new beginning for Marisol and Ethan.

Lone Star Ranger by Renae Brumbaugh Green

Elizabeth Covington will get her man.

And she has just a week to prove her brother isn't the murderer Texas Ranger Rett Smith accuses him of being. She'll show the good-looking lawman he's wrong, even if it means setting out on a risky race across Texas to catch the real killer.

Rett doesn't want to convict an innocent man. But he can't let the Boston beauty sway his senses to set a guilty man free. When Elizabeth follows him on a dangerous trek, the Ranger vows to keep her safe. But who will protect him from the woman whose conviction and courage leave him doubting everything—even his heart?

Printed in Great Britain
by Amazon